Praise for Adam Christopher

"Adam Christopher has d[illegible]ur modern super-hero fasc[illegible]at reads as beautifully as th[illegible]all the power, creativity, and force that both mediums can muster. This is traditional heroism with a decidedly wicked and iconoclastic twist. Inventive, engaging, bewitching, and delightful, a feast as much for fans of the tropes as for the innocents amongst us."

Greg Rucka, New York Times bestselling author of Alpha, The Punisher *and* Batman

"*Seven Wonders* is everything that's great about superhero novels – a fast pace, a complicated plot, iconic characters, and an unlimited effects budget. Absolutely wonderful."

Seanan McGuire, New York Times bestselling author of Discount Armageddon *and* Ashes of Honor

"A cool, clever, wickedly twisty superhero story… You can, and will, provide your own pictures…"

Mike Carey, New York Times bestselling writer of The Unwritten *and* X-Men

"A blast of pure pleasure. This is Watchmen meets *NYPD Blue,* while *The Incredibles* stroll by; fast-moving action infused with Christopher's infectious love of pulp fiction and the superhero genre."

Philip Palmer, author of Version 43 *and* Hell Ship

"Rocketing ahead on a super-human combination of lightning-fast story, sharp-witted writing, a supervillain who will give you chills and a superhero team as diverse and complex as the Avengers or the Justice League, *Seven Wonders* is, quite simply, the superhero novel we've all been waiting for."

Caitlin Kittredge, author of The Iron Throne *and* Street Magic

"*Seven Wonders* is the exploded view on superheroes. Set pieces are described in colourful visuals like enhanced comic frames and the heroes' physical vulnerability is deftly shown in a way only novels can. Adam Christopher forges superhero glamour with the gritty proceduralism of police noir."

SL Grey, author of The Mall *and* The Ward

"Superheroes, we've always been told, are far above the common man in both powers and nobility, but Adam Christopher unrelentingly tells the story of heroes struggling to guide the world long after they've lost their own way. *Seven Wonders* slams readers in the gut from the very first page and then just keeps on firing cannons, giving readers the same choice as every single citizen of San Ventura – either duck and cover, or ride along with the laser."

Paul Tobin, author of Marvel Adventures: Spider-Man

"Witty and cinematic, packed full of spectacular set-pieces, labyrinthine plot twists and devious double-crosses, and populated by an imaginative array superheroes as flawed and fallible as the citizens they're sworn to protect, Adam Christopher's *Seven Wonders* is the literary equivalent of a lazy Saturday morning with a stack of your favorite comic books: pure, unadulterated fun!"

Owen Laukkanen, bestselling author of The Professionals

"A novel with the best of superhero traditions: cool adventure, great action, and heroes and villains with genuine personality."

A Lee Martinez, Alex Award-winning author of Emperor Mollusk vs the Sinister Brain *and* Gil's All Fright Diner

"An exhilarating, rocket-heeled ride. Adam Christopher grabs the super hero story crashes through the comic book frame and carries it straight into your mind's eye. These pages are filled with gleaming spandex, sinister motives and explosive action. *Seven Wonders* is wry, sly and ready to fly."

Tom Pollock, author of The City's Son

"*Seven Wonders* is a modern day superhero novel done right. Never too dark and never too campy, this book's just the right amount of fun."

Stephen Blackmoore, author of City of the Lost

"Adam Christopher is a bold new voice in the prose world, merging the literary with genre into a explosive new vision for modern fiction."

Joshua Hale Fialkov, Harvey-, Eisner- & Emmy-nominated writer of *I, Vampire, Echoes* and *Tumor*

"*Seven Wonders* is a rollicking roller-coaster of a novel – Christopher has created characters you care about and a plot that doesn't let up, all wrapped up in prose as feisty as its superheroes... Ka-pow! I loved it. A must-read."

Alison Littlewood, author of A Cold Season

"With *Seven Wonders* Adam Christopher has proved himself the master of a new type of noir for the modern age. A noir where Chandler meets the Avengers on pages of delightfully crisp prose. A noir flavoured with echoes of *Sin City* and *Watchmen*. A noir that's simply marvel-ous and entirely his own."

Sarah Pinborough, author of The Chosen Seed *and* Mayhem

"Adam Christopher grabbed everyone's attention with his debut novel *Empire State*, and his follow up *Seven Wonders* will surely please all of his readers who have been waiting breathlessly for more. A smart, entertaining, energetic take on the superhero genre."

Victor Gischler, writer of X-Men *and* Deadpool

"An awesome heroic adventure that cannot slow down. This book was so much fun!"

Mur Lafferty, John W. Campbell Award-nominated author and editor of Escape Pod

BY THE SAME AUTHOR

Empire State

ADAM CHRISTOPHER

SEVEN WONDERS

ANGRY ROBOT
A member of the Osprey Group

Lace Market House,
54-56 High Pavement,
Nottingham,
NG1 1HW, UK

4402 23rd St., Ste 219,
Long Island City,
NY 11101
USA

www.angryrobotbooks.com
Up, up and away!

An Angry Robot paperback original 2012

Cover art by Will Staehle (lonewolfblacksheep.com)

Distributed in the United States by Random House, Inc., New York.

ISBN 978-0-85766-196-8
EBook ISBN 978-0-85766-197-0

Printed and bound by CPI Group (UK) Ltd, Croydon, CR0 4YY

9 8 7 6 5 4 3 2 1

For Sandra, always and forever.

AUTHOR'S NOTE

Head down the Pacific Coast Highway in California and you won't find a turnoff for the city of San Ventura; it doesn't exist, although you might reach San Buenaventura – more commonly known as Ventura – if you go far enough south. Any resemblance between the real seat of Ventura County and the fictitious Jewel of the West Coast as presented in this book is entirely coincidental.

Likewise, you won't see the Draconid meteor shower if you look to the night sky in summer, in the Northern Hemisphere at least; you need to wait until early October in our universe.

"Forgive me, Father, for I have sinned.
It has been ten years since my last confession.
In that time, I have murdered and terrorized.
I have destroyed the city."

***SAN VENTURA, CALIFORNIA** – Jewel of the West Coast! The Shining City! A modern metropolis of industry and commerce, a city synonymous with progress!*

*And a city in thrall of **THE COWL**, that superpowered supervillain whose identity is concealed by the famous dark hood, that evil-doer who enacts his reign of terror with the help of the enigmatic and mysterious **BLACKBIRD**, the Mistress of the Night, her features concealed behind a bird-like mask!*

*But hope is not lost, for the Shining City is home to the last group of superheroes, that band of marvels who keep the city safe as they prepare for the ultimate showdown with their arch-nemesis! Watch the skies, for they are **THE SEVEN**...*

Wise is their leader, that champion of champions who carries the amazing atomic power of the very sun itself within him! No villain is a match for the supreme strategies of Earth's superman, ***AURORA'S LIGHT!***

Out of the ordinary, her mental powers read the secrets of the criminal mind, and in her anger unleash a psychic lightning storm that none can weather! Villains can hide nothing from the penetrating gaze of ***BLUEBELL!***

Night-stalkers, take flight! For there walks among you a magical warrior woman, born of a lost tribe of Arabian nomads blessed with a supernatural link to the animal kingdom! Beware the claws of ***SAND CAT!***

Defying the laws of physics, gifted with access to the Slipstream, that *n*th dimensional plane beyond the ken of modern science that bestows speed and flight! There are none who can outrace the silver speedster ***LINEAR!***

Exiled from Mount Olympus – the sole survivor of the Hellenic Pantheon! Carrying the Hammer of the Gods with which he creates his magical weapons, this Architect of Power is ***HEPHAESTUS!***

Robotic... yet alive! Forged from a mysterious alloy known only to his creator Hephaestus, no foe dare challenge the Supra-Maximal Attack-Response Titan, the giant machine-man ***SMART!***

Strange is the cold light she wields from the unfathomable depths of space-time, that esoteric energy that illuminates her mighty power-staff! Mystery surrounds this visitor from another world, for she is ***THE DRAGON STAR!***

"Thanks, Mary, and good morning San Ventura for Thursday the fourth. I'm Sarah Nova and here's a recap of your top headlines this morning.

"Astronomers at the South Cal Catadioptric Observatory say that this year's Draconid meteor shower will be the biggest and brightest on record, with up to five thousand meteors an hour predicted to hit the skies over the West Coast at the shower's peak. With just seven weeks to go, the hills of North Beach are expected to be even more crowded this year as spectators vie for the best vantage point, with officials advising people to get there early. Traffic restrictions will be in place on the North Beach suspension bridge and City Hall has called in extra buses to run on the free shuttle route.

"Shares in Conroy Industries are set to open this morning at a record high after late trading yesterday pushed stock above the $1,000 mark. The price represents the highest ever achieved by the San Ventura technology company, which is the county's leading employer, and puts Conroy Industries' market capitalization nearly $10 billion ahead of Apple Inc., its closest competitor in terms of value. Conroy Industries' performance stands in sharp contrast to other tech firms, which are..."

MEANWHILE... ON AN ORDINARY **WORKADAY** MORNING IN AN ORDINARY **WORKADAY** BANK IN DOWNTOWN **SAN VENTURA**...

...

...

...

CHAPTER ONE

It wasn't until the following week that Tony realized he could fly.

He knew it was coming, of course. Well, *hoped* it was coming. Hell, the last week had been one wild ride, so it was inevitable – he dared to suggest – that the most glorious, most *enjoyable* of all superpowers would hit sooner or later. Typically, of course, it had been later, the last of his powers to manifest. But who was complaining? Tony could fly, game over.

Sure, he could freeze a can of beer with a glance and light the gas hob on his stove with a flick of the wrist. He could chop firewood up at his old man's lodge in the hills with his bare hands. He also thought, maybe, that if the skin of his hand was like the steel blade of an axe, perhaps he was bulletproof as well. That would sure be handy in a city as dangerous as San Ventura, but hardly the kind of superpower you could just test, unless you were the kind of guy who got a kick out of Russian roulette.

A city as dangerous as San Ventura. The Shining City, right? Uh... yeah, right. Tony shifted his weight, trying – failing – to get more comfortable in the awkward squat in which he found himself on a warm Thursday morning. He wobbled, momentarily losing his center of gravity, but couldn't risk moving his hands from the back of his head. But, under the black, empty gaze of the gun barrel that very quickly appeared in his face, he found his balance again and remained quite, quite still. Unspeaking, but apparently satisfied, the gunslinger pulled the barrel of his Kalashnikov upwards and walked on, the wet creak of his leather combat boots loud from Tony's low position near the floor of the bank.

Tony really hated Thursdays. And didn't this one just take the cake.

With the thug's back moving away, Tony glanced around. A few desperate eyes were on him, wide and white, furious that he'd attracted the attention of one of the raiders, but relieved in a shaky kind of way that he hadn't got them all shot. Tony wasn't sure if an apologetic smile was appropriate, so decided not to bother and returned his attention to the cheap carpet tiles in front of him. A distraction came anyway as the leader of the robbers threw a few more heated words out of the window at the cops gathered in the street outside.

Robbers? The word stuck in Tony's mind. Fuck that. *Robbers*? What the fuck kind of robbers walked around with AK-47s, or whatever the hell their guns were? They were big guns; automatic assault rifles, with the distinctive curved magazines that only weapons bought on the Kazakhstani black market had. As far as Tony was concerned, the name "AK-47" applied to all that kind of shit. It was a bad, bad scene.

Which meant they weren't bank robbers. Bank robbers wore black jeans, and balaclavas, or maybe pantyhose (over their heads, anyway). Bank robbers ran in, maybe three or four, waving handguns and shouting at everyone to *get the fuck down* and *fill this fucking bag, bitch,* and *nobody fucking move*. And a few kicks and punches later, out the door, leaving old ladies to cry and bank clerks to comfort each other while the police carefully crunch on the scattered candy of broken glass spilt from what's left of the front doors.

Machine guns, combat boots – hell, combat *uniforms* – weren't the purview of bank robbers. These guys were pros.

No, thought Tony. Even more than that. Organized, disciplined, efficient. There had been no shouting, no running. A dozen men, black-booted, black-suited, each identical and anonymous behind something approaching a paintball mask crossed with a respirator. They came in silence and calmly took up what must have been pre-assigned positions, before their leader clicked something on the side of his mask and told everyone to crouch on the ground with their hands on their heads. Two of his men broke off and brought the bank manager from his back office, and the leader began politely asking a series of questions.

It was surreal, dreamlike, which at first gave an illusion of safety. It was only when the cramp started to bite that reality began to crystallize.

So not robbers, professionals. *Soldiers,* masked and uniformed. In San Ventura. Soldiers? No, *henchmen.* Which meant…

Shit. The one day I go to the bank, the one day I go to the bank in, like, a whole *year,* and I walk right into a classic piece of San Ventura villainy. Because henchmen and AK-47s and raiding a quiet bank with overwhelming firepower meant just one thing.

The Cowl.

"Your threats are noted, officer, as is your lack of understanding and situational awareness. Discussion terminated."

The leader turned away from the window and walked behind the main counters, through the now-open security door, around to the main lobby where his eleven soldiers stood over two dozen civilians. One AK-47 for every two members of the public. Tony felt sick.

The bank manager wasn't talking. Normally, Tony would have seen him as a proud man, defiant to the end, captain-going-down-with-the-ship kind of loyalty – if he was watching this on *World's Most Awesome Bank Robbery Shoot-outs 7.* He could imagine the manager's smoking, bullet-ridden body being stretchered out at the end of a day-long siege, with mugshot and eulogy in Friday morning's *San Ventura Ledger-Leader,* with quite possibly a civic funeral the next week complete with police honor guard and respectful mayor in attendance. The mayor would later give one of his all-too-regular press conferences decrying the Cowl and swearing justice would be served, and the citizens of San Ventura would shake their heads and turn off their televisions and lament the dark times that had fallen on the Shining City.

But right now, the bank manager was just being a dick. It's just a bank, it's just money, Tony thought. The anger and frustration rose as he watched the Cowl's mercenary orbit the bank manager like a panther looking for an opening. *Stop being such an asshole.* Tony's lips almost shaped the words, willing the bank manager to suck it up and open the safe. Give them the money.

Except… money? It wasn't money. Couldn't have been money. The Cowl's resources were legendary, his ill-gotten wealth rumored to be as close to infinite as any human being could ever hope to approach. The last thing he needed was cash. Diamonds, perhaps? Jewels, or gold? Because all supervillains liked to dive into a vault of treasure and swim around like Scrooge McDuck, right? No. There must have been something else, something locked in a safety deposit box in the vault. Something small, but important; important enough for the Cowl to take it by force, something important enough for the bank manager to risk his life and the lives of his staff and customers, even in the face of a dozen machine guns from central Asia.

"I don't know what you're talking about." The bank manager lifted his chin and pushed his dated, square-framed glasses up his nose a little. A small, defiant act.

"Oh, I think you do, Mr Ballard," said the leader. "Sure, it's well hidden here. Who would expect such a small, average branch of an average bank to hold such a priceless artifact. But that's the whole point, isn't it? That's why the Seven Wonders entrusted you with it. Locking it in their own citadel would prove, eventually, to be too much of a temptation, even for them. So, the solution is to lose it somewhere in the city – what, they gave it to you, then Bluebell did a mindwipe on everyone, so even they had no idea where or even *what* it was? Everyone, except you, Mr Ballard."

Mr Ballard said nothing. But he wasn't a professional, not like the mercenary. As the leader spoke in an odd, almost synthesized voice that echoed from underneath his respirator, a hundred emotions flickered over Mr Ballard's face. Satisfaction turned to doubt turned to fear. Even Tony could see that the mercenary was right on the button.

"Interesting, Mr Ballard." The leader walked away, casually. After a moment of nothing at all, he gestured slightly with a gauntleted hand. Instantly his eleven men prodded each of the two hostages in their charge with their guns, indicating for them to stand.

Each trio – mercenary plus two hostages – was separated from the next by a couple of feet, the whole group arranged in a neat semicircle in front of the counters. To Tony's left, a young woman, homely and mid-twenties but with that odd thinness that suggested eighteen with three kids, began to cry. With her hands still behind her head, her face turned red and the tears flowed freely, dripping onto the carpet tiles. Tony looked away, focusing instead on the mercenary leader.

Tony had superstrength, he had freeze-breath. He had superspeed. The only thing he wasn't quite sure of was whether hands of steel translated into torso of Kevlar. And even if it did, what about the other twenty-three hostages? Perhaps he was faster than a bullet, but he wasn't really sure – how fast did a bullet fly, anyway? Fast enough not to be visible in flight, but Tony had seen his own reflection in the water yesterday as he'd skipped from one side of the bay to the other. But faster than the high-velocity shells spat by the heavy-duty weaponry carried by these guys? Too much of a risk. Hold back, bide your time. Jeannie's training was sure going to come in useful, he knew that now.

The leader seemed to be watching the hostages, although it was hard to tell; the wraparound visor of his mask meant that his head only had to turn very slightly to give any indication that he was looking for something. For *someone* – picking a target.

"You see, Mr Ballard," the leader continued, turning back to the bank manager, "the method I'm about to employ may well be a cliché. In fact, I guarantee you'll have seen it plenty of times on the television. Do you watch much television, Mr Ballard?

"Anyway, it's simple, but effective. You have twenty-four chances to get the answer to my next question correct."

Mr Ballard didn't move, but he started breaking a hell of a sweat. Tony felt his anger melt, replaced instead with indignation. The Seven Wonders, he thought. I bet those bastards never told you this might happen.

There was a crack – not a gunshot, but an organic splitting, like a young branch bent off a new tree. One of the hostages – a nondescript man in an ordinary gray suit, the color of which matched his neatly parted hair, mid-priced black leather slip-ons from a mall shoe shop on his feet – twisted, ever so slightly, arching his back almost like he was stretching out a stiff muscle. Then he dropped, knees folding up and his body telescoping almost vertically down beside his paired hostage.

The crying woman moaned loudly, trying to turn her head away from the body. Several others swore and muttered. A couple of people remained silent, unmoved, staring at the body. Tony included. Then he said: "Holy fuck."

"Oh, language, please." A new voice now, from the back of the bank, from the direction of the manager's office. It was male, low and hoarse, not artificially modulated like the mercenaries, but a rasp put on deliberately, naturally, to disguise the owner. "And that's twenty-three chances, Mr Ballard. My… *staff*… were never good with numbers."

The Cowl stepped forward into the bank lobby. He couldn't have been there very long, certainly no one had entered since the place had been raided an hour ago. Nobody was really sure what the extent of his powers were, but sudden appearances and disappearances were a regular feature of his exploits reported with depressing regularity in the pages of the *Ledger-Leader*. Tony had only a few days' working knowledge of superpowers, but here, witnessing them with his own eyes, he began to reel off possibilities in his mind. Teleportation? Had to be.

The scalloped edge of the Cowl's cloak brushed over the dead man's face, catching in the wide, rolling red of blood that had started to ooze from his mouth, nose, ears. His infamous hooded head turned down toward his victim, killed without a finger laid.

Psychokinesis. Fucker was a supervillain, all right. The best – well, the most powerful – and the last. The last, because not even the Seven Wonders could take the bastard down.

Even in the bright daylight of a summer morning, the Cowl was a walking shadow. He had his back to Tony now, and somehow Tony couldn't quite focus on the inky depth of the black cloak that streamed seamlessly from the villain's hood and flowed out over the arms. It shimmered, matte black on matte black, with the finesse of silk but with something rubbery, leathery about it. It was high-tech, clearly.

With his appearance, the atmosphere of the siege changed. Fear and tension, fuelled by adrenaline, metamorphosed into something else, something colder. Tony felt quiet calm and he sensed the other hostages around him relax. Then he realized what it was. With the Cowl here, people no longer had any hope. The feeling was one of total, emotionless surrender. Tony didn't like it.

The Cowl turned with a sweep to face Mr Ballard, whose neck muscles visibly tensed. Under the black hood, the Cowl's face was obscured by a half-mask which left the mouth and chin exposed, the bare skin peppered with a healthy stubble. The eyes were unfathomable, empty white ellipses against the black of the face-hugging mask. And on the chest, vivid scarlet against the pitch dark of the bodysuit, the famous emblem: an inverted pentagram, the bottom point skewed to the left, the central pentagonal space enclosing the Greek capital omega. And within this, two stacked equilateral triangles, aligned with flat sides vertical to form a runic letter "B". Inside the open space of the top triangle was the Eye of Horus, while the bottom triangle included some miniscule script in an unknown language.

Nobody knew what the complex symbol meant, but everyone had a theory. It was referred to by most just as the "omega symbol", including the various criminal gangs who roamed the city, claiming to be doing The Cowl's work.

Tony's heart raced. He thought it was probably the same light-headed sensation you might get seeing a famous movie star or your favorite celebrity in the flesh. Surreal, exciting. Only here, now, in the East Side branch of the California Cooperative Bank, terribly, terribly dangerous.

The Cowl raised a gloved hand, the silky cloak swishing aside as he moved his arm. He gently pressed a finger into Mr Ballard's chest, as if he wasn't making his point clear.

"Simple, but effective, Mr Ballard. But we're not going to do it my way. Too... quiet. I want show. I want screams. So now my colleague here will execute another."

The leader of the mercenaries leapt into action, a blur of precise military training. Without further instruction, he squared his body into battle stance, raised his machine gun, and sent a single round into the head of another bank customer. The woman cartwheeled backwards, blood erupting behind her as the back of her head shattered and her brains evacuated, post-haste. Her body nearly flipped over completely before crashing over a faux-velvet queue barrier, sending two of its moveable metal supports toppling together.

The speed and noise of the execution was shocking. The young crying woman screamed, and several others shouted in surprise. One man, older, turned to the Cowl, protesting the situation. The Cowl did not respond. On the floor, the front of the dead woman's pants stained darker as her bladder emptied. Tony's bladder nearly did the same thing.

Mr Ballard looked like he was trying to speak, but shaking in fear he seemed more likely to hyperventilate. The Cowl's dead eyes regarded the bank manager with indifference, then the corner of his mouth raised in a mocking smile.

"Actually, I've changed my mind," he said. "Guns are a little... unsophisticated, aren't they? Still too easy, too quick. Loud, though. I like loud. But let's try the hands-on approach."

The Cowl looked over the remaining hostages. Each man and woman shrunk into themselves, trying to look as nondescript and invisible as possible, knowing full well that their self-consciously averted gaze betrayed them, that their body language was a giveaway, that if they shifted position even a quarter of an inch it would have been the equivalent of shooting their hand towards the ceiling and calling out *Pick me! Pick me!*

All save the crying woman. She was quieter now, head bowed, face red, eyes black with streaked mascara. The weakest member of the pack, the easiest target.

Son of a *bitch*. The Cowl knew picking her would cause the most offence. That was his intention. He strode over and, grasping her chin forcefully with one hand, yanked her head up in a sudden movement. The woman stared into the Cowl's unreadable mask, her eyes wide and mouth stretched in what almost passed for an apologetic smile. Her shakes now rocked her whole body, the effect exaggerated by the supervillain's firm grip on her jaw.

At the opposite end of the hostage circle Tony caught a movement from a woman in bad make-up and not-quite-right brunette bob wig. Almost without thinking, he shifted to X-ray vision. Instantly her outline was bleached into a white and blue haze, her bones almost mathematically detailed. Her bones, and a brilliant white shape, narrow and rectangular under her right arm, pressed tight against the now-invisible flesh. A small gun.

Purple spots spun in Tony's eyes as his vision switched back to the regular spectrum, the morning daylight painfully bright. He blinked, tried to process what he'd just seen, and blinked again. The Cowl was still holding the crying woman's head, but now raised his other hand to her neck. The other woman, the one with the gun, shifted her balance, just a little.

Whoever she was, she was going to try something, and get everyone killed.

Fuck it. This was it. Tony had the power, he just had to use it. He knew it and Jeannie had encouraged him, had faith in him. Sure, he didn't know how far he could push his abilities, whether his steel skin would protect him from the high-velocity AK-47 rounds, whether his superspeed would be fast enough to remove the hostages from the bank lobby before any bullets reached them. Whether he could possibly even match the Cowl for strength, speed and firepower.

But he had to try. He felt… responsible, even duty-bound.

Without time for a proper plan, Tony launched himself at the Cowl. From a standing position, he hit sixty miles an hour in the five yards it took to reach his target. Relying on his opponent's not insubstantial frame to right his deliberate overbalance, Tony tackled the Cowl at the waist, wrapping both arms tight around the silk cloak. It was like driving a truck into a cinder block wall, but Tony had readied himself for the shock of collision, knowing full well that the Cowl would hardly feel it at all. All Tony heard was a surprised "Oof!" as he collected the supervillain and kept running.

Fifteen yards, and the reinforced front doors of the bank evaporated into glass dust as Tony and the Cowl crashed through them at two hundred miles an hour. The road had been closed off, with a rank of police cars arranged at angles in front of the bank in the classic standoff position. The bank was right on the corner of Galileo and Kuiper, a wide, multilane intersection right in the heart of San Ventura's business district, which afforded plenty of room for the SVPD to set up a mobile headquarters to manage the hostage situation. Tony hoped that they had left plenty of room for a supersonic runner to get through without killing anyone in the way.

Problem. Tony couldn't really see. His head was buried in the Cowl's flank, cold black leather pressing into his face and blocking all forward vision. Tony squinted sideways and caught nothing but a glimpse of the police cars and blue sky.

Shit. This wasn't how it was supposed to go.

Tony had figured on saving the crying woman first, then whipping the other civilians out of the bank, then back for a third trip to disarm and disable the mercenaries. But now several seconds had already passed, and he didn't know what to do with the Cowl. Dump him? Hand him to the police? Maybe run out to the middle of the Pacific and drop him? Was he even that fast?

This wasn't working. *Fuck.* Tony shifted his arms and managed to get his head around the Cowl's side for a quick forward glimpse.

Buildings, people, cars. They were right in San Ventura proper.

Tony turned left, but was going too fast. He cut a near ninety-degree angle and only just managed to avoid slamming into the corner of an Apollo Coffee, skimming a table and a lamppost instead as he pushed off down another street.

Buildings, people, cars. Getting busier.

Shit.

Tony spun right, attempting a circle so he could get back to the bank and finish his botched plan. They were now maybe three miles from Galileo, heading out to the coast. The tall spires of the big hotel chains that lined the waterfront filled his forward vision.

And then Tony tripped. For a second he saw nothing but concrete pavers, then the pink marble tiles that clad one of the swankier hotels, and then the clear blue sky. A second later the black void of the Cowl's cloak flashed into his vision, and Tony panicked, and turned *up*.

Tony felt rushing air, felt his legs cycling into nothing. The Cowl was still in the way, but now Tony could look down. He gasped at the perfect – *aerial* – view of the beach curving against the hotels of Charles Fort Boulevard. Beyond, the cityscape sparkled in the brilliant sun.

San Ventura was beautiful.

"Holy fuck."

Tony's exclamation was met with a punch in the side. The Cowl, for the first time, began struggling in Tony's grip. He managed to turn so Tony's face was now stuck in his stomach, and freeing his other arms, struck downwards directly onto the top of Tony's head.

The blow would have killed anyone else, crushing their skull like an eggshell. Tony's vision doubled momentarily and he felt a hot, sharp sensation in his mouth as he sliced his tongue on a tooth. But he didn't let go, didn't relax his hold on the Cowl for even a second. If anything, the blow snapped Tony back to his senses.

He was flying.

He was flying with the world's greatest supervillain in his grasp. Which meant…

Tony wasn't flying, the Cowl was.

Shit.

Tony fought to tighten his grip, but now the Cowl had his hands inside Tony's elbows and was forcing his arms apart.

Tony was in luck. His superstrength held against that of the Cowl's, their powers apparently equally matched. And Tony had no intention of letting go. This high over the ocean the water would be as hard as stone if he hit it, and Tony hadn't really had a chance to test that steel-skin-bulletproof thing yet. And even if his skin was that resilient, surely the impact would scramble his insides and kill him anyway.

Up they went, the city receding with surprising speed. Above, past the Cowl's flapping hood, Tony could see the sky get darker and darker, and right overhead, right where they were headed, the blue became black. My oh my, *that* was high.

It took Tony a moment to realize the Cowl was saying something, shouting right at him, but the roar of wind in his ears was a solid wall of sound. The Cowl's cloak was slick against Tony's sides and his hood had stopped flapping and was now flattened in the jet stream as they accelerated upwards.

The Cowl had stopped struggling, and now seemed to be focused more on heaping abuse at Tony. Or at least that's what it looked like – the lower portion of the Cowl's face seemed to look angry whether he was speaking or not. Now he was shouting, yelling at Tony, arms pushing against the wind as he gesticulated. Tony smiled and let his eyes drift to the inky blackness ahead of them.

What an asshole, Tony thought. The exhilaration of flight made him giddy, and the view around them rendered their struggle insignificant. What a view that was. And Tony had done it, saved the day, tackled San Ventura's number one terrorist single-handedly. Wasn't so hard.

The sky was quite dark now. Or was it the Cowl's cloak enveloping him? The black leather and spandex was actually tinged with white, when you looked closely. Tony's nose was half an inch from the miraculous, high-tech fabric. Black and white and crusted with icing. Maybe it was lemon flavored. Tony wondered if he should taste it.

After a minute, the Cowl stopped shouting. His head hung loosely, pushed into his chest by the wind. Tony smiled, possibly cruelly, before his eyes rolled white into his head and his oxygen-starved brain lost its grip on consciousness. His ice-frosted cheeks held the smile for a moment, then Tony's arms relaxed, and he let go.

Tony and the Cowl drifted apart by perhaps half a yard, momentum carrying them upwards but at a rapidly declining pace. Gravity eventually won, robbing the pair of their speed. Tony and the Cowl reached the top of the curve, and, their bodies massaged into the most naturally aerodynamic position by the winds of the mesosphere, they fell to Earth.

CHAPTER TWO

Joe Milano was keeping his mouth shut, although – for the moment at least – this decision was purely academic. Sam Millar hadn't stopped shouting yet.

Joe eased back onto the hood of the unmarked Lincoln Town Car, folded his arms, and peered into the clear blue sky as he waited for his partner to calm down. This was going to take a while, because Detective Millar had started to go around in circles, spitting out a high-rotation greatest hits of what went wrong on the bank job. The bank job that had taken weeks to gather intel for. The bank job that was going to – finally – nab Sam her quarry, the Cowl. The bank job that was so important she put her own *life* on the line in a cheap brunette wig. The wig was still on her head; that and the bargain-basement drab gray suit and white T-shirt made her look like an underpaid paralegal.

Joe coughed, and Sam paused, arms mid-air, stream-of-consciousness rant interrupted. A few uniforms idled by uncomfortably as Sam set a murderous glare on Joe.

"Something to say, Detective Milano? Got an angle on the fuck-up of the century?"

Joe coughed again, and glanced around the mass of marked and unmarked police cars, half of which had their lights on a slow cycle. The intersection was still blocked off, and straddling the now-dark signal lights, the brilliant yellow of a school bus blazed in the midday sun. Through the windows he could just make out the hostages from the bank seated in the dark, cool interior, a few capped shapes walking up and down, notepads and radios in hand.

"Where the hell did we get that bus from?"

Joe's question was an unwelcomed distraction. If Joe had something to say, some theory to offer as to how their meticulous weeks of planning had got so totally screwed, Sam wanted to hear it. The requisitioning of a brand-new school bus to safely ship the hostages away from the crime scene was, in all honestly, the last thing on her mind.

One of the uniforms, Officer Braithwaite, nudged Joe discreetly, then backed off to a safe distance, head bowed so the peak of his cap hid his eyes from Detective Millar's glare. Joe sighed, realizing he'd picked the wrong opener, and tried again before Sam's face got any redder.

"Sam. Look, it... We were fine. We'd planned it out, our information was good, we had a solid. Perfect placement, perfect timing." He sighed and tapped the underside of his wedding ring against the hood of the car. "It was in the bag, Sam. But the only thing we didn't count on – *couldn't* have counted on – was the Seven Wonders screwing with us. Again."

Sam lowered her arms and stepped towards Joe, the anger melting away to be replaced by an uncomfortable anxiety. He was right, dammit. Joe knew that this operation had been an obsession of hers recently. In fact she'd lost track of the number of times he'd covered her ass, the number of times he'd fudged his reports and taken on various bits and pieces of unauthorized work that Sam passed to him. She'd taken quite a risk, using members of one of the Eastside Omega gangs as informants, although how they'd got the info was anyone's guess. All so she could finally take down the Cowl.

But he was right. Sam's work had been on the button, and the operation had been faultless in the planning. Yet again, the city's sworn protectors had dipped their oar in where it wasn't wanted.

"The Seven Wonders?" Sam almost hissed the name like an insult. She tilted her head, looking Joe in the eye like he'd just cast doubts on her mother's lineage. "So now the Seven Wonders go undercover, do they? I suppose that was Linear depositing pennies from an arcade machine?"

Joe shifted his backside on the car and adjusted his belt as he thought.

"Well," he began. "He's the only speedster. We've got reports from all over the city. Hundreds of people – hell, the whole damn city – saw this guy take the Cowl airborne over the bay. Must have been quite a struggle up there. Thirty seconds later both fall into the drink." Joe scratched his cheek. "Who else could do that, if not Linear?"

Sam sighed, and she let her body relax. Her whole posture sank, the fight sapped from her body. She swore and sat on the car's hood next to Joe. She pulled the wig off, and fiddled with the polyester fibers in her lap.

"We were close, Joe, real close. Screw the Seven Wonders."

Braithwaite slipped back into Joe's eye line. The officer mouthed something that neither he nor Sam understood, then quickly stepped away and stood smartly, if not quite to attention then damn close. From behind him came the voice of an older man who liked his cigarettes. Joe and Sam jerked into life, pushing themselves off the car simultaneously.

Captain Gillespie had decided to poke his nose in, in person. Which, in a situation like this, was entirely expected but exactly what they didn't need.

The chief of the San Ventura Police Department was a chain smoker who, over the course of a glittering career spanning more than twenty years, had carefully cultivated the kind of angry police chief persona normally found on cheap late night made-for-TV movies. It would have been hilarious, had both Sam and Joe not felt his cold temper on more than one occasion. It didn't look like today would be any exception; if anything, things were about to get very unpleasant indeed. Today Captain Gillespie was well within bounds to blow his stack.

The chief's walk was brisk from his newly parked car, a car exactly the wrong shade of turd brown that no civilian in their right mind would ever order, marking it as a police vehicle as clearly as any standard black-and-white paintjob, even without the nub of the Kojak strobing silently over the driver's side. The chief hadn't even bothered to close the door.

In the growing heat of a California summer's day, Captain Gillespie couldn't have looked more out of place. Sam often wondered whether he had a whole closet full of plain black suits, the color of which was just a tone darker than his skin. In the few short steps it took to reach his subordinates, he'd broken into a sweat, beads of sticky perspiration pebbling his bald head.

Sam self-consciously clasped her hands behind her back, an action to hide the brunette wig, but it was too quick, too obvious, doing nothing but making her embarrassment even more apparent. Sam felt her partner tense beside her and out of the corner of her eye saw him shake his head. It wasn't his fault, and not for the first time, Sam felt ashamed at the way she dragged Joe into her... obsession.

Gillespie took a long drag on his cigarette. The end flared as he pulled air through the burning tobacco, taking a long, deep lungful. He was making a point, and Sam knew it. He was in charge, and they would just have to wait until he was good and ready. End of story.

"No one dead, at least." When Gillespie finally did speak, it was quiet, calm, polite even. Sam and Joe looked at each other, unsure who should speak or what the response to the chief's inaccurate observation should actually be. While they fumbled for an answer, Gillespie dragged again, finishing the cigarette and tossing it to the tarmac where it lazily smoked like a spent shell. He held his breath for a moment and Sam watched, imagining the rush of nicotine and wishing she hadn't quit the habit six months ago. Then Gillespie exhaled over Sam's head and smiled.

"Oh wait, two civilians dead. One missing half her head, the other with brains turned to scrambled egg by the Freak. God knows how many fuck-ups are sitting in that shitty bus." He gesticulated at the glowing yellow transport. "Marriage break-ups. Suicides. Who can tell. Seeing someone's brains blown out at close range can do that to the average Joe. Did you know that? Shock. Post-traumatic stress, that kind of thing." He paused, eyes flicking to meet Joe's but quickly focusing back on Sam. "And for... what, exactly?"

Gillespie's voice remained low, quiet. The chief wasn't one to rule his department with loud voices and popping blood vessels. In fact, the quieter he got, the worse the situation. Right now it was looking pretty ugly.

Gillespie sighed. "I don't want to see you guys in the precinct today. Consider it an unofficial half-day suspension." He looked the pair over again, head to toe, then took a step closer to Sam and turned so his back was to Joe.

"Go stew in your own juices and come back tomorrow with a damn good explanation as to why you made this poor sucker–" Gillespie jerked a thumb over his shoulder "–complete your reports and alter the department work plan for the last three months to fit this little party in."

Oh, *shit*. The chief knew. He knew all along. Sam glanced at Joe and saw him looking down at his feet, covering his eyes with a hand.

The chief knew about the swapping of work, about the screwy timesheets, about Sam neglecting her regular duties to pursue the "Freak", the chief's name for San Ventura's public enemy numero uno, the Cowl.

"Sir, I'm sorry," Sam began, "but this was a watertight operation. Our intel was right on the money, the Cowl was right there, and we had him. Dammit, almost had him." Sam's eyes joined Joe's on the tarmac. She gave up. "I'm sorry, sir, Joe was just helping a friend. I take full responsibility."

"Really?" To say the chief's tone was unsympathetic was one hell of an understatement. "You know how much this jazz all costs?" He waved his arms around, not really looking, but his point was clear. "The SuperCrime department's budget isn't unlimited. I might just have to start taking some deductions from your pay check, officer. Now, before you get out of my sight for the rest of this miserable day, tell me what happened. Why do I have a damn school bus full of terrorized civilians and not a single suspect in powercuffs?" The chief was already reaching for another cigarette. Joe folded his arms, sat back on the hood, and left it all to Sam.

She took a short, shallow breath, clearing the events in her mind before assembling them into some kind of order.

"Sir. 10.30am, two black SUVs pulled up and twelve combatants we assume are in the Cowl's employ entered the bank. Detective Milano and his teams were positioned in the area. I was embedded in the branch as a customer."

The chief snorted at her use of the term "embedded".

"With the raid in progress, Detective Milano established the police cordon as though it were any other armed robbery call-out. As expected, they required information from the branch manager, Mr Ballard..."

Gillespie held up a hand, and Sam stopped short, quickly, lips pursed in the formation of her next words. The chief made a show of dragging on his cigarette. This time he was less careful where he blew the smoke. Sam's eyes narrowed as the irritant cloud wafted around her face.

"What you didn't expect, detective, is that they'd start killing hostages almost immediately." He shook his head. "You, you of *all* people, should have known better. The Cowl is an evil, insane little man, and his hired help are usually the lowest form of sadist. Sure, they're trained, they're resourced, they've got the latest and the greatest, but they're lowlife, Detective Millar. You know this. So what the hell were you doing?"

In the bright sunshine, Sam's face was a flat gray. The chief was right. Joe knew it. Sam knew it. She'd known three months ago that people were going to die, but part of her shut it out. She wanted to take the Cowl down herself, and damn the consequences.

No, that wasn't true. Sam knew what would happen but was actually quite relieved that the bloodbath hadn't been even worse. But whenever it came to the problem of the Cowl, some cognitive center in her brain started to skip unpleasant but necessary details. She had known people would die, but she went ahead anyway.

She felt sick. The chief was right. But more than that, she had no right, no right at all, to serve the city making judgment calls like this one.

Sam reached into her seconds-store suit jacket and took out a small black rectangle of leather. Sewn into the stiff material was the badge of the San Ventura Police Department. On the reverse, a laminated photo ID card. Sam offered it to her boss.

Gillespie looked at the badge, shaking his head. "What do you think this is, detective? *The Wire*? You don't get out of it that easily. Stop making meaningless gestures because you feel bad, and tell me what happened."

Sam retracted the badge, glancing sideways, not at her partner but to see if any uniforms had been watching. She felt her face grow hot in embarrassment, but nobody was paying the trio any attention. She quickly pocketed the ID and cleared her throat.

"The Cowl entered the bank by unknown means, through our cordon. Probably some kind of teleportation. He killed the first hostage remotely – psychokinesis we assume. He then made threats against Mr Ballard, and ordered one of his men to shoot a hostage. Mr Ballard refused to cooperate and the Cowl was going to kill a third civilian himself when..."

Sam paused, hesitating.

"When what, detective?"

"When the Cowl was attacked by one of the civilians. It was impossible to see clearly, sir, it happened so fast. But the man charged the Cowl and carried him straight through the doors, and out into the city."

"And the mercenaries?"

"They must have been acting on standing orders. They immediately abandoned their hostages and their leader used some device. There was a flash... and I woke up on the floor. They were gone, along with Mr Ballard, the manager."

"Uh-huh." The chief turned his back on Sam and Joe, and walked a few steps around the front of the car, towards the bank. Almost the entire stretch of the plate-glass frontage had been shattered by the impact of the Cowl and whoever it was who ran him out of the building. On the right and left, in almost perfect symmetry, were the abandoned black SUVs. Police tape had been stretched around them, but they had been left otherwise untouched for the forensic team which was on its way.

Sam knew from past experience that the vehicles would not be booby-trapped, but she also knew that they wouldn't provide any data. The Cowl rarely left anything behind, but when he did, it was scrubbed clean. Just another couple of pieces of expensive non-evidence to take up space in a police storage warehouse.

Gillespie walked over to the first SUV, peered into the windows, then beckoned Sam and Joe over, away from the other police.

"If they had some kind of teleport facility, why did they make such a show of arriving in these things, waving guns around? Why didn't they just zap straight into the vault, take what they wanted, and zap out again. Why the theatrics?"

Detective Joe Milano considered for a moment. "Because the Cowl is an asshole, sir?" Sam sighed, but amazingly the chief allowed himself a small chuckle. Joe folded his arms and continued.

"It's part of his modus operandi; it's how he controls this city – with fear."

Gillespie's reflection loomed large in the SUV's tinted window.

"So what did the Cowl want here anyway? What's in the vault?"

But Sam was already shaking her head before the chief even finished. "Nothing of interest, sir. Cash, customer records, nothing else. But the Cowl didn't want the vault, he wanted Mr Ballard. The Seven Wonders had entrusted him with something. That's why they took him."

Gillespie turned from the vehicle and popped another cigarette into his mouth. "The Seven Assholes."

Joe nodded. "Yeah, the Seven Wonders. Since when do they go undercover? Their identities are secret, they make damn sure of that. We've got CCTV angles covering the whole branch, so we should have a good record of the guy that took out the Cowl and dumped him in the ocean. But... could it really have been Linear, on his day off, or something? We'll have his face on the tape, but he would have known his actions would reveal his identity. I don't see a member of the Seven Wonders pulling a stunt like that. They'd just sit tight and let people die before revealing their real faces. They've never acted like this before."

Sam laid a hand on Joe's arm, a dangerous thought sparking in her mind. "What, you're saying we have another superhero in San Ventura?"

Joe nodded. "Could be. The secrecy of their identities is paramount. Linear wouldn't perform on camera, even in the middle of one of the Cowl's schemes."

The chief sighed, a deep, hollow sound like wind rushing through an underground cave. "That, detectives, is *all* we need. Now, go. Ponder on what you are going to put on your reports. I don't want to see you until tomorrow. Let uniforms clear this mess up. I'll get them to send you the bill."

Dumping his unfinished cigarette to the sidewalk, Gillespie scuffed his shoes as he turned and headed back to his car. Joe unfolded his arms and walked off, leaving Sam alone by the SUV.

She felt her heart race. To come so close, to plan everything so perfectly, only to be foiled by something they could never have foreseen.

San Ventura had a new superhero.

Then she smiled, just a little. Because if there was one thing guaranteed to piss the Seven Wonders off, it was a new hero on their turf.

CHAPTER THREE

Tony had always been frightened.

A Friday, a couple of months back, and San Ventura at night was just as hot and muggy as San Ventura during the day, the only obvious difference being that it was dark. At 11pm the city was just hitting its stride, getting as busy as it was at midday with the surge of diners and drinkers, partygoers and clubbers, people hitting the night shift and people late leaving the office. At 11pm the night was young for a lot of folk.

Tony was not one of them. Retail was hardly a bountiful career choice and he was resigned to taking as many extra shifts as he could to make ends meet. Friday night was no exception. As the city came to nocturnal life, just the same as every other city in the country, Tony's only thought was to get home as quickly as possible. Attract no attention, speak to no one, get on the bus, the subway, then home. Safe.

Park Boulevard was illuminated as bright as day, the weird monochrome of the yellow sodium lamps on the main street outshone by the more natural white glow emanating from restaurants and bars. Added to this was the orange and red of neon signs, the blue from a few all-night internet cafes – there were three of them here, all in a row. Tony knew that they were all owned by a large Mexican who liked to be called Leroy in one shop, Jesus in the second, and Arnold in the third; Tony was half-convinced the man was a retired superhero with a quick-change closet between each of the premises. This part of town was practically floodlit.

This was no comfort for Tony. Pulling up the collar of his jacket, he buried himself deeper into the shadowed corner of the bus shelter, unconsciously sucking his stomach in to reduce his profile as much as possible. It was a token effort, but Tony felt better, convinced that perhaps if he slowed his breathing he'd practically vanish. What a superpower that would be.

In reality, the way he folded himself into the corner of the bus shelter just made him look like a crackhead on a comedown, but the effect was much the same. The three other people waiting at the shelter for the 300 to Maryville were judiciously gathered at the other end of the shelter, away from Tony, ignoring him completely.

For just a moment, Tony allowed himself to relax and focus inward. He tried to cut himself off from the hustle of the street, find his center, and let his brain switch off after a particularly numbing day at the Big Deal megastore.

He sighed quietly. Even the name of the store was appropriate. Big Deal. Sure, he was working with computers – selling the damn things. He'd had such ambition once. Computers, programming, IT, a trendy dotcom company and a lot of neatly stacked bundles of cash next to the bed he shared with a Californian beauty queen.

But Tony knew that some dreams were never meant to come true. Six months into computer science at UCSV and his math gave out on him. Switching to an arts major, he lasted another two months before quitting altogether and deciding to focus on the important things in life: eating, sleeping, avoiding the dangers of San Ventura. And Big Deal was the state's largest electronics and home entertainment chain, so theoretically he was still in computers. So really, what he told his mom wasn't entirely untrue.

Big Deal. Oh, how the name of the store mocked him. Tony never thought he'd be bothered by his lack of ambition. He really had no interest in career progression or business development or working any longer than the end of his ten-hour shift. But four years selling cheap bloatware PCs to unknowing soccer moms and their eager seven-year-old sons was becoming a real drag and the pay was lousy. And the lack of money presented issue number two.

Tony pondered on this with just a hint of resentment as the 300 pulled up. He let the other waiting pedestrians board first, keeping a distance between himself and the young suit in front just slightly too wide to be natural. Even the bus driver seemed to see it, squinting slightly at Tony as he climbed the three steps, presented his pass, and slipped down the vehicle's aisle to find a seat on his own. He was in luck – back third, right-hand side. Tony swung onto the bench seat quickly, and sank into the corner. As soon as the doors of the bus clacked shut, the interior light automatically dimmed. Tony felt better already, off the street.

Money. If Tony had money he could buy a car and not have to take first the bus then the subway and if he had money he wouldn't have to work in Big Deal but more than that he wouldn't have to live in San Ventura the most dangerous fucking city in the world and you think Mexico City is a piece of work or fucking Skid Row but neither of those places have their own fucking supervillain and...

Breathe, Tony, breathe. He closed his eyes and exhaled, and decided that he was tired and brain-dead after his shift. Sure, San Ventura was a dangerous place, but if a couple million other people could survive it, so could he. He wondered if he needed to see a doctor, maybe get something for anxiety, but as the bus rolled gently around the city center he couldn't help but smirk at his own paranoia. Sleep was the solution. Everything would be better in the morning.

Tony was jolted forward, the bus rocking on too-soft suspension as it came to an abrupt halt. Heart attempting to drill out of his chest cavity, Tony gripped the top of the seat in front and half-stood to get a better look out of the front window. A car beeped, and another responded, and somewhere outside a man was swearing. Then the bus jerked again and coasted forward, journey resumed.

Tony flopped back into his seat heavily. Holy *fuck*. Getting freaked by someone cutting in? Maybe it wasn't a doctor he needed, maybe it was a shrink. No, OK, sleep soon, no problem, then tomorrow is Saturday and the sun will be shining and maybe I can even go down to the beach.

Tony opened one eye. He knew it, he goddamn *knew* it. At the front of the bus, on a backwards-facing seat, was an old black man in a black suit underneath an overcoat. There was an old-fashioned hat, a Homburg maybe, perched on his head, and his hands rested on the black handle of a thick walking stick.

The old man was *looking* at him. It wasn't a glance, it was a *look*. The man held it for maybe three seconds, then blinked and turned his attention to the rainbow fuzz of city lights that flickered through the window.

OK, he didn't look dangerous, but looks were deceiving in San Ventura. He looked *odd*, which was reason enough to fear. Tony had never seen him before; he wasn't a regular on the bus and he hadn't noticed whether the man had been waiting at the bus shelter with him or had been on the bus already.

San Ventura was not a city you took risks in. Tony thumbed the bell and immediately stood, awkwardly walking down to the doors by the driver as the bus lurched around a corner. Tony stood in the short stairwell and closed his eyes, nose practically touching the rubber flap that sealed the two halves of the door together. His stop wasn't for a while, but he had to get off the damn bus and lose the old man. Had to.

Tony snapped his eyes open as the bus doors slid apart, cooler air suddenly rolling over his face. He took a second to check where he actually was, then hopped off the second-to-last step and stood, hands in pockets, until he heard the bus doors close and the vehicle hum off down the street.

Tony was alone at this stop. This part of town was much quieter, a collection of nine-to-five businesses now closed for the weekend. The street was busy in one direction, people heading into the beating heart of downtown, but not so much in the other. Tony oriented himself and saw a subway sign down on the corner ahead. On this route he'd have to make an awkward train change, which would extend his journey time by quite a margin. But tonight that wouldn't be a problem.

By the time he reached the station stairs, Tony was in a jog. He checked his speed as he approached, checked over his shoulder (just in case), then trotted down into the light.

The A-line was heaving, as always, a combination of people coming and going as the day's train timetable drew to a close. Tony was happy in the crowd this time, as there were enough people to get lost in. He politely pushed himself to the front of the platform and waited for just half a minute before a train rumbled to a halt, the doors not quite in front of where he stood. Tony let himself be carried by the mass of people shuffling slightly to the right, and swung himself into the train car.

The train was very brightly lit, and without thinking Tony headed straight for the semi-alcove provided by the curve of the wall and the sliding doors on the opposite side of the car. There were no shadows to hide in here, unlike the bus, but nevertheless he squeezed himself against the plastic frame of the car, hands in pockets and arms held tight against his sides. People filled nearly all of the space around him, packing the train almost as full as the five o'clock rush hour.

Two stations later was his change. He wasted no time in moving between platforms, and safely inside the next train Tony returned to his corner and closed his eyes, counting the stops in his head as the train ploughed through them and feeling the other passengers thin out around him as the doors slid open and shut and open and shut.

When Tony opened his eyes, he swore quietly under his breath.

There, on a folding seat that was really only supposed to be used when the train wasn't quite as full, sat the old black man. Tony couldn't get a clear view, but as the train rocked he could alternately see the man under an armpit and behind a head, walking stick clutched so tightly the man's knuckles were bleached white.

And he was looking at Tony.

Fuck. This was trouble. Who the hell was this guy? Not just a crim, not a mugger, nothing so petty. Maybe a mark, a decoy, a finder, an old peaceful man working with one of the Omega gangs, the groups of violent youths who thought they were doing the Cowl's good works. Tony had been ID'd as a target. The gang would be waiting for him on the streets above. He could see it now, teenagers, probably not more than five years younger than himself but, really, just children. Dressed up like their hero, omega symbols sprayed onto their T-shirts. Damn it, every black hat in the city thought they were in the Cowl's gang. This old man, oh so innocent, must have watched Tony from the bus then got off at the next stop and managed, somehow, to intercept him from another subway stop farther uptown. It couldn't have been a coincidence.

Tony focused on his breathing. The air was hot and damp, and in his tight corner filled with sweat and perfume. He tried not to move, not to draw attention to himself, for all the good it would do as the old man was still looking straight at him.

The train screeched a little as it punched the bright light of the next station – Tony's stop – and glided to a halt. The car was packed but Tony wasn't really interested in being nice to little old ladies, not tonight. As soon as the doors were half an inch apart he dived forward, using speed to catch the other passengers by surprise so they offered no resistance, and slipped out first. Tony's thin-soled sneakers slapped the cement floor as he shot for the station exit.

It was much darker up top than it had been in downtown, even though Tony lived, in theory, within the central city area. Pedestrians here were few and the street traffic was light. Tony wasted no time, and after a perfunctory check of the roadway, sprinted across it from the station steps to the almost entirely black shadow cast by the still-unfurled awning of his local grocery. Back flat to the plate-glass storefront, Tony checked ahead, left, right.

All clear.

Tony waited a few more minutes. Two people emerged from the subway and walked off together in the opposite direction, but that was it. Tony counted to ten, then up to twenty, before finally settling on thirty. Holding his breath, he peeled off the window and headed up the street towards his apartment.

Tony slowed as he approached his building. He expected it to be fairly quiet – dead, in fact – at this time of night, but there was no need to burst into the lobby in any kind of rush, just in case. The safest place in the city was Tony's apartment, and priority number one was getting up there in good time and with no suspicions raised.

Of course the elevator took forever. The building wasn't particularly new, but then it wasn't exactly a rundown dump – Tony had struck lucky finding the place, especially on his limited means. It was just a hair above average, in an OK area with a manageable rent provided he kept up the extra shifts at the store. It wasn't five star living, but it was clean and tidy. And safe.

The imaginary chase – and it was imaginary, surely – and the interminable wait for the elevator tore at Tony's nerves. He jumped from foot to foot as the elevator rattled upwards, balancing on his toes, almost unable to contain his impatience. As soon as the elevator dinged his level he was tapping at the chromed doors with his door key. His taps left tiny pale marks on the shiny surface, which vanished with a rub of his thumb, and then the doors slid open.

The next few seconds were a brown blur of communal hallway carpet, slightly muted fluorescent lighting and a parade of gray doors flashing past on either side. At his own door Tony pushed his hand forward, without pause, letting the key mate with the lock in perfect, practiced alignment.

In the dark of his apartment, Tony leaned against the reassuring solidity of the door, bumping his head back onto it and breathing heavily from his sudden burst of activity. He was panicking again, and he knew it. An overreaction, an irrational fear, a phobia. He closed his eyes, allowing the dark of his apartment to melt into total blackness behind his eyelids. He cleared his mind, slowed his breathing, and focused on the pinging in his calf muscles.

He stood like this for a few minutes, enjoying the semi-meditative state. Total relaxation, his mind floating free. After a spell, his attention turned to thirst. It was late, and bed called. A pot of tea, a little reading, then tomorrow was a Saturday in summer. If Tony wanted, it could be a perfect day.

He flicked on the light and, squinting at the sudden brightness, walked into the kitchen. Operating on automatic, he grabbed the china pot from on top of the fridge, spoon from the drawer, and jar of loose leaf from the pantry. He reached for the jug, gave it an experimental waggle to judge the amount of water, then moved to the sink to refill it. His friends at Big Deal ribbed him for his taste in English tea, something he'd picked up from his Anglophile parents. But Tony knew there was just nothing quite like it.

There was a window above the sink. It wasn't much of a view, just down onto the main street, a windowless beige office building across the way covered with a giant, though dated, mural. If you leaned out a bit to the left, you could see the corner of a small park with a brightly colored plastic playground. It wasn't a bad part of town, not really. But then did San Ventura actually have any good parts?

Tony caught the thought as it arrived, and stifled it. Enough already. Tea, book, bed. He hit the faucet and filled the jug, then glanced out of the window again.

Outside, across the street, the old man with the stick was standing, a black silhouette against the milky monochrome of the office block.

Tony froze. Even at this distance, the man was nothing more than an indistinguishable dark shape, but Tony could see his old, wet eyes glint, just a little, in the street lighting.

Holy shit. Fuck paranoia, he'd been right. *Damn. It.*

Distracted, Tony let the jug overfill, sending lava-hot water cascading onto the back of his hand. He swore, knocked the faucet off, and dumped the kettle in the sink. With his uninjured hand he reached up and released the window blind, sending the thin metal slats snapping down almost instantly.

Tony jumped in fright, and abandoning his tea making, went to the bathroom – where there were no windows – to run his burnt hand under the cold faucet.

He'd been right all along. He had to get out of San Ventura.

On the street, in the shadow of the office block, the old man clacked his tongue as Tony's kitchen blinds zipped down with a bang.

The man sniffed, shuffled the stick into his other hand, and walked away.

CHAPTER FOUR

"Where the hell have you been?"

Blackbird spun around in the wing-backed swivel chair to address the man as he entered the chamber. Illuminated as she was in the spotlight installed high in the vaulted ceiling of the cavern, she couldn't actually see him after he had disappeared from the security feed displayed on the Cowl's computer and communications deck which towered behind her. The only approach to the platform on which she sat was a narrow bridge of metal gridwork crossing a natural chasm that split the repurposed cave neatly in two. A nice, simple line of defense, she supposed, but then if an enemy had managed to get within a hundred yards of the Cowl's own chair, a sheer drop of a few hundred feet – with the walkway retracted – wasn't really going to pose much of a barrier.

The platform opposite, like the rest of the cavern, was swathed in darkness. Blackbird knew that aside from pandering to the theatrical side of her boss's personality, the shifting shadows that the place was carefully draped in had a very practical purpose, disorienting any enemies who *did* manage to penetrate the complex, giving her and the Cowl the upper hand. Of course, such an infiltration had never happened, but there was no point in taking any chances, especially if you were the last supervillain in the world.

There was a cough from the platform, and Blackbird frowned under her mask. The beak-like protrusion that had given rise to her name – that contained a complex image-processing GPU that fed directly to the large circular OLED screens that covered both eyes – didn't allow much facial movement beneath it. Blackbird felt the headpiece tugging at her jaw as her mildly surprised expression pushed against the snug lining. With a thought she switched her mask's powerful optics to night vision, throwing her view of the cavern into brilliant shades of violet.

"It's getting worse."

The Cowl's words echoed across the chasm that separated him from his accomplice. As he stepped forward onto the bridge and into her spotlight, she noticed that he was holding his right arm across his chest, the hand hooked over his left shoulder. His walk was slow, hampered by a slight limp. But worse, perhaps, his cloak was missing entirely, the famous hood gone. Without it, the black skullcap and half-mask looked incomplete, unfinished.

Blackbird leapt from the chair, rushing to meet the Cowl halfway across the gangway. His eyes were unreadable, hidden behind the lenses in his mask, but the corners of his mouth were downturned and twitched slightly as she looped an arm around his waist and led him back to the computer.

"So where did he take you?"

The Cowl reached for his chair and slumped into it, sending it spinning about its axis. He corrected the rotation against the computer workstation with his good hand, and let out a deep sigh.

"Over the bay. He was fast... too fast. Knocked me out cold when he hit... *hrmm...*"

The Cowl gingerly felt his side, palpating the skintight black spandex at the base of his ribs. He hissed when he found the sore point, but brushed Blackbird's hands away when she tried to help.

"It's fine," he said. "Broken ribs on both sides. They'll heal overnight. I still have that power, at least. You got back OK?"

Blackbird backed off and, standing straight, folded her arms. She nodded. "Used one of the emergency one-shot teleport buttons. The hired help should be back in Argentina, memories blanked. And what do you mean, 'they'll heal'? They shouldn't even break! How much have you lost?"

The Cowl leaned forward, his face hidden from his partner. He breathed deeply, more in exhaustion than pain. She watched his shoulder muscles move underneath his bodysuit and realized she was still seeing the world in night vision. Responding to her thought, the bird mask switched back to the regular spectrum.

"Fifty percent. Maybe sixty. I can get hurt now, but it heals, maybe a little slower than it used to. Not sure how much damage I can take. Strength is nearly all there I think. Transference gone."

Blackbird swore and the Cowl looked into her round, expressionless goggles. She dropped to one knee, leather catsuit creaking, so her beak was almost touching the masked triangle of the Cowl's nose.

"Transference? But you got *into* the bank as planned… How did you get back here? You didn't…?"

"Walk?" He cut her off, then nodded and almost laughed. "Yes, I walked. It's a long way from the bay." The Cowl took Blackbird's delicate, thin hands, and curled his fingers through hers as best he could. His reinforced gauntlets were almost as thick as welding gloves and his left hand was wrapped tightly in a string of black rosary beads. Blackbird's fingers pressed sharply against them. He must have had a rough time if he'd got those out. She didn't understand it herself, but then there was nothing wrong with clinging to a comfort blanket, no matter what form it took. She preferred hers in a small glass with ice.

"You walked?"

"I can't fly anymore."

"Can't fly?"

"Nope." The Cowl looked up into the invisible dark of the cavern ceiling, as if he were replaying events in his mind. "When I came to we were well on the way to orbit. Up, up, and away! I get the feeling it wasn't intentional. He was holding on, tight, almost as if he was afraid to let go. But it wasn't me providing the power – he was the one doing the flying. I managed to turn and push him off, but we were high. *Very* high. He went out cold, must have been lack of oxygen, and let go. I think I blacked out too, for a moment."

"And?"

"And, my dear, it was a one-way ticket to ground zero. I couldn't fly. It was all him, whoever he is. If he survived the fall – we were up a good few miles."

"The Seven Wonders?"

The Cowl shook his head, then sat back and spun the chair around to the computer. Pulling the small wireless keyboard towards him, he idly tapped for a few moments, bringing up a variety of windows on the giant display almost randomly. Sensing he was deep in thought and not really paying attention to what he was doing, Blackbird reached over and placed her hand on top of his. He stopped typing, looked at her, almost startled, then smiled. She returned the expression, forgetting her mouth was hidden from view.

The Cowl's smile dropped. "Did you get a look at him? He was one of the customers. I know the Seven Wonders. We both do. It wasn't Linear. Too short. And I don't think I recognized any of the others in the bank. You?"

Blackbird sat on the lip of the desk. "No, I was preoccupied playing Universal Soldier. We should use machine guns more often. They're fun." She giggled, the sound echoing metallically through the filters in her mask. The Cowl chuckled, but stopped quickly and wrapped a hand over his side as he coughed.

"Oh, don't make me laugh. You won't like me when I laugh."

He resumed his one-handed tapping at the keyboard; four keystrokes later, a new folder opened on the gigantic screen. The Cowl leaned forward, just a little.

Blackbird watched him for a moment, tapping the panel beneath her.

"What happened to the cloak?"

"It weighs a ton when it's wet. I dumped it upstairs. You been busy?"

Blackbird stood, and moved behind the Cowl's chair. Reaching around the wide, winged back, she rested her hands on his shoulders and her chin on his head. Her voice fell to a whisper.

"Oh yes. We've received the second transmission. Two to go and we'll be able to plot the coordinates exactly. I've also extracted the data from *that*."

She pulled his chair around and pointed it off to the right. Ahead, on a third shadowed platform apparently floating above the cavern's abyss, was a long table surrounded by medical equipment. On the table lay the mortal remains of Mr Ballard, late of the California Cooperative Bank. The man's head was missing.

The Cowl swiveled the chair around to face Blackbird. She reached forward, behind his neck, and tugged. The Cowl's skullcap and facemask came off in her hands; his eyes were bloodshot, with dull purple bruises around the sockets. Blackbird ruffled his hair and he smiled.

"Mask-hair, sorry."

Blackbird reached behind her own neck, running her fingers down a concealed seam. The black beak in front of her facemask sagged forward, and she pushed the mask up and off. She dangled it from the strap on two fingers and blew her short fringe from her eyes.

"Me too," she said coyly. "But when we rule the world, we won't need masks, or secret identities. Two more transmissions and we've won."

The Cowl's smile creased his eyes into thin slits. Oh, she loved that. Blackbird let her mask drop to the floor and pulled a glove off before running her naked finger over his stubbled cheek.

"Come on, we need to get ready. We've a big night ahead."

"Oh, that I do not doubt, Blackbird."

He smiled, and she smiled, and they leaned towards each other, supervillain and sidekick locking together in a deep kiss.

CHAPTER FIVE

Joe spilled his coffee, swore under his breath, and said hello to Gillespie.

The coffee station was mostly in darkness, the main overheads off but with just enough light leaking through from the open-plan precinct office to enable the safe preparation of hot beverages. Joe smiled weakly as Gillespie paused in the doorway, keeping outside of the mini-kitchen but fixing Joe with a look that wasn't entirely friendly.

"How did I know you'd still be here?" Gillespie's eyes returned to his cell phone, the four-inch screen lighting his face from underneath like he was about to recite a campfire ghost story.

Joe turned back to the sink, mind racing as he set about attempting a second cup of coffee. Not quite able to multitask to the required degree, he ended up tipping his own fresh cup down the sink. He paused, resisted a sigh, and peered at the faint, worn LEDs on the coffee robot on the countertop next to him. He cleared his throat and spoke to the wall.

"Y'know, in some lines of work, a bit of unscheduled overtime is considered to be a good thing."

He heard Gillespie chuckle to himself, and, confidence buoyed, turned to follow up his joke quickly – and *naturally*, he hoped – but the captain's attention was back on his phone.

Joe sighed again. Gillespie's eyes flicked up to him, their whites green from the LCD light, then back to the phone. The captain began texting while talking. Now *there* was multitasking.

"It's considered a good thing in this police department too, detective. Except when it's a Friday night and you're hiding in the dark, which means Sam's here using the taxpayers' electricity for work which isn't on her books." He paused and his phone bleeped as the mystery text message was sent. When he looked back at Joe, it was with *that* look. Head tilted down, Gillespie peered up at his detective through thick black eyebrows knitted together into a single featureless furry spacebar.

"Uhh..."

"She at her desk, or have you stalled me long enough for her to get to the ladies' while I go to my office, grab some paperwork, and get out? Is that how it works?" Gillespie waved his hand at the sink. "Is the coffee-spilling something to do with it? You running interference, detective?"

The captain took just a step into the coffee station, glanced around the perfectly serviceable – if simple – area and gave a snort of derision. Joe knew that it was nothing to do with the mini-kitchen and its amenities, or lack thereof. Gillespie made his coffee here just like anyone else during the day.

This was establishing his seniority, his authority.

"Uhh..."

Joe wasn't good at this, but then he was a little surprised that Gillespie knew what the game was anyway. Fuck. Who was he kidding? A John Le Carré spy novel this was not.

"I don't want to hear it." Gillespie abruptly turned and headed towards his enclosed office. "It's the weekend. I'm going to play golf. I'm only here to take some papers so I can pretend I'm important to my wife. If you guys are into some kind of kinky career-retardation fetish, I cease to give one shit. Goodnight, detective."

Joe followed his boss out into the office; Sam was nowhere in sight, but her computer monitor cast a white spot of light on her empty chair, and her traditional green-shaded desk lamp was on.

Shit.

"Sir, I..."

"You need to learn to quit while you're ahead, detective." Gillespie kept walking, shaking his head. "If I remember this on Monday morning I'll call you to the principal's office. But just make sure you get him. I don't care if it's for mass murder or tax evasion, bring me something to pin on the Cowl and then we'll take it to the Seven Wonders to handle. We're their guests next week, don't forget. You got that, detective?"

Joe nodded, fresh cup of hot coffee in one hand and heart racing in his chest. Gillespie turned and looked his detective up and down, then sighed and walked out, banging the door to his office closed behind him. A second later the bubbled glass of his partition lit brightly as the captain began shuffling papers on his desk. Joe squinted and looked away.

"Safe?"

"Safe."

Sam's blonde hair appeared around the edge of the short corridor leading to the bathrooms. She looked confused for a second, then her eyes widened as they traced the source of the light to the captain's office. "Fuck!" She pulled back around the corner a little. "I thought you said it was safe?"

Joe sighed, and shook his head. "Chill, detective. He knows."

The lights in the captain's office snapped off, and Gillespie strode out. He glanced at Joe as he passed and then at Sam, frozen in the doorway. He paused for a second, gave her a curt nod, then kept walking.

"Milano can fill you in. Have a good weekend."

And then the captain was gone; Joe and Sam had the office to themselves once more.

Sam slowly made her way back to her desk and sank into the chair. "Fill me in?"

Joe rolled a nearby chair over, sat heavily and leaned back, stretching his legs out. Arms behind his head, he whistled without a sound and looked at the ceiling.

"He says we can get him if we take our investigation to the Seven Wonders."

Sam's jaw worked up and down for a second or two as she processed the information.

"Since when are the Seven Wonders interested in what goes on in this city?" She paused. "And since when is the chief interested in cooperating with them?"

"Hey," said Joe, his arms collapsing onto his lap. "Don't you get it? Gillespie just gave us the go. We're attending that civic thing next week. They'll all be there, so let's gather the case up and make sure we have something to present."

Sam looked at him blankly. Joe sighed.

"Come on, Sam, we have a chance here. For the first time in months. This might be the so-called SuperCrime department, but we're redundant, our services mostly farmed out to Homicide or other places that actually need good detective work when we're not just pulling yellow tape around another of the Cowl's battlegrounds. And it might be our last chance. If we blow this, Gillespie isn't going to let it slide any longer. The Seven Wonders may be ineffectual but they're the city's official guardians. And they were good once, remember? Hell, they were great – the best."

Sam nodded, slowly. Joe watched her for a moment. Finally, she got it. Sink or swim, do or die. Joe quite liked his SVPD pay check and wasn't too keen to lose it. And if that meant taking everything to the city's resident superteam, then so be it.

"OK."

Sam shifted her monitor around a little, waving Joe in.

"Look at this."

Joe swung forward, the rollers of the office chair banging loudly on the floor. It was late. It was Friday. Tomorrow was Saturday. He wanted a drink. And something to eat. And some sleep. And to watch ESPN. And to generally have a life. Then he looked at Sam's face, alive with concentration, focus, passion. Another all-nighter digging into the SVPD files on the Cowl, filling Sam's own private file on the supervillain. A private file that now had possibilities.

On their own, he really wondered what Sam thought she would be able to do. Locate his lair, reveal his true identity, present the case without Gillespie's knowledge, and force the Seven Wonders into action? The captain had been right there, at least. The city's superteam may have been a mostly invisible, idle presence for years, but there was no way in hell the SVPD could do anything about the Cowl. The supervillain was untouchable. It'd be like handcuffing God.

As much as he hated to admit it – as much as he knew Sam refused to believe it – they needed the Seven Wonders on their side. They had no choice.

"So, we got something we can run with? Something new?"

Sam nodded, and smiled. The shock of Gillespie's visit forgotten, the old excitement was returning. The Cowl really was her reason for being a cop. Joe glanced at the tiny portrait frame on Sam's desk. She never mentioned him when they were working, but David was an invisible presence, always at Sam's shoulder. Joe felt it – he and Sam had a partnership, an understanding about not just the job, but about *life*. Sam didn't talk about David because she didn't need to. Not even on the anniversary of his death, which… *Fuck* it, it was the day of the bank job. Joe sighed and pulled back a little out of Sam's light, but his partner didn't notice. Or if she did – she was a mighty fine detective, after all – she didn't show a damn thing.

"I've pulled the CCTV from the bank. Here's our mystery man."

Joe squinted at the monitor. Like all CCTV recordings, it seemed, the tape from the bank was black and white and fuzzy. Sam tapped the screen over a young man with dark hair kneeling beside another hostage. The man was glancing left and right, shifting slightly on his knees.

"There's no match on our system for our new speedster."

Joe frowned. "Are you going to ask them about this guy?"

"Leverage. They'll want to see this, and maybe we can use it to get some cooperation out of them."

"Do you think he is Linear?"

Sam leaned back. "If he is, knowing his face is a card in the hand for us. If he isn't, they'll be spitting tacks. Either way, they might start taking us seriously."

Joe whistled again. "Blackmailing the superteam. Nice plan, detective."

Sam laughed, then closed the CCTV and brought up the SVPD's CRIMESCENE database. A saved search displayed a series of mugshots, arranged in a tiled display. Sam had stacked files on a dozen recorded criminals. Joe couldn't see any connection in the collection of faces – black, white, Asian, all male, some young, most old.

"I ran a new keyword search," she said. "Check it out."

"You think one of these could be the Cowl?"

Sam smiled. "You bet. Here, listen."

Joe leaned forward, eyes on the screen. It was going to be a long night.

CHAPTER SIX

Tony remembered the night he met her.

He remembered looking around the bar, and saying to Bill: "This was a bad idea." Bill was sitting on his left, his smile a mile wide. Clearly he wasn't letting Tony's negativity ruin a night on the tiles, and Tony watched as Bill's head bounced a little to the music even as he shook it in despair at his friend's attitude. Bill swigged his beer then breathed malt-toned bubble-air into Tony's face. Tony tried not to react, but moved his own glass a little farther away from his chin, which was practically on the bar anyway. He knew he was being a killjoy in a club full of happy people, but part of him liked the fact that he was being contrary. The other half of him felt bad for Bill, who was making a superheroic effort to cheer him up.

"Lighten up, bro," Bill said. "And drink up. You've been nursing that glass for an hour. What the hell is it, anyway?"

Tony pulled the glass in and sniffed it, reminding himself but also making a show that this really wasn't his scene.

"Gin and tonic. Too much gin."

Another disbelieving shake of the head, another swig of beer. Bill drained the bottle and waggled it between two fingers in Tony's face.

"Gin and tonic? Who the hell drinks gin and tonic?"

"*I* drink gin and tonic, Bill."

"Yeah except you're not tonight, are you? Or do you wait for it to evaporate from the glass and breathe it in?"

This Tony smiled at, and in defeat he took a sip. He didn't go out much – didn't go out at *all*, truth be told – and he'd forgotten that bar staff sometimes didn't quite understand the complexities of alcohol beyond beer, Southern Comfort, and whatever cocktail with sexually explicit moniker was popular among the underage drinkers this month.

"Screw you," said Bill, slapping the bar and sending his empty bottle rocking. "I see ladies of a female persuasion. See you in a bit." Bill's fourth/fifth/sixth beer arrived in his hand, ice-cold beads running into his fingers. He patted Tony slightly too hard on the shoulder, and casually sauntered away, taking an elliptical course that looked natural but would eventually lead him to the other side of the dance floor where two girls were doing their best to look like high school jailbait. Tony's eyes followed his friend's progress, and he craned his neck around as he refused to shift his quite comfortable arm from where it was supporting him on the black glass of the bar top.

"Huh," came the voice from behind Tony's back, to his right. "Bill is such a dick."

Tony laughed and dragged himself upright. He swallowed some more G 'n' T, clacked the glass down onto the bar and turned to his other work colleague, Nate.

"Ain't that the truth."

Actually, Nate was more than just a nine-to-five work colleague. Tony had been at the Big Deal for four years and had been avoiding making friends there from almost day one. Work wasn't a place for friends, work was work, it just "was". But four years in shit-pay retail is practically a lifetime, and Tony, Bill and Nate had accidentally found themselves the most senior floor staff in the local store's history. But while Tony and Nate *tolerated* Bill, there was still a slight, almost uncomfortable distance between them and him, as apart from their shared experience of selling computer junk to soccer moms, they had very little in common.

Tony and Nate, on the other hand, were firm friends. Kindred spirits, battling the oppressive corporate world, talking about music and books and gaming strategies while they stalked the almost endless shelves of cheap, shiny plastic laptops and the towering pyramids of free, shiny, printer/scanner/fax combos.

Tony and Nate both watched Bill for several minutes. Neither of them could understand it. Bill was fine in small doses, but not the kind of person you'd ever really choose to be around. Nate called him the Neanderthal. Tony didn't bother with a name. True, Bill annoyed him, but Tony really couldn't muster enough energy to think about him much. It seemed better that way.

Nate sniffed. "Sooo…?"

Tony regarded Nate with a raised eyebrow. Nate paused, bottle almost but not quite at his lips, eyes wide like he'd been caught naughty.

Tony frowned. "So what?"

Nate sighed, completed his drinking maneuver, and set the bottle down, *clink*. "So the old man who followed you? You seen him again?"

"Oh, that." Tony's mouth felt thick, the bitter aftertaste of juniper sticking to his tongue. "No, not since last Friday. And gee-whizz, thanks for reminding me that I have a stalker. I've been trying not to think about being bashed to death with a walking stick for a whole week."

Nate shook his head vigorously, drinking as he did so. Tony raised an eyebrow. How did people manage to fill themselves with so much weak beer?

"Yeah well there's something you really need to know. Your stalker? He was in the shop today. Oh yes, Carlos the Jackal wants a laptop for his granddaughter."

Tony almost choked. He waved at the girl behind the bar, not quite making coherent sentences, but eventually she got the message and extracted a green bottle from the neon-lit fridge behind her. Tony slapped a ten-dollar bill on the bar and took a long, cool draught of Mexican beer. His throat cleared and his head felt light.

"What the *fuck?* When exactly were you planning on telling me this?"

"Calm down, sister. I'm telling you now. I figured you might want some alcohol at hand first."

Tony sucked the bottle again, draining it in three gulps. The bitter taste was gone but his molars ached from the cold.

"What did he want? Was he looking for me? Did he stay long? When did he come in? Who did he speak to? Was it you? What did he want?"

Nate waved his friend down, and tried to resist laughing but failed, miserably. He half-turned away out of politeness.

"Dude! Easy, tiger, easy! Like I said. He wanted a laptop. Bill saw him, I was on the other side of the shelf and kept an ear out. He was there for about twenty minutes, no he didn't ask for you, I don't know what time it was, and he left with some brochures. He sounded nice."

"Nice?!" The music in the bar was loud, but not so much that his outburst was lost. A couple of nearby drinkers turned in his direction, forcing him to smile politely and pretend nothing was wrong. But his heart was hammering out of his chest again. Anxiety, panic, adrenaline. He had to do something about it or get out of the city. This was it, last straw. The Shining City could take a jump.

"Yeah, nice. Smelled of lavender."

Tony sat back on his barstool, brain processing the new data but having quite some difficulty. "My would-be murderer is a nice old man who smells of lavender? Thanks a lot."

Nate laughed, patted Tony neatly on the head like he was a little boy, and swung off the barstool. "I'll make sure I mention it at your eulogy. I need to pop the cork." Tony was alone at the bar.

The stool behind Tony creaked a little.

"You have your own stalker? I'm jealous, I've always wanted one."

Tony turned around.

The girl leaned in on the bar, mirroring Tony's own lazy slouch. He reflexively shifted, sitting up almost politely, but the girl didn't move. She grinned, and sipped from a shallow clear glass. Tony recognized the scent, and matched her expression.

"I thought nobody drank gin these days?"

"You're so right." She swirled the remainder around the glass and swigged it back. "You know I had to actually point to the bottle on the shelf? Jesus, I don't know why I come here. Don't they use it for 'Sexual Assault and Misdemeanors in a Dark Alley'? Or is that vermouth?"

Tony couldn't help but laugh. For the first time that night, in the company of a total stranger, he felt relaxed, his fear of the city and of the old man evaporating as the girl's eyes met his own.

"Let's see if they remember how to make it this time." Tony leaned in on the bar, grabbed the attention of the same girl that had served him a beer, and placed his order. He watched as her face creased with thought for a moment, then she turned and reached for the little-used bottle of blue gin.

"Blue gin? You must be rich. I think I like you." The girl on the barstool nodded appreciatively at Tony's selection of top-shelf liquor. Tony found himself grinning like a little boy, so busied himself with his wallet, avoiding her gaze.

"Yeah, real rich. Who knew retail slavery would be put me at the top of the Fortune 500." He extracted another twenty – his last bit of cash – from his wallet. He didn't try to hide it. He'd had enough of pretending to be social for one month anyway. He glanced around and saw Bill still trying it on – apparently quite successfully – with the maybe-underage girls. Nate had yet to return from the men's room.

Tony raised an eyebrow towards his new friend as he fingered the money. She smiled, shook her head, and waved her still-full glass at him. Tony nodded, part of him relieved to learn he'd have a couple of bucks left over for the rest of the weekend. A moment later and he parted with his hard-earned cash for this unnecessarily expensive G 'n' T.

"Retail, eh?" The girl's tongue rested on her upper lip. Tony found it to be the most attractive expression he'd ever seen. And really, this girl was something else – short dyed-black hair that shone with a bluish tinge in the dingy light of the bar, ruffled, spiky. It went with the angles of her face, sharp cheeks, pointed chin. Various clichéd descriptors floated in the front of Tony's mind – he wanted to say "elfin", maybe "birdlike", but aside from a pleasing bone structure there was nothing delicate about this girl. She wore a white T-shirt with sleeves torn off at the shoulder, exposing toned, muscular arms, clear evidence of a healthy gym routine. Each bicep was a multi-colored mural of tattoos – blacks and reds and yellows, a mix of abstract symbols and patterns on one arm, sharp leaves, thorns and flowers, and stylized birds on the other. Hunched over the bar as she was, legs folded over each other, the silver-capped toe of one of her Beatle boots almost touched his leg as her foot bounced with her heartbeat. The ensemble was finished with black tights and black mini, and an enormously wide belt, studded with silver.

She was exactly the kind of girl that Tony had always wanted to meet, and exactly the kind he never expected to. Cool, edgy, part of the alt crowd, part of a *scene,* hip but not a hipster. Tony shrank inside as he caught himself thinking those actual words. Good God, was it that long since he'd met a girl?

Tony raised his glass, noting again the volume of heady spirit overwhelming the amount of tonic. The girl laughed at his expression and raised her own drink. The pair clinked a toast, then swigged. Then their eyes scrunched, faces twisted in only slightly exaggerated displeasure, and both burst out laughing.

"Yeah, retail." Tony found his voice again after the harshness of the poorly prepared drink. "Been selling computers at Big Deal for four years. Not quite the high-powered career I had in mind, but it's easy enough. I can handle being bored and being paid to be bored. Work is work."

The girl nodded. "Work is work." She whispered Tony's mantra back to herself. "I like it. Jeannie." She held out a hand. Tony hesitated, thinking he'd misheard what she said, then took her hand. Her grip was light but there was strength in the fingers. "Tony. So, genie in a bottle?"

She smiled and sipped her drink, carefully this time, really only letting the liquid bathe her lips. Tony found himself imagining that she enjoyed the warmth the strong spirit imparted, the hint of bitterness as she ran her tongue around her mouth. He took another sip of his own drink and found his hand was shaking, just a little, and the front of his jeans were suddenly uncomfortably tight.

"Wow, a Fortune 500 retail monkey and a comedian as well?" Jeannie's smile was like a summer's day. "This is my lucky night."

"You and me both, huh?"

"Wanna dance, monkey?"

Before Tony realized what he was doing, realized that dancing was the most horrible thing that he hated the most, Jeannie had slipped off the barstool, grabbed his hand, and dragged him onto the dance floor.

CHAPTER SEVEN

The night belonged to the Cowl; he *owned* it. It was his kingdom, his domain; everything he did revolved around it. His costume was black, non-reflective, and the long scalloped cloak could envelop his entire body with a twist of an arm, reducing him to nothing more than a shadow. The famous hood, pulled forward, could hide most of the lower part of his face, the only section of bare skin visible. Give him an alley-way, a rooftop – hell, give him the shadowed overhang of a shop front – and the Cowl could vanish, becoming one with the blackness.

He'd been doing it a long, long time, and life on the night side of San Ventura was easy. Indestructible, invulnerable, able to fly, to run, to manipulate energy, to see through people and walls, to eaves-drop on every conversation on the West Coast of North America. Life was easy.

Or had been. His powers were ebbing, one by one, almost according to some predefined checklist. The unexpected curtailment of the bank job had come as something of a surprise, the lack of power a terrifying, paralyzing moment of realization. As much as he tried to pretend it was age, or tiredness, or just some weird phase that would pass, he knew, really, that something was up. It wasn't natural. It occurred to him that perhaps it was some kind of act of God, that He was judging him. But... no, he was doing God's work, he knew that. And besides, there was a probable cause much closer to home.

The Seven Wonders. It had to be. They'd finally found a way to take him down without getting their brightly colored hands dirty.

But the Cowl was the Cowl. And so he ignored his fading powers, pushing the problem to the back of his mind. He didn't need powers to rule the night. He was an expert in terror and combat. Nobody could touch him, superpowers or no superpowers.

And… and in a way, it added something. A new thrill. It was almost like he was doing it himself, getting his hands dirty, going back to basics like he did when he first started on his mission to control the city ten years ago. Maybe this *needed* to happen. Strip it down, take it back to basics. The feeling was strange, but it drew him close to his beloved city, the city he had guided, shaped and terrorized for a decade. San Ventura was his city, and nobody could take that from him. And, for the moment at least, he could still heal, although it was slower now. He'd recovered from his drop in the ocean, but his shoulder still ached if he lifted his arm too high.

He thought of this as he waited in the shadows of the alley, a dozen blocks south of the main strip, heading out towards the less salubrious suburbs but still within the city limits. An area of dark parks where crackheads did deals with prostitutes, where police calls often went unanswered, where the law feared to tread after a certain hour thanks to the Cowl's personal fan clubs. If only he'd thought of it first, it would have been a genius piece of marketing: all you needed was a black hooded sweat top and a black bandana to tie around your face, and some red spray paint to scrawl an Ω on your chest and that was it, you were in the Cowl's gang. He'd even seen some shirts with the logo – the *brand* – properly screen-printed, some even attempting to copy the entire sigil. Now that was commitment to the cause.

None of it was his doing, but it pleased him nonetheless. As his grip on the city tightened, so more and more gangs – just kids, really – came out at night, dressed in black, calling themselves the Hoods, or the Executioners, or the Black Hats, or the End Times. He liked those names. They sounded like metal bands. No one in San Ventura dressed like the Seven Wonders, or formed vigilante justice groups to patrol the night. It wasn't that kind of city. The night belonged to the Cowl and his admirers. The night was what everyone feared.

The Cowl snapped out of his reverie at the sound of slow, soft footfalls. They were a block away still, but he'd been waiting for them and his subconscious tuned the sound in, focusing on it, judging speed, distance, direction. He wasn't sure whether he still had superhearing or whether he was running on pure instinct and years of experience. The footsteps were matched with a third sound. It was hollow, brittle, muted. A walking stick with rubber foot. The target was getting closer.

It was a bad area of town, but even so, the man with the stick walked it every night, late, late. He even left the street – which was at least doused with the tobacco smudge of yellow sodium streetlamps – and walked down the dark alley. A suicidal shortcut in any large city in America, surely, the very kind of cliché that delighted fans of every cheap B-movie thriller.

But the man was never afraid and never hesitated, and for good reason. The Cowl knew he had the protection of the Seven Wonders – the *personal* protection of them. Or at least he had. The old man always walked the same route, closing his laundromat at 7pm precisely and heading home via the same street and the same alley. The Cowl knew about the arrangement with the city's protectors, and that was why he'd always warned the gangs off the man. The more usual kind of criminal, the regular or garden-variety mugger, had tried a few times, but more often than not had found themselves at the end of Linear's silver supersonic fists, or being held by a rapidly tearing shirt front from two hundred feet in the air, Aurora or the Dragon Star still climbing high.

But that hadn't happened for a while. No one had tried anything in forever. Perhaps the word had got around the bums and drunks that this guy was too much effort and not worth the risk. The impossible crime.

But tonight… well, tonight the Cowl had something he needed to collect. He could be in and out before the Seven Wonders were alerted. And he knew for a fact that most of the superteam were otherwise engaged, prepping security with the SVPD for the annual grand police charity ball tomorrow, which was due to start in just a few hours. The city's rich and famous and beautiful would all be in attendance. The Cowl allowed himself a smirk at this, and stretched out his arm, trying to exercise the pain out of the joint.

The target turned into the alleyway. The Cowl was practically invisible in the night to most people, he was sure of that, and he also knew that the target was a frail seventy year-old man with bad eyes and bad hearing. As far as the old man was concerned, the alley was empty.

And besides, while the Cowl had declared the man a no-go for the gangs, he knew that someday, one day, he'd need the information he carried, locked in his elderly mind.

Were the Seven Wonders stupid, or just arrogant? Both, probably. The whole purpose of these protectors of knowledge was that their secrets would be kept from the Cowl. The ease with which he'd taken the bank manager had proved that perhaps the Seven Wonders really were that stupid. The Cowl had known about the "vaults" for years, the living strongboxes, entrusted with individual elements of a single secret. He imagined the superteam scrambling in a blind panic as the bank job went down.

The Cowl allowed himself a smile. All too easy.

The second "vault" was just feet away. Despite the heat of the night, the elderly man was wrapped in a heavy woolen overcoat, black homburg pulled down tight. He wore glasses with thick plastic rims that were probably new in 1963. His cane was a thick walking stick, the expensive kind, fashioned out of a single natural shaft of wood. The Cowl could see the grain and the knots of the branch that were left in the surface as a decorative touch, and was pleased to note his supervision was still in operation.

The man passed by, walking slowly but not shuffling. The Cowl observed his movements. He was old, sure, but seemed in good shape. The coat was filled out, the shoulders straight, the head up if it weren't for the deep tilt of the hat. The walking stick was being used for the intended purpose rather than just for show, but aside from the slow pace, he looked like a rather spry elderly gentleman. Something like an ex-boxer, or maybe someone who had served his country in an overseas theater back in the day.

The Cowl pushed himself off the alley wall, allowing his cloak to fall away. Although he knew he'd be silhouetted by the light streaming into the alleyway's entrance behind him, his costume would still keep him featureless and dark. And if the man were to turn around, there was nothing wrong with a touch of fear instilled by the sweeping shadow of San Ventura's resident supervillain.

Immediately the old man in front of him stopped. The Cowl stood still, completely silent. It occurred to him that perhaps another reason why the vault was untouchable was because, perhaps, he wasn't *just* a regular old man. Although he knew about the failed attacks, how various members of the Seven Wonders would appear as if by magic as soon as their secrets were threatened and fight off any attacker, other stories of dead gang members and failed muggings crossed the Cowl's mind.

He dismissed them. Mr Ballard had just been a man, after all. And while there were more than enough retired superheroes in the world, the whole purpose of the vaults was to hide the information *out* of the reach of those who may be tempted to use it.

The Cowl smiled again. Even the Seven Wonders themselves probably didn't know about it, mindwiped by that stuck-up bitch, Bluebell. Hide the secrets in the city, mindwipe everyone so not even they can remember anything about it, but leave a latent post-hypnotic suggestion to protect the locations at all costs.

Although...

The old man shuffled. Still the Cowl didn't move.

Although none of them had shown up at the bank. Maybe the Seven Wonders were sleeping on the job.

Or maybe they had an eighth member, that mystery speedster. The Cowl frowned again. He'd have to look into that. First things first...

"I figured you'd try it sooner or later, boy." The old man coughed, clearing his throat wetly before continuing. He didn't turn around. "Didn't figure on it being so damned long, though. You got some patience, I'll credit you that. I guess that's part of why you're in charge of this otherwise mighty fine city." He turned slowly until he was facing his ambush, then switched his walking stick over to his other hand.

The old man harrumphed. His accent was deep, molasses-dipped, each word drawn out like an oil painting. He wasn't a local. Alabama perhaps. Somewhere south-east.

The Cowl took a step forward, stopping when the old man raised his stick up and pointed it directly at him.

"Now hold on there, fella," said the old man. "You might be faster than a speeding bullet and stronger than a locomotive, but even you might want to think twice afore you do anything you might regret in the morning."

The Cowl swept his cloak behind him, intended to intimidate, but the old man just laughed drily. The Cowl stepped forward again, annoyed.

"I extracted the secret from the first vault without much trouble," he said. "What makes you so different?"

The old man placed his stick back on the ground and leaned on it as he ran a hand around the rim of his hat. "Oh, I'm plenty different, no mistake. Each vault is different, y'see? The first was hidden. Well, you found him right enough, sittin' pretty in the bank. Me, I'm hidden in plain sight, but my secret is what you might say a little more important, so the heroes didn't just give it to no one. You ever heard of Death's Head Angel?" The old man paused, expecting a reply.

The Cowl didn't have time for this. It was a snatch-and-grab, in and out. "The Black Angel? Superhero from South Carolina. Missing in action twenty years now. And?"

The old man laughed drily again, like his throat was full of grit. "The Black Angel. Haven't heard that one in a while. It started as an insult, you know, until I claimed it for myself. You're right, I was active in South Carolina, but I never went missing. I just... retired and relocated. Seems even an old man is useful for something."

This information was new, and the Cowl had been quite, quite mistaken. The old man – the second of the Seven Wonders' walking "vaults" of knowledge and data – was a retired superhero. Death's Head Angel – the Black Angel – running a laundry on Bull Street.

The Cowl took a deep breath. No problem. He knew about the Black Angel. He was more powerful by an order of magnitude and thirty years younger at least.

The fact that he was missing a range of superpowers crossed his mind, but he dismissed it. Even so, the Black Angel was an old man. His skin would tear like dry leaves. The Cowl didn't need superpowers to take him on.

"Ah, I figured on that," said the old man.

The Cowl blinked behind the lenses in his mask. What, the Black Angel was telepathic now?

"I'm an old man and my powers are fading fast, that's the truth," the mark continued. "You could kill me with a mean look from that mask o' yours." The old man stepped forward, removing his glasses and carefully tucking them into the top pocket of his overcoat. He waved the stick again, punctuating each point with a jerk of his gnarled hand. "If it weren't that your powers were a-fadin' too. Am I right? You ain't as fast as you were, you ain't as *strong* as you were. You can't even fly." He laughed, shaking his head and leaning back on his stick. "Hell, you'll still kill me, but listen to me, boy. This isn't going to be easy. Consider it first, and if you stay true to your decision, then so be it. The Black Angel retired and went missing years ago. I'm just an old man mugged in an alley. Nobody will miss me. But sure as hell I'll make it difficult."

"Enough!" The Cowl couldn't help the outburst, but fought to control the irritation. How did the old man know what was happening to him? He was a superhero entrusted with a secret, so perhaps he was still in touch with the Seven Wonders, even if the superteam didn't actually remember doing it.

But did they know about his powers fading? The Cowl sucked on his teeth. He'd been right. They must be responsible for it. He clenched his fists.

The old man sighed, looking to the ground. "Well, there's your decision then. I hope the secret is worth it."

The old man ran forward, stick raised like a club. He didn't cry out or say anything else, his face fixed with a firm, purposeful expression. The Cowl immediately crouched, timing a punch that would snap the man's head from his shoulders. The Black Angel came into range, stick above his head, and then he let out a yell.

The Cowl's fist flew forward, but was met by the downward curve of the walking stick. The wooden shaft flexed alarmingly, the impact forcing the Cowl's arm downwards and throwing him forward off balance. A stab of pain shot through the Cowl's shoulder as bones jarred together in the joint, but after a second he put it out of his mind and tried to swing his other arm around. But the Black Angel had kept moving and the Cowl's fist whistled past his head. The old man ducked left and brought the stick down and out to his right, then pulled it back with both hands like he was a champion rower.

The stick's shaft slipped between the Cowl's legs, twisting them and sending the supervillain sprawling forward. As his cloaked back presented itself, the Black Angel spun and threw out both his legs, balancing on his walking stick with superhuman agility as he ploughed both feet into the small of the Cowl's back. The Cowl bent in the wrong direction and cried out in pain as the force of the kick propelled him through the air to the far end of the alley. A large yellow dumpster, already pitted and dented, took the brunt of the impact, collapsing around the Cowl like baking foil as he crashed into it.

The Cowl slumped downwards and hit the ground, but his cape was pinched in a tear in the dumpster's side. He grabbed it and yanked the fabric free, but it took two strong tugs.

Dammit. Not good. His strength was borderline normal. The old man had been right, it was going to be difficult.

But not, by the Black Angel's own admission, impossible. He'd known the Cowl would be able to beat him. The key was to get it over with as quickly as possible.

The Cowl stood and tasted something sour on his lip. He ran his tongue over his bottom teeth, discovering with surprise that his mouth was filled with a liquid that wasn't saliva. It was... blood?

OK. Blood. There goes the invulnerability.

The old man was on his knees at the end of the alley. He was completely out of breath, and was forcing his walking stick into the pavement as he tried to pull himself up. His laugh was still dry but much weaker now.

"Now that's something I haven't had to do in a long, long time. I have to say that while I know you're going to kill me, at least you do me the honor of letting me go out fighting. Perhaps the time has come after all."

The Cowl ignored him and conjured a fizzing orb of plasma between his hands, the alley suddenly illuminated with brilliant white light. He grew the energy ball in his hands like a balloon, noticing that the light had dazzled the old man while his own mask had instantly compensated. The Black Angel was standing now but looking down, holding both arms in front of his head to shield himself from the light.

"Goodnight, Gracie," said the Cowl, throwing the ball of energy toward his enemy like a World Series baseball pitcher. Even before it had reached its target, he began to walk forward, ready to claim his prize.

The plasma ball exploded, early. The Cowl stopped and his mask struggled this time as the alley was enveloped in a rainbow flash of light. As the remnants of the energy crackled against the damp brick walls of the alley, he could see the old man standing straight with the walking stick held in both hands, like a batter, the shaft smoking from where it had hit the plasma ball. The old man had his eyes closed but was smiling.

The Cowl couldn't help but laugh. He had to hand it to him. Even nearing, what, eighty, the Black Angel was a class act. The fight was beyond him and it was starting to show, but he kept it up and would battle until his last breath. Just like a superhero.

But every second that passed was time for him to recover, and this had already taken far longer than the Cowl had hoped. As the old man stood there and wheezed, the Cowl charged forward. His fists flew, left, right, left, right, left again, cracking the Black Angel's jaw and cheekbones. The old man was thrown backwards, each successive punch tossing him higher into the air, each left and right hook arcing blood in either direction, spraying the already wet alley with hot liquid.

But the old man didn't fall. As soon as his feet touched the ground he stumbled backwards and, to the Cowl's surprise, ducked the final punch then jabbed his own fists in a sharp uppercut against his attacker's chin. The Cowl cried out in surprise and hit the alley wall, pins and needles crawling over his whole face and neck. He blinked to clear the spots and saw the old man shambling forward, zombie-like in the half-light, blood dripping thickly into the shadows.

The Cowl pushed off from the wall to renew the attack, but each punch was blocked with a forearm or an open hand. In the near-darkness of the alley, the two scuffled like prize fighters, a mix of boxing, martial arts and no-rules brawling as the Black Angel made his final, glorious stand. For every hit that landed on the Cowl, the Cowl managed to get four into the Black Angel's body. Bones cracked audibly on both sides, but the old man took the worst of it. Finally he swiped drunkenly for a gut-punch, but the Cowl eased back out of range. With the old man's head bowed, he pummeled downwards with both hands, striking the Black Angel between the shoulder blades. There was a *crack*, and the old man slumped, leaning forward against the Cowl's stomach.

The Cowl kicked a knee up, throwing the old man off him, and stepped back. Acid-sharp pain coursed down his side, and he leant forward, cradling his damaged ribs with both arms. There was more of the unfamiliar metallic taste of blood in his mouth, and looking down he saw exposed flesh underneath tears in his costume, dark and slick with more blood. The Cowl hadn't had a fight like that in… in *ever*.

The old man twitched on the ground and, slowly, stood up and arched his back, like he'd just finished his warm-up and was ready for round two.

The Cowl flinched backwards, and felt the alley wall against his back. How was this possible? Clearly the old man thing had been an act.

The Black Angel looked around and scooped his hat up, replaced it on his head, then bent down and picked up his walking stick. The wheezy, brittle chuckle sounded again.

"You're doin' good, son. Real good."

This was a mistake, the Cowl knew now. Underpowered and injured, he should have brought Blackbird and taken the old man in an instant. No games. No terror. Just in and out, job done. With Blackbird's help even a superhero as powerful as the Black Angel wouldn't have stood a chance.

Back against the wall, the Cowl felt for the armored compartments around his belt and, after depressing a catch, slid out a short, shaped handle. Another flick, and a blade materialized in the air, twelve inches long but blue and translucent and not quite *there*. He swept it in front of him and the non-existent blade trailed blue and white mist.

The Black Angel looked up, still smiling, but the laugh was gone. His eyes were on the weapon. Neither moved or said anything for a moment, until the old man removed his hat and scratched his head, then replaced it.

"There's another hero in the city. You've met him once, in the bank, but the Seven Wonders don't know about him. He's not like them, believe me, and he'll be nothing but a world of hurt for you. In fact, he seems to have some of the powers you so carelessly mislaid. Been watching him a while now, even before he got all special. Got a touch o' the second sight, see – even saw my end comin', tonight. But I reckon you might have a match sooner or later. Take some advice and consider your ways."

"Thanks. I'll think it over."

The Cowl stepped forward. There was no time for any of this. He had a schedule to keep and already this particular expedition had gone on far longer than he'd anticipated.

The knife arced in the air, each cut and slice leaving a trail that lingered on the retina for longer than it should. The old man dropped first to his knees, then forward onto his face, and lay unmoving, and Death's Head Angel was no more.

CHAPTER EIGHT

There was a pop, and the audience *oohed* appreciatively. Aurora sent another glowing ball of energy up towards the ceiling, this one a spinning teardrop of many colors. It went out with a bang, and as the leader of the Seven Wonders took a deep bow, the crowd showed their appreciation with applause. Aurora stepped back and joined the clapping as the mayor of San Ventura took to the stage. It was cheesy shtick, but everyone loved it. Especially on a night like this.

"Thank you, everyone," said Curtis Leonard Smith III, thrice-elected mayor and as impressed by small tricks as anyone. "A toast, now, to the brave men and women of the San Ventura Police Department, in whose honor we are gathered tonight. Policing in this city is a unique challenge, and has been since the first powered criminals appeared in our fair city in 1958. Now, more than sixty years later, San Ventura is safe, is secure, and is happy, protected by the best law enforcement agency in the country. To the Shining City's finest, the SVPD!"

Joe raised his glass to the mayor's toast, broad grin on his face. Sam winced, and joined him out of politeness only. She was self-conscious enough as it was in the backless, sleeveless cocktail dress, and really didn't want to draw any more attention than she already was by not at least *pretending* to join in. She'd seen the looks all night. Even now, Dennis and Watts from the fourth floor chugged back the free champagne, thinking the glasses obscured their wandering eyes from her notice. Wrong. *Pricks.*

Joe drained his glass and gave a satisfied sigh of appreciation. He held it by the stem, looking around for one of the roving waiters to receive another.

"I can't believe you bought that bullshit, Joe."

Joe's smile didn't falter, his eyes still tracking the packed hotel ballroom. Sighting his prey, he adjusted his bowtie just a little and waved his glass in the air, waggling it by the stem in a faintly ridiculous "More please!" gesture.

"I don't." His teeth remained set in their smile, a gleaming band of white against the dark brown of his face. "Thing is, Sam, I know when to play the game and how to act like I mean it." He paused as an attractive waitress barely in her twenties switched his empty glass for a full one. Joe's grin stretched a little farther, and as the waitress walked away his gaze lingered on her rear, just a little. Sam caught the look and slapped him on the shoulder. Joe took a sip and turned to his friend and colleague, abandoning the fixed grin of his ventriloquist act and dropping his voice to a discreet whisper.

"This is the annual police charity ball. We all have to be here, Seven Wonders included. We know the mayor and the commissioner are in their pocket, and there's nothing we can do about it. We're also in the chief's little black book of naughty people, so we don't want to get noticed. We want to fade into the background and get this stupid charity event over and done with, and then front up with our case before we turn into pumpkins. Do you get it now, Detective Millar?"

She did, and she swore at Joe. She was sure his surprised reaction was also fake, as it didn't stop him bringing the glass to his lips and taking another gulp of champagne.

He was exactly right, and she should have known he was playing from the moment they walked in together. There was a reason that she and Joe stuck together both on and off the job. His ability to juggle difficult tasks and unusual requests, all the while presenting the facade that he and Sam were just a couple of regular cops doing their normal job, enabled her to continue work on her "extra-curricular" activities. It was a risk, but they'd managed for a couple of years. In reality, all it meant was longer hours for the both of them as they kept the official detective work up while Sam continued her investigation into San Ventura's most infamous criminal, the Cowl. SuperCrime, it turned out, was mostly clean-up, which meant she had to follow her own lines of enquiry if she was going to nail the bastard.

Which, it turned out, their chief had known about all along. And given that he hadn't given any indication that he did until the failed operation at the bank, perhaps they had tacit approval. The Cowl was a problem for everybody and Sam knew the chief wanted to get rid of him as much as she did.

Well... maybe not as much as she did. Sam sipped her champagne and pushed dark memories out of her mind.

"Captain Gillespie, how are you doing, sir?" Joe's hand steered Sam by the elbow around a ninety-degree arc so the pair were facing their boss. Gillespie looked just as fierce as always in black tie, and cast a quick look over Joe and Sam with a sour grimace before nodding in greeting.

"Good evening, detectives. I'm glad you were able to drag yourself away from your desks to be here."

Sam did her best to look demure. "Of course, sir, we've been looking forward to this for weeks." Joe nodded with a smile, and raised his glass. Sam wondered how much he was going to drink tonight. Or her, for that matter.

Gillespie's glass was full to the brim; Sam suspected it would remain so all night. The chief turned slightly and whispered something to a tall man behind him, with his back turned. The man immediately spun on his heel and joined the conversation.

"Detective Milano, Detective Millar, I would like to introduce the police charity's largest benefactor, Geoffrey Conroy. Mr Conroy, these are two of my finest detectives. Sam has been in the SuperCrime department for six years now, Joe for four. They're inseparable, and quite the dynamic duo."

The man was tall and had broad swimmer's shoulders that filled his expensive jacket admirably, despite one arm being held in a rigid cast. His chiseled features, an echo of 1940s Hollywood glamour, were marred only slightly by two dull black eyes. His tuxedo was expensively nondescript, save for a small gold crucifix lapel pin.

Sam knew exactly who he was. Everyone in the city did.

Conroy smiled and raised the glass in his free hand.

"Is that so, captain? Enchanted, Miss Millar. Detective Milano."

He bowed to Joe, and delicately took Sam's hand. Sam shivered slightly as one of the wealthiest men in the world, one of the most successful CEOs of one of the most successful industrial tech empires, kissed her hand. The smile on her face, for the first time that night, was now completely genuine.

"That's some cast you've got there, Mr Conroy." Joe prefaced the statement with a low whistle of appreciation. The billionaire industrialist grinned broadly, the lines around his eyes creasing into the dull purple bruises that circumscribed each. Conroy waggled the tips of his fingers, the only part of his left arm that was left out of the cast. Despite herself, Sam found the way the immaculate dinner jacket hung loosely over one shoulder rather rakish. Feeling her cheeks redden, she buried her nose in her champagne flute.

"You ever been waterskiing in the Virgin Islands, Mr Milano?"

Joe shook his head. "A detective's salary doesn't usually stretch that far, I'm afraid. Although if you want to have a word with my chief here I'm sure he'll be all ears."

Conroy laughed. "It's amazing at this time of year, let me tell you. But if you do get down there, just make sure you pay attention to your instructor. Or... well!" His fingers waggled again, and his laugh was shared with Captain Gillespie. Sam felt one eyebrow go up on its own. Gillespie, laughing? Wonders would never cease. She turned back to the billionaire.

"I'm glad you could still make it, Mr Conroy. That eye looks fresh and sore." Sam hoped it was a polite observation. Socializing with the city elite was not her favorite pastime, nor her most practiced.

Conroy nodded behind his drink, presenting Joe and Sam with just the waggling crystal base.

"Uh-huh." His voice echoed in the flute. "Took the fall yesterday, just got back this morning. I might be busy and rich and have, oh, sixteen hundred invitations to charity balls and auctions and bake-offs every year, but the most important is the SVPD Benevolent Fund. No way I was going to miss this. It's been in my iCal for eleven months!" He laughed with Sam and the others, but stopped to press the side of his empty but still-cool champagne glass to one black eye. "Ouch. But please, if you'll excuse me, it looks like I'm wanted."

Joe and Sam waved him off as Conroy bowed again and ducked off to talk to a young woman in hotel uniform, who was discreetly waving a white envelope to get his attention.

The trio stood in silence, avoiding eye contact for a while. Sam really needed another drink but there was no sign of a nearby waiter. If anything, the captain's customary scowl grew ever deeper.

Finally a waiter arrived; Sam and Joe switched their empty glasses for full ones while Gillespie actually took a real sip of his drink.

"Will you guys relax? You come to the ball every year. Does it always have to be like this?"

Sam turned but found Joe heading to the buffet. Under Gillespie's withering glare, she felt even more ridiculous in the little dress.

"Sorry sir, it's fine, really. No, really." She sucked on her fresh glass and found it emptied faster than she had intended. She gulped the mouthful awkwardly and hoped the chief hadn't noticed. "I've never met Mr Conroy before. Not in person, anyway. He's not what I expected at all."

Gillespie grunted, and, having now broken his no-alcohol rule, allowed himself a generous mouthful of drink. "He's rich, he's young. Ish. Good-looking. Some people have it all, I guess."

Sam raised an eyebrow. "C'mon, chief. He was nice."

This raised a smile. "Yes, he's nice. Looks like he sure must've taken a tumble. The perils of the rich and famous, eh, detective?"

Sam clinked her glass with his in mock toast. "Who'da thunk it?" She spun idly from side to side on one heel, turning enough to see Joe heading back toward them at some pace, holding his cell phone to his ear with one hand and balancing a pile of food on a far-too-small plate with the other. As he approached he looked up, shaking his head at his partner as he finished the call.

"What's up, Joe?"

Joe pocketed the phone. "Sorry to bust up the party, but we're needed back at the precinct. Body's been found in an alley off Main and Descartes. Homicide are on the way but Jackie Chan wants us to take a look. Irregular, could be one for our department."

"Main and Descartes?" Sam flapped her arms against her sides.

Work, just as she was beginning, perhaps, maybe, to enjoy herself. "Well, great. Sorry sir, duty calls."

Gillespie nodded. "That's not far. Check the scene and if it's not too much of a mess, come back here and send out Starr or Luigo. I'd rather have my two best detectives here representing the department than spending too much time on a routine case. And don't forget, we have an audience with Aurora at 11pm sharp. That's something we can't miss."

"Understood, sir." Sam turned to leave. Joe looked at his plate, reluctant to abandon the luxurious surrounds for the cold night. Gillespie held out a hand. Joe glanced between the chief's pale palm and his plate, before finally surrendering to his superior.

Joe met Sam in the lobby just outside the ballroom, where she was waiting for an attendant to fetch her coat from the cloakroom.

"Wait a second..."

"What?" Sam kept her eyes on the retreating form of the attendant as he disappeared into the cloakroom.

"Did the chief just call us his best detectives?"

"Don't worry, he was joking."

"The chief never jokes. It's those eyebrows. They're an alien parasite that exerts some kind of mind control."

"Is that a fact?"

"Sure is, partner. Aurora told me himself."

"Oh, Aurora now? Well, I'll be damned." Coat retrieved, Joe helped her into it and patted her on the back.

"Yep," he said. "We go way back. First-name basis, y'know. And besides, 'Aurora's Light' is a real mouthful."

Sam laughed. "That mouthful saved his ass from that superpowered copyright lawsuit, remember."

"Ah, the lifestyles of the superpowered and litigious."

Sam sighed.

"Let's go."

"Mr Mayor."

With one last wave to the assembled guests, Smith turned from the podium. Behind him, his personal staff and colleagues were still applauding his third (fourth?) toast. He smiled at them all, and raised his glass again. It was empty.

A red gauntlet holding a full glass appeared in front of him. The mayor took it gingerly, careful not to touch the fabric of the glove as it shimmered with energy, then made to playfully slap the provider on the shoulder before pulling his arm up short, theatrically. His staff laughed politely.

"And they say you can't get good service in San Ventura?"

This was the mayor's show, although perhaps not everyone was looking at him now. Beside him, a deep, hearty laugh emanated from the barreled chest in bright red and yellow that stood next to him. Aurora's Light, leader of the Seven Wonders, husband to Bluebell, and the most powerful superhero left in the world. Everyone called him Aurora.

The superhero's smile pushed his half-mask up his face a little, the flaming halo above his head flickering as he chuckled at the mayor's joke, tugging his thick salt-and-pepper hair like he was swimming in deep water.

"I hope I didn't warm that up too much for you, Mr Mayor." He raised a glove, palm-upwards, and created a small translucent yellow sphere of plasma, hovering an inch above his hand. It wobbled slightly, and Aurora let the crowd get a good look before quickly forming a fist and squeezing the ball of energy to nothing. There was an appreciative murmur, and sporadic applause broke out. The mayor laughed.

"Can I book you for my son's ninth birthday party? Our magician had to cancel."

"The Seven Wonders serve the city." Aurora gave a tight bow. "Now, sir, if you'll excuse me?"

The mayor waved his glass, and Aurora left the group of councilors and city staff.

He would have stayed to chat a while longer, maybe done a bit more with the plasma – middle-aged housewives loved it, and middle-aged housewives were, according to the mayor, the most influential group of voters. But he couldn't ignore the alert buzzing in his ear. As the most famous – and imposing – person in the entire room, he had no trouble reaching the quiet edge of the ballroom, the crowd parting to let him through without pause before closing in again in a wake of appreciative gossip and beating hearts.

He reached a pillar near the buffet, and turned back to face the charity ball. In the crowd, but at the periphery, he caught sight of a tall black woman in an ochre dress. She caught his eye and nodded, imperceptibly, before turning and casually taking another glass of champagne from a passing waiter.

Aurora touched his belt, the alarm clicking off with a sharp beep.

"Report, SMART."

"Citadel of Wonders to Aurora. Tracking on the Angel Vault has been lost. Vault breach presumed." The voice that entered Aurora's head was metallic, artificial, but not without inflection, simulated though it was.

Aurora took a breath. "Confirmed. Stand by."

He clicked the communicator off, and looking up saw the black woman moving slowly towards him. Happy that no one was observing with any particular interest, he began to walk towards her.

"Oh, excuse me."

Aurora stopped and smiled broadly, inwardly cursing at his own distraction. The man in front of him had a broken arm and two black eyes.

"Mr Conroy, a pleasure as always." Aurora bowed in acknowledgment. Looking up, he allowed a small smile to cross his face. "I heard about your Caribbean excursion. No permanent damage, I hope?"

"Only my pride, Aurora!" Conroy laughed, then with a grimace passed his uninjured hand inside his open jacket to rub a cracked rib. "Anyway, how's it going, big guy? The city keeping the Wonders busy?"

"Well," Aurora began, looking around the charity ball meaningfully, "the SVPD are the country's finest, I have no doubt about that. But San Ventura is no ordinary city. With the Cowl still at large..."

Conroy hissed, shaking his head. "We can't let that son of a bitch hold this proud city back, Aurora. That's why charities like this are important, that's why the Seven Wonders are important, that's why Conroy Industries is committed to the future of San Ventura."

Aurora held up a hand. His eyes were blank white ellipses in his mask and his chin was the only bare skin visible. Aurora's expressions were nearly impossible to read. That was the point. Superheroes – like supervillains – had to have one hell of a poker face.

"Don't worry, Mr Conroy, I know how committed you are to the future of our great city. You keep the place running from the bottom. We'll keep it running from the top. The Cowl doesn't have long now. One man – superpowered as he is – can't stand up to the seven of us much longer. Now, if you'll excuse me, I'll let you get back to the party."

"You got it." Conroy shook Aurora's hand as the superhero dialed back the swimming haze of heat around it enough not to burn. Aurora then gave his customary curt bow, and walked on.

Conroy watched the hero's receding back for a moment, then headed over to one of the plate windows that lined the entire east face of the ballroom. San Ventura glittered at night, a million points of light twinkly in the misty sea air. And at the center of it, towering above the skyscrapers of the business district which reflected its light back from their tall glass walls, the Citadel of Wonders. Tonight, the night of the SVPD ball, the thin triangular sliver that was the headquarters of the Seven Wonders was illuminated in a rotating display of blue, red and green light, mimicking the colors of the Police Benevolent Fund's logo.

Conroy gazed at the Citadel for just a second, then took a cell phone from his inside jacket pocket and put it to his ear.

"I hope," he whispered, "you're calling with good news?"

CHAPTER NINE

"*Stone cold,* is what."

"Murder is what it is, detective. Stone cold or not, makes no difference."

Sam kept her distance. The large pool of blood, black on the alley floor, was no longer spreading and the leading edge had been demarcated clearly with a little plastic triangle. But she'd never got used to the butcher's-slab stink of a stabbing, and until the scene lights were up, God only knew what she might step in. Joe was less cautious, squatting within reach of the body, enough to poke and prod with a pen. Sam seriously hoped it wasn't the same one he used to write up his notes.

Joe abandoned his incredibly thorough scene investigation, and – to Sam's dismay – replaced the pen in the top pocket of his jacket. Hands in pockets, he walked back to where Sam stood with her arms wrapped tightly around her in the cool San Ventura night.

Now Jacqueline Chan, SVPD's finest forensic examiner – and *please,* don't ever call her Jackie – could finally get on with her job without the clumsy frame of Detective Joe Milano at her elbow. Her blue-latexed hands were immediately on the collar of the old, worn coat that the body was wrapped in, not so discreetly checking that Joe's inept fiddling hadn't disturbed anything important. Sam had to smile. She knew how much Jacqueline hated it when cops touched things.

"What's the news, Jackie?"

Jacqueline tensed visibly, and Sam's smile only grew wider, knowing that Joe was using the nickname deliberately to get a bite. The doctor sighed loudly, and when she stood and turned around to face the detectives her own smile was pretty tight and thin. Behind Sam, Joe sniggered under his hand.

"What you have here, *Detective Milano,*" said Jacqueline, stressing Joe's name in the same way a disappointed schoolteacher would address a problem student, "is what we call a dead body. Scientifically speaking, of course. Please stop me if I'm getting too technical."

Joe pulled a face and Sam suddenly wished she'd taken that reassignment to San Diego when she'd had the chance. It was late, it was a Saturday, and it was colder than a summer's night should be. But San Ventura kept her close, and she knew she could never leave. Not while *he* was on the loose. And at least this had got her out of the charity event. Sam idly wondered what the dictionary definition of "workaholic" was before she took a step forward to get a better look at the body and dragged the conversation back to a professional level.

"Cause and time of death, Jacqueline?"

The good doctor unfurled the protective gloves slickly from her hands.

"Time? Difficult, but he's pretty fresh. Maybe only in the last two or three hours. Actual cause will take a bit longer to get the detail, but if you want the Cliffs Notes, it's pretty easy. He was cut up, and cut up good. A sharp blade, very long. Actually, *very* sharp – sliced his gut like jello."

Sam winced at the image. Unusual causes of death in San Ventura were not, well, unusual. Plasma incineration, bones powdered with a superpowered punch, flesh rendered molecule by molecule: the SuperCrime department had seen it all. Including, on very rare and significant occasions, the results of a knife so sharp it *fell* through solid objects. It was the preferred hand-to-hand weapon of San Ventura's finest and most upstanding citizen, the Cowl.

Except...

"It's not him."

Sam snapped out of her thoughts. Jacqueline was looking right at her. Sam held the gaze for one confused moment, then blinked and asked what she meant.

"The Cowl. I know what you're thinking, girl, and it ain't him. Can't be. You want to get down closer and see the mess that the perp made of the body. The Cowl is clean, perfect. When he uses that magic knife of his it's with precision, finesse. He uses it because it leaves no trace, unless you know what to look for. Which we do. But he and that side-kick of his never leave any evidence. You and I both know that."

Sam nodded. The Cowl's famous knife was, mostly, a weapon of last resort, used only if the supervillain didn't have time to unleash the array of incredible superpowers at his disposal. When you have superstrength, superspeed, invincibility and a dozen other abilities that were beyond the understanding of science, there usually wasn't much a knife could do that you couldn't do yourself with a flick of a spandex-wrapped wrist.

Not for the first time, Sam completely failed to understand why the SVPD – normal, ordinary, unpowered people with regular families and lives – were left to deal with supercrimes while the city's great protectors, the Seven Wonders, were not.

A second later and the thought evaporated. It was something she had felt every day for the last five years. All the cops in the city did. They had a job to do just like anyone else, and damn the Seven Wonders.

"Hey, Jacqueline, you seen this?"

Joe was at the end of the alley, which terminated in a chain-link fence, beyond which lay a courtyard and an outhouse with a low roof, most likely the back-end of a restaurant. Against the fence a squat rectangular dumpster had been pushed, filled with damp cardboard boxes, folded or crushed presumably by whoever worked in the brick building that formed the west-facing wall of the alley. The dumpster had seen better days, for sure – it looked like a delivery or more likely a collection truck had reversed into it at high speed, crumpling the front side of it.

Joe was squatting again, poking at the side of the bin with his pen. He stood as Jacqueline and Sam approached and gave the dumpster one final drum. The sound rang out dully in the still night air.

"Well, well, well..." Jacqueline peered closer at the side of the dumpster. Joe moved out of her way, and shot a grin at Sam.

"I think we got us some evidence, detective."

Sam blinked, and watched Jacqueline's hunched back as she worked at something on the dumpster. After a moment she stood and turned, brandishing a shining set of tiny tweezers in both hands. Between their claws, a triangular strip of what looked like black plastic. Sam squinted, unable to see it clearly, but Jacqueline fished out a pen-sized flashlight and trained it on the find. The plastic shone in the beam, the curved surface of the fragment smooth and patterned with a tiny triangular gray weave.

"What is that? Fabric?"

Jacqueline shook her head, and shuffled to one side to let Sam have a clear look at the dumpster. She played the flashlight over the surface, revealing patches of shiny bare metal all over the damaged area. Fresh, clean damage.

"Look," said Jacqueline, pointing to a thin gash that penetrated the dumpster's wall. "Looks like it's been cut with the knife too." The edges of the cut were thin and most likely razor-sharp. Sam reached forward then pulled her fingers short as she thought better of touching it.

"The plastic, or fabric, or whatever it is, was embedded in the cut." Joe pointed with his pen, indicated the point at which the knife had stopped as it sliced into the metal.

Sam stood, thoughts racing in her head. Evidence? Impossible. The Cowl never left anything concrete. But something had clearly gone very, very wrong here. The quantum knife was an easy weapon to wield, yet there were signs the victim had put up a hell of a fight. And now a bent dumpster and a scrap of fabric.

Sam felt her chest going tight. Did she dare think that the fabric came from the Cowl's famous cloak?

"Detective? Hello?"

Sam blinked as Jacqueline clicked her fingers in front of her face. Sam jerked back in surprise, and then a smile began to creep upwards, very slowly, from one corner of her mouth. Jacqueline nodded and smiled herself.

"Do you know what this means, Sam? You've got what you always wanted. Evidence linking the Cowl to a crime scene."

Sam exhaled. "Sonovabitch."

"Damn right, detective." Joe laughed. "Ladies and gentlemen, we have a *trail.*"

Sam clicked her tongue in thought, then nodded, a small smile beginning to play over her lips. "Come on, partner," she said, as she took a step back towards the cars. Joe nodded, then turned to Jacqueline and gave her a wink. The doctor laughed and touched his shoulder.

"Off you go, big boy. Hey, you still free Tuesday?"

"I think you might need to ask Detective Millar about that."

Sam laughed and headed off, Joe stalking behind her, the pair leaving Jacqueline to continue her work long into the night.

Evidence.

Goddamn solid, concrete, *real* evidence.

Sam felt like her grin was a thousand miles wide as she tripped down the alley towards the police cars.

Screw the Seven Wonders. Leave Gillespie to blow them off, there was no time to go back for their meeting at the hotel. She didn't check her watch but it must have been after eleven now anyway.

Detective Sam Millar had evidence. She was going to solve this case herself, and catch the Cowl.

She was going to save the city.

CHAPTER TEN

The black woman in the brown dress brought the champagne to her lips, but didn't drink. It was a pretense, a charade to satisfy curious glances, nothing more. Even if she wasn't here undercover, Sand Cat would have acted the same. This society was not hers, and it still confused her. All the city's most important and most wealthy people, each with their own conceits and vices, secrets and affairs, tax dodges and off-shore accounts, gathered in artificial celebration of a law enforcement service that none of them would dream of relying upon, of trusting. It was ridiculous. Pretending to drink champagne was nothing. Everybody in the whole room was pretending.

But this was the way of the world. Aurora and Bluebell had taught her that, and she accepted the fact that as an outsider she could never understand, and importantly, never take part. She had an honor-bound duty to uphold the law and defend the city, and for her this was more important than her own life. And if, occasionally, she took pause from her mission to observe the city's inhabitants in their natural environment – specimens to be examined, *studied* – then this was all part of her ongoing education. Aurora would be pleased.

"I know that look."

Aurora's arrival at her side surprised her, lost as she was in her own thoughts, but she did not allow herself to show it. With instincts honed to virtually supernatural levels, her body remained entirely still in the casual pose she had copied from another woman in a similar dress on the other side of the ballroom. Sand Cat held her glass to her chin, gazing out across the crowd with a knowing smile. This she had also copied. Inside, she cursed herself for letting her guard down. Aurora was a walking nuclear reactor. To not notice him walking up behind her was unacceptable. She was a warrior like no other.

She repented her failings to the Goddess, and vowed never to let it happen again. She continued to scan the room in front of her.

"I too received the alert. What did SMART report?"

Aurora moved closer, standing by Sand Cat's side and casting a smile across the room. To anyone watching, it was just the city's most famous superhero having a casual chat with just one of the many beautiful women in the room. Although Sand Cat's face was never obscured by a mask, with the dress, hair and make-up, she was unrecognizable to anyone who didn't know her personally.

He dropped his voice to a whisper.

"The Angel Vault is offline. We must assume the worst."

Sand Cat flinched at the news, her previous vow temporarily forgotten. The vaults were hidden, scattered throughout the city. It had been Bluebell's greatest achievement. If someone had been able to not only identify the vaults, but breach them, it... well, it was unthinkable.

"The Cowl?"

"There is no one else."

Sand Cat placed her still-full glass down on the edge of a table behind her.

"Understood. We need to head back to the Citadel."

Aurora nodded. "Agreed."

Sand Cat stalked off, her powerful stride cutting a path directly across the packed ballroom.

Aurora watched Sand Cat leave, then clicked a control on his belt again. There was no need to worry about drawing undue attention now. The city needed its protectors, and there was no harm in letting the assembled guests see the call to arms.

Aurora's halo pulsed and changed from yellow to red. Several nearby guests gasped and stared, in awe of the powerful superhero and his fiery aura.

Aurora raised a hand in apology. He clicked the communicator on his belt again, and this time spoke with a voice loud and clear, a voice known to everybody in the room from the television news and, for some, from seeing Aurora battling the Cowl out in the streets of the city.

"Seven Wonders, unite!"

CHAPTER ELEVEN

Tony remembered the first day the powers manifested.

It had been a hot night, and Tony had drifted in and out of sleep. He turned over and frowned into his pillow. He'd dreamed of a bus ride home and the night he'd met Jeannie. He'd been dreaming about the recent past more and more frequently. Maybe, he thought, it was a side effect of his new situation, of being happy and of feeling safe. It was all new to him.

He screwed his eyelids tight, but it did nothing to block the brightness of the morning light. He sighed and rolled to the left, then curled to the right, then turned onto his stomach and pushed his face into the pillow, drawing the edge of it over the back of his head. But no matter what position, the day was a red glow that told him he needed to get up, that it was very late, and that the day was being wasted. A Saturday too. Tony hated sleeping in at the weekend – weekends were a precious gift that only came once a week, and every hour had to be savored. But it *had* been a late night… so maybe just another five minutes… maybe ten… maybe…

The red light pulsed painfully. Had he left the curtain open in his tiny bedroom? It was so bright, it had to be nearly midday. Shit.

"Um… Tony? Tony, wake up."

Tony's body jolted at the voice, and he swung up onto one elbow. Jeannie was sitting up in the bed beside him, under the covers but with the sheet drawn fully to her chin. He noticed first her clenched hands holding the sheet up, almost like a shield. Then he noticed the look of fear on her tired face. She looked like she'd only just woken as well.

Tony reached a hand towards her. "Jeannie? What's wrong?" She backed away farther against the bedstead, eyes fixed on Tony's outstretched hand. Tony stopped, and raised his hand to his face.

It was glowing bright yellow.

His skin hadn't changed color; he could see his hand and bare arm quite clearly. But they were surrounded by a bright aura, a shimmering corona of pale yellow light. Tony gawped, and raised his other, glowing arm.

"Tony?"

Tony leapt off the bed. "What the fuck? Shit. *Shit shit shit shit.*"

His entire body shone with light, illuminating the room in the yellow-white glare of a midsummer's day. Tony saw that the curtain on the one window in the room had indeed been left open, the square window beyond nothing but a black mirror, reflecting Tony's image back at him. It was still the middle of the night.

"What's the time?"

Jeannie scrambled for the clock on the dresser with one hand while the other kept the sheet taut at her neck.

"4.23." She let the clock clatter back to the bedside table. "Are you OK? What the fuck is going on?"

Tony walked around the bed to the full-length mirror that was propped up against the bare patch of wall by his built-in closet. He stared at himself, turning his body experimentally to get a good look.

"What the hell is this?" he whispered, half to himself. His entire body was surrounded by a white-gold halo. The aura didn't seem to touch his skin, it *surrounded* him, starting at about two inches out from his body, extending for another six, and flaring out to a moving, ragged edge. As he moved his hands, arms, legs, head, the aura moved with him, flaring slightly at sudden motion but otherwise remaining a near-perfect, encapsulating field.

Behind him he heard Jeannie shuffle in the bed, then heard her bare feet on the carpet and the pulling of fabric as she came to stand behind him, wrapped in the bed sheet. She appeared in the mirror over his shoulder, standing outside the range of his glow, but close enough to touch. Their reflected eyes met.

"Well, this is San Ventura," she said. "City of fucking weird shit. Do you feel OK? Does it hurt?"

Tony swung his arm back and forth across his front, mesmerized by the reflected glow in the mirror. It was a few seconds before he answered.

"No... no, it feels... it feels good. I feel fine, I mean... Welcome to the Shining City..." he breathed. In the mirror he saw Jeannie reaching out to gingerly touch his shoulder. When she did, her worried face cracked with a hesitant smile.

"It tingles, like putting your tongue on a battery."

Tony smiled. San Ventura, city of fucking weird shit?

"You think something is going on? The Seven Wonders up to something? Like that time all the grass and leaves in the city turned orange for a day?"

Jeannie stroked his shoulder and bit her bottom lip. In the mirror Tony saw the hairs on her arm stand on end, and Tony thought he could smell the smell of the ground after a thunderstorm.

"I don't know," she said. "This city is fucked up. But... I kinda like it."

Tony turned around. He felt good, refreshed somehow. Who the fuck knew what the glow was, but it lit the room like an aurora, and his girlfriend liked it.

"Well now, that a fact?" Tony grabbed Jeannie's rear through the thin sheet, and drew her close to him. She yelped and he felt her quiver involuntarily as their bodies touched. He pulled the sheet that separated their naked bodies away.

Jeannie smiled and laughed as Tony pushed her back to the bed. He reached over and closed the curtain, cutting out the San Ventura night.

Jeannie turned the bedside clock around so the display faced away from the bed. "I'd say we should do it with the lights off, but I don't think we have much choice tonight."

Tony laughed. "I think I love you."

CHAPTER TWELVE

Four-four-seven-four-four.

The Cowl tapped at the numeric keypad. Gloveless and maskless, he was nonetheless clad in his combat suit – it wasn't a *costume*, its design was purely practical, but hell, if the lowlifes of the city got a fright whenever they saw him, then fine. And by lowlifes, he meant everyone in San Ventura. But it felt good to be wearing it again, now that his arm and ribs had healed. The Black Angel had given him quite a beating and it had taken two days for his body to repair itself. He'd been working all night, and it was nearly dawn.

His fingers flew over the keyboard, transcribing the complex pulses of static-laced code that pumped into his ears. The transmissions were automated and repeated, and once he had been taught the pattern it was easy enough to transcode into something usable. Hell, it was too easy. He could have set up a script on the Lair's computer, but he wanted to do this himself, to check the code as it came in, to analyze the blueprints and instructions as they were assembled, to make sure (of course) that he wasn't being tricked. But he wasn't, and in the end the manual encoding was a real chore.

So he let himself listen and type on autopilot – the computer would check it later – and with the other half of his brain (the half that was easily bored), he scanned three large LCD displays in front of him. Two were tuned to news channels, one local, one national, while the other showed a web browser. He wasn't looking for anything in particular, but he leafed through a few websites of electrical component manufacturers and research institutes. He wasn't changing targets – he and Blackbird had firmed up the final hit list just the other night – but it paid to shop around.

He paused a couple of times as items of interest popped into view, but tabbed on through when he saw they were not suitable. On the news screens above, *San Ventura Today Tonight* was doing a background filler on the Draconid meteors which made him smile, while the national channel was showing fluff about an amazing new wonder drug that could cure pancreatic cancer. In rats. Fascinating stuff. The Cowl stifled a yawn. Not long until the final transmission was transcribed, then he could run the verification algorithm on it while he grabbed some breakfast. Blackbird was due in half an hour or so, or at least she'd said so when she'd called the previous night.

He paused the incoming data stream, leaving the computer to timeshift the transmission while he cycled back through. Maybe this was why he insisted on doing it manually. He pulled the earbuds from the side of his head and muted the news channels. Rotating a finger around the touch-sensitive panel above the numeric keypad, he ran the transmission back fifteen seconds and replayed. With his left hand, he stretched thumb and forefinger across the main keyboard, calling up a series of shortcuts to display data analysis and recent input.

There it was. A repeated pattern, corresponding to a new section of blueprint. Weeks of half-listening to alien garbage had attuned him to the code, and with a little effort he could translate it, slowly, as he read.

Interesting. This new section, describing some kind of coupling cradle, required a very specific kind of component. And there was only one place in the world where one could come from, and he knew about it only because his girlfriend had invented the damn thing. He rocked the touchpad back and forth a few times, double-checking the message, while he highlighted the visual representation of the signal on the main monitor and started the computer verification. He normally left it to the end, but he had to be sure of this part now.

He kept working until a discreet double bleep announced Blackbird's arrival. Moments later, she was walking along the bridge that linked the outer ring and main doors of the Lair to the towering control area. The Cowl smiled, listening with superpowered hearing to the thick, spongy softness of boots on the tiled floor.

"Another all-nighter at the lab, my dear?"

"Yes, darling. Uh-huh. Whatever." There was a metallic snap and Blackbird's mask landed in the Cowl's lap. "Final transmission?" Her gloved hands found his shoulders, her hot chin resting on the crown of his head.

"You bet. Almost done, but I thought you might like to see this bit." He pointed to the main screen, reverse-tabbing back a couple of sections. Green machine code on a black background, a large block outlined in reverse highlight.

Blackbird pressed down on the back of the Cowl's chair as she folded her arms on its back. The Cowl could hear the saliva in her mouth move as she frowned. He smiled, then turned his hearing down to normal human levels.

Blackbird shook her head slowly, rocking the chair just a little. "No," she said. "I might be a goddamn genius, but I'm not good with the code. You'll have to fill me in on that one."

The Cowl pointed again, leaning in a little so his intention was clearer. He waved a finger along the lines of code in the highlighted section. "We need to steal that."

"And what is 'that'?"

"It's a black light converter."

Blackbird stood up, quickly. Behind him, the Cowl could hear her laugh quietly into her hand.

"Is that so? I think I know where we can find one."

"Oh really?"

"Ya really."

"No way!"

Blackbird playfully tapped the top of the Cowl's head with the flat of her fingers, then pushed at the corner of the chair. The Cowl raised his feet, allowing himself to be swiveled around.

Blackbird reached into her belt with a finger and thumb, extracting a white plastic card featureless except for a black magnetic strip.

"The Clarke Institute of Technology. I has a key, too."

The Cowl feigned surprise. "Whoa!"

"Shall we?"

The Cowl looked back over his shoulder, checking the twenty-four-hour clock on the control board. His eyes flickered over the highlighted code again, and beside the monitor the light on the satellite receiver winked, showing that the transmission was ongoing but being recorded.

"No, it's early," he said, swinging back around. "And we've both had a hard day's night." He stood, planting a kiss on Blackbird's nose. "Let's get breakfast. Wouldn't want to plan a daring heist on an empty stomach now, would we?"

CHAPTER THIRTEEN

Over the next few nights, Tony's magic light hadn't reappeared. But he was waking up with new... *skills,* each morning.

"Too hot!"

"Oh, sorry... it's just that I..."

"Too *friggin'* hot!"

Jeannie pogoed around the kitchen, mouth open, tongue out, waving at Tony to keep back. She just managed to keep enough control to drop the cardboard coffee cup into the sink rather than onto the floor. It hit the stainless-steel tub and buckled, lid dislocating and the superheated contents filling the kitchen with mocha-flavored steam.

"Are you OK?" Tony kept his distance, but reached a hand out. Seeing the heat shimmer coming off his knuckles, he stopped, squeezed his eyes shut in concentration, and dropped the temperature of his hand. "Maybe I can cool it...?"

Jeannie stopped hopping and looked at Tony, her expression of half-surprise, half-fear made ridiculous by her open mouth and exposed tongue. When she spoke it was like her mouth was numb from the dentist.

"Cool id? Are you therious? You jus burd ma face off."

Tony's shoulders rose stiffly in defense, and he decided to stuff his hands in the tight pockets of his jeans. Although he couldn't feel the heat generated by his hands himself, he felt the denim go dry and stiff over his skin.

"You said your coffee was cold," he offered by way of explanation.

Jeannie laughed, throwing spit at him and dribbling. This made her laugh more, and she gingerly retracted her tongue and wiped her mouth.

"Yeah, well given the choice between cold and lava from the fiery bowels of hell, I'll go with cold next time."

Tony smiled. "Good point." He shrugged. "But practice makes perfect, right?"

Jeannie nodded slowly, the incredulous look spreading over her face again. "Yes, Tony, practice makes perfect. Just try not to practice on your girlfriend in the future."

"Oh, I don't know." Tony got a little closer, hands still in pockets but raised shoulders turned into what he hoped was a cool, rock 'n' roll pose. "You said you liked it a couple of nights ago."

Jeannie laughed as she poured herself a tall glass of water from one of the many bottles Tony had in the fridge. Taking a sip, she slapped Tony's shoulder with the other hand. "Tiger, tiger, burning bright." She walked past Tony and flopped onto the couch, just managing not to spill her drink.

Tony turned and followed, but stopped to lean his back against the breakfast bar with his hands still deeply embedded in his jeans. "Seriously though, I seem to be getting a new power almost every day. I need to be able to control them if only to stop myself killing somebody by accident. Yesterday I got on the bus after work and almost wrenched the rail off the door as I walked on. I managed to convince the driver it must have been loose rivets, but I'd love to know what the bus garage is going to make of my hand print embossed into the steel bar."

Jeannie finished her water, experimentally opening and closing her mouth, moving her burnt tongue around. "Point. So what do we do? Some kind of training?"

Tony nodded and scooted over to the couch. "Yeah, why not?" He sat down and gestured around his apartment. "We can do most of it here. Hot and cold touch for example." He sat back. "The rest, well, we can do one thing at a time outside. Strength, speed, you know."

Jeannie nodded. "You're right," she said. "Control is the key. OK, sounds like a good idea. And who knows, maybe the Seven Wonders have room for one more."

Tony laughed. "Get out. The Seven Wonders would cut me up for experiments. They've got the city sewn up tight."

Jeannie leaned forward, turning on the leatherette to face Tony. "I know how you feel about San Ventura, Tony, and the superteam."

Tony's face darkened, and he shook his head in frustration. "Let's not talk about it. The Cowl is tearing the place up and the Seven Wonders are just playing his game. Won't change. Can't change."

Jeannie tapped Tony's knee. "Can't it? You've got powers. Why don't you do something for the city?"

Tony looked blankly at her, then blinked, then blinked again. "Take out the Cowl?"

"Why not?"

"Why not?" Tony sat up, back straight. "He'll kill me. I'm not a superhero."

Jeannie shook her head and smiled. "Not yet, no." She raised her half-full glass of water to Tony's face. "But practice makes perfect. Let's start."

CHAPTER FOURTEEN

The city morgue was Jacqueline Chan's domain; Sam never liked it when she had to visit.

Attached to a side of the city's central hospital that was out of public view, the morgue looked like nothing more than a loading bay and a set of concrete stairs leading up to wide double doors. The only people who really knew what the nondescript back entrance was were morgue staff and the police. And of the police, Sam was more familiar with the area than most. Being in the SuperCrime department meant cleaning up after the Cowl, and the Cowl rarely left anyone alive when he was done.

Sure, visiting the place was sometimes part of the job, but the peculiar quietness of the loading bay was still unnerving. The only vehicles that made it around to this part of the hospital were hearses. It was purely psychological, but waiting around outside this part of the medical complex, on a grass square that passed for some weird kind of garden of the dead that nobody ever visited (complete with never-used park bench), made Sam edgy. She was already breathing through her mouth rather than her nose, her subconscious prepping her senses for the chemical stench she knew was waiting inside.

"You never get used to it, do you? I can't imagine what it would be like to work here."

Sam turned at the voice. It was familiar, but she couldn't place it at once without a visual cue. There was no one around, and then realization hit – she hadn't heard it at all, the voice had been inside her head. She looked up as Bluebell gracefully descended on a vertical to land on the grass next to Sam.

"Bluebell, what can I do for you?" Sam tensed immediately; Bluebell was by far the most pleasant of the Seven Wonders to deal with in person, but her habit of intruding on your own thoughts, accidentally (as she usually claimed) or not, was deeply unsettling. Not that their paths had crossed that much: thanks to her psychic powers, Bluebell tended to act mainly behind the scenes. There was no need to get your hands dirty when you could scramble someone's brains from half a mile away. Bluebell made Sam nervous.

Bluebell also made Sam feel... frumpy. It was a brilliant clear morning, and she was at work in a nondescript dark gray suit and white shirt. Smart, certainly, even stylish, but it was nothing next to Bluebell. The superheroine's short blonde hair was perfect, her face applied with just the right amount of make-up to make you think she wasn't wearing any at all. And in the morning light, her skintight blue and white bodysuit almost shone, the pattern of bold lines running vertically up the outside leg and curving in to the waist, then out again over her bust to the shoulder, then down each arm. On the wrong figure it would have looked like some second-rate gym costume worn by a hopeful Olympic gymnast from the Soviet era. On Bluebell, in the bright sunshine, Sam couldn't take her eyes off it.

"Tell me about it." Bluebell smiled a film-star smile. "Appearances are important for us. But it's practical."

Sam paused, mid-thought. Of course, Bluebell was reading every single thought that raced across the front of her cerebral cortex. Her eyebrows dipped in annoyance. She really hated it when Bluebell came to visit.

"Sorry." Bluebell looked away politely. "I'll try not to eavesdrop. I can't turn it off, but I can point it someplace else."

Sam sighed. Bluebell was nice, and maybe she was being too hard on her. Hearing every private thought going on around you whether you liked it or not couldn't have been the easiest of superpowers to come to terms with. "No, I'm sorry, I didn't mean to be rude. Gray suits seem to go with the job though. I think I need a change of career!"

Sam and the superheroine shared the joke just as a large, black Lincoln pulled into the parking lot designated for morgue staff and police only. The driver, in silhouette through the darkened glass, appeared to lean to look out the passenger window and survey the scene, then flung the driver's door open. Detective Milano's shaved head bobbed over the car roof.

"Ladies," he said with a smile, his voice ridiculously low and husky. He flipped the door closed and swept his sunglasses off in a single cool move. Sam couldn't resist smiling at his efforts.

"Detective Milano, I believe you've met Bluebell before."

Joe strode towards the pair, extending a hand just a little too early for a handshake. "I have indeed, Sam. Bluebell, always a pleasure."

He took Bluebell's hand in his, turned it over, and planted a kiss that raised Sam's eyebrow. Bluebell's smile was as wide and as white as ever. Sam really, really hoped Joe was keeping his thoughts to himself as much as possible.

Bluebell laughed politely. Everything about her body language was posed, affected. It was all an act, the kind that film stars did on a red carpet, but Sam could see how it worked. It made Joe feel good, proud, but also submissive. He'd do anything Bluebell said, but more importantly, his mind was completely unguarded. She could *make* him do anything she wanted.

"Detectives, I apologize for the unannounced arrival, but I understand you are here to discuss autopsy results on a recent homicide with Dr Jacqueline Chan? If you don't mind, I'd like to attend. It's just routine; we hope to take a more active role in city policing."

Who cooked up that half-baked piece of PR? Sam instantly regretted the thought. Bluebell looked at her, clearly listening in, and nodded.

"I understand completely. But believe me, we are always seeking ways to better support your fine work. I won't intervene, I'll just observe. Shall we?"

Joe gestured for her to lead the way towards the loading dock, the schoolboy grin firmly plastered to his face. He said nothing, waved at Sam to follow, but as she looked at him she caught a glance, nothing more than a flicker in Joe's eyes. She nodded, allowing the corner of her mouth to raise slightly. Joe was deliberately filling his mind with lustful thoughts about Bluebell. It was drowning out everything else in his mind. He was a clever boy.

With Bluebell walking ahead, Joe's eyes drifted to her spandex-clad rear. Bluebell's stride changed rhythm, just slightly, but Sam noticed. It was working.

Clever, clever Joe.

It was the same every time. It didn't matter how prepared Detective Sam Millar thought she was, inside the morgue the heady mix of formaldehyde and disinfectant was rich in the air and made her cough as soon as the plastic-sealed doors flapped closed behind her. Dr Chan appeared through a side door, latex-covered hands glistening already.

"Come on through." She waved them after her and disappeared back into the dissection room. Bluebell held back, allowing Sam and Joe to take the lead. Sam wondered why Jacqueline hadn't said anything about the uninvited presence of the superhero. Perhaps she was a more regular visitor?

There were four slabs in the morgue; all were empty save for one, the form covered in a blue hospital sheet. Jacqueline strode up to the table and pulled the shroud off completely, revealing the naked remains of the black man from the alley. Joe instinctively looked away from the destroyed torso, focusing instead on the man's face. Sam and Jacqueline, meanwhile, bent low over the body as the pathologist pointed out individual injuries. As much as Sam thought she hated this bit, she knew she had a job to do.

"The torso is dissected into four sections. It's not precise, but then with the weapon used you don't need to be."

Sam tried to follow the parallel cut lines that carved the man's chest up. Dr Chan had done her best to tidy the body up following the autopsy dissection, the stitched skin forming a grid of thick twine, delineating the cuts.

"The quantum knife?"

Dr Chan nodded. "The quantum knife. It's unique. You can't mistake it."

Sam stood back. "That settles it. The Cowl."

"I don't want to make any assumptions, detective, but nobody else has one of those toys."

"We got an ID yet?" Joe was still looking at the man's dead face, and frowned. "Something doesn't add up. Why would the Cowl kill an old man, and why did he use his knife? Dude is superpowered." He gestured to the body. "This guy must be pushing eighty. The Cowl could have turned him to cat food without even touching him."

Sam shook her head. "Nice, Joe."

Jacqueline took a manila file from the wheeled cart next to the table. She opened it and flipped through the autopsy check sheets to get the police report on the victim.

"Oh, there was a fight, all right. Whoever this guy is, he was no ordinary old man. We've IDed him as Ernest Crosby, seventy-six, lives down in..."

Dr Chan trailed off. After a moment, Sam and Joe both looked at her, awaiting the continuation. Dr Chan was looking at the papers, shuffling back and forth between the autopsy sheet and police report. Bluebell had moved from the door to stand behind her.

Jacqueline clacked her tongue against her cheek. "Nope, no ID. Looks like we've got a John Doe here."

Sam and Joe blinked in unison, then returned their attention to the body.

"He wasn't carrying anything?" Sam looked back to the body. He'd been wearing a black suit in the alleyway, and she was surprised that nothing had been found on him. Joe picked up the thread.

"Yeah, no wallet? Keys? Money?"

Jacqueline reached the end of the manila file. Bluebell moved forward. The superhero said nothing, but glanced quickly at each of the three policemen.

Jacqueline selected a sheet of paper and stared at it for several seconds. Her mouth moved, forming words as she... as she *tried* to read the report.

"A set of keys... a building society savings card and a library card under the name of..."

Jacqueline sniffed loudly and dropped the sheet back into the folder. "Nothing." She tossed the folder back onto the cart.

Sam nodded. "Cause of death?"

"Gunshot to the stomach." Dr Chan pointed to the body's abdomen, indicating a non-existent wound on the one part of the man's body that was intact. "Ballistics is looking at the bullet now."

Sam nodded again. Bluebell stepped in behind her, standing very close to the detective's back.

"Looks like a mugging, nothing new in this city. The Seven Wonders are taking the body in, they think the victim is part of a... a..." Sam paused in mid-sentence. Neither Joe nor Dr Chan noticed; both remained motionless and without expression.

"The FBI are taking the body in. Here's the forms." Sam held her empty hand towards Dr Chan. The pathologist grabbed at the empty air, and slotted nothing into the manila folder. Mime complete, she pulled the blue sheet back over the body.

"Thank you, detectives." She pulled off the latex gloves and tossed them into a yellow biohazard bin. Sam and Joe thanked the doctor, and went to the exit.

The morning outside was as brilliant as ever, the summer sun starting to bake the city. Joe and Sam stood in the small garden, Bluebell beside them. Joe blinked.

"Wanna grab some eats at Curran's Diner on the way back?"

Sam smiled. "Sounds great. I'll follow." She waved and headed off to where her car was parked around the front side of the hospital. Joe walked to his car parked nearby, and hopped inside.

Standing on the grass, Bluebell relaxed her grip on the minds of the two detectives just enough for the pair to resume normal activities without requiring her conscious control, but still masking the true nature of the autopsy report. Later she'd work on making the memory adjustment permanent.

But for now, the Seven Wonders had secured the remains of the Angel Vault, with no danger of police interference. The last thing they needed was the pathetic efforts of the SVPD hampering their own investigation.

The last thing they needed was the SVPD getting close to the Cowl.

CHAPTER FIFTEEN

Blackbird blinked behind her mask and felt a tear trail down her cheek. She blinked again to clear her vision and returned to concentrate on the job at hand. It had never even entered her mind, but seeing *him* stalk the corridors of the Clarke Institute was... hard. It was an invasion of her world, and an invasion of her memories. But she knew it had to be done. She knew it *all* had to be done, and that the ends justified the means.

She just had to be patient, and wait.

The job had been messy – messier than usual, anyway. By the time she'd led the Cowl to the secure laboratories at the center of the CIT, built low in a hard-to-reach valley in the mountains just east of San Ventura, the trail of dead numbered in the dozens. Most were guards, variously armed, variously dispatched. Some cleanly, some not so. With the Cowl's superpowers now almost non-existent, fighting was much harder work. It would have been quicker if Blackbird helped out, but she didn't. The Cowl was too preoccupied to notice.

Still, Blackbird had to commend the guards. At least they had all tried to do their job, and do it well, even if the more they fought, the more blood ended up on the floor. They were military and paramilitary, trained and tough and packing heat. Enough to keep the place safe and secure from criminals and terrorists. The defenses had certainly been beefed up in the last few days, but with the news of the other high-tech raids racing around the city, this wasn't surprising. With this level of security, even Blackbird would only have been able to penetrate so far before being overwhelmed by sheer force of numbers.

Blackbird smiled. Even with his powers at minimum, none of them were even remotely capable of dealing with a supervillain like the Cowl. She half-wondered why a superhero wasn't stationed here on permanent rotation if the place was so special, so important, so clearly a target. Oh yeah. Because the only supervillain left was the Cowl, and there was nothing here for him to take.

Wrong.

Blackbird held back in the last corridor. She knew the place like the back of her hand, and they were heading straight to the pay dirt, but she was careful to keep her caped, hooded boyfriend ahead of her, removing any obstacles.

She pressed her back against the wall, pointing silently. The Cowl nodded and darted forward. Blackbird smiled as she heard the *whoosh* of his cloak swirling around as he tackled the guards. A second later, the Cowl casually walked back around the corner, looking something like Darth Vader, except his black gauntlets were dripping with blood, leaving a dotted trail on the floor behind him.

Blackbird's smile evaporated. She glanced down and saw his footsteps thick in the stuff. It didn't matter. Everyone would know who did it, so there was no point in worrying about evidence being left behind. Besides, the footprints would be untraceable. The costumes of the Cowl and Blackbird were designed very, very carefully indeed.

Blackbird peeled off the wall and walked towards the Cowl. They met in the middle of the corridor and she glanced down at his hands. In the half-light their wetness was nothing more than a gloss finish. She let out a breath that echoed metallically from behind her mask. The voice modulator kicked in as she spoke.

"I didn't hear any guns?"

The Cowl shook his head. "These ones weren't carrying any. Scientists. Seemed quicker to remove their hearts." He smirked.

Blackbird's mask tilted towards him, but behind the goggles and beak her expression was dark. Her heart wasn't as black as his. Those scientists, quite possibly, were the ones she worked with day in and day out. She pushed the thought from her mind and pushed past him in the corridor, trying to avoid getting blood on her.

The ends justify the means, the ends justify the means, the ends justify the...

Of course, her parents had worked here too. And they'd also met the Cowl, although unlike the scientists lying face down in the corridor in what looked like gallons of blood, they had survived the encounter.

Initially.

The ends justify the means.

Blackbird flicked the audio output of her mask off, in case she made a sound that might have given a reason for the Cowl to take pause and ask questions. She stepped over the two bodies in white coats, now stained vivid scarlet. She didn't recognize them from the backs of their heads, but she had a fair idea of who they were. It wasn't uncommon for researchers to work late. She knew; she'd done it enough times herself before her "calling" had started eating into her time outside of the day gig.

It hadn't been uncommon for her parents either.

"In here," she said.

Blackbird remembered the day her world had ended. She remembered it well.

Alone in the Cowl's Lair, she held her arms out in front of her, keeping her elbows bent carefully so not to lock them when she hit. She closed her eyes and gave another firm push.

For any normal person, the extra velocity would only be slight. For someone with augmented, above-normal strength – not actual super-strength, but more than you could ever get by working out 24/7 and chugging protein shakes – the push was something significant. She squealed, as did the tiny wheels beneath her, rocketing across the narrow bridge and straight into the edge of the Cowl's computer desk.

She reached out and stopped the chair, but forgot about momentum and her body keep going, smacking her face-first into one of the aluminum panels above the computer control deck. She swore and flopped back into the chair, pulling her mask off with one deft movement. The stylized, beak-like front of her headpiece had prevented a broken nose and was undamaged itself, and with no visible mark on the panel, her boss would never know. She laughed, spinning around on the chair, but her pleasure quickly evaporated into the dark, empty space of the Cowl's Lair.

She was alone, and bored, and pissed off.

OK, she was new, had only been on the job a few months, but she wasn't a rookie, oh no, sir. But she also knew she was not an equal – and never could be, not to him. Not even the Seven Wonders – *seven* of them – could beat him, a single superpowered badass. But still she thought she was a step up from "sidekick". She could handle herself, she was powerful if not superpowered, and well trained. Hell, if she could take charge in bed (he liked that), then she could be relied on to have his back on the night streets of San Ventura.

Powerful, but not superpowered. OK, so as good as she was – and she *was* good, just ask that blonde bitch Bluebell about the time her blue and white spandexed ass was handed to her on a silver platter – it didn't really make sense for the Cowl to need a sidekick. He could handle anything on his own. And clearly he still could and even preferred it, because when something was mission-critical, he went alone. Like now. Leaving her, the Cowl's apprentice, alone in his Lair. Perhaps he'd have preferred a young ward in tights. Blackbird wondered if she should alter her costume to accommodate.

Then again, when you're *that* powerful and have *everything*, not all decisions need to be logical or efficient or have a deeper meaning. The Cowl just liked her around, and her scientific knowledge *was* useful; that's how she'd been recruited in the first place. She was one of the most respected scientists at the Clarke Institute, she knew that, even if she feigned ignorance and pretended to ignore the reverence with which her work colleagues held her. And as for companionship... well, even a supervillain gets lonely. It's not much fun sitting on your throne of skulls when you can't tell someone about how great you are. Not that the Cowl had an ego. No way. The Cowl was, well, a really nice guy. Sweet. So he killed people? So what? So did she. Besides, he had a calling, he said. He was doing "good works". And if that was the justification he needed, then who was she to argue?

She spun the chair around idly again. It stopped after six revolutions, pointing her at the Cowl's supercomputer. It was impressively large, and impressively expensive. The main display itself was truly huge, more like the kind of projection screen rich people install in their basements, along with some comfy armchairs and a beer fridge (which, Blackbird considered, would have made an excellent addition to the Lair). It was framed in aluminum, and she had to look up awkwardly to even see the upper edge. Nearly the whole wall of the cavern was dedicated to this device. On each side of the main display, six smaller screens were stacked, five of which were dark, one of which was on but just displayed a command prompt and a flashing cursor. Blackbird wondered if she could get Netflix on it.

The thing's control deck was, at first glance, a complex collection of keyboards and control panels, but having watched the Cowl at work, Blackbird had a fair idea of what everything was. It was logical, after all. Aside from a standard keyboard and mouse, there was a color-coded keyboard linked to the Cowl's video systems, allowing editing, replay and analysis of video streams. Linked to this was a small audio mixing desk. Next along, an oscilloscope and an old-fashioned panel of tiny twist knobs and sliders – controls for the secret satellite surveillance array in orbit above North America and the communications system the Cowl had secreted around the city. Then some flat panels consisting mostly of LEDs and digital readouts, controlling power systems and the underground environment itself, some with their own mini-keyboards. Easy.

Blackbird idly tapped the spacebar of the regular keyboard, hoping to wake up the main display. It remained resolutely off, but another of the smaller displays – a mere fifty inches diagonal – on the left of the main screen lit up with a white flicker. It showed the desktop of the Cowl's private operating system, some exotic build of UNIX that he'd compiled to suit his purposes, and which Blackbird had helped code.

A folder was open. The Cowl had left himself logged in before he'd vanished on his night errand of terror.

Not recognizing any of the files listed, Blackbird clicked the window shut, and out of sheer boredom rather than curiosity opened the hard drive icon and scrolled through the file list. Maybe he had some movies, or music at least. Or porn. He was only human, after all. And Catholics lived off guilt, didn't they?

Nothing. Folders with codenames, filled with RTF files on people and places, PNG files of blueprints or designs. Dull, dull, dull.

And then she found a folder labeled CIT 2014, and she paused, hand on the mouse, finger poised over the scroll wheel. CIT. The Clarke Institute of Technology. That was where she worked – where her parents had worked. She'd been there three years. Six years ago her parents had disappeared. In 2014.

Blackbird hesitated. There were also folders called CIT 2003 and CIT 2002 and CIT 2008 and CIT 2016. It probably stood for something else. It was nothing, there was no connection.

She double-clicked. RTF files, PNG files. Audio files. Two, labeled Sarah and Patrick. The names of her parents. She moved the mouse pointer over the Sarah file, counted to five in her head, trying to reduce her heart rate, then double-clicked again.

The file opened. It was an hour-ten long, with the triangular indicator stopped around the halfway mark. Blackbird clicked the play button, and the Cowl's Lair was filled with a scream, a woman's horrific cry, so loud Blackbird practically leapt out of the chair. Then the screaming stopped and the recording played on with a hiss. Something moved, shuffled, then another voice.

"When I ask a question, Doctor Ravenholt, I expect an answer," said the Cowl.

The door wasn't anything special, white with chrome handle and the kind of standard lock you'd see on a high school chemistry room and a frosted, wire-reinforced window. If the Cowl had expected hermetically sealed rooms, *Star Trek* doors that swished and whistled, and giant keypads for giant key codes, Blackbird thought he must have been sorely disappointed.

She took the key card from her belt, but he reached out and held her wrist just as she moved to unlock the door. She turned towards him, the beak of her mask almost touching his nose. He shook his head.

"I've changed my mind about that. There's nothing to suggest you were here. All this," he gestured to the bodies under his feet, "was me."

Blackbird pulled back her hand, and the Cowl reached for the door handle. He grabbed the chrome lever and pulled downwards, pushing the door open as though it were unlocked. With no effort at all, the wood around the handle and lock exploded in splinters, the door swinging open with the locking bolt still attached to the doorframe, the mechanism orphaned from the body of the door itself. He stepped past Blackbird and into the laboratory. Blackbird watched his back for a moment, unsure whether his demonstration was the last remnant of his superpowers or just due to his natural strength.

The laboratory was as ordinary as the door. White cupboards with glass doors lined most of the walls, interrupted at intervals by a couple of emergency water showers, two large industrial sinks and two fume hoods. It was obviously a chemical lab rather than an electronic one, which made the clutter that covered the bench running down the center of the long, rectangular room all the more obvious. The tools of an electronics engineer were everywhere – soldering irons, volt meters, bulky oscilloscopes, and miles and miles of cable. Plastic crates ranging from beer cooler size down to matchboxes were spread over the available floor space and much of the bench tops, filled with neatly sorted and filed componentry and construction material. Someone had clearly moved in quickly, requisitioning a spare laboratory for a purpose other than what it had been designed for.

All of this was unimportant. The Cowl kicked tubs of resistors and transistors out of his way as he approached the center bench. With both arms he swept the detritus from the work surface clear so he could get a good look at the device G-clamped into position.

It was long and narrow, a cylinder that widened to a cone at one end. It looked like a slightly larger-than-life model of an anti-tank rocket, although instead of camouflage green the object was shiny piano black. It had to be, as the reflective quality of the surface was essential to its function.

Blackbird spread her hands. "One black light converter. Help yourself."

The Cowl reached out to touch it, paused, then brought his hand back. Without turning to Blackbird, standing behind him, he asked: "The whole thing? It's bigger than I expected."

Blackbird nodded, moving forward so they stood next to each other at the bench. "Yes. The design was modified as it was built. Most of the cylinder is a modified housing for the conductor rods."

"Presumably the converter coil itself is in here?" The Cowl patted the top of the wide cone section, much like a car enthusiast admiring an old classic.

Blackbird flicked a panel open on the side of the cone. The access was only big enough for a single hand to pass through, but the end of the conductor rod array, converging in a glassy, squat trapezoid like the tube from an ancient TV, was clearly visible. Sitting on the flat end-surface of the tube was a black metal box, studded with input ports and held in place by aluminum struts.

"The convertor coil?"

Blackbird nodded. "Coil and prism, yes."

"That's what we need." The Cowl reached into the panel, felt around for a moment, then yanked. The entire bench rocked in protest, and the G-clamps loosened, but after a second pull the black box came cleanly from its cradle. He held the box up in front of Blackbird.

"Pay day."

"Is that really all you need?"

The Cowl looked at the main body of the converter machine. "That's it, sweetie." He frowned. "Looks like you'll have to put in some late nights to get it fixed. Some more late nights, I mean."

Blackbird's mask clicked sharply, the sound of a quick intake of breath for a laugh, but amplified and spookified through the bird mask's synthesizer.

"I don't think I'm coming back here again."

It was the Cowl's turn to laugh. He laid a heavy hand on her shoulder. "You got that right. Shall we?"

His companion nodded, and the Cowl turned on his heel and strode confidently out of the laboratory. Blackbird lingered a moment, surveying the wrecked machine and the components scattered on the floor, some cracked and split from the Cowl's blood-spattered boots. She remembered the damage she'd seen in the lab her parents shared, the morning after they'd vanished. The police had let her in under the yellow tape across the door, and had warned her about the blood, although she hadn't listened.

Blackbird stopped and tried to remember the last thing her parents had said to her, but she couldn't, and she wondered whether this should have bothered her or not. After a few seconds she discarded the thought and gritted her teeth.

Focus, focus.

Before she left, Blackbird ducked around the central bench to a smaller worktop, mostly hidden from view thanks to a large movable magnifying screen that hung on a dolly arm over it. Nudging the screen aside, she glanced over the small device currently under construction, a cat's cradle of fine wire and circuitry. Beside it, one of the component bins, this one the size of a shoebox. She rifled through the contents for a couple of seconds until she found what she was looking for, a blue circuit board with a large cuboidal CPU embedded at the center.

"Forgotten something?" The Cowl stood in the doorway. Blackbird stopped mid-stride, then straightened up and calmed herself. There was nothing to be afraid of.

"Spare processor. Anything happens to the converter coil, I can fix it, but the processor burns out we're back to square one." She held up the circuit boldly. It looked innocuous enough, but it was no part of the black light convertor. She just hoped he didn't realize. Blackbird was grateful her mask covered her entire face, so the Cowl couldn't see her trembling lip or the cold sweat running down her face.

After a thousand years the Cowl smiled, his cheeks creasing and pushing his half-mask up slightly. "Good thinking, Batman."

Blackbird smiled beneath the mask. Her synthesized voice snapped on. It hid her fear well.

"Lead the way, Boy Wonder."

She watched him when he returned. He walked across the bridge towards the computer, the Lair apparently empty. The swivel chair was askew at the desk, and two screens were on. She watched him from a doorway swathed in shadows, her catsuit blending her into the dark completely.

The Cowl glanced across the control desk like he always did, eyes taking in key readings and indicators out of habit. But she had left nothing amiss.

He jerked his head back, throwing the infamous hood back, and with one hand he swiftly unhooked his mask and skull cap from the back and shucked it off, dumping the sweaty piece to the control desk. With the other hand he tabbed one of the active computer displays through open applications and folders. From the doorway, Blackbird could see the music directory flip into view, the only folder she had left open.

She stepped from the dark.

"Good hunting?"

The Cowl flicked a switch on the desk with a theatrical flourish, like she wouldn't notice his surprise at her approach. Nobody could get past the Cowl, but, of course, that was a key design point of her costume: complete stealth. Nobody could get past the Cowl but her.

He flicked another switch, adding to the illusion, then turned to reply. Blackbird stepped into a sharp triangle of light cast from halogen hidden high above. She almost made to rub her face, to get rid of the puffiness she could feel from an hour of tears, but stopped herself, realizing her face was still in shadow. He couldn't see the redness of her skin or the state of her hair.

He flipped a glossy black oblong from a compartment on his belt. He held it up, and rubbed a thumb across the surface. Responding to the gesture, the device's small screen flicked into life, displaying a set of diagrams. Blackbird couldn't see what they were, exactly, but she guessed they were part of the machine her partner was gathering the parts for.

"Oh yes, my dear, good hunting indeed. No resistance, easy job. I can start feeding the design algorithms into the computer in the morning, and we can work on the next part."

Blackbird padded over to the Cowl. As soon as she was near enough, he swung his arms around her neck and drew her in. She resisted, just for a second, then relaxed and returned the gesture. They hugged.

"Boring night for you, huh?" His breath was hot on her neck, and he was damp with sweat. Whatever he'd been doing, he'd had a good workout, even with his powers. "I'm sorry, I've been neglecting you. Us. We're a team, we're partners. I should have taken you tonight, I'm sorry. But I need you for the next one for sure. You OK?"

Blackbird hesitated again. Over his shoulder, her face was impassive, emotionless, her eyes dry and sore, her mind emotionally spent. But he couldn't know. Not yet. There was planning to do.

"Yeah, of course. I've just had myself for company the past six hours." Her fingers found the edge of his suit around his neck, and then the silver chain. She tugged it out from under his costume and squeezed the crucifix in her hand. "So, tell me about the job."

The Cowl had killed her parents after they refused to cooperate. Blackbird allowed herself a little smile.

Revenge would be sweet.

CHAPTER SIXTEEN

To run like the wind, went the proverb. A phrase never used because, well, it was the worst cliché around.

Tony laughed at the thought but found himself gasping almost instantly as the breath was snatched from his lungs. His heart raced, not from exertion, but from the sheer thrill of it. It really wasn't hard – if you could run this fast, then your brain was also capable of navigating around the obstacles registered even fleetingly by your optic nerves. People, animals, trees, park benches, skyscrapers. The rocks on the hillside south of the city. He hadn't meant to cut straight down from his dad's lodge, but he couldn't help himself. It had been the most direct route back to the city, and he was still buzzing a little after reducing a pile of dry logs stacked against the house to neatly split firewood. He knew his dad wasn't going to go anywhere near the lodge until the winter, and by that time he wouldn't remember whether he'd cut the logs himself or not.

Tony slowed enough to suck in a proper, full breath, his chest tight. That was interesting. Was it an insurmountable problem? Back when the railroad first opened America to high-speed travel, people thought you wouldn't be able to breathe at thirty miles per hour, and be dead at sixty. Perhaps they had the right idea, born out of fear and superstition rather than science, but they were off by a factor of ten. Tony could only guess his speed, of course. Maybe Jeannie had some gadget he could carry, some kind of pedometer or speedometer that would give him an actual reading. As part of her training regimen, as she had called it, it would make sense to actually collect some kind of data.

He slowed, then stopped. The wide sidewalk stretched ahead of him, curving along the back of East Bay and the famous golden sands. He jogged a little, momentarily just one of many, carefully checking around him as discreetly as possible before coming to a stop at a bench. Nothing. Nobody had seen him virtually pop into existence out of thin air. He sat and watched bathers on the beach, and joggers on the walkway. Everything was OK. Situation normal.

He felt... well, he felt fine, although his feet were hot. He crossed one foot over his knee to examine his old shoes. The rubber, amazingly, hadn't melted, but the soles were worn. That was probably going to be the limiting factor. Footwear. He'd have to mention that to Jeannie, get her to program it into her design.

Tony leaned back, enjoying the morning sun, and laughed then tempered his humor, glancing self-consciously to the left and right. For years, he'd felt apart, distanced from his home town. The Cowl held court, the Seven Wonders were never there, the city government was corrupt, the police force impotent.

And then he'd woken up as the most powerful man in the city. Well... *one* of the most powerful, although he didn't really know what powers each of the Seven Wonders had. How this had happened to him, he had no fucking clue. It didn't matter. What did matter was that in the last week he felt part of San Ventura in a way he never had. No fear, no regrets. No limits.

No motherfucking goddamn limits.

Feet restless and quadriceps pinging pleasantly, Tony stood. No limits? He looked across the beach, separated from the walkway by a concrete retaining wall and some elegantly arranged palm trees. The beach itself was deep yellow sand for maybe fifty feet, turning to harder wet sand for the next fifty before the breakers licked land. On his right, the great North Beach suspension bridge, based on the grand design of the Golden Gate of San Francisco far to the north. The sun glinted off the swanky North Beach suburbs that studded the hills across the bay, maybe a forty-minute drive away by car if you stuck to the coastline.

But directly across the harbor it wasn't so far. A couple of miles? Maybe a bit more. And the harbor wasn't exactly deep. San Ventura was a pretty spot and a popular tourist destination, but the channel wasn't capable of letting cruise ships of any size into the port. And Tony could swim, and there was coastguard, and plenty of people around.

Could he do it? Could he run fast enough across the water? Skip over it like a stone, and reach the other side? If he got across and then back he could meet up with Jeannie at the coffee shop like they'd agreed, only he'd have to step on the gas even more so he wouldn't be late. Even better, an incentive. And Tony hated being late, *hated* it. And he had time to spare. He needed to go to the bank, but he could run that errand tomorrow. Thanks to a change of shifts at Big Deal he had Thursday off too.

Tony hopped the wall and landed ankle-deep in the sand of East Bay. Shaking his shoes, he trotted towards the sea.

CHAPTER SEVENTEEN

The precinct house was air-conditioned as all modern buildings in San Ventura were. This was southern California. It was hot in June. Everyone knew this. But the SVPD were funded by the good taxpayers of the county... which meant the air-conditioning units, each individually working at maximum capacity, were inherently unable to cool the air inside the police offices due to their cheapness. Detective Sam Millar lamented this fact every day in summer, and was grateful that she at least had a window, and one that even opened. True enough, it did seem that all opening it did was funnel hotter air from outside *in*, but Sam figured that the psychological benefits of seeing the gently swayed blinds behind her desk outweighed the purely practical – if non-existent – effects.

Joe was slumped at the desk facing hers. The two of them had shared the same corner of the open-plan floor for a handful of years now. She got the warm breeze, he got the view.

Her partner was sagging a little too much in his chair, which he'd pumped low so he could put his feet up more comfortably on his desk. He was gingerly sipping a hot coffee while Sam sucked down an ice-cold mint frappé. She didn't quite believe his explanation of how a piping-hot drink actually cooled you down in summer, and had politely declined his offer of a jumbo grande Americano from the Apollo Coffee across the street, opting instead for something cooler. Joe certainly looked like he was suffering as he attempted to down the drink. Sam, on the other hand, was feeling remarkably refreshed.

"I wonder why the FBI were interested in that shooting?" Joe lifted the lid on his drink, apparently admitting defeat as he gently blew across the surface of his coffee.

Sam kept the straw of her milkshake in her mouth. "What shooting?" She took another delightfully chilled mouthful.

"That black guy. The one we went to see this morning with Jackie."

"Oh yeah." Sam thought as she pulled on the straw. How did she forget what she was doing that morning? The more she thought, the more her mind clouded over. She took another suck of milkshake. Boy, it was hot today. The heat made her fuzzy and tired. "What did the FBI report say?"

Joe shrugged, and re-crossed his legs. "No clue. Jackie saw it and signed it."

"Oh, OK then." Dammit, why was she so lethargic? This drink was supposed to wake her up. Perhaps Joe was right about the coffee.

"Still." Joe stretched, swinging his legs off the desk and reaching to an evidence box with one hand, fingers dancing on the hot cardboard held in his other. "We did get this. I wonder if we should send it on to the bureau?"

"What's that?" Sam sat up in her chair, the spring suddenly tilting her forward as she moved, making her realize she was slouched as lazily as her partner.

Joe tossed the sealed plastic bag onto Sam's desk. She sat her half-done drink on one of the few empty spaces on her crowded desk and picked it up. Inside was an elliptical strip of something black and plasticky. She moved it around through the bag between her thumb and forefinger. It was some kind of fabric that shone in the light coming in from the window behind her.

"Material? A scrap? Did we pick this up from the scene?"

Joe nodded quickly, then slowly as his eyes widened. "Yeah, yeah we did. Do you remember the dumpster, it was all... smashed in. That was on it, like it had been torn off. The dumpster had also been cut up, like with a knife."

Fascinated with the tiny piece of scene evidence, Sam brought it right up to her eye to get a close look. She grabbed the frappé with her other hand and leant back in her chair.

"What do you mean? What kind of weapon can slice into a metal dumpster?"

Joe blinked, and rubbed his forehead. "I... can't remember. No, wait, a quantum knife. And that guy, he wasn't shot, he was sliced up." He took a quick gulp of coffee and coughed, shook his head, and took another. "What the fuck is going on?"

Sam hadn't moved from her position. She thoughtfully pushed and pulled the straw in and out of the tiny hole in the transparent plastic dome that topped her cup with a sound not entirely unlike fingernails on a blackboard. Her mind was full of a montage of images from the morgue – the body of the victim, with gunshot wound to the abdomen... and the body of the victim, abdomen *intact*, but chest from ribcage to throat stitched up coarsely, a grid pattern that followed the incisions from a knife that passed right through from one side to the other.

Sam squinted, not looking at the evidence bag, but searching the images in her mind for something else. Another person, just a blurry form, something at the edge of her vision. She took another sip. There. Blue and white, blonde and radiant, and standing in the morgue between her and Joe and Doctor Chan.

Bluebell, The Seven Wonders' psychic warrior. Sam drained the remnants of her drink and slammed the cup down onto her desk, throwing the evidence bag down in frustration.

Joe and Sam looked at each other for several seconds, mouths wide in surprise.

"Bluebell! That bitch... Shit, Joe, the Seven Wonders only went and brain-baked us."

Joe half-stood, then sat, face wide in surprise. Then he clicked his fingers and slapped his own desk.

"Mother*fuckers*. Sorry."

Sam waved away his apology. "Don't. That descriptor is entirely appropriate. Those interfering *motherfuckers*."

"So what do we do?"

"Oh, that's easy, detective." Sam tapped her laptop awake and started the too-long process of getting the department intranet up. "The Seven Wonders have taken the body. We can't do anything about that, they'll have covered their asses good and proper. But, we have this." She pointed to the evidence bag. "If the murderer was the Cowl, it was unusual, totally out of character. Which might be why the precious Wonders are so interested. But if we can get anywhere with analyzing this scrap – components, manufacturing process, whatever – we might be able to get to the perp first, Cowl or no Cowl."

Joe's smile dropped a degree.

"Trying to track down the Cowl with a little piece of cloth? I don't think he buys his capes at Walmart. It's custom, high-tech. How are we gonna trace... well, *anything* from that scrap?"

"Ever the optimist, detective."

"Realist, detective. Realist."

Sam folded the evidence bag in half, and again felt the black material between her fingers through the plastic. "We've got to start somewhere. So, what's logical? He probably uses the costume as some kind of light armor. So, ballistics, and ballistics textiles, we start there."

Joe clapped his hands together, the smile reappearing. "Ballistics, yes! Let's get down and see Lansbury, she can take a look."

"Detective Milano, you read my mind. Let's go."

CHAPTER EIGHTEEN

"Thanks, Mary, and good morning San Ventura for Monday the twentieth. I'm Sarah Nova and these are your headlines this morning.

"Fifteen dead in the fourth high-tech raid this year. The Clarke Institute of Technology remains closed this morning after the high-security government energy research unit was attacked in the early hours. A fire later gutted the main office block. San Ventura PD have no leads but Seven Wonders' chairman Aurora's Light said the raid was clearly the work of his arch-nemesis the Cowl, and that the superteam would be assisting local and state law enforcement officials in their investigation.

"Detectives from North Beach sheriff's department are searching for two teenage girls who disappeared from their home near Lee Springs Friday and haven't been seen since. The pair were last seen walking home from their local high school in the mid-afternoon. The parents of the pair said it would be completely out of character for their daughters to run off. SVPD are appealing for anyone who knows of the girls' whereabouts to come forward.

"And later today, Geoffrey Conroy, CEO of Conroy Industries, will present the Build-A-Home Foundation with a check for $150,000, raised from the Police Benevolent Fund charity auction last month. The money will go towards upgrades of two community centers in El Simona. Mr Conroy hosted the auction himself in June at the annual San Ventura Police Department charity ball. The check handover will take place at a garden party hosted by Mr Conroy at his North Beach hillside residence.

"And now our top story. Seven Wonders' chairman Aurora's Light has repeated his call for the supervillain known as the Cowl to give himself up, following the murders of fifteen personnel at CIT in a raid early today. The dead were a mix of security and research staff at the High Valley complex, which has been conducting defense research for the federal government since 1996. The brazen attack was, according to the Seven Wonders, masterminded by the supervillain and his accomplice, known only as Blackbird. While neither felon – both holding joint number one on the FBI's Most Wanted list – left any physical evidence, the leader of the city's superteam told *Good Morning San Ventura's* Leroy Martin earlier today that the raid is part of the Cowl's latest evil plan."

"There is no doubt that this is the work of the Cowl. This is the fourth raid on government and privately funded research institutes this year, with each attack bearing his hallmarks. We are continuing to investigate and are assisting the San Ventura Police Department in their investigation, with my team lending specialist equipment and personnel to try to trace the whereabouts of both the Cowl and Blackbird and of the stolen equipment and components."

"When asked about what the Cowl's plans might be, Aurora's Light said the matter was still under investigation."

"I would like to personally reassure the people of San Ventura that the Seven Wonders exist only to serve and protect, with the cooperation of the SVPD and City Hall. We have been gathering intelligence on the Cowl's activities for some time now, and while we have no knowledge of credible, specific threats at the present, we must keep the city's terror level on red for the time being, and I've put all members of the Seven Wonders out on public patrol. I would also like to put a call out to the Cowl and to Blackbird: we may not know your true identities, but if you come forward and give yourselves up to the Seven Wonders or to a representative of the SVPD, this will count in your favor. Thank you, Mr Martin."

"*Good Morning San Ventura* was unable to verify what has been taken from the institute, but a source close to the sheriff's department said that it fitted the pattern of the previous raids where high-tech experimental electronics had been snatched. The four raids in total have claimed twenty-seven lives.

"Detectives say the disappearance of two teenage girls from Lee Springs is completely out of character. The two girls, aged fourteen and fifteen, have not been seen since Friday afternoon when they appeared on CCTV leaving their high school..."

CHAPTER NINETEEN

With a two-handed key combo, the message was replayed for perhaps the twentieth time. Two displays showed two graphs each, the points plotted and connecting lines drawn as the recorded data were analyzed again. A smaller readout projected a green circular grid with a wildly wavering orange line across the dark computer room, an abstract but highly mathematical interpolation of the transmission pulsing in time with the audio playback.

The audio was down low, because she didn't want anyone to hear. In a building occupied by at least two people with superhearing, keeping things a secret was difficult. At least she didn't have any brain activity that could be read by Bluebell. But to cover any eventuality, the Dragon Star's powerstaff, propped against the desk, was generating a signal-cancelling dome a few yards in diameter, enough for her to work on her own project without drawing attention to herself.

The message finished, she tapped some keys, then started from the beginning again.

The Citadel of Wonders was a building far, far too large for just seven occupants. In reality, only a small part of it was used as the headquarters of San Ventura's superteam. The main purpose of the edifice, a giant, triangular glass skyscraper standing square in the center of the city, was to inspire awe and wonder. Only a few civilians had ever been beyond the cathedral-like atrium, and even those who had had no idea that eighty percent of the one million, one hundred square feet of usable space inside the fantastic construction was completely empty.

Mayoral tours, military meetings, presidential galas. It didn't matter what rank or office you held, the Citadel was a castle of secrets.

Deep in the bowels of the building, SMART completed some routine tasks for its master Hephaestus in the Forge, a large, hangar-like room that descended under the city and formed a cuboidal void reaching six stories high through the center of the Citadel. It was here that the Greek god worked on tech for the superteam – it was part workshop, part R&D lab, part test bed. The Supra-Maximal Attack-Response Titan – SMART, the only artificial member of the Seven Wonders – had been designed, built and tested in the room. As far as it was possible, the Forge was the robot's home.

With the Forge computer on sleep, SMART lumbered to the exit, the next part of its nightly routine to take the service elevator to the uppermost floor of the Citadel and install itself into the custom port in Control One, the master nerve center in the building's tetrahedral apex. From there it could monitor not only the city, but patch into the entire global network of superheroes, communicating with operators both machine and living all over the world. Despite worldwide retirement, the Seven Wonders had assigned a few heroes dotted around the world a series of surveillance tasks, just in case a supervillain decided to reappear or, somehow, managed to escape from one of the world's three superprisons. In addition, the Seven Wonders' own surveillance extended into space by several tens of thousands of miles, thanks to their covert satellite network, again designed and built by Hephaestus, the greatest engineer and weaponsmith the world had ever known.

The service elevator was slow, but given SMART's eight-foot bulk, it couldn't get around the building any other way. The journey would take two minutes; in that time SMART routinely ran a remote systems check of the empty building. It was the middle of a quiet night, and as the superteam's mobile supercomputer and operations core, directly linked to the main systems in the Citadel, SMART was the only one who never went off duty.

SMART scanned, cancelled the process, then scanned again. The result was the same – at seventy-five per cent progress, there was an anomaly, the scan sticking on something odd, before continuing uninterrupted until the robot halted the command before completion. A third time, the same. SMART re-launched the application. It hiccupped at seventy-five per cent, again.

The elevator was not quite halfway to the fiftieth floor. SMART tried something different, an old-fashioned short-range wireless scan, reading regular Wi-Fi fields and comparing the data with something similar to a radar scan. The requisite data was gathered in 0.015 seconds, and correlated with the seventy-five per cent scan results in 0.07. SMART stopped the elevator, and patched in the Citadel's internal security computer.

If SMART had been given a simulated sense of humor by its creator, alongside its simulated emotion, the appropriate response might have been "*Bingo!*" But the robot remained silent, accepting the logical conclusion derived from the available data.

Someone was in Subcontrol Three, and was shielding themselves from detection by deflecting all electromagnetic energy waves in a small umbrella which formed a small blank spot on the robot's scan. But logic also told SMART that the "intruder" was really one of the other six members of the Seven Wonders, and that as all had authority to carry out their duties precisely as they saw fit, there was no problem. Deflection shield or not.

SMART redirected the elevator to level thirty, just four floors up. As soon as the doors slid open, it activated a second set of gyros and couplings, transforming the usual slow, heavy and loud gait of the slow, heavy and square white robot into a lithe, smooth motion. Stealth mode was taxing on system memory and couldn't be used for extended periods before SMART's processor heatsinks got hot enough that they could be detected by infra-red through the reflective armor plate. But for sneaking around the Citadel, it would do admirably.

Subcontrol Three was hardly more than a small cupboard housing a redundant bank of servers and a small control desk, a simplified version of the room-sized panels available in Control One. But depending on what systems you wanted to use, the subcontrol rooms dotted around the Citadel made for comfortable and quiet workspaces, the required controls and systems mapped from the master deck on the top level.

The door was open as SMART rounded the corridor. Under stealth, only Hephaestus would have been able to sense SMART's presence. The machine had no mind for Bluebell to read and the white armor deflected any energy signature that Aurora or the Dragon Star might have been able to detect. But unlike the hero working in Subcontrol Three, this included the visible spectrum. The eight-foot-tall robot was a vague shimmer of heat in the corridor.

The person seated at the panel, hunched over in their task, was totally oblivious to the robot's presence. SMART zoomed its optics in. There was the tall golden powerstaff, and the superhero's face was hidden by a huge flowing hood which continued down into a billowing robe over skintight white and red spandex. From the corridor, SMART was only able to see one leg, bare skin visible through a series of geometric – and very revealing – holes in the costume.

SMART knew that the Dragon Star's costume was designed to be attractive to male humans. Part of the Seven Wonders' mission was PR, and the citizens of San Ventura, rightly or wrongly, wanted to be protected by the perfect and the attractive. The Dragon Star was certainly that, although some logical argument worming its way through the back of SMART's CPU suggested that if the general populace knew that the Dragon Star's body was the corpse of a teenage cheerleader stolen from the city morgue and reanimated by a sexless alien entity, then the athletic, spandex-clad form in enigmatic flowing robes and hood would be a lot less attractive.

SMART paused, its CPU completing a full cycle with no processes. SMART... SMART *felt* something. It was impossible, of course, and as soon as the errant cycle was detected SMART launched a full array of diagnostic applications and processes, cleared terabytes worth of caches, and restarted several systems.

Two seconds later the robot's systems were back up and... the *feeling* remained. It was almost disgust. SMART considered, then accepted the logic. It was an assimilation of data based on its knowledge of the Dragon Star and of human society. All the robot needed to do was correlate one with the other and *simulate* a predicted response. This was within its operational parameters, and was therefore entirely logical.

SMART was disgusted, and shrank back a little in the corridor as it watched the Dragon Star at work.

SMART *hid*.

The crystal set into the top of the Dragon Star's powerstaff pulsed rhythmically, generating the electromagnetic shield that covered her and the computer desk. SMART cycled its optical filters through a range of wavelengths, recording the data as the Dragon Star alternately appeared and disappeared from view depending on the spectrum.

SMART considered again. All members of the Seven Wonders had the express permission of their leader, Aurora, to do what they liked to protect the city, within certain bounds – that each superhero was independent and free to pursue justice when the superteam was not "united", as the catchphrase went; that every action had to be within the law, unless an emergency was declared; that the no-kill rule was unassailable.

But the Dragon Star was hiding under a deflection shield as she worked in Subcontrol Three, and as no one except the Seven Wonders had access to this part of the Citadel, it meant that the Dragon Star didn't want the others to know she was there.

The Dragon Star was keeping a secret. SMART considered and felt...

SMART's processor skipped a cycle again, and the robot moved slightly in the dark corridor.

Another logical deduction and more of this new process, this *simulated* emotion. SMART considered. It was not thinking for itself, it was thinking on behalf of the humans it was programmed to protect. What would the people of San Ventura think if the reanimated body of a dead girl was carrying out secret work at the Citadel, hiding it from the superteam she had sworn her allegiance to? Did the honorable vows of an alien to protect the city count, anyway? What would the *people* think?

After three hours, the Dragon Star stood, powerstaff held firmly in one delicate hand. SMART's optics crash-zoomed to follow her every movement and gesture. There. She took a data stick from the computer and pocketed it in her cloak. Powerstaff still pulsing, the Dragon Star shut the subcontrol room systems down and closed the door, heading down the dark corridor towards the regular passenger lift, and out of SMART's visual range. The robot continued to track her movements for a while afterwards, seismic detectors registering her movements in the floors above, Citadel security systems feeding video and audio. Not that there was much to see, or hear. The Dragon Star moved through dead corridors silently, and with her staff still throwing the cone of invisibility around her, each night vision camera went black as she passed. The trail of active and inactive cameras was a more-than-adequate tracker for SMART, linked as it was to every system in the whole building.

Thirty minutes after leaving the subcontrol room, the camera in the Dragon Star's private quarters came on suddenly. She was lying on her futon, asleep, or at least resting the human body. SMART watched for a few minutes but her form remained still. The Dragon Star was the only one of the Wonders to make the Citadel their permanent home. Well, her and SMART, but then SMART *was* the Citadel, in many ways.

The robot allowed itself to make noise now, clicking loudly as it refolded the stealth mechanisms away and reverting to its regular, cumbersome gait. At an even walking pace, it thudded into the subcontrol room and, pushing the high-backed swivel chair aside, extended a powerful arm towards one of the custom computer ports that were studded throughout the entire building. As soon as SMART connected, the Subcontrol Three came to life, readouts changing and displays scrolling through data as SMART flipped the system back through its last actions. Reaching a selected time point of four hours past, SMART rolled through the residue of erased data still clinging to the solid-state hard drives and computer memory. There. A pattern, an unknown program run, and data from one of the surveillance satellites routed past the main system in Control One and fed directly into the subservers on level thirty.

SMART saw the message buried in the high-frequency noise of the raw satellite data quickly, like a person focusing on a magic eye picture puzzle. As the graphs changed on the room's two widescreen displays, SMART threw in various filters and decryption algorithms.

There. The Dragon Star's secret message, a transmission received from the stars.

SMART rewound the data and replayed.

CHAPTER TWENTY

It was like a scene from a movie.

Tony sighed. No, it was worse – it was like a scene from a chick flick. *Gabrielle Gets Hitched*, or *My Fat Cashcow Wedding Franchise VII*.

His arms were sore. Why, he wasn't sure. He was a superhero, invulnerable, having woken up with superstrength, flight, heat vision, the whole damn works. A superhero who, just a couple of days ago, had taken on the Cowl in a downtown bank. Who had flown up, up and away, carrying the supervillain in the wild blue yonder. Who had survived the fall in the sea with nothing more than a sore head and who had walked, rather than raced – well, look where racing had got him – soaking wet back home.

Gee-whizz, that had been a fun day!

So why holding his arms out for fifteen minutes was such a strain, he had no real idea. It was probably psychological. It was probably because having Jeannie pull and shove his groin with a mouthful of pins just inches away from his... well, made him uncomfortable. He wanted to fidget, to move, to do anything to change position and relieve the stiffness in his muscles, but he dared not break the statuesque pose his girlfriend had put him in.

Jeannie wanted to make the costume, and make it she would. It was bizarre, to say the least. Jeannie had clothes-making skills worthy of an old-fashioned seamstress, but was using high-tech fabrics acquired from her day job... whatever that was, exactly. Tony wasn't sure. Jeannie had mentioned it was to do with military research and was mostly classified, and she hadn't exactly been laughing when she said it, so he didn't push the issue. It was a little early in their relationship to be breaking official secrets, but he knew the pins in her mouth were a secret tantalum/protactinium alloy. The industrial sewing machine clamped to the kitchen table – looking more like a heavy-duty drill from a factory – used a needle made of the same substance, superheated with two green lasers.

So yeah, Jeannie was taking it seriously.

Tony felt her hands pull his waist around. He went with the movement, and turned, finding himself looking out of the window. He wondered if he should close it, but then it was late and there was never anyone out on that side of the street, abutting the old warehouse like it did. The sight of the city's latest superhero getting his new kit made would have been an amusing sight.

Tony turned his mind to an equally important matter.

"Been thinking about the name."

"Uh-huh," said Jeannie. In fact she might have said something else entirely, but with a mouth full of nuclear pins Tony couldn't tell.

"I like names that have 'The' in front of them."

"Mmm."

"The Judge."

Jeannie stopped, removed the pins from her mouth, and looked up at Tony. "No." She resumed work.

"The Judge and Jury?"

Pins out. "Yes, that's great! No wait, the other thing. Fucking terrible." Pins in.

"Well OK then," said Tony. He looked back out the window. Names weren't his thing. All of the good ones were already taken. Not that there was any kind of registry, like domain names or trademarks or anything, but superhero names *could* be copyrighted. Even Aurora had fallen foul of that one. It had been a supervillain's plot, back when there had been more than just one supervillain and one superteam. Red Tape, he had called himself. He'd been second-rate... no, *third*-rate, at the very least. But he'd been a real handful and although he'd been taken down easily, he'd caused no end of trouble for the Seven Wonders. And since then, Aurora's full name was the slightly awkward Aurora's Light to avoid the rights issues over the original, shorter version laid down by Red Tape's final act of bureaucratic terror, a superpowered contract that promised the Pacific and North American tectonic plates would suddenly wrench the West Coast apart should Aurora's name be incorrectly cited in any official document from now until ninety-five years after Red Tape's death.

But now Tony knew he needed a superhero name. Something original, something with impact and which also reflected his aims and intentions.

Shit. It was hard work.

Jeannie finally embedded the pins into three sheets of gray fabric that were loosely wound around Tony's middle, stood up, and tapped his biceps. Tony took that as an indication he could lower his arms and get off the chair.

"Done?"

"Done." Jeannie nodded, adjusted the pins, and directed Tony to step out of the costume template. Tony then swung the chair around on one leg and sat on it backwards, resting his arms on the back, watching Jeannie align the panels of top-secret material on the table.

"You seem to have this sewn up. Oh, I'm a funny guy. But seriously, what did you have in mind?"

Jeannie fiddled with the atomic sewing machine. "If you like the letter 'J' – and I have no idea why – then Justiciar. Or even 'the' Justiciar. It's original and it means what it means."

"Sorry, I forgot to do my Latin homework this morning."

"It's not Latin, that would be *justiciarius*"

"Of course. My mistake."

Jeannie poked her tongue out at him. "The Justiciar was a law keeper in medieval Europe. Sort of like a policeman and judge, an officer of the law."

Tony clicked his fingers. "Judge and Jury!" he said again. His smile was ridiculous.

"Yeah, because Judge Judy is a great nickname."

"Judge Judy is a superhero? I fucking knew it."

"You bet. Why do you think her show starts with that voiceover? 'Real people. Real cases. Judge Judy.' It's a secret identity."

Jeannie reached for a set of heavy industrial goggles that lay next to the machine. "The Justiciar is shit cool though, yeah?"

Tony's mouth worked the unfamiliar word. It sounded odd and memorable. He nodded. "Let's run with it for now. See how it fits." He stood and walked behind Jeannie, peering low over her shoulder as she fitting the special fabric under the foot of the sewing machine. "I don't even know what I'm going to look like. You sure you know what you're doing?"

Jeannie nodded, eyes tight in concentration as she prepped the machine. "Trust me, I've had a lot of experience."

"Ah yeah. Amateur dramatics at the company? Christmas shows, that kind of thing?"

Jeannie looked up for a moment. "Yeah, that kind of thing."

"Cool, cool." Tony stood. "I'll leave you to it." He walked to the kitchen and came back with a beer.

Jeannie carefully adjusted the alignment of lasers and needle, slid the goggles down her forehead, and started bonding the Justiciar's armor together.

CHAPTER TWENTY-ONE

Unlike the morgue at the central city hospital, which acted as the SVPD's main processing center for bodies, the ballistics department was housed in the main precinct building itself in downtown San Ventura. And unlike the morgue, the ballistics department was a place that Sam liked to visit.

She wasn't sure why, exactly, because while it lacked the stench of formaldehyde and racks of chilled bodies in various stages of decomposition or examination, it was still very much a laboratory. And laboratories had never been Sam's thing. She'd taken chemistry at UCSV as her major, but had only lasted a single semester. The sterility of the place, the whiteness of the appliances, the humming of refrigerators, the need for gloves and lab coats and safety goggles, and the silent lurking presence of emergency showers spaced at intervals along the big undergraduate chemistry laboratory had terrified Sam. She'd known it was irrational – a phobia, pure and simple – and had even gone to see the Dean of Studies about it, but unable to shake it off she'd switched to a paralegal course which eventually got her interested in law enforcement. So it goes, and here she was.

Perhaps then it was the feeling of an enemy defeated, the satisfaction that came with overcoming her phobia in the course of her job. Because – like the city morgue – visiting the ballistics department wasn't an uncommon task for a detective in SuperCrime.

"Ballistics" wasn't the official name of the department – it was the Forensic Ballistics and Materials Science, which made more sense as there was a lot more to it than just looking at guns and figuring out who had fired them and what they had fired. The department had its own single-alley shooting range, deep in the basement underneath the main street where the sound would be adequately baffled, and three large laboratories attached to it. The labs were ringed with six offices, in one of which sat Diana Lansbury, the head of the section.

"You realize what you've got here?"

Sam found her lips tightening as she watched Lansbury finger the ziplock-sealed evidence bag on her desk. Within was the strip of black curled fabric.

Joe sighed next to her and Sam knew the feeling. Lansbury was someone you might call... old-fashioned. For as long as Sam could remember, Lansbury had ruled her basement empire, and for as long as Sam could remember, Lansbury was about due for retirement. She was one of those older women who had stayed fresh-faced and bright-eyed, her hair still refusing to gray. She was also a scientist, one of the best on the force, and perhaps that explained her eternal youth as well – she was, as Sam well knew, fulfilling her passion, which was her job. Only someone with such absolute single-minded focus on her career could put in such long hours, become such an expert, and apparently be so energized and revitalized by the sheer volume of work.

That, or she'd been granted eternal youth by a superhero back in the Middle Ages. Perhaps she *was* one herself.

Sam licked her lips. At least Lansbury got job satisfaction. So few people in life achieved their aims. She idly wondered if there was more to her own than the pursuit of the Cowl, but then wondered if there was anything about that that was particularly wrong anyway.

So it was a shame in many ways that Lansbury was a pain, as Captain Gillespie often said, in the fanny. Sam choked back a snort of laughter as she remembered the chief's quite serious appraisal when she'd told him they were heading downstairs to get the results of Lansbury's analysis. The captain said it each and every time, with a fixed look and a tight forehead, like he was offering a vital warning to an intrepid explorer heading into the unknown. Sam knew well enough the ins and outs of Lansbury's manner, and she'd learned through a couple of years of painful trial and error how to deal with her.

The method was simple: keep quiet, look interested and let Lansbury do all the talking.

The problem was that Joe hadn't quite got the hang of it. Sam glanced at her partner, sitting with one leg wrapped over the other in the short space between his chair and Lansbury's desk, an ancient and valuable specimen that was far too large for the pokey underground office. The muscles along Joe's jawline pulsed as he stifled a yawn. Sam looked back at Lansbury, but it was too late. Lansbury had noticed Joe's apparent boredom.

"Low on oxygen are we, detective?" said Lansbury, flicking the evidence bag on her desk and leaning back in her chair, another piece of furniture of the kind they just didn't make anymore. It occurred to Sam that they'd probably been installed in the building's basement when it had been built back in the 1930s. Perhaps Lansbury had signed for the delivery herself.

Sam leaned forward in an attempt to bring herself back to the task at hand. She sniffed. It wasn't hot in the office, but the air was thick and stale and smelt of browning paper and lit fireworks.

"I'm sorry, Doctor Lansbury," she said with a smile that the scientist viewed with some disdain before, apparently, deciding it was genuine. "We hoped *you* were going to tell us just what we had."

Lansbury sniffed loudly and began shuffling through a manila folder. Sam noticed for the first time that there was no computer in the room.

"I'll send the full report up to you tomorrow once I get it typed up, but I can give you a summary now." Lansbury found the right piece of paper. Sam saw it covered in a thick handwriting with large letters.

"It's synthetic, a ceramic–plastic polymer."

Joe jerked in his chair like he'd just woken up, but when Sam turned to face him she saw his face creased with serious focus.

"That means a superhero?"

Lansbury's right eyebrow went up. Sam clicked her fingers.

"Or supervillain," she said. "Right?"

Lansbury sniffed a third time. "The material is similar to that used by some superheroes, both retired and still active. As you know, this department cooperates with the Seven Wonders on a number of city-wide initiatives, and in exchange we have part of their database on reference. This material is similar, but not the same to the material used for Aurora's suit."

Sam sank back into her chair. Well, she'd thought that would be the case – not that the sample would be the same as, or similar to, Aurora's suit, but that it was a high-tech fabric that could have only come from one source. The Cowl.

But she knew how limited their access to the superhero database was. That was probably as far as Lansbury was able to go. Confirmation of a theory, but nothing that could be acted on.

"Don't be so keen to make assumptions, Miss Millar."

Sam froze in her chair, realizing after Lansbury did that her muscles were tense, part-way to lifting herself from the chair, eager to terminate the discussion. The fact that Lansbury had called her "miss" rather than "detective" was noted with irritation.

Sam relaxed back into the chair. She exchanged a look with Joe, but Joe still had his poker face on. He turned back to Lansbury.

"What are we trying not to assume here?"

Lansbury rubbed an eye; Sam watched the skin over her cheekbone move too much under her finger. Sometimes Lansbury showed her real age.

"You're assuming that I've spent the best part of three days analyzing this sample and getting zero results. But actually I can tell you more than just its composition. I can tell you where it came from. In fact, I can tell you who invented the base compound."

Sam blinked. "I was under the impression that these kinds of fabrics are either the work of the superhero community, or some government or military authority, access to which requires security clearance well above our collective pay grades?"

Lansbury hissed like a bicycle tire with a slow puncture.

"Impressions, assumptions. See? Just wait until you get some experience under your belt, then you won't be so quick to make your mind up on a case. Particularly a case as important as this."

Zing. Sam felt her face beginning to heat. Lansbury knew exactly where to place that barb – the whole precinct knew about her history with regard to public enemy number one, the Cowl.

Her and David Millar's history.

The laboratory phobia began to return, crawling into the edges of Sam's vision like black snow. They were underground, it was stuffy, there was no natural light. Sam wasn't claustrophobic, but she had limits.

Lansbury waved a hand. "At ease, soldier," she said. Her eyes were closed and she was sitting back in her pre-war office chair again. "This material was developed by a researcher at CIT, a Doctor Ravenholt. CIT is a contractor for the US military but also for the FBI, for whom this material was designed. As one of the country's foremost experts on ballistics fibers I was involved with testing. There is no mistaking this weave – it comes from that project."

Sam and Joe exchanged another look, but it was Joe who found his voice first. "So, the FBI use it for... what, vests?"

"Nope," said Lansbury, with an unpleasant smack of the lips. "The project was cut short due to funding reallocation. Doctor Ravenholt moved on to something else. But..."

"But...?"

Lansbury paused and eyed Sam. Sam bit her tongue and gestured for her to continue.

"The field tests were, oh, six years ago, maybe more. I forget. This fabric is new, though. The base polymer is slightly different, but the process by which it is made has only been around for a year. Someone is manufacturing this stuff, in small quantities, for something."

Sam smiled. "For a suit."

"For a suit," said Lansbury, and for the first time in the last half-hour her smile was real.

Joe shimmied to the edge of his chair and had his smartphone in his hand already, tapping out notes.

"This Doctor Ravenholt, he still at the CIT?"

"*She*. And I believe so," said Lansbury, her face dropping slightly along with her interest; they were starting to move from ballistics and science and into police work and Sam knew Lansbury didn't much care about how that all worked.

"Well, we can find out," said Joe, his attention returning to his phone.

Sam frowned. There was something missing from the picture. Something that felt like it was right in front of her, if only she could come at it from a different angle and see what it was.

And... Sam sucked in a breath. Could it really be so simple... so... *stupid*?

Simple, but not unusual. Back when there had been a world full of superheroes, this kind of thing was actually pretty common. It was like some kind of standard operating procedure for meta-humans, a superheroic in-joke.

"Joe," said Sam, speaking slowly, running the theory through her head again and again in quick succession, making sure she had it exactly right.

Joe caught the pause and put his phone down.

"You thinking something?"

Sam was indeed. They had a scrap of high-tech fabric developed by a scientist contracted to the US government, now being manufactured possibly in secret for the purpose of making a suit – a *costume* – for someone other than a member of the Seven Wonders. A scrap of fabric that was placed at the scene of a crime carried out, as far as they knew, by the Cowl.

The Cowl, and his accomplice...

"This fabric was developed by someone called Doctor *Raven*holt?"

Lansbury nodded. "Doctor Jean Ravenholt, yes." But Sam was looking at Joe. Joe's eyes flicked to Lansbury then back to Sam. Lansbury's smile was as wide as the ocean and showed a shark-like array of yellowing tombstone teeth.

Sam blinked.

"Doctor Ravenholt is Blackbird?"

Joe sat back in his chair and sighed. Sam looked at Lansbury, who winked.

Joe had his phone out again and was halfway out of his chair. "Let's get digging, talk to Gillespie. If this is right we've just found a direct link to the Cowl's operation."

Joe excused himself and was talking into his phone even before he was out of Lansbury's office. Sam sat a moment longer, not looking at anything except the air in the room.

"Being superpowered must come with a superpowered ego, I suppose."

Sam blinked. Lansbury's fingers were steepled.

"To adopt a pseudonym like that, I mean. To base it on your own given name."

Sam stood. It was time to get to work.

"Welcome to San Ventura," she said.

CHAPTER TWENTY-TWO

"Hey, Tony."

"What?"

"Make a wish."

The sound of the gunshot in the apartment was appalling. Tony saw the walls and ceiling spin, Jeannie appearing momentarily upside down before the floor reared up and the back of his head connected with it. He was completely deaf, and his mouth was full of the taste of metal and vinegar.

He said: "What the fuck?" In fact, he was pretty sure he shouted it, but he could hear nothing after the hardwood hammer-snap of the gunshot but a ringing of infinite depth. He kept his eyes open, and when he was fairly sure the ceiling wasn't going to move anymore, he chanced a look up. He couldn't crane his neck far from his tumbled position against the couch, but could just see Jeannie from the knees up. She was smiling, one hand plucking a plug from her left ear, the other holding a pistol. It was sleek, rectangular, something modern and police-like. Where she had got it from, who knew. Maybe she'd always had it. Fact remained, his girl had just fucking shot him in the chest.

Huh. The ringing faded, and as he inhaled through his nose, the tang of the gun smoke was actually quite pleasant. He'd never used a gun himself, never been anywhere near a firearm being let off, but it reminded him of fairgrounds and wet grass, when he was a kid. Fireworks and jet fuel; the smell of an airport.

He uncurled himself, hands at his chest, expecting to find carnage and blood. He didn't feel anything in particular except a slightly deep, dull numbness over his heart, where the bullet had entered. Must have been bad. They say you don't feel it when you die. Soldiers can get their legs blown clean off and die quietly in the arms of a comrade. This was it. His girlfriend had shot him. The end.

He heard Jeannie's boots on the wooden floor before he looked up and saw her close, leaning down, and still with the fucking smile. The wrong crowd, she was it. He'd met her in a bar, and he knew nothing about her. He didn't even know where she worked or what she did. "Military research"? Damn. Of course she had a gun. She was a fucking soldier. He should have paid more attention.

"You gonna stay down there forever?" Jeannie's nose almost touched his own. She stood, put the gun on the coffee table, and turned back to him. Her smile turned into a frown, then she stood and walked out of his field of vision. "You wanna eat?" she called from the kitchen. "Maybe we can go down to Sherrod's for some pizza?"

He was alive. He stood, supporting himself carefully on the sofa arm, only to realize he didn't need supporting. The hands that clutched at his chest were not smothered in blood. He looked down, pulling his T-shirt out with both hands. There was a hole, the edges crisp, about the size of a quarter. Around it, about a hand-span across, the black cotton was shiny and smooth where the discharge and powder from the barrel had burnt it. Having opened the front door to let her in, Jeannie had actually been at point-blank range when she fired. The force of the blast had sent him reeling, but that was it. Loud and hot, the shot had done nothing but put a hole in his shirt. God knew what the neighbors were thinking.

"Sherrod's?" Jeannie emerged from the kitchen, drinking a glass of water. She reached for her jacket. "Fog coming in from the bay, might be cold out. You should change your shirt."

"Ah. OK. Um. What the fuck was that?"

Jeannie's face broke into a wide grin as she brought the glass up to her mouth. She gulped too soon, some water trickling from the side of her mouth.

"So you're bulletproof." She shrugged. "You said you wanted to know, after the thing at the bank. And we had to find out sooner or later, if you're gonna fight like a real superhero. Now we know. Let's go, I'm hungry."

Jeannie disappeared through the bedroom door. Tony stood for a moment, slack-jawed. He glanced down at his chest again, and then saw it on the floor – a shiny disc of metal, the black edges crinkled with a thicker coppery nub at the center. He stared at it for a handful of seconds, trying to reconcile the flattened object with the bullet that had left the barrel of Jeannie's gun and hit him square in the chest.

"Hey."

Tony looked up, then his vision went black as the T-shirt Jeannie threw enveloped his face.

"I said I'm hungry." She knocked his shoulder. "Come on!"

CHAPTER TWENTY-THREE

It was late, but this was a summer in San Ventura and the heat was unlikely to let up, no matter what the hour.

It was well after midnight when Jeannie and Tony walked out of Sherrod's pizza and into *And Then I Dreamt of Yes*, a stereotypically dark and noisy bar-stroke-club just off Vincent and Abnett, but the place wouldn't reach maximum capacity for a few hours yet. At the moment it was just nicely busy, with no queue to get in and relaxed bouncers happy to let Jeannie by. Perhaps they gave Tony a look, pausing just a little as they checked the quality of his replacement shirt, but seeing as he was attached to a far more attractive, far cooler woman, they waved him through without anything more than a raised eyebrow.

Why they were there, Tony wasn't sure, as Jeannie knew he didn't like dancing. But he felt happy, exhilarated even, and was willing to give anything a shot. He was invulnerable, and powerful, and now he had nothing to fear. Strangely it had been the little incident at the bank that had done it; the ultimate test, and while he might not have aced it, he'd at least managed a C+. Add to that some hard evidence now that he was bulletproof, and hell, he was a goddamn superman.

And, you know, San Ventura was actually pretty nice when you didn't have to worry about the Cowl or the thugs pretending to be the Cowl's thugs jumping you from the alleys. Actually, it was more than pretty nice. San Ventura was fucking *awesome*. Downtown was lit and full of people, young and old, almost busier than it was during the peak shopping hours of the day. It might have occurred to him that the hundreds of citizens happily playing in the town after hours were not superpowered, were not invulnerable, were not fearless like he, and none crept along the shadows, watchful for imminent attack. Maybe some part of his brain did notice, but his conscious mind was too busy having a fucking great time to pay it much heed. That kind of bolt-of-lightning resolution was usually best served in the morning, when all was silent and there was nothing to do on a Sunday but sit in the sun and mull over the problem of life and drink tea.

Tony wasn't sure what he'd ordered, but the barman nodded, the large black onyx ring in his nose swinging as he turned to prepare something. His shirtless back was heavily tattooed with snakes and gargoyles. At the center, between the shoulder blades, a cloaked, hooded figure was shown perched on the lip of a fairy-tale Gothic cathedral. The Cowl? Surely not... but... was that the Seven Wonders etched into the man's skin around the supervillain, like a double-page comic book splash?

The barkeep turned, and Tony smiled as nonchalantly as possible, pretending to be fascinated by the myriad colored bottles that lined the back of the bar. As the barman selected bottles and glasses it looked vaguely as though Tony had managed to order two gin and tonics and two tequila slammers. As the barman dropped ice into two of the tumblers Tony watched the cubes vibrate in time with the bass that filled the air.

Jeannie tugged his elbow, and Tony turned, two glasses in hand. Jeannie's eyes lit up in appreciation and she said something he couldn't hear, but she grabbed the shot glass first and chugged it, set it back on the bar, then took the gin glass and sipped it more sedately. Tony followed her lead, the raw tequila flavor mixing with the gin pleasantly. He hadn't tried that particular combination before, but he added it to his list of "not bad at alls".

Jeannie led him to a booth by the elbow – despite the crowd, most were standing or dancing, leaving plenty of seats. They slid in, sitting opposite each other, the walls of the booth baffling the music well. Jeannie only had to shout at the top of her lungs to be heard now.

"Not a bad day then?"

Tony smiled and sipped his drink. "I guess not. Speed, strength. Um, a gunshot to the fucking heart." He absently rubbed his chest, just to make sure – for the millionth time – that there wasn't a gaping bloody hole there. "Not bad at all."

Jeannie laughed, silently again. She'd taken to the whole superhero thing rather well. In fact she seemed pretty happy about it. As did he. No fear, no limits. Anything was possible. San Ventura would not know what had hit it. As the alcohol worked its magic, Tony's mind idly drifted around the possibilities.

"So what's left?" Jeannie swirled her straw around the rapidly melting ice in her glass.

Tony paused, drink halfway to his lips. "What do you mean?" he asked.

"Oh, you know," said Jeannie, waving one hand around her head. "What have we got? Strength, heat vision, speed, invulnerability, flight. What comes next? Lasers?"

Tony nearly choked at the thought. He crunched down on an ice cube accidentally, but was pleased to note his molar shattered it without any effort. Did that count as superstrength or had he been able to do that before?

"Lasers? Are you serious?"

"Sure! Why not? What's a superhero without laser beams coming out of their eyes?"

Tony frowned, checking off the Seven Wonders in his head. "Well, if you put it like that... the Greek dude with the beard doesn't. Nor does Sand Cat."

Jeannie snorted. "Oh, her. *'Tremble in fear or I put da voo-doo on ya, mon!'*"

"She's Middle Eastern, isn't she?"

"Haitian I think."

"You sure?"

"How do you think she turns into that big cat? It's voodoo, has to be."

"Aren't sand cats from Iran or some shit?"

"Huh." Jeannie took a long gulp, setting the empty glass down afterwards. She crunched on ice for a moment. "What the fuck is a sand cat anyway?"

Tony considered for a moment before he found Jeannie pulling at his arm. "Worry about it later, flyboy." Jeannie was already standing. "Now to test another superpower: dance."

Tony felt the adrenaline stab his chest. One hand fingered his T-shirt, just checking that gunshot hadn't appeared on a six-hour delay or anything.

"You have got to be kidding me."

"No, come on, it's easy!" Jeannie pulled at his arm.

"I'm serious. Dancing? What the fuck? I don't dance."

"Yeah but you're a superhero now, and superheroes dance. I have it on good authority. There was even a hero called Dance Dance Revolution, I'm pretty sure."

"That's a video game," said Tony, shaking his head and pretending to drink from his empty glass while he raised his other hand. "Uh-uh. Not happening."

Jeannie stuck her tongue out at him. "Well fuck you, superhero. Come join me when you grow a pair." But she was smiling as she turned, and Tony couldn't help laughing at his own lameness. He was such an ass.

Jeannie found a spot relatively close to the booth, and did her very best to gyrate seductively for Tony's pleasure. Her come-hither looks frequently collapsed into laughter, which tended to spoil the effect, but Tony enjoyed the show anyway.

Jeannie turned and Tony suddenly smelt cut grass. The world wobbled sideways, and he was on his feet in an instant.

The back of Jeannie's head was devoid of her glossy black hair, and instead showing a ghastly gray-white expanse of bone. He stared, following the jagged fuse lines of her skull, then his eyes dropping lower and lower. Her spine, embedded in moving, undulating sheets of striated muscle. As she moved her arms back and forth, the sleeves of her black shirt vanished, replaced by red and white muscle through which the rounded white ends of her elbows protruding sickeningly. Tony blinked again and her limbs became entirely devoid of flesh, creamy bright bone showing now in perfect anatomical alignment. Her radius and ulna rotated around each other, held together, Tony presumed, by tendons and ligaments which were oddly absent.

Tony felt bile rising and fell back into the booth. He had not the fucking clue what was going on, except that he felt sick and his X-ray vision had turned itself on by itself. He screwed his eyes shut, but it made no difference – he could still see, clearly and without impediment. He sank the heels of his hands into each eye socket – this worked for a moment, then the layers of skin and muscle separated in front of him like the layers of a dry old onion, until he was staring into an alien, rocky terrain that looked like the bleached surface of the moon. With a start, he realized he was looking at the bones of his wrist.

Tony cried out, but nobody could hear him. He looked left, right, straight ahead. The dance floor in front of him was a heaving mass of jumping, bouncing, twirling skeletons. No clothes, no flesh, nothing, just skeletons bouncing, floating an inch or more above the floor. Shoes! Some of the skeletal forms teetered on the tiny bones of their toes, Tony realizing they were girls in ridiculously high heels. The tattooed barkeep seemed to notice Tony, and craned his neck up. Tony doubled over at the sight of his stripped bones, a wave of nausea sweeping over him.

Hands on his shoulders. He looked up, staring into the bare skull peering down at him, revulsion pulling his face into a grimace. The skull was talking, the jaw bone flapping without meaning or form. The skull shook, and the figure dropped onto one horribly sharp knee. The empty nostril swung into his eye line, and he shrank back again. The old taste of tequila filled his mouth. Here it comes...

"Tony! What's wrong?" the skeleton shouted – it was Jeannie. Tony felt a little relief and managed to keep his stomach contents where they were, if just for the moment.

"I don't feel so good," he said. Jeannie leaned in, Tony closing his eyes – uselessly – as he imagined the sharp ridges of her skull scratching his ear. What he imagined and what he felt were two different things entirely. Her lips brushed his earlobe, and he felt the tickle of her hair on the side of his face. He pulled away, too quickly and regretting it, but he had to look. Beside him, skeleton Jeannie looked at him with empty eyes, her surprised expression completely invisible to him.

The effort of shouting pulled the energy almost physically out of him, causing him to pause after every pair of words. His ears rang and his vision – skeletons aside – was growing shadowed at the edges. Unconsciousness wasn't far off.

"I can see skeletons. Bones, nothing else, just skulls and ribs and shit. I can't even close my eyes, I can see through my own hands. My X-ray vision has gone batshit crazy."

The jaw of Jeannie's skull rattled up and down like bad CG. Laughter. Tony burped, thankful that nobody could hear. The gin and tonic and tequila and pizza from Sherrod's was about to make an uninvited reappearance.

Jeannie kissed Tony on the cheek, the warm wet of her lips surprising him again. Her humid, hot breath in his ear told him she was alive and normal and it was just him.

"Don't worry," she shouted. "You can't expect to just know how to control everything. Some things will need to be learned!"

Tony smiled, head clearing just a little, then his mouth opened and he puked salami, cheese and tequila over Jeannie's shoes. But he felt better, and he opened his eyes, and saw Jeannie's face of flesh and blood frowning at the mess. He smiled, sheepishly, and glanced over her. There she was, black haired and black shirted. Around them, the bar was populated with people, fully clothed and full dressed. He felt better.

"Sorry."

She shook her head. "Tomorrow we're taking your feeble Big Deal pay check and going shopping for new Chucks. Roger roger?"

He nodded. She stood, shaking the worst of the vomit off inelegantly. "Let's go, party animal. And no peeking at my coccyx, promise?"

CHAPTER TWENTY-FOUR

Fucking hell, it hurt. It hurt so bad his vision was white at the edges and he felt the inside of his head pinging with static. He spat blood into the dirt of the infield, then swung around with his full bodyweight, good arm outstretched. It connected with something small and hard which yielded, resulting in a cry of pain that, this time, didn't come from his own throat. He managed to keep himself upright as his opponent hit the deck awkwardly. Beyond, in the dark, his accomplice lay unconscious and face down.

The victim didn't stay down. Instead, almost bouncing from the dirt in a cloud of orange dust, he dived back towards his attacker. One outstretched fist collided with the attacker's eye socket, dropping him immediately. The attacker managed to get to his knees, but the white mist in his eyes was turning red, and with every tiny movement of his face there was a nauseating scraping underneath the muscle of his cheek.

The fight paused, and without the sounds of two men scuffling somewhere near the third base of Leicester Field Ballpark, the night was silent. Concentrating, the attacker could just make out the legs of the victim walking away from him through his double vision. A moment later the legs stopped, then the man bent over and picked up something discarded in the fight. The man seemed to fiddle with it for a few seconds, then replaced it on his head and pulled the front of it down over his forehead. A baseball cap.

This was it, do or die. With the victim's back turned, the attacker removed a piece of black plastic from his belt that was shaped like a handle. There was going to be just one chance. He was left-handed, but his left arm was numb and swung like a lump of rubber from the shoulder. He fumbled with the handle for a moment, then a blue blade, almost white in what little light there was in the ballpark, materialized with a *shick*. The victim paused, and turned, drawing up something long and gray into a defensive posture. It looked like a baseball bat, but then it turned in his grip and shone brightly, the thin edge of the weapon disappearing into nothing.

The Cowl allowed himself a sly grin. A katana? Was that all? He adjusted his grip on the handle of the quantum knife and, holding his breath, leapt forward.

The existent/non-existent blade of his weapon passed through the sword in complete silence, entered the man's body and only stopped when the Cowl's gloved fingers hit the man's baseball jacket. The victim hissed like a deflating balloon and the Cowl rotated the blade one hundred and eighty degrees and dragged it upwards from stomach to chest. The blade met no resistance, and the Cowl had to pull his arm short so he didn't cleave the man's torso completely in half. Another twist, then another, then another, and the victim's chest and upper abdomen were divided into neat cubes which slid and squelched, soaking the ground with pints of blood in mere seconds. Finally the man dropped his sword and fell, head cracking on the rubber mat of third base, his baseball cap flipping up and off his head again to lie in the pool of blood.

So ended the secret retirement of the Flyball Ninja. The Leicester Nighthawks were going to need a new mascot.

The Cowl swore, and lifted himself to his feet. His broken arm was beginning to tingle, almost vibrate, which was something because that meant it was starting to heal already. He could move it now, just, so held it as best he could against his waist as he bent over the disemboweled victim. Just a few weeks ago his ribs had taken two nights to heal. With his powers even further gone, he had no idea how long this break would take. But at least, as far as the pins-and-needles told him, he wasn't yet down to regular, human metabolism and he wouldn't need a cast. For that fact he was grateful, because there was hardly any time left at all, not before they arrived, and there was lots still to do.

The Cowl hissed and bent double. *Pain.* He knew what it was, experienced it occasionally, but only in the rare event that the heavy artillery was rolled out, and then it was more abstract, an interesting sensation rather than his body's natural warning and defense system. This was different. Very different. *This* was pain. This was his nervous system alight with signals it had never transmitted before.

And as the Cowl was – had been – indestructible and invincible and could heal in seconds, the new sensation was all kinds of wrong. It took effort not to panic, not to scream at the sky. It took effort not to black out from the pain, but the Cowl closed his eyes and breathed, breathed, breathed, for a while.

He coughed again as he considered how, or even if, he could receive medical attention. Luckily Blackbird had trained as a doctor before shifting from medicine to physics. The problem is, he thought, she seemed to be dead. She hadn't moved since the Flyball Ninja had pitched a high-density *n*th metal baseball at her. He'd been right on target, the projectile clocking Blackbird on the forehead and throwing her back at least twenty yards towards the pitcher's mound.

The Cowl knelt heavily by the body of the Flyball Ninja and reached for his dislodged cap. He flipped it over, and tugged at the lining. There, a small square of transparent plastic, a tiny blue LED glowing within. What a stupid place to hide something so valuable.

A sigh from the darkness. So, Blackbird was alive. Things were looking up. Still on his knees, the Cowl crawled from the corpse to her body, then carefully felt along her sides, her neck, her arms and legs for any obvious injury that would preclude movement. Nothing seemed to be broken, but of course who knew what internal injuries she might have sustained? A concussion at least, although her heavy mask showed only a faint smudge where the baseball had impacted.

He turned her over, and she sighed again but did not cry out loudly, as he would have half-expected her to had her injuries been more severe. Released from under her body, her left forearm was gashed, the fabric of her catsuit ragged from where her arm had been caught by a hailstorm of tiny ninja stars. One was still caught in her suit, the razor-edged flower a bright silver with the logo of the Leicester Nighthawks proudly enameled in yellow and green on the hub. The Cowl plucked it from Blackbird's arm and tossed it onto the ground.

Sliding his good arm underneath his accomplice's back, and leaning forward to rest her shoulder against his chest, the Cowl staggered to his feet, pulling Blackbird's unconscious frame across his upper body, balancing her weight on one shoulder. Satisfied that the night was still quiet, he left the ballpark at a trot, vanishing into the unlit shadows under the nearest bleachers.

CHAPTER TWENTY-FIVE

The first four roofs had been fine. Flat, spacious and clean. Just air-conditioning units, the occasional skylight. Easy.

Tony thudded over the last one, judged the distance across the street, and leapt the next gap in a single bound. The roof he landed on was angled a little and Tony found himself crashing through a forest of metal. He instinctively covered his face with his arms as he rolled through a complex web of aerials and satellite dishes, but they didn't slow him much. He'd landed on a block of restaurants, and realized he'd crossed into San Ventura's Gaslight Quarter. The area was a pretty half a square mile of historic buildings and interesting architecture, a mecca for tourists and one of the best spots in the Shining City for eating. Tony hoped the patrons in the bars and restaurants below wouldn't be too upset now that he'd busted their TV reception.

He saw the Cowl up ahead. The bastard had stopped and was actually waiting – waiting! – for Tony to catch up. Tony couldn't see his face from this distance, but he imagined the villain smiling and letting out an extra evil chuckle, just for himself, before turning on his tail and resuming his escape across the roofs. The Cowl had something large slung over his shoulder, a man-sized sack of spoils or something.

Tony sighed. This was bullshit. He could fly. The Cowl could fly. This foot chase – albeit one across the rooftops of San Ventura – was bullshit, a cliché. The Cowl was playing with him, refusing to make an airborne escape. Tony had taken off a couple of times, but from the air it became impossible for him to spot his quarry in the night, even with supervision and infra-red and whatever. Clad entirely in a black fabric that played tricks with the eye even in broad daylight, it was easy for the Cowl to avoid his pursuer. The only option for Tony was to run, run across the goddamn roofs for who the hell knew how long. This wasn't crime fighting… or, thought Tony, the right way to start his battle with San Ventura's supervillain. It was just a game for the Cowl. Tony began to get an idea of how the cat-and-mouse of superhero versus supervillain, Seven Wonders versus the Cowl, might work. An unending conflict, more entertainment for both sides than a serious mission for justice/anarchy. Why the Cowl wanted to run was beyond him. Maybe, thought Tony with a grin, the Cowl was scared. He probably just wanted to get his bag of goodies back to his secret hideout.

Tony laughed. He'd teach that hooded prick that things were different now, that his grip on San Ventura was loosening, that there was a new hero in town who would pick up the slack left by the Seven Wonders. No, more than that. He would show the whole city exactly how much it needed the Seven Wonders (a clue: not at all).

Tony grinned under his new mask and accelerated, feeling the air parting in front of his face, carrying with it the scent of a hundred award-winning restaurants wafting from kitchen chimneys and air vents. The first night out in the costume and he had to run straight into his mark. He couldn't have asked for a better field test.

He had to pick his way carefully across the roof of this block – the whole area was divided by open-air courtyards and glass ceilings, the perfect design for hot summer evenings – but with a renewed enthusiasm to teach that sonovabitch who the new boss was he found his way forward with surprising speed. He jumped a couple of courtyards and then one of the glass ceilings, but misjudged the timing slightly, his foot missing the support beam and landing on the glass instead. He heard the glass crack, but not break, and as he hopped forward onto a studier surface he chuckled at the thought of fifty diners looking up at the sound and seeing the city's new superhero chasing his quarry. The thought tickled him, and at the next courtyard he powered higher in his jump than was strictly necessary, making a head-over-heels somersault in mid-air, and smacking down on the other side on his knee. The old building vibrated, enough to rattle some wine glasses, Tony thought. He was almost having fun.

His focus snapped back. The Cowl was gone, out of sight. Shit. Tony skidded to a halt, surveying the block in front. He was almost at the next street, at the opposite side of the Gaslight Quarter. A couple of streets farther up, the light from the street below was particularly bright and flecked with red and blue. It crossed Tony's mind that it was probably the police, but a second later distraction came as something pushed his head, at speed, into the brick of the chimney next to him.

The chimney cracked but stayed upright. Tony blinked the dust out of his eyes and cried out in surprise before finding a gloved hand at his throat and a second forming a clenched fist in his peripheral vision. Tony turned, but was pinned in place; straining his eyes to the right he saw only a black silhouette and hooded head. Something was said in a hoarse whisper, but before Tony registered the words the raised fist connected with his jaw, pushing not just his head but his entire upper body clean through the chimney. Off balance, Tony was pushed off his feet, bricks exploding around him as the chimney collapsed entirely. The rubble pummeled Tony's head, although now the hand around his neck was gone. After a few seconds, he shook his head clear and raised himself back upright, spitting the dust from his mouth. There was a hiss from nearby, and Tony looked up.

The Cowl stood, arms folded in a classic, action-figure pose that Tony suspected he might have practiced in front of the mirror. It was imposing and impressive, designed to strike fear and dread into the city's general populace.

Tony realized with a start that that used to be him.

He'd been the guy on the street running for cover when the Cowl flew low overhead, the one ducking into a shop doorway when the Cowl's sidekick Blackbird sped down the street on her motorbike, one hand on the accelerator and the other reaching back, emptying the magazine of an MP5 at pursuing police. Tony felt his heart racing and took a moment to calm. He wasn't tired from the chase, far from it, but he regulated his breathing and relaxed his muscles. There was a tight feeling in his chest, one of excitement. And, perhaps, despite himself… fear.

But things were different now. He was the Cowl's equal, he knew that from the little to-do down at the bank. Tony was prepared to do whatever was necessary to stop him. The Seven Wonders weren't prepared to neutralize the Cowl, the last supervillain on the Earth, or they'd be out of a job. Tony wasn't like that. Tony was the Justiciar for a reason. And that reason was standing right in front of him. This was it. His big moment.

The Cowl didn't move when Tony took a step forward. The naked mouth and chin under the Cowl's mask were fixed in an arrogant snarl, not dissimilar to Aurora's smirk made famous by countless television appearances and promotional material. On Aurora it was the carefully calculated expression of grim determination. On the Cowl it was the smile of an asshole who thought he knew better.

"The 'Eight Wonders' doesn't quite have the same ring to it, does it?" The Cowl's teeth shone in the dark, the flash of white matching the blank ellipses of his eyes and the only things that weren't jet black against the night sky behind. Even the famous red sigil on his chest was invisible.

Tony paused and leaned back slightly, biding his time, choosing his moment. He was going to tear this motherfucker's head off, there was no doubt about it, but he wanted to play the game, just a little. He was on the same level now.

Tony – the *Justiciar* – straightened up and lowered his voice to match the Cowl's own theatrical growl. It seemed like a good way to disguise his real voice. And, hell, maybe it sounded pretty cool too.

"You'll have to explain that joke," said Tony. Then before he could stop himself he added: "Creep" and instantly regretted it. This wasn't a comic book show-down.

The Cowl laughed. Tony was a little surprised, as it wasn't an evil, calculating chuckle. Of course not. The Cowl *wasn't* evil. Nobody was. Everybody in the whole world was the center of their own life drama. Everybody was their own superhero, everybody was a good guy. It just so happened that the Cowl's "good" was the opposite of most people's. Even the tag, "supervillain", had been given to him by the news media of San Ventura. Not even the Seven Wonders had ever used that terminology. As far as the Cowl was concerned, he was the city's benefactor and savior.

Huh. Just like Tony. Except Tony knew he was right and the Cowl was wrong.

"Superheroes are regulated," said the Cowl. "Self-regulated, sure, but that means you're either with them, or against them. You're the eighth Wonder, or you're a crook like me. Which is it, boy?"

Tony balled his fists and raised himself up on his toes, ready to charge. "The 'boy' that took down the Cowl, that's who. You can call me the Justiciar."

He sprinted forward, allowing just a touch of flight power to push him forward over the roof and towards the Cowl. He moved quickly, too quickly for the Cowl it seemed, who hunched over ready to take the impact force. Tony's shoulder connected with the Cowl's lower abdomen, forcing the air from the villain and causing a cracking sound so loud Tony thought they'd stepped onto another glass ceiling. It was like the bank all over again; remembering what had happened on their first encounter, Tony cleared his mind and concentrated on what he was doing.

Tony kept up the pressure, pushing the Cowl across the roof and impacting the cinder block outhouse of an emergency stairwell exit. The wall buckled inwards, but stayed intact, and Tony bounced back, ready to block the Cowl's attack.

Nothing. Tony tiptoed like a boxer for a moment, then relaxed his posture. The Cowl tried to pull himself from the wall, and eventually succeeded but not without quite some effort. Disengaged from the split concrete, the Cowl toppled onto one knee and breathed heavily, sucking the hot night air. Tony thought he heard a nasty popping sound with each gasp and he could see his quarry was favoring one arm as he supported himself in a crouch.

Tony saw his opportunity. Somehow he'd hit harder than he intended and had incapacitated the Cowl, even for just a minute. This was more than the Seven Wonders had ever managed. He *was* more powerful than them, this proved it.

Well, holy shit and praise Mary.

Tony grabbed the Cowl's hood and yanked him to his feet. Immediately the Cowl twisted and threw an awkward punch towards him, but Tony ducked to one side and the fist flew past his face and into only empty air. The Cowl grunted with the effort and the arm fell loosely back to his side.

Tony lifted the Cowl's face to his own. The Cowl laughed, showing a mouth full of blood. Tony's heart raced at the sight, but caught up in the moment he chose not to dwell on the level of violence he was inflicting. He let go of the Cowl, who sagged on his feet before Tony punched once, twice, three times, and ended with a kick that sent the Cowl tumbling over and off the roof, down into the street below. A second later he heard the villain hit the pavement, and then he heard running, booted feet. The red and blue lights continued to flash. The police were on the scene. They must have had reports about the chase and had swept in.

Well, good. He'd done it. He'd taught the Cowl a lesson and had dropped him right in the lap of the police. He straightened up and dusted the rest of the brickwork from his costume. Time to introduce himself to the SVPD, but rather than walk and jump, he flew upwards and backwards, keeping out of sight of the street below, then once he'd reached what felt like an appropriately impressive height, he flew forwards and descended vertically with his arms folded, as he'd seen Aurora and the other flight-capable members of the Seven Wonders do many times. There was something to be said for making the right entrance.

He touched down, looked around, and realized his mistake. The blue and red light hadn't been flickering at all, it had been steady: the red halo of Aurora, the blue glow of the Dragon Star. Tony had landed behind the Cowl, who lay in a crumpled heap on the ground.

On the other side of the supervillain, the Seven Wonders stood in an arrow formation, Aurora at the head, flanked to his left by the Dragon Star, Bluebell and Linear, and to his right by Sand Cat, Hephaestus and SMART. Bluebell and Linear looked surprised, Sand Cat angry. The Dragon Star lifted her huge golden staff in one hand and floated about six inches off the ground, her wide hood and white clock swirling behind her in some invisible field streaming off her weapon.

Tony stared. Holy shit. What had he been thinking? The Seven Wonders were, well, *superhuman*.

Aurora stood with arms folded. He stared at Tony, white eyes unreadable but his aura pulsing scarlet in what, to Tony, looked like a decidedly pissed-off way. The Cowl's words came back to him and he suddenly felt very small and in a lot of trouble. Superheroes were regulated, and he wasn't a member of the Seven Wonders.

Bluebell stepped forward, breaking the superhero formation to kneel beside the Cowl's prone form. The supervillain stirred, pushing himself up from the ground. He saw Bluebell looking down at him, and smiled to show his injuries. Bluebell's eyes widened at the sight of his bloody mouth, and she looked first at Tony, then back at Aurora.

Oh *shit*. Tony puffed his chest out but it was more to make himself feel better. He could escape, get away, live to fight another day. The Seven Wonders now had the Cowl in custody, and they surely couldn't deny the opportunity to lock him up and recover whatever it was he'd dumped on the roof before he'd jumped on his pursuer. His job was done, for now, and maybe later he'd approach the superteam and introduce himself properly, in better, more controlled circumstances. Yes, that was a good idea, now that he had shown his mettle. He was well disguised in the costume Jeannie had made for him, so they couldn't find him in his civilian identity. Up, up and away, no problem.

Aurora started to speak but Tony was already half a mile away and didn't catch all of it. He ground his teeth in concentration, shooting straight up as fast as possible. After five minutes he looked down, and didn't see any glowing superheroes following him. He was high in the stratosphere, where it was freezing and the air was thin. But he wasn't making that mistake again, either. He stopped his flight, relaxed, and let gravity pull him back towards San Ventura.

Bluebell rejoined the Seven Wonders, and none moved for a while. The Cowl pushed himself into a sitting position and spat blood onto the pavement.

"Is this it?"

Aurora unfolded his arms.

"You're hurt."

"It'll heal. But it's Blackbird. She's hurt and she's not like me. I need to get her back to… to my facility."

Bluebell glanced at her husband, who nodded and refolded his arms.

"Where is she?"

"I left her on the roof."

"Then go," said Aurora. "We will meet again."

Following their leader, The Seven Wonders jetted skywards, leaving the Cowl bleeding in the alley.

CHAPTER TWENTY-SIX

Bluebell paused. The sharp clicking grew in volume and the doors to the conference room slid open. The Dragon Star padded in, her footfalls silent but her powerstaff ringing loudly against the hard floor of the Citadel. The five other heroes assembled at the elliptical table watched their colleague walk in and take her designated chair, a few nodding in acknowledgment before returning their attention to Bluebell.

The Dragon Star sat stiffly, staff making one final *clack* before being held upright and still. She glanced up, and saw that Aurora's attention wasn't on his wife, it was on her. But the white eyes and set expression – the famous, odd smile, half grim determination, half arrogant condescension – made his face impossible to read.

Bluebell resumed the briefing, placing the thumb and forefinger of one hand against her forehead and her short, spiky blonde hair. She rose maybe six inches from the floor as the air above the center of the conference table shifted and blurred as the event replay was resumed.

"There!" An empty conference chair was left rocking as Linear blinked into existence on the opposite side of the table to where he had just been sitting. His silver-clad form melted into a shiny blur as he spun around the table several times, examining the three-dimensional replay from several angles.

"What do your eyes tell you, speedster?" Hephaestus now, stroking his ringlet beard with a massive hand, his chair creaking as he leaned his bulk back into it. All eyes moved between the Greek god and the slightly fuzzy outline of Linear, who was buzzing with excitement.

All eyes except Aurora. The Dragon Star tilted her head down slightly, letting the peak of her hood cut the top of his face from her own view. She didn't like the attention.

Did he know something?

Linear's form solidified as he slowed down and he pointed at the playback. "Back one-fifteenth of a second, Bluebell. One-fifteenth more... There it is."

Hephaestus harrumphed theatrically.

"There *what* is?"

Linear pointed at the paused image. The image changed depending on the angle, so each of the Seven Wonders seated around the table saw a slightly different aspect. Overall, the image most showed the interior of a small city bank. There were several people standing around a semicircle, civilians flanked by what looked like soldiers in black combat uniform, faces obscured by respirators. In the center of the image was a blur, one wide black smudge that seemed to taper to sharp points on either side of a more solid center. Next to this, an elongated blue and white translucent smear, almost like a double exposure. The different perspectives around the room showed the same frozen moment, intersected with walls, furniture and other objects that obscured the three-dimensional psychic scan. Bluebell's eyes narrowed and she rose a few inches higher, bending one blue and white spandex-clad leg behind her at the knee as she concentrated. The image shimmered and the focus seemed to sharpen.

The inference was clear. It was the same man calling himself the Justiciar, the man who had engaged the Cowl in the rooftop battle and, it seemed, got the better of the supervillain.

"He has superspeed. We know." Aurora's statement sounded final, but Linear shook his head. His body vibrated a little in excitement.

"No, no, no. It's not just superspeed. He can access the *Slipstream*. Look at the image. This is just when the Slipstream is punched. See that?"

He pointed to the blue and white smear, tracing a finger along two white threads that were slightly more opaque than the rest of the blurry form. "The Slipstream. Trust me, I see it every day."

"Observation noted but incorrect. Slipstream access limited to two individuals."

Everyone's attention moved to SMART. Its creator, Hephaestus, sat up and looked at the white domed head of the robotic superhero. Towering over the others, even when seated, the robot's head rotated, the two rectangular red eyes scanning the faces of everyone in the room, the supercomputer buried deep under the armor plating analyzing all expressions and responses. Hephaestus waited until the robot's head turned to face him before issuing his command.

"Explain statement."

Aurora raised a hand, the hazy glow of the plasma that constantly surrounded him catching everyone's attention admirably. "No, SMART's observation is correct but the deduction is false."

"Exactly!" Linear cocked a finger at Aurora. "Whoever this guy is, he can access the Slipstream. That makes him both dangerous and unusual."

Bluebell returned to the ground and sat at the conference table, allowing the bank raid recording to continue at normal speed. The black blur and the blue and white smear vanished, then the soldiers apparently lost interest in their hostages and lowered their weapons. A man in a gray suit was grabbed by one of the soldiers and dragging along with them as they left the bank foyer and headed into the back office behind the teller counters. The psychic recording changed perspectives, looking back into the teller area from the office. Through the doorway, the civilians could be seen, looking around in shock. Of the uniformed raiders there was no sign.

"Mass teleport. Effective but illogical. The Cowl's methodology never fails to fascinate." Aurora stroked his chin.

Linear buzzed around the room before returning to his seat. Even sitting, he continued to vibrate. Bluebell waved her hand at him, already tired from controlling the psychic condition. Linear muttered and slowed his molecules down enough that his indistinct form wasn't so much of an eye strain for everyone, superpowered vision or not.

"There is a more important issue at stake, Aurora." Sand Cat's entry to the discussion drew everyone's instant attention; if she had something to say, you'd better be listening.

Sand Cat gestured to Bluebell, who wound the recording back through to the beginning, before the mystery speedster took out the

Cowl. Image paused, she studied the scene carefully. The speedster was a young man with black hair and a floppy fringe, wearing a blue checked shirt and dark jeans. Mr Ordinary.

Sand Cat pointed, then turned to Aurora, and said nothing.

Aurora had drawn his hands to his face, clasped together with index fingers outstretched, tapping the triangle of mask that covered his nose. Then he stopped tapping and nodded.

"A new, unregistered human with powers. One who disguised himself last night but was apparently not so careful earlier."

Linear drummed his fingers on the table, then shook his head. "A new one was bound to appear, sooner or later."

Reaching behind his neck he grabbed at the back of his mask and pulled the skintight covering off. Unzipping the top of his tunic, he reached underneath and extracted a glasses case and, with almost painful slowness, opened it, took the thick-framed glasses out, and slid them onto his face. The Dragon Star watched as the old man's hands shook. It looked like he was almost due for another round of rejuvenation. Access to the Slipstream was a very rare power indeed, but the consequences were dire. Linear's accelerated metabolism had trapped the twenty-five-year-old hero in a body that was around fifty years older. Although the Dragon Star didn't quite understand the nuances of human society well enough to fathom the rationale, she knew that was why the star of college track and field had taken to wearing a mask with his costume. Superheroes were young and vigorous, not old and arthritic.

Sand Cat leaned forward, regaining the attention of the superteam. "Forgive me if what I say is already known, but our words are flying in circles around themselves. Our problems are twofold. One, the Cowl has compromised all but one of the vaults, which means he knows what is hidden within each, even if we do not. Two, an unknown powered agency is operating in San Ventura, and he appears to be targeting the Cowl. We must protect the secrets hidden in the city, and we must prevent this newcomer from taking rash action. Both are critical."

SMART's head whirred to face Sand Cat, who raised an eyebrow as the machine-man commented. The Dragon Star watched in silence.

She knew Sand Cat, who drew her powers from a supernatural source, was less impressed with artificial technology, even though SMART was a fully-fledged and independent member of the team. Out of the corner of her eye she saw Bluebell's expression flicker as the psychic member of the team picked up on Sand Cat's unspoken opinion of the robot.

SMART's eyes flashed as it spoke. "Sand Cat's assessment is accurate. Recommendation one, immediate action to retrieve the final remaining vault; vault to be placed in protective custody within the Citadel of Wonders. Recommendation two, immediate action to disable or recruit unknown power agency."

Hephaestus frowned. The Dragon Star looked to Aurora, but again he seemed to be staring right at her. Not that it was possible to see exactly where his eyes were looking behind the opaque lenses of his mask.

Bluebell stood and gestured toward the recording. The image broke up momentarily, and when it reformed it had zoomed in, showing the speedster's face in close-up.

"Well, the second part should be no problem," she said. "There he is." Bluebell's forehead creased as the image rotated in space to give the best view of the man's face.

SMART beeped. "Subject file accessed from CIA internal database. Tony Prosdocimi, aged twenty-three years. Occupation: retail assistant, according to IRS records. Last known address accessed."

"Wait, wait." Linear's agitation caused him to buzz again, rattling the glasses perched on his nose and causing him to place two liver-spotted hands on the conference table to stabilize his chair. "Identification is easy, sure. But apprehension might be a little more difficult. We have no idea what his powers are – he's got superspeed and flight, and he did a number on the Cowl which suggests superstrength and some level of invulnerability. He might have energy powers. Or he might even be psychic." He tapped his temple and nodded at Bluebell. The superheroine nodded and turned to her husband.

"Linear's right. We need to take him in, but avoid collateral damage. He must know who we are, but if he's going up against the Cowl, chances are he'll listen to us. We're the good guys, after all."

"Agreed," said Aurora after a beat. "We need to account for all eventualities. Bluebell, Sand Cat, Linear: pay a visit to Mr Prosdocimi in the morning, put him to the test, see how he reacts and what he's got, and depending on the outcome, make him an offer. We want him fighting on our side."

Bluebell nodded, as did Sand Cat. The two stood together.

Aurora brought his gloved hands together in front of his face again in thought. The halo of fire over his head began to darken from a white-red to a deep orange.

"SMART, Hephaestus: calculate possible locations of the remaining vault, and work to protect it on-site, or to bring it into the Citadel."

"As my lord commands." Hephaestus stood and bowed, and picked his blacksmith's hammer from the table. He turned to leave, then paused.

"It would help if we knew what we had hidden, would it not? To know what the Cowl was trying to steal?"

Bluebell's eyes widened. The other heroes turned as one to Aurora, but their leader's expression was set in the enigmatic smirk.

"Perhaps," said Aurora, "but some knowledge is too dangerous, even for us. Bluebell hid the knowledge from our minds – from *all* of our minds, and such an action cannot be undone."

Hephaestus frowned and adjusted his grip on his hammer. Aurora's smile widened.

"All we need to do is stop the Cowl taking the final vault."

"So," the Greek god began, "why did we let him go, again? If his accomplice was injured we could have treated her here."

Aurora's expression was unchanged. "While we are – were – able to track the other vaults, the location of the final secret was designed as a mystery, even to us. We need to locate it as much as he does. Perhaps he can lead us there."

"Ah." Hephaestus glanced at the others, then back to Aurora. "You have been expecting this to happen, my lord?"

"Sooner or later," said Aurora, tilting his head just a little, almost in amusement.

Hephaestus nodded, then waved at SMART to follow. The two lumbered out, followed by Bluebell, Sand Cat and Linear.

The Dragon Star did not move. She sat at the opposite end of the conference table from Aurora, and, alone together, she finally met Aurora's blank gaze, raising her head until the wide hood slipped back. Still she said nothing. The two heroes sat, staring, for ten seconds before Aurora broke the silence.

"Dragon Star, dismissed." He rose and, sweeping his cloak around his wide frame, strode from the room.

The Dragon Star relaxed, just a little, one hand sliding down her powerstaff a little, the other fingering the data stick hidden underneath the fold in her cloak. She sat for a few more seconds, then left the room, staff clacking loudly on the floor.

CHAPTER TWENTY-SEVEN

"Are you sure about this?"

Sam frowned and she heard Joe's chair shift next to hers as her partner tried to get comfortable. They'd been in Gillespie's office nearly all afternoon, had spent hours trawling through the data, through surveillance reports and summary sheets prepped by Joe, through request forms and requisition orders filled out by Sam. All the evidence was there, laid out on the small conference table that filled the space of the police chief's office that wasn't taken up by his actual desk.

They had it all there, no problem.

"Is there a problem, captain?" Sam's eyes roved the table top. There were the surveillance photographs showing the target, an athletic-looking young woman with spiky dyed-black hair coming and going from a nondescript apartment building out in the eastern side of downtown. Other photos of her in the CIT parking lot. She'd been trailed all over the city, but the plainclothes out in the field had reported several times when she'd somehow dropped off their radar altogether. She was clearly hiding something, and was doing it with some skill.

It had taken a full two weeks to gather enough evidence – a relatively short space of time, all things considered. Aside from the supposed connection between the names and the information from Lansbury down in ballistics about the fabric, there was nothing to actually link Doctor Ravenholt with Blackbird, nothing more than coincidences and circumstantial evidence. But they needed to talk to her about the fabric, and the best option was a raid. Under any normal circumstances that was probably well over the top, but considering who the suspect most likely was – and who she was partnered with – they needed decisive action.

Gillespie's office was stuffy, but at least he had a window and a view of the city. Sam hadn't been back to ballistics since she and Joe had gotten the results of Lansbury's analysis. Since that hot afternoon underneath the city streets, Sam's laboratory phobia had come back – or, more likely, her phobia of aged ballistics experts who went by the name Lansbury. Speaking on the phone was no better – every time she'd done it in the last two weeks she could just imagine the scientist in her antique office, sitting on the antique chair that no way in hell could have been either comfortable or good for her back, eyes closed and with the confident smile that people who thought they knew everything had.

"Sir, I'm happy with the data we have, and I think we can proceed." Sam knew the chief was just testing. They hadn't gone over everything for nothing and Gillespie had been the model of attention. It was on his neck too, she realized – they'd blown the Seven Wonders off once already and were now going to proceed with their investigation without them. Which was, Sam had argued, essential, given the interference from Bluebell. But on that matter, at least, their hands were tied. While there was no authority they could have complained to about the actions of the town's superteam, they were at least within their rights to do their job and take the Cowl – and Blackbird – down, should the opportunity arise. If the Seven Wonders wanted to complain about that when they handed them Blackbird, or the Cowl, or both, Sam wanted to see them try to mindwipe a whole country via the dozens of television cameras she hoped would be watching.

Gillespie grunted and sat back, which was as much indication as he was ever likely to give that he was satisfied. He put his hands behind his head and looked at Joe.

"Teams ready?"

Joe slid to the edge of his seat. "Picked and ready. We just need you to sign the warrant application and we can get it to a judge. Once everything is stamped we'll be good to go tomorrow morning."

Gillespie looked at Sam. Sam said nothing... but for a second or two she thought her chief was in tune with her perfectly. No more hiding, no more fudging reports and – quite frankly, committing federal offenses in her furtive pursuit of the Cowl.

"This is it, Sam." He never called her Sam. Sam felt heat pricking behind her eyeballs. "This is for David."

Sam nodded and the world seemed a thousand miles away.

"Go bag us that sonovabitch and save the city."

Sam smiled.

"Yes, sir."

CHAPTER TWENTY-EIGHT

She was beautiful, of that there was no doubt. Not unconscious, but sleeping, helped along by a carefully calculated cocktail of pharmaceuticals. Eyes closed, lips apart, she looked angelic and peaceful. The red mark on her forehead was already fading; the Cowl was grateful for the protection Blackbird's mask had provided, because she was unpowered, unsuper, and the impact from the Flyball Ninja's *n*th metal baseball would otherwise have killed her. It seemed that some superheroes took risks when things got desperate.

The Cowl pushed his half-mask off and ran a hand through his hair, becoming Geoff Conroy once more. He stood by the side of the infirmary bed and counted the seconds between Blackbird's breaths. She would sleep for a while. Thankfully she had remained unconscious throughout their entire flight across the city, from the ballpark via the Gaslight Quarter. During his meeting with the Justiciar, as he had called himself.

Now, that was interesting. A new superpowered man in the city… just as he had lost his own powers. Very interesting indeed.

She would sleep for a while, and when she woke up the city would be a different place. The Cowl would be no more. Of that, he was certain.

Conroy wanted to hold her hand, but to do so while she slept and with the thoughts racing through his mind, it seemed inappropriate, an invasion. He closed his eyes and thought of God and squeezed the rosary beads in his right fist.

And oh, what had he done? Abduction, coercion, rape – not physical, far from it – that wasn't the kind of villainy the Cowl was known for. But, in essence, he felt it was the same. Manipulation of the mind, of feelings, emotions. He'd abused his sidekick from the very start, subjecting her to a subtle mental assault. He had terrorized her just as he had terrorized the city; broken her to his will, drawn her down the dark path. All the while she had come, willingly. Perhaps that was the hardest fact to bear.

She'd been brought up well by her parents, taught values, principles, her duty as a citizen, her pride at being a native of San Ventura, the Shining City.

Her parents' death had shattered her life – pride turned to bitterness, and the feeling that the city had betrayed her and the Seven Wonders had abandoned her began to grow. Her duty became a cause, her anger became a mission.

The Cowl killed Jean Ravenholt's parents and had spawned Blackbird. A word here, a motion there, and she was in his grasp. Her technical skill was needed and he'd piloted her rage at the city and the world into something far colder, far more dangerous. She'd united with him. He'd promised her the city. He'd promised her revenge.

Conroy reached for her hand again and this time he did not hesitate. His hands were cold and hers were warm and dry. Her breathing did not alter. He could see the pulse gently ticking in her neck. Her injury was superficial but she would wake up with a headache. And she'd wake up to find herself alone.

Conroy jerked his hand back. His eyes were wet, but he felt nothing but calm inside. He stood like that for some minutes, listening to Blackbird breathing, aware of a growing tightness in his chest.

Without powers, he was nothing. Oh, he was smart, he knew secrets, he was rich and had resources. But he was suddenly mortal, suddenly at risk. Everything was now dangerous. He couldn't continue as he was. But more importantly, something stirred within him. A feeling, fleeting only but still there, that he had taken the wrong path himself. That whatever he wanted to achieve… he had done it wrong. Made a mistake.

Committed a sin.

If he was at risk, so was she. If he had been powered as normal, none of this would have happened. The Flyball Ninja would have been dead in a second.

How many others had he killed without a thought?

Oh, Blackbird was fine, would be fine; had a mild concussion but nothing life-threatening. But it was the thought of what *could have been* which filled Conroy's veins with ice.

He may have created her, but Blackbird was special to him. Their love, at least, was genuine.

Conroy left the infirmary.

When he next took a breath, he was standing on the narrow grille bridge that connected the central platform of the Lair, with the big computer and control station, to the main exit. The air was slightly damp and when he finally breathed in he could taste something organic and could smell something musty, the two together combining to form something softly choking, the residue of bat droppings, perhaps, or something dry and moldering at the bottom of the Lair's deep pits.

He didn't remember walking from the infirmary to the platform. When he turned he saw the computer was on, the main display showing a view of San Ventura's main shopping plaza patched in from one of the city's CCTV cameras. San Ventura was well covered by them, supplied and installed by Conroy Industries.

San Ventura. He thought he ruled it. Well... didn't he? As Geoff Conroy he controlled most of the large business in the city and had influence over the mayor, the police commissioner, the city council and a dozen other key personnel at City Hall. As the Cowl, he controlled most of the underworld, the criminals and villainy, all part of his ultimate goal, to remove the Seven Wonders.

Well, not all of the city's dark underbelly, but those he didn't control directly were influenced, inspired by his actions to take up his omega sigil and form their own groups and organizations.

The city was in his thrall.

Conroy felt dizzy. Years of work had got him... nowhere. He had money, minor fame, major infamy. But the Seven Wonders were still there. And while they showed little interest in his daily affairs, whenever he tried something big, they put him down.

Conroy laughed and the sound was ugly and reverberated around the cavern. Put him down? No. They poked their noses in, did the minimum required, then let him go. They'd done it just tonight. There he was, deposited right in front of all seven of them – *all seven!* – by that newcomer, and they'd told him to leave. No arrest, no admonishment. He was free to go and come back another day.

And the newcomer. He was violent, brash, uncontrolled. Sooner or later he was going to do something that even the Cowl would have balked at, and then the Seven Wonders really would have to do something.

Conroy reached into the pocket of his linen suit. He stopped and glanced down, not remembering when he got changed out of the Cowl's suit, not remembering taking a shower and cleaning himself up.

He stood still for a few minutes, then blinked.

He was not only losing his powers, he was losing his mind.

His hand continued its journey into his pocket, and his fingers touched something bulky and smooth. His fingers gripped the object tightly, then he pulled the rosary beads out and began to count them.

Conroy turned back to the main display and watched the city for a while. It was late, but it was busy. Always busy.

He descended into hell; the third day He rose again.

Geoff Conroy walked to the exit and began to pray.

CHAPTER TWENTY-NINE

The knock was the classic pattern – *da-da-da-de-da... da da*. The kind employed by friends who weren't quite in the top league, or by mailmen too cocky for their own good. Whoever it was, it got Tony's back up the instant he heard it. It announced, quite clearly, that someone Tony didn't know and didn't invite was at the door. And Tony hated, fucking *hated*, the unannounced and unexpected.

He rolled out of bed, leaving Jeannie asleep. The long and late hours she pulled at her mystery job left her whacked most mornings, and today was no exception. He didn't know what time she'd come in, but there was an odd bruise on her forehead and he was tired himself from the previous night's exploits on the rooftops of the city. He pulled on a pair of sweatpants and one of the ubiquitous black T-shirts that littered the floor, and took a breath to call out to the unwanted visitors, telling them in no uncertain terms to get lost before he came to the door and told them the same face-to-face.

Tony stopped, catching the call in his throat. Something wasn't right. He could hear it. The morning was quiet and it was easy to focus his suped-up hearing on the hallway outside. He didn't even really think about it, it came naturally to him now. He was growing into his new powers.

There were three people in the hall, waiting by his front door. But they didn't sound like normal visitors. The slippery sound of cotton and denim was missing, so it wasn't a postman or neighbor or one of the guys from the Big Deal. The harsher scratch of synthetics like nylon or polyester was also absent, so it wasn't a Mormon or some cold caller trying to get him to change power companies. He listened for the air currents, but it was mostly still, no breezes or streams caused by coats swinging or jackets being straightened. Whoever was outside the door wasn't wearing ordinary fabrics. Aside from the floor creaking beneath three pairs of feet, the visitors were almost silent, wearing something tight. Something like... spandex?

Superheroes. The Seven Wonders. Well, *shit*. He shouldn't have been so naive to think they wouldn't have managed to work out who he was. They were here to dress him down for last night's little escapade.

Wait, that was good, right? OK, they weren't perfect. In fact, the superteam were part of the whole problem of San Ventura. But they'd seen him dealing with the Cowl, and they'd traced him back here. They wanted to meet him and talk, and explain how everything wasn't working how it should, how they needed new blood, how they were impressed with his work in the Gaslight Quarter, how they saw he had the courage to stand up to the Cowl and had delivered the supervillain right to them (and boy, didn't that feel grand?), how he'd fundamentally changed the way they saw crime and their responsibility to the city, how they needed his help to make a case to put the Cowl behind bars and clean the place up and make San Ventura the best city in America and...

A second knock, shorter this time, just three raps, but much louder. Tony cleared his head, and realized that his heart was pounding a little. He pushed himself forward, toward the door. Now he felt nervous. They were here to kick his ass, right? Well, he could deal. He was more powerful than all of them put together.

He called out this time, the standard stalling tactic of "Hold on!" He reached for the handle and his ears pricked at a subsonic *whoosh*, a thin envelope of air parting quickly then collapsing again. The floor creaked again, revealing only two people now. Linear had stepped into the Slipstream and left. Well OK. One down, two to go.

Tony opened the door. In front of him, in the narrow hallway, stood the lithe warrior woman, Sand Cat, her brown and ochre suede-like catsuit, dark skin and black hair a sharp contrast to the electric blue and white stripes of Bluebell's equally figure-hugging outfit, pale skin and short peroxide hair. Sand Cat's expression was pleasant but guarded, a thin smile and a raised eyebrow the only greeting offered. Over her shoulder, Bluebell's face was creased in a wide smile showing perfect teeth. Tony wasn't sure which he preferred. But one thing was clear: both were very fake.

"Ah, hi there," he said. He wanted to play it cool. They'd only seen him in his Justiciar suit, and while they'd obviously discovered his identity, he wanted to find out how. It was time to play dumb, let them do all the work. Sit back and enjoy the game.

Sand Cat said nothing. Bluebell's eyes flickered beyond Tony, into the apartment, for just a second. The air whooshed again, at a volume far below the detection of normal humans. Tony realized this too late, spinning around to find Linear relaxing on his couch, his featureless silver face looking in Tony's direction. Tony could see the man's jaw move under the mask, like maybe the hero was smiling at something.

Tony didn't realize his mistake until he felt a small, dense fist impact the small of his back. As he staggered forward and over, Sand Cat followed with a sweeping kick to Tony's knees, forcing his legs out from under him and sending him awkwardly to the ground.

Tony hit the hardwood floor, and while there was a second of sharp pain first in his spine and then in his knees, it passed quickly. He was beginning to understand how invulnerability worked. You felt pain, at least a little bit – you had to, because it was your body's internal communication network lighting up, telling you what was going on to which parts of your body – but it passed as his body quickly healed the microdamage, allowing him to continue the fight.

Tony jerked himself to his feet, using his overbalanced momentum to propel himself forward, back toward the bedroom. But Linear was already in his way, Tony catching just a glimpse of his blank mask before an uppercut traveling at Mach 3 lifted him into the air and sent him tumbling back toward Sand Cat. Sand Cat raised her elbows, and even as Tony was airborne, darted to one side and hit him in the arm, the shoulder, the kidneys.

Tony twisted in the air and found himself lying on the floor on his side. He looked up, just in time to see Bluebell stepping over his body, exchanging smiles with Sand Cat. The assholes were actually enjoying it. Sand Cat looked down at him, her expression darker than her companion's. She placed a foot on his chest and applied just enough pressure to tell him to stay down. He could take her out, and she knew it, but the message was pretty clear. Linear and Bluebell moved to flank the mystical warrior.

"What the fuck is this shit?"

Three heads snapped around to Jeannie, standing in the bedroom doorway in her pajamas. Tony craned his neck to see, noticing that he could push up against Sand Cat's leg with no effort whatsoever. Sand Cat glanced down at the movement, displeasure crossing fleetingly across her face. Jeannie held her gun loosely in one hand, the same weapon she'd fired into Tony's chest a couple of weeks back. He saw her finger wasn't on the trigger; pulling a handgun on members of the Seven Wonders was probably a very bad idea indeed, and thankfully she seemed to realize that.

"Apologies for the intrusion." Bluebell stepped around Tony again and toward Jeannie, holding out her hand in greeting. "We understood that Mr Prosdocimi was in fact single and lived alone. I can see our intelligence was incorrect." She paused expectantly, but Jeannie did not move to accept the handshake. Bluebell lowered her own arm, but her smile did not flicker. "My name is Bluebell, this is Sand Cat and Linear. We represent the Seven Wonders."

Jeannie folded her arms, gun held awkwardly against her body, and narrowed her eyes.

"I know who you are. What are you doing here, and what are you doing to Tony? Is harassment one of your superpowers?" Jeannie's look was black, but Bluebell was unfazed. The superhero turned away and indicated to Sand Cat. The warrior woman removed her foot from Tony's chest, and reached down toward him. Tony looked from Jeannie to Sand Cat to Bluebell, then grabbed the proffered arm and allowed himself to be lifted to his feet. He made a show of brushing himself down, even though he was dressed only in a dirty tee and dirtier sweatpants.

"I'd kinda like to know what you're doing here myself," he said. "I'm thinking that was a little impolite, even for government officials."

Bluebell laughed, her voice light and airy, the voice of someone without a care in the world. "Mr Prosdocimi, we're well above the government, as you well know. Now, do you prefer Tony or the Justiciar?"

Tony shook his head, laughing through a clenched jaw. Ignoring his superpowered guests, he brushed quite pointedly past Linear and made his way into the kitchen, where he threw the faucet on and filled the kettle.

"Word gets around," he said. "So now what? You want me to stop, right? This town ain't big enough for all of us, right? Orders to ship out by sundown? Or do I get a medal for handing you the Cowl?"

"The Cowl is not in our custody," said Bluebell. Tony snapped the faucet off.

"Excuse me? I dumped him right in front of you. How can he not be in your custody?"

Bluebell and Sand Cat exchanged a look, the same kind of look that adults swapped when dealing with a particularly stupid child. For all Tony knew, Linear might have had the same expression on behind his smooth silver face.

"Our operation is running according to plan," said Bluebell, before changing the subject. "You'll forgive our abrupt entrance, but we had to be sure. The Seven Wonders are impressed with your powers. Genetics, magic or technology?"

Tony turned back to Bluebell, leaning back on the kitchen counter and folding his arms. His lips moved as he ran Bluebell's options over again. "Huh," he said, finally. "None of the above. I stack shelves at Big Deal. I woke up as Superman. End of."

Linear buzzed around the room before returning to where he was standing. The other two superheroes didn't even seem to notice. Bluebell's smile flickered off, just for a second, confirming to Tony it was as real as her platinum hair and her turbocharged tits.

"Interesting," the superhero said. She pursed her lips slightly. "Unusual, but not unheard of. But the offer still remains."

"Offer?" Jeannie met Bluebell's vaguely disparaging look before turning to Tony. "What did I miss?"

"Ah, come on." Linear stepped forward, shaking his head at Bluebell. "Cut to the chase. All this cloak-and-dagger stuff cheeses me off." He looked at Tony, holding his hand out to shake. "Join the Seven Wonders. See the world, et cetera, et cetera."

Well, *ho-ly she-it*. Tony had been right the first time. He could show the Seven Wonders how the city deserved to be treated. He grasped Linear's hand firmly, allowing just enough power to show him that he wasn't a mere mortal.

"Done."

Easy.

"Good man." Linear slapped Tony on the shoulder then tugged his mask off, revealing the face of an old man, lined and worn, with goatee beard the same color as his silver suit. Tony raised an eyebrow and Linear's face split into a huge grin. The speedster ran his fingers through his short hair and winked at Sand Cat. He leaned in on Tony and whispering loudly in mock conspiracy. "Don't mind her. Heart of gold, strength of a lion. She was just playin' with ya, the kitten."

Bluebell kept to the back of the group as Linear joked with Tony. Jeannie had ducked back into the bedroom and returned wearing something more substantial, minus, Tony noticed, the gun. As Tony watched she saw Jeannie catch Bluebell's eye, but the superhero looked away quickly, immediately calling her companions to order.

"We'll be in touch, Justiciar. Welcome to the defense of the city." She let Sand Cat and Linear out first, then paused at the threshold. She turned, nodding at Tony, and then holding her gaze on Jeannie. She smiled the fake smile again. "We'll talk later, Doctor Ravenholt." She turned and left, leaving the door open. Tony reached and swung it shut, while Jeannie went to the kitchen to finish making the tea. Tony heard her rattling china in the cupboards. They'd been spooked, the both of them.

But... what a way to start the day. Then he paused.

"*Doctor*? You didn't tell me you were a doctor. She knew your name?"

Jeannie's voice floated around the partition. "She's telepathic, remember? Bitch probably read my mind."

Tony clicked his tongue. "Oh yeah. Now that would be some freaky shit, poking around in *your* head." Tony paused again.

Jeannie reappeared, holding two steaming mugs of tea. "Yeah, real horror show," she said, but her voice wavered without conviction. "And I'm a PhD, not an MD." Tony nodded in appreciation, and shuffled back to the bedroom.

Jeannie held her mug to her hand as she sat next to Tony on the bed. He was saying something, but she wasn't listening. The hot liquid in her mug vibrated as she trembled.

Bluebell had read her mind and knew the truth. She had to get over to the Lair ASAP and warn Geoff.

CHAPTER THIRTY

"Hello?"

She'd been asking the same single-word question for the last half-hour. There was never an answer; hers was the only voice in the whole place. The question rang around the Lair's main cavern and its less natural ancillary rooms. The echo changed to flat muffled tones as she went up the main stairwell that ended in Geoff Conroy's hillside mansion. In the house itself her voice seemed to hang in the air. The furniture had sheets over it, and it creeped Blackbird out like nothing else.

But the sheets were good, right? The sheets meant he was coming back, because if he'd fled in some kind of panic then he wouldn't have made the arrangements, right? When she'd woken in the infirmary the night before, the Lair was empty, but that wasn't unusual. Satisfied that her head injury was nothing more than a purple bump, she'd headed back to Tony's apartment. She'd catch up with the Cowl and find out what happened with the Flyball Ninja's component later. Now she needed to talk to him about their little visit from the Seven Wonders.

But she didn't remember all the sheets in the house, although it had been a couple of days since she'd gone upstairs. The sheets meant that maybe he wasn't coming back for a while.

This wasn't quite what she had planned.

Blackbird completed the fourth circuit of the house. The doors and windows that she had tested were locked, but the alarm wasn't on. She wasn't even sure there was an alarm. Maybe he had security staff coming to keep watch or patrol or whatever. She'd never seen any before, but that didn't mean he didn't have them. Maybe he had staff that came in and put sheets on everything when the house wasn't being used in a while. Who the fuck knew about the lifestyles of the rich and famous and their army of housekeepers?

Returning to the study which housed the top end of the Lair's stairwell hidden in a grandfather clock, she found herself staring at the ghostly outlines of the furniture, all draped in white. The house was still, and quiet, and she didn't think about anything in particular. After a few minutes the hair on the back of her neck began to crawl and she spun around, as if the Cowl had made one of his famous silent entrances and was waiting behind her, hands on hips, mouth set into the tough-guy grin.

But Blackbird was alone. She turned and headed back downstairs.

This wasn't quite what she had planned. Not at all.

Then again, what *had* the plan been, exactly? Remove the Cowl's powers, transferring them to a stooge carefully selected – someone with a *reason* to act and someone who could be controlled. With the Cowl de-powered and the stooge powered-up, the balance in the city could be shifted and a new supervillain would take over.

Of course it sure as hell wasn't going to be her. Firstly, if she suddenly replaced the Cowl as a *gin-you-ine* supervillain, then perhaps the Seven Wonders would change their policy and take her out. They had the power to, it was obvious. But it was almost as if they'd come to some arrangement with the Cowl – don't kill anyone too important, and you can run around the city at night scaring the little people all you like.

Secondly, the device hidden in Tony's closet wasn't something she wanted to use on herself. Sure, it worked, but she wasn't sure *how* it worked, and what it would do to you long-term was a total mystery. She might have been better off sticking her head in a microwave for all she knew.

Tony... well, Tony was the stooge, the mark, the target, the someone who could be controlled. If his brain turned to jello in a year then what did she care?

It sounded simple enough. But she hadn't thought through every angle. She hadn't expected the Cowl to pick up sticks and get the hell outta Dodge, although in retrospect that was probably one of the most likely outcomes.

But did it matter? He was out of the way, that was the primary goal. It hadn't even taken that much – just the loss of power and a hint that there was a new guy in town who wasn't going to take any shit like the Seven Wonders seemed happy to do.

Blackbird was back in the Lair. She sat at the main console and saw that all systems were on security shutdown, the computer locked. That was annoying. Here she was, having apparently inherited, well, everything, and she couldn't even turn the main lights on.

Fear. She'd gone and done it with the Cowl's own favorite weapon – they'd scared him shitless and sent him running. There was something to be enjoyed about that. Poetic justice or irony or whatever the hell it was. And even if he'd fled San Ventura to maybe build himself a supervillain army from all the contacts he had around the world, by the time said force returned to the city she'd be ready for him. So would Tony. The stooge.

Blackbird made a mental note to check on Conroy's financials, to see if he could be tracked on his travels. He had plenty of money and plenty of friends, but chances were he'd need to use an ATM or credit card once in a while.

Blackbird had seen enough. Wondering if they could move in to the house above without anyone noticing, Doctor Jean "Jeannie" Ravenholt headed back to Tony's apartment.

CHAPTER THIRTY-ONE

It was funny. Summer in the city was always looked forward to with great expectation. In the lead-up to the "official" start, the weathermen on TV went into overdrive with predictions, radar images, statistical comparisons with past seasons. This was going to be it, the summer of summers, the barbecue summer, the summer of the beach. Pack your bags and head to the house in La Jolla. But if you didn't have one – and really, why the hell not, you poor, godforsaken layabouts? – stick around San Ventura, North Beach. This was it, we were in for a sizzler. And don't forget the lightshow of the Draconids. The meteor shower was going to be better and bigger and brighter than ever before (as they said each and every year), so stock up on ribs and beers and invite your friends.

Of course, it wasn't that winters in southern California were anything approaching harsh, or even cold. But if you were a local, born and bred, the mid-seventies were just not warm enough. Praise the sun god and all who bask in his glory.

And then summer arrived, and after a few days of delight the novelty wore off. Bright, hot mornings were great, but by early afternoon the concrete of the city had heated, turning the whole place into a kiln. Those not on the beach retreated inside to sit in front of air conditioners and start checking predictions for a cool fall with pleasant sea breezes. Who needed summer? It was too hot to do anything, to go outside even.

Tony was, in general, ambivalent. His apartment's AC hadn't worked for years, so the heat outside was actually a slight relief to the stuffy oppressiveness inside. It crossed his mind that when the heat arrived he should probably switch out of his customary black attire. Yeah, probably should. Maybe next year.

Summer meant frequent trips to the convenience store. It was only a block away, and for this Tony was grateful. At this time of the year, the water from the faucets in both kitchen and bathroom actually came out hot. Tony didn't much like to drink the city's water when it was cold anyway, so stocking the fridge with bottled water was his number-one summer hobby.

The store's AC was in fine form, and by the tall standing refrigerators it was even better. Tony knew exactly what water he wanted, the kind he always got (one of the more expensive ones, imported from somewhere fancy), but he lingered over the shelves, opening doors to check labels but really to stand close to the arctic blast of air that swept over him. It was probably only forty degrees or something, but it was sheer bliss. He wondered if eventually his superpowers would grow until any temperature at all – hot or cold – would have no effect on him whatsoever. He hoped not. He liked standing in front of the convenience store fridges in summer.

Tony knelt down to check the bottom shelf. The store was almost empty, an afternoon lull, except for two pairs of legs that he could just see out of the corner of his eye, loitering around the laundry goods shelves.

There was a sharp click, a mechanical sound that was out of place, followed by a cry of surprise.

"Open it! Open it! Dude, *open it*!"

Tony stayed low, out of sight. He slowly closed the refrigerator. Water selection could wait. He dropped to the floor and pressed his face sideways on the sticky linoleum – some of the shelves in the store were solid, others sat on tiny legs. Through the mucky, dusty underside of these, he could see two pairs of feet standing in front of the counter. One wore shiny sneakers, not an inexpensive pair, all red and gold metallic plastic, with white socks pulled tight. This person stood on their toes, jiggling up and down. His companion wore much cheaper footwear, black unbranded sneakers with Velcro straps, the bottoms of black sweatpants just visible.

Tony relaxed. He'd walked into a robbery. No problem. He was the newest member of the Seven Wonders. All he had to do was incapacitate the perps and then let the police pick them up, just like he'd seen the superteam do countless times. Well, countless times before they'd let the city go to hell as their obsessive cat-and-mouse game with the Cowl took priority. Tony wondered if they even knew what had happened, had even realized how they'd let San Ventura slip away from them.

And speaking of slipping away – letting the Cowl go, after he'd handed his sorry ass right to them? What the fuck was going on there? Well, he'd find out, soon enough. He was one of the team now. He'd press for some answers, and then maybe press for some changes. Things were different now the Seven were the Eight.

Tony raised himself slowly upwards until he balanced on his toes. Peering over the top of the shelf, he got a clear look. Two guys, one disheveled, too-thick black coat and dirty baseball cap, long hair, goatee. The other was dressed in a mismatched combination of basketball and baseball gear, all baggy and street and gangsta. He waved a tiny gun over the counter at the store attendant, who stood back, as far as possible, with his hands raised tightly by the sides of his face.

The gunslinger was getting more and more agitated. If the attendant didn't start cooperating, the robber would start to panic. It was a classic scene Tony had seen countless times, played out on late-night TV police shows that consisted of nothing but security camera footage of robberies. Apart from the incident at the bank, Tony had never actually been directly involved in any kind of crime, no matter how bad he thought San Ventura had become. But, unlike the Cowl's bank job, this was nothing. This was two jerks getting money for dope.

Easy.

Tony glanced around and found the security camera. It blinked above the counter, providing a clear view not only of customers, but of the cash register and the attendant, keeping tabs on both. Tony licked his lips. As a member of the superteam, he now had to protect his identity. He was in street clothes, and one public performance had been enough. If another little show joined the recording from the bank, which no doubt would eventually make it first online and then on TV, Tony would be feeling the heat, not only from the Seven Wonders but maybe the Cowl too, if he was, apparently, still at large.

The idea that the Cowl might approach him and make a counter-offer entered Tony's mind and tickled his funny bone for a second. It was all he could do to keep from sniggering in the quiet store.

Tony held his breath and rolled his neck. If he was going to do this, he needed to take out the camera first to prevent identification. He nodded to himself. No problem. The shop was pretty small, which meant he could make it to the counter, taking out both the camera and the robbers in just seconds. The two guys doing the stick-up had picked their moment well, as the store was also empty of other customers, which meant the only person Tony really had to watch didn't get caught in the fight was the attendant. And really, in these situations, Tony knew he could make compromises. Sometimes bystanders got hurt. That was part of living in a city caught in the perpetual battle between crime and justice.

Right?

The companion of the gun-toting robber was getting jittery and nudged his friend. His friend didn't seem to like this and swore loudly, waving the gun in front of him like he was trying to get rid of a bad smell. The other man backed off a little then leaned in, whispering something, and checking over his shoulder. His hands were stuffed into the pockets of his hooded sweat top, fists clenching and unclenching within, stretching the spongy fabric already worn thin and shiny.

Tony shook his head. Fucking crackheads.

The store attendant still didn't move, though in defiance or fear, Tony wasn't sure. He couldn't smell much – the dust and grime around the shelves and the BO-reek of the robbers blocked out any hint of sweat or fear pheromones from the cashier.

There was a pause, a split-second beat when the moisture in the air seemed to hang, the posture and body language of the robbers changing slightly, relaxing almost. This was it. Their patience had come to an end, and the next event would be the hammer of the gun striking the cap on the end of the bullet, and then it would be game over for the attendant. It was now or never.

Tony skidded as he ran, losing his balance as the thin soles of his

Chucks burnt into the ancient linoleum of the shop floor. He compensated, but it cost him a few milliseconds. Accelerating to two hundred miles an hour in the space of a dozen feet, he realized the near-trip had set him off course. He corrected, ankles rolling as he pushed himself at an angle, aiming for the space between the two robbers. From there he could clothesline the pair then jump up over the counter, taking out the camera on the way before sweeping the attendant to the ground and out of the path of any bullet that managed to leave the gun. As he approached the counter at superspeed he realized he could really have done it all from afar, shooting the camera and the crooks with a bolt of energy, but... well, now he was here, maybe a hands-on approach would really be faster and less likely to go wrong.

His path correction ran true. His superpowered synapses processed the incoming optical data at a colossal rate, telling his muscles to raise his arms at just the right time. The backs of his forearms connected with the necks of each of the robbers, one on the left, the other on the right. The pair didn't have time to register the attack and crumpled instantly.

Tony was going too fast, again. He realized the fact and tried to slow, but he hardly felt the impact on his arms, the thought arriving too late that he'd probably reduced their cervical vertebrae to fragments. The main perp hadn't fired his gun though. Tony saw the store attendant directly in front of him, completely motionless. At the speed he was going, the entire world was almost frozen in place, hardly even moving at more than one frame a second.

As the crooks fell, Tony hopped up, his knees crashing into the front of the counter. He gained just enough height to reach up and slap the security camera with the tips of his fingers. The cheap black plastic box exploded, bright sparks and dark shards radiating outwards at a snail's pace. Tony kept going, now airborne and unable to stop. Instinct made him cover his face with his arms, even though nothing could scratch his diamond-hard skin, as he crashed into the cigarette stand that adorned the store's rear wall. Most of the display came down around him, but the wall was thick and he'd lost some momentum by jumping upwards. Consequently, his face was only embedded an inch into the white-painted concrete when he hit it. Tony pushed off instantly, feeling suddenly the heat against the soles of his feet as the bottom of his shoes melted.

The universe accelerated as Tony slowed. The store attendant was now lying on his side behind the destroyed counter, eyes blinking as the dust and debris clouded around him. His hands were raised above his head and when he looked at Tony, his mouth was open in fear. Tony felt the world lurch as he returned to normal speed.

"Hey, it's OK, I'm not here to hurt you." Tony reached down to help the man, but the attendant whimpered and shuffled backwards a little, cracking his head against the counter. Tony sighed. The cops would be here soon as his attempt at foiling the robbery hadn't exactly been discreet. There was no time for this. He leaned over and grabbed the man's arm, pulling him to his feet. The attendant's eyes screwed shut but he made no attempt to pull away. Tony drew him up to his face, and noticed tears running from the corners of his scrunched eyes. Dust or fear, he couldn't tell.

"Come on, snap out of it. You're safe." The man opened his eyes, but there was nothing behind them, no light of understanding. He was Hispanic... perhaps his English wasn't that good? Tony fumbled for a moment over a handful of bad Spanish before giving up. Of course he knew English. The attendant just looked blankly at him as Tony realized he was holding him by the collar, not just to his toes but almost an inch off the floor. He muttered an apology and set him down. The man's mouth began working as soon as his feet hit the floor.

"Anything, anything you want, take it, *take it...*" The attendant turned around, rolling himself along what was left of the counter and to the register, murmuring his offer over and over again. Tony folded his arms, not quite sure he had heard right.

The register shot open with the familiar clatter of small change and a digitally simulated ping of a machine fifty years older. The attendant turned, hands full of green bills. He pressed them into Tony's folded arms, ignoring the fact that nearly all fell to the floor. Turning back to the register, he swung back with another two handfuls, then another. And now coins. Money scattered all over the floor. Cash register empty, the attendant turned around again, pressing himself back against the counter. He screwed his eyes tight, raised his arms above his head in surrender, and began to softly sob.

What. The. Fuck.

Tony didn't move, arms still tightly folded with bills stuffed between them, as he regarded the weeping man. He'd tried to help him – hell, he'd done more than try, he'd taken out two dopeheads and saved this guy's goddamned life. Now he was crying and throwing cash on him, like he thought Tony was some kind of superpowered robber. How could someone be that weak?

Well fine. Fuck it, let him deal with the bodies. Tony went down on one knee, scooping up the bills on the floor. He waggled the fistfuls of dollars in front of the attendant's face, but the man's eyes remained closed, and his mouth moved in some silent prayer. Tony sighed, and swore, and sighed again. Fuck this shit. He stuffed the money into his jeans, gathered up the rest of the loose cash, and filled his back pockets. He walked out from behind the counter, stopped by the fridge and took two bottles of water, and left the store with the panicked attendant and two dead bodies and wrecked tobacco stand and counter.

It was hot outside, and Tony was hot from his little exertion. He pressed one of the bottles to his forehead as he walked, and realized he'd taken the wrong brand.

He'd tried to help, and he wasn't welcomed. Well, wasn't that nice? San Ventura could go to hell. This motherfucking town *owed* him, dammit. He'd had to talk to the Seven Wonders about how to… adjust the city. Change its outlook. Teach the citizens a little respect.

He flipped the lid off one of the bottles and took a long swig as he walked back to his apartment.

CHAPTER THIRTY-TWO

"Good evening, San Ventura. You're watching *The Shining City Today Tonight*. I'm Sarah Nova and these are your headlines this Tuesday evening.

"The business community is in shock after Conroy Industries announced its chairman and CEO, Geoffrey Conroy, will be taking unexpected and indefinite medical leave.

"The police crackdown on the Omega gangs has been totally ineffective, says the chief of the San Ventura Police Department Captain Charles Gillespie, as he called for closer ties between local law enforcement and the Seven Wonders.

"And a third suspicious fire in Tempest County has local residents worried that an arsonist is on the loose. Our man Dex Brubaker is on the scene and has been talking to locals.

"Our top story tonight: members of the San Ventura Chamber of Commerce are meeting this evening after Conroy Industries announced its chief executive, Geoffrey Conroy, is to take indefinite medical leave, starting immediately. Speaking on an unscheduled conference call with investors just hours ago, Conroy Industries' CFO Bruce Anderson revealed that Mr Conroy, whose business concerns include Conroy Computer Inc. and the Big Deal chain of home appliance stores, had been absent for the last week before submitting notice of leave, although sources close to the company have revealed to *The Shining City Today Tonight* that Mr Conroy has not been at the company for nearly two weeks and is believed to be seeking treatment for an undisclosed ailment somewhere out of state.

"Geoffrey Conroy is a major contributor to the mayor's Keep San Ventura Beautiful charity trust and to the San Ventura Police Benevolent Fund, and just last month made a sizeable personal donation to both. Mr Conroy also sits on the board of directors of a number of California's Top 50 companies. The Chamber of Commerce is expected to meet with executives from Conroy Industries later tonight to request assurance that their CEO's absence will have no effect on the company's short-term commitment to San Ventura, where they are the largest single employer. CI shares were down three points at the close of play.

"The Omega gangs are 'out of hand', says police chief Charles Gillespie. Speaking with the mayor on the steps of City Hall, Gillespie today said that the criminal gangs – who take their name and colors from the symbol worn by the Cowl – are entrenched in several poorer areas of the city, terrorizing residents and causing millions of dollars' worth of criminal damage. Gillespie took the opportunity to publically call on the Seven Wonders to take decisive action, as the problem was now beyond the capacity of the SVPD to deal with effectively.

"Investigators tonight are looking for a suspicious car seen driving in the Tempest County area following the latest of a string of arson attacks..."

CHAPTER THIRTY-THREE

San Ventura mornings in summer were generally foggy, the hot air sweeping off the desert inland mixing with the cool air from the Pacific, the resulting condensation dumped right on top of the coastal city. For those up early enough, before the thick gray mist was burnt off by the Californian sun, it was a pleasant relief from the egg-frying temperatures overnight. The cooler temperatures brought joggers, commuters, and old people out for a walk through one of the city's many parks. Early morning in San Ventura was the best part of the day.

Tony stood at the kitchen basin, looking out of the small window at the mural on the flat cinderblock wall of the building opposite. The ocean scene was a peculiar mix of Sixties surfer art and traditional Japanese illustration. It was beautiful, and perfectly positioned to be enjoyed from the row of apartment buildings that lined this side of the street. That it hadn't been whitewashed by the city wasn't too much of a surprise. San Ventura had a strong art community, and while the mural was probably listed on a chart of graffiti problems, the city council would have given a tacit agreement to not get around to erasing it for, oh, thirty or forty years.

"Hey," said Jeannie, padding into the kitchen. Tony turned from the window and smiled, then reaching out, took her hands and spun her around to embrace her from behind. With his arms around her waist, he planted a kiss on the back of her neck.

"Hey yourself." He said, then: "Time for tea. Hot and black!"

Jeannie shook her head and laughed. "The one time of the day the temperature is livable, and you want a hot drink? Are you sure your superpowers don't include retarded in the head?"

Jeannie pulled away, and Tony smiled knowingly at her as she turned back around. He held a finger upright in a mocking gesture of silence, then grabbed the electric jug. After filling it from the faucet and replacing it on its base, he touched its metal side with his hand. Almost at once, the sound of boiling water echoed from inside, steam billowing from the spout. Five seconds later he had poured the water into a teapot, the side of the still disconnected electric jug glowing a faint orange.

"Wow!" Jeannie's faked surprise made Tony laugh. Mouth wide, she raised her hands to her face in pretend shock, then almost jumped on Tony in a bear hug. "You're my hero! Superhero tea-maker extra-ordinaire!"

"What*ever*." Tony laughed and they kissed. After a while he extricated himself and moved to the sink to finish making his tea. He glanced up out of the window instinctively. Now there were a couple of black vans parked in front of the mural. It briefly crossed Tony's mind that this was odd, as it was a no-stop zone, but he also knew that parking violations in this part of town were not uncommon.

"I'm on the afternoon shift at work today," he said, still looking out of the window. "How's your head? You feel like doing anything this morning?" The bruise on Jeannie's forehead was fading fast but he knew that a bump like that took a while to come right.

Jeannie leaned back against the counter. "Yeah… no… maybe. It's early! How do you manage to be so alive after just two hours' sleep, anyway?"

"Tea and apples!" Tony opened the small fridge and took out a small red apple. "They can make up for a lot of lost time, you know. People think coffee is the answer. *Uh-uh*." He waggled his finger again. "Apples. Tea. A magical combination."

Tony stirred the teapot, and the apartment front door exploded inwards. He dropped the apple and jerked his other hand, overturning the pot and sending scalding hot liquid across the bench and splashing Jeannie's bare feet. "The *fuck*…?" was all he managed before the shouting began.

The door had come completely off its hinges and was buckled at the center, and lay at an angle like a makeshift skateboard ramp. In the corridor beyond, Tony could see a black-clad, helmeted man step backwards, pulling a two-handed battering ram out of the way as two similarly attired comrades rushed in. These ones were carrying formidable automatic weapons, their laser-assisted sights firmly pressed against their protective goggles, eyes expertly trained along the stub barrels. Four letters in bold white advertised their affiliation across each armored chest.

SVPD.

Tony blinked. Yesterday, superheroes. Today… this?

Behind them, lingering for a moment longer just around the edge of the doorway, were two plainclothes police – detectives; a man, dark and Latino, and a platinum-blonde woman – with black Kevlar vests strapped over their shirts, regular pistols held close and at the ready. Both wore clear protective eyewear.

"San Ventura Police Department! Do not move! Do not move!" The command from one of the armored police was screamed at Tony's direction, and seemed perfectly unnecessary. Tony was frozen in shock, hand and arm still outstretched from when they had been holding his freshly brewed tea. He blinked away the dust from the shattered door and glanced over his shoulder, towards the kitchen, but Jeannie was nowhere to be seen.

The two detectives moved into the apartment. Both kept their guns pointed at Tony as the heavily armed cop who had given the order gestured for his colleague to explore beyond the room. Behind, the male detective backed off a little, and started looking around the room. His companion's gaze never shifted from Tony.

"Where's Jean Ravenholt?" she asked.

Tony coughed. The question was something of a surprise. Apparently, they weren't here for him, they were here for… wait, what?

"You mean Jeannie? What do you want with her?"

The male detective paused in his survey of the room. "This your apartment, Mr Prosdocimi?"

Tony nodded. The female detective adjusted her grip on her gun. "We don't have time for this. Is she here? We'll turn this place upside down if we have to."

Tony's mouth twisted into a smirk. He just couldn't help it. He saw the reaction it provoked in the detective, one of surprise and suspicion, her head moving back a little as her eyebrows dipped together over the bridge of her nose.

Three guns? Easy.

"Something funny?" asked the male detective, casually stepping closer.

Condescending prick.

There was a cry from the kitchen. Tony turned to see the armored policeman return to the front room, machine gun in one gauntleted hand, the other wrapped around Jeannie's upper arm. She looked pissed, but didn't struggle.

The female detective adjusted her aim, moving her gun from Tony to Jeannie.

"Jean Ravenholt, aka Blackbird, you are under arrest for murder, conspiracy to commit murder, terrorism, conspiracy to commit terrorism, treason, conspiracy to commit treason..."

"Blackbird?" Tony interrupted the detective's recitation of charges. Nobody spoke. The detective's eyes flicked up and down Tony, standing barefoot in pajama bottoms and black T-shirt.

"Somehow I don't think you're the Cowl, but we're taking you in as well. We have you on CCTV from the California Cooperative Bank."

Tony ignored her, and took a step forwards. All four guns instantly moved in his direction. The policeman who had used the battering ram appeared in the apartment's doorway, his own gun now raised.

Tony glanced sideways at Jeannie. Her demeanor had changed, her face now white, eyes wide, her whole body trembled gently in the policeman's grip. Tony's expression had turned from surprise to anger.

"Tony, it's... I..."

"*You're* Blackbird? You're the Cowl's bitch? What the *fuck,* Jeannie? Please tell me she's full of shit." He jerked his head towards the female detective.

Jeannie took a step backwards. Tony watched the fear spread over her. Things began to make sense: her schedule of training, her mysterious job, how she had access to the tech required to make his Justiciar costume. All of it. It all made sense. Clearly his new superpowers – which, somehow, she must have had a connection with – including gullibility and falling for any old made-up shit.

Tony clenched his fists and Jeannie flinched. Tony saw the look in her eyes. She was afraid, not of the police. Afraid of *him*. She knew what Tony was capable of now.

Huh. Superpowers. It had to be her. This might have been a strange city where weird shit could happen, but it couldn't be a coincidence, could it? Tony shook his head, amazed that he could have been so blinkered.

The male detective sniggered. "Hold on, lovers, save it for the station. Officer?"

The first armored policeman stepped towards Jeannie, unhooking a set of powercuffs hanging from his belt as he did so. The restraints were wide manacles, complete with mini keypad control and winking LEDs, and had been developed by Hephaestus for restraining superpowered criminals. Given that Blackbird and the Cowl were the only two left, and had been for a couple of years, Tony realized this must have been the first time they'd be used in quite a while.

Tony kept quiet, ignoring the cops, and returned his stare to Jeannie. A hundred emotions coursed through him: anger, jealousy, love, and fear were just a selection.

"Tony, we need to get out of here." Jeannie's voice was low, not a whisper, but quiet and slow, emphasizing each word clearly so there could be no misunderstanding. "I know somewhere we can go," she continued. "I can explain everything."

Tony just shook his head. The cop with the cuffs paused, then raised his gun again and took another step forward.

Jeannie looked at Tony. Her eyes were wide, pleading, but otherwise she seemed calm.

"Please, Tony. *Please*."

"Enough already," the female detective snapped. "Let's go."

"Fuck you." Tony's hands flew towards the cop with the cuffs. One hand grabbed the gun, the other the man's forearm. He flicked upwards, bending the gun barrel and snapping the man's hand almost off. The policeman screamed and hit the floor on one knee. As his helmeted head got close to Tony's right knee, Tony kicked outwards, sending the man careering full across the apartment to slam into the wall. The man slumped in the corner, and didn't move again.

One down.

The two less-protected detectives stepped backwards as one, towards the front room's large main window. Showing years of ingrained police training, they raised their pistols in unison, and after a perfunctory warning shout, began firing, not even pausing for surrender. At the same time, the cop in the doorway opened up, sending high caliber rounds two at a time, almost experimentally, perhaps realizing that Tony was no ordinary civilian but unsure how much punishment he could take. The one holding Jeannie spun her around and forced her to the floor on her front, shielding her with his own body.

The bullets were hitting Tony, there was no doubt about it. In a few seconds his black T-shirt was torn and smoking. He took a moment to focus on the hot water tapping on his skin as the slugs were compressed to molten slag, and dripped off, burning away his thin clothing as they did so. The pistol rounds were surprisingly sharp, but felt small, like someone flicking his skin with a fingernail. The automatic weaponry packed more of a punch, each burst of paired bullets more like being hit by a fast-thrown tennis ball. He closed his eyes, counting the shots, nostrils flaring as the tangy smoke from the burning cloth of his top curled around his face.

The detectives stopped shooting first. Sensible. The woman was on a radio. Standing ten feet away, Tony reached out with one arm, and the radio's plastic casing split in the detective's hand before the device was wrenched from her grip and tossed against the wall.

They really weren't prepared for anything like this, Tony thought. As he accelerated towards the cop in the doorway at half the speed of sound, he considered how botched the raid had been. They clearly lacked any more operational intelligence than a basic connection between Jeannie, Blackbird, and – somehow – Tony's apartment. Blackbird was only moderately powered, and they'd come with powercuffs and small arms. That was it. Which meant they had no idea that the Cowl's girlfriend was also shacked up with the Justiciar. They had no clue who Tony was. The female detective had recognized him from the CCTV footage, but there had been something in her eyes, a sign of sudden recognition, of hesitation. They hadn't been expecting him.

Tony brought his arms up and hit the policeman with his own body at Mach 0.7 before stopping almost instantly. There was a surprisingly loud and wet crunch as the man's chest imploded, his head thrown back and helmet knocked clean down the corridor with the force of the impact. Tony spun and flicked out three globes of blue plasma, the force of their impact sending the policeman's burning body after it.

"Tony!" Jeannie's cry for help refocused him. He was beginning to enjoy himself, but he snapped out of it. Destruction was addictive, it seemed.

Already the male detective was radioing for superpowered assistance – Tony swore as he realized he'd overlooked the second detective's radio – and there was a very real possibility that the officer pinning Jeannie to the floor would get nervous and not look when he started shooting.

Tony took three steps forward, his bare feet sticking slightly to the melted carpet which had been seared an inch into the floor by his burst of superspeed. The officer was lying directly on top of Jeannie. Without a second thought he reached down, grabbed the man by a booted ankle and, swinging him directly upwards, embedded him in the ceiling. He was still moving, so Tony pulled him back down, snapped his automatic weapon clean in half, and broke his neck in one clean sequence of moves. Dumping the body, he carefully helped Jeannie up, concentrating on winding his superstrength down so he didn't throw her across the room too.

Tony looked Jeannie in the eye. She smiled, looking almost apologetic. Tony sighed, and shook his head. The cops had got it wrong, there was no way Jeannie was the Cowl's dumb bitch. No way.

Right?

"We have to leave," she said at last, quietly. Tony nodded.

The pair turned around. Behind them, the two detectives had retreated into the corridor, but if help was on the way, the front door was not the best exit. Tony turned, glanced around the apartment, and decided on the main windows that led out to the street below.

"Mr Prosdocimi," called the female detective from the corridor. "I don't know who you really are or why you're protecting her, but Blackbird is wanted on multiple counts. We need to take her in, to stop the city being torn up. It's just one step from her to the Cowl."

Tony smiled. "You really don't know who I am?" He looked at the wrecked bodies of the two armored cops. Smoke curled around the apartment's front door as the body of the third continued to smolder out of sight.

"You're not one of the Seven Wonders," she said. "You're not the Cowl either."

Tony puffed his chest up and addressed the empty room.

"How do you know I'm not the Cowl? If I'm shacked up with Blackbird…"

There was a sound from the corridor. Tony turned his hearing up and caught the end of a whispered conversation between the two detectives. The Seven Wonders, apparently, had acknowledged their call and were on their way. Then the female detective answered Tony's question.

"We know you're not the Cowl, Tony."

Jeannie pulled on Tony's arm, but he shook it off and glared at her. So he wasn't the Cowl. Well, he'd be something else. Something worse.

"And how do you know that, exactly?"

The detective's snort echoed down the corridor. "Come on. You're too short, too young, just for starters. Don't flatter yourself."

Tony's lip curled. "You're right, detective. I'm not the Cowl. I'm the Justiciar."

There was a pause. Tony had hoped for some reaction. The silence was insulting.

Then the male detective spoke up. "The Seven Wonders are on the way. All of them. Give it up before they teach your sorry ass a lesson." The words were slightly braver than their delivery.

Jeannie grabbed Tony's arm again. He flinched, irritated at the interruption to his thoughts. He was calculating an escape, working out whether the detective was right or not. Maybe he was… it would only take a second to kill the pair, evaporate them with a plasma blast perhaps, but if that second was enough for the superheroes to arrive, they'd be finished. So much for becoming the Eighth Wonder. In his haste he'd killed three police already. But… he'd had to, hadn't he? It was necessary, to control the situation and to stop them all making a big mistake, thinking that his girlfriend was Blackbird.

A... mistake, right?

He turned to Jeannie.

She looked him in the eye, and nodded at the window. Tony grabbed Jeannie in a bear hug that buried her head in his chest and under his arms, and exited the apartment via the apartment window. The force of the impact tore half of the exterior wall open as well.

The Justiciar and Blackbird made their escape.

Detectives Sam Millar and Joe Milano gingerly walked back into the apartment, now half in the open air. The pair stood there, unmoving for a moment, then lowered their guns. Sam ran to the hole in the wall in time to see Tony and Blackbird speeding across the sky. Then the wind from the opening changed direction and caught her hair, pushing it in front of her face. She brushed it away, and gasped. Floating in the air outside the apartment were Aurora, Bluebell, Linear and the Dragon Star. Aurora's arms were folded and his face set as he floated forward, stepping onto the apartment floor, the others following. Sam stepped back, giving the team room and trying to get away from the heat of Aurora's rippling corona.

Joe slapped his thigh. "Gee, thanks for coming, but you're too late!" He waved at the partially demolished wall in frustration. "Pardon me for saying this, Mr Aurora sir, but Blackbird and that new creep with superpowers just took off, and you don't seem to give a shit. You should be chasing after them right now!"

Aurora stepped closer to Joe, his gray hair swimming with agitation in the plasma that flared off the top of his head. Still his mouth was set in the expression that wasn't quite a smirk, his eyes empty white ellipses in his half-mask. Now the context of the conversation had changed, Aurora didn't look quite as friendly as the noble leader of San Ventura's finest should.

"Don't worry, Detective Milano," the superhero said after a beat. "Hephaestus and SMART are tracking the felons, and even now are moving to apprehend the pair with Sand Cat." He glanced at his team, then turned back to Sam and Joe.

"I think, detectives, we need to talk."

CHAPTER THIRTY-FOUR

Humility.

Our Father who art in heaven, hallowed be thy name. Thy kingdom come, thy will be done, on Earth as it is in heaven.

He'd hidden during the day, afraid of being seen, afraid of the fact that it was all out of control. He'd seen the headlines on the newspaper displays on nearly every major street corner. Geoffrey Conroy had vanished: medical leave, a mystery illness, the famous businessman was in Mexico seeking alternative therapies or had gone to Canada to seek a renowned doctor.

He knew he couldn't be seen, so he'd kept a low profile, waiting for the night. The night felt comforting, homely somehow. He wanted to see the city at night. In the meantime, he sat in the shade behind a closed-down factory and said his prayers and counted his rosary beads until the sun went down.

He'd made a mistake, taken the wrong path. But he knew there was hope, somewhere, deep down. Hope, forgiveness, salvation. And then justice and punishment.

But it was… the right thing.

It was after midnight when Geoff Conroy found himself in Moore–Reppion Plaza. Someone said something and he scooted to one side, realizing too late that he was walking far too slowly along a sidewalk that was bursting with life despite the hour. A drunken hen-night swaggered by, ignoring him completely, while a not-so-drunken couple power-walked across the street, heading in the direction of a tall parking garage. With Conroy out of the way, the traffic on the sidewalk picked up the pace appreciably, and the street itself was as busy now as on a Saturday shopping morning. San Ventura was a big city. It was called "night life".

Conroy knew all this. Most of his work as the Cowl took place under cover of darkness, usually in a seedy corner of the city populated by freaks and crackheads and police patrol cars nervously crawling the curbs. But not always. Sometimes an audience was important – you couldn't instill fear if there was nobody to see. He'd loosed killer robots on San Ventura's club scene back in 2009. Just last year, Sand Cat had uncovered Blackbird mapping the sewer system under Maass and Decker, and their fistfight had exploded into the middle of the Gaslight Quarter at ten on a Friday night. The Cowl had cruised in and forced Sand Cat's retreat, but he remembered the sizeable bar crowd out in the street, jeering and hooting at the superpowered catfight.

But this... this was different. People walked, talked, ran, sat, laughed, drank, ate. People were noisy. People were quiet. But all of them were getting on with their lives. None of them, as far as he could tell without superhearing, were talking about the Cowl. None of them wondering where the next attack would come from. None of them were looking over their shoulder in fear. None of them were creeping slowly under the brightly lit streetlamps.

Business – *life* – as usual.

And the Cowl realized just how *wrong* he'd got it.

He thought he owned the city. Ruled it. He was the country's number-one terrorist, a home-grown superthreat. People feared him. Even the Seven Wonders were too scared to take him on, content instead with a policy of appeasement, happy to let him get on with his business, and only limiting his more audacious schemes. As Geoffrey Conroy, billionaire industrialist and charity king, he was known among the city elite, although not quite famous enough among the general populace for anyone to take that much notice here. A few heads turned here and there as they passed him, but the newspapers said he was out of town and the stock photo they'd used of him was a few years out of date. And besides, everyone was more concerned with their drink, or the next club, or to get home, and it was more likely they were just glancing at a guy in an expensive linen suit counting rosary beads absent-mindedly with one hand, rather than the sick Geoffrey Conroy. Just another weirdo, albeit one with better taste in clothes than most.

He stood in the street as a completely normal, vulnerable human being. Nobody knew he was Geoffrey Conroy, city benefactor and leader of commerce. Nobody knew he was the Cowl, the criminal mastermind behind San Ventura's reign of terror. Nobody gave a shit.

He'd got it *wrong*.

Hail Mary, full of grace, the Lord is with thee.

Conroy sat on a fire hydrant and watched people walking, talking, sitting in the open-air spread of restaurants and bars, dancing in multicolored silhouettes behind the windows of clubs. Nobody was scared of the Cowl. Life was too important to stop and worry and fear. Everybody ignored the danger and got on with it.

He'd failed.

Had he really fooled himself that much that he hadn't seen what was right in front of his eyes? Perhaps. Drunk on power? Or high on his own superpowers, locked away in his underground Lair and his hilltop mansion, plotting, scheming, calling himself a king... yet doomed to irrelevance, a mere mischief-maker that made the news in the second before the viewer flicked the channel? A mischief-maker who killed, yes, but if you do something often enough it loses its punch, you get desensitized.

Well, how's that for a comedown?

He stood and loosened his shirt collar, the rosary beads clacking against the ring on his right hand. It really was hot. So many people, too many. Conroy suddenly felt alone, despite the crowds, and stupid, and vulnerable. What if someone knew who he was? Not just the super-rich Geoffrey Conroy, with a thousand dollars of loose change in his wallet, ripe for robbery. What if someone knew he was the Cowl? What if someone knew he didn't have superpowers anymore? Someone had to be responsible, of that he was sure. The loss of flight, invulnerability, superspeed – it wasn't a natural phenomenon. The Seven Wonders claimed publically to have never uncovered his identity, although he knew that to be a lie. And who else could be responsible for draining the powers of a supervillain? In fact, he was surprised they hadn't done it earlier. Maybe they'd needed time, perhaps entering into a covert alliance with another superteam? Perhaps the superheroes of the world were all about to come out of retirement and turn the tables.

He wracked his brains, trying to remember who else had ever discovered his true identity. Silverlord – but he was dead. The Ultimate Hero – dead. Lady Daylight and Kingkiller? No, supposition on his part. Kingkiller wasn't exactly a hero either, and he was locked in the bowels of the Earth in the supercrime prison built by the United Nations. Lady Daylight was missing, either off-world or, more likely, dead.

"Hey bud, you OK?"

Conroy turned his head slowly, trying to focus on the portly, bearded man in front of him. His face showed concern behind the whiskers, and he was wearing a plain dark suit, the white shirt glowing almost fluorescently in the neon strip light of the bar opposite. There was a black nametag pinned over the left breast, indicating the man was known as Brother *somebody somebody*. The man smiled but the smile was weak, and Conroy watched as the man's narrow eyes flicked to the rosary beads.

Glory to the Father, and to the Son, and to the Holy Spirit.

"Ah, yeah, fine," said Conroy. The Samaritan's face swam in front of his own. Maybe it was him? Perhaps the Mormon suit was fraudulent, the concern a sham? Conroy backed off and almost tripped over the curb behind him. Shit, it could be anyone. He turned on his heel, dodging past another gaggle of partygoers, and headed uptown. He needed to get away.

Uptown was quieter. A mix of small businesses and apartments, the only activity at this time of the night/morning was centered around a convenience store on the corner. Beyond was a small park, playground and basketball court visible under the streetlights, but the trees vanishing into the gloom beyond. A pinprick of light flared, suggested the presence of a cigarette smoker. A drug dealer, or maybe a would-be murderer or rapist. Conroy couldn't say. Maybe one of his faithful fans, a member of one of the Omega gangs.

Conroy's fingers found the next large bead on the rosary, and heart pounding, he ducked into the store.

• • • •

Love thy neighbor.

The bright artificial light inside stung his eyes, causing him to blink to adjust. His vision was now human-normal. This was going to take some serious getting used to.

It was quiet in the store, just the hum of the refrigerators and the slush machine at the counter. Conroy was surprised to see the counter was unprotected, no after-hours screen or hatch. Then he saw the damage.

The counter was new, as were the shelves behind it. So new they hadn't been restocked with cigarettes and condoms yet. At first Conroy just assumed it was ongoing maintenance, but then he saw the spider-webbed glass on a cabinet to the left of the new counter, clearly part of the older, original structure. The floor in front of the counter was marked with two distinct patterns – regular, almost rectangular burn marks, where the linoleum had been torn and then melted, and an irregular series of blobs with soft edges. Conroy had seen the second set of marks before, many times. The telltale afterimage of spilt blood. The convenience store had been robbed, and recently.

The attendant made a good show of reading a newspaper, but her eyes were clearly following her only customer. Conroy smiled self-consciously, and moved to browse the shelves. His eyes didn't focus on the groceries – rows of beans and laundry detergent went unseen. He wanted to savor the calm and the quiet, the reassuring purr of the drinks fridge, the dust and pine-fresh smell familiar from childhood.

But he'd picked the wrong neighborhood, clearly.

Holy Mary, Mother of God, pray for us sinners, now and at the hour of our death. Amen.

He reached for a tin of something unappetizing, and found it heavier than he expected. He hefted it in his palm, and noticed that his hand was shaking, just a little. He raised his other arm in front of his face. That hand shivered slightly as well.

Conroy exhaled loudly. Now he knew what this was: fear. He was terrified.

The newspaper rustled. Conroy emerged from behind the shelf and saw the attendant watching him. She wasn't that old – possibly kissing sixty, at the most – but she was frail and despite an attempted hardness in the eyes, Conroy could sense something was wrong. She was afraid too. Afraid of him.

Conroy glanced at the store damage. The wrong neighborhood, all right. And what was this woman doing here, running a store, apparently unprotected? Hoping that lightning doesn't strike twice didn't seem like a sensible business decision.

He took a step towards the counter and the woman jerked back, fast enough to bump her back into the empty cigarette rack behind her. Conroy didn't need superpowers to estimate her increased heart rate and respiration. She was going to have a damn heart attack.

Conroy flicked a bead with his right hand and held his left up, in a gesture of what he hoped was peace. The woman didn't seem to notice. She was shaking visibly now.

The blood, the damage. Given the state of the woman Conroy realized that she probably wasn't the regular attendant. No... something had happened, something had happened *recently*, which had left the regular worker incapacitated, and she'd had to come in and take over. Probably the mother. They had no choice, the shop had to stay open, they couldn't afford to close it even for a day. Conroy just hoped that the blood on the floor hadn't belonged to the shopkeeper. The damage and the burn marks on the floor suggested that a hero had been here. Linear, perhaps.

"Everything's going to be all right," said Conroy. His voice was suddenly loud in the shop and the woman jumped with a small cry. As Conroy watched, tears welled at the corners of her eyes.

Conroy felt sick. What right did people have to come in and attack a family-run business? What right did people have to cause fear and terror? People were just trying to live. All of them, everyone in the city. People had a right to freedom and to mind their own business.

As it was in the beginning, is now, and will be forever. Amen.

Conroy swallowed and found a lump in his throat the size of a grapefruit. He lowered his hand and walked backwards, towards the doors.

The Omega gang, out in the park. That was probably as close to a permanent HQ as the group had. Which meant they must have seen something. When he explained who he was they'd give him information, and even help him track down the perps.

As the woman behind the counter collapsed weeping onto her knees, Geoff Conroy returned to the night outside and ran across the street to the park.

Detachment from the things of the world.

The park really was dark. The lone streetlight cast a sickly yellow glow over the playground and basketball court, rendering everything a faded monochrome. Conroy could only assume everything was bright and cheerful in the daylight, because right now it was like something out of a Stephen King movie.

The path through the park led off out of the dull light and towards the trees, vanishing with surprising abruptness as the darkness beyond swallowed everything. Conroy knew that was an illusion, that the yellow streetlight was actually brighter than it looked and that once his eyes had adjusted to the gloom, the park would be easy to navigate. But that was also why it was the perfect spot for an Omega gang – they could lurk, maybe dozens of them, near the trees and watch the world go by, safe in the knowledge they were completely invisible to anyone who looked their way.

A firefly in the dark, a tiny flaring red that grew like a bloodspot in the air and just as quickly shrank back to nothing.

Hiding in the tree line was no good if you were a smoker.

Another large bead, another *Our Father*, and Conroy held his jaw up and walked into the black maw.

It was dark, and it was quiet. The trees moved constantly, their leaves a faint curtain of white noise that added to the odd feeling that he was walking into a soundproof chamber. Conroy listened to the trees and listened to his own footsteps; glancing down, the pale concrete of the path managed to capture the dregs of the yellow light from the playground, and was practically the only discernible object around him. Glancing back, the playground and basketball court were a tiny faded vignette. Beyond, the street and the convenience store. The store was brightly lit, the white of the interior and the red of an advertising sign for soft drink in the window the only color in Conroy's field of vision.

Conroy turned back to the darkness, bunched his shoulders, and took one step forward before stopping, quickly. The cigarette flared ahead, much closer now. Above the sound of the trees came the suck and crackle of someone taking a long drag.

"Nice suit, my brother," said the smoking man. Conroy could see him vaguely – a washed-out gray figure in a puffer jacket and wide jeans. There was no sign of any costume or uniform or insignia that he knew the Omega gangs wore, but it was too dark to see clearly, and the chances were such an emblem was on the back of his jacket anyway.

"You got a quarter for a coffee?"

Conroy glanced to his left. There was another person there, tall and thin, the voice young and deep. As the cigarette flared again, Conroy heard the trees rustle, too close to his back. He turned on this heel, carefully. There were two more men – youths – behind him. They were silhouetted sharply by the yellow light at the end of the tunnel formed by the tree-lined path. One was wearing a baseball cap. Conroy watched as its outline moved, the wearer looking him up and down.

"Oh my Jesus, forgive us our sins. Save us from the fires of hell. Lead all souls to Heaven. Especially those most in need of thy mercy."

Someone laughed and Conroy felt his mouth dry out completely. He hadn't meant to speak that out loud. The smooth wood of his rosary beads cut into the knuckles of his hand as he squeezed it into a fist.

"You on your way to church, mister?"

Three of the youths laughed. The fourth, the one with the cigarette, sniggered in an unpleasant falsetto and waved the hand holding the smoke. The dry-leaf smell of the park was joined by the strong, sweet aroma of weed. Conroy watched the end of the joint glow faintly as it was dragged through the air, and wondered whether this really had been a good idea.

He rolled the next rosary bead over a knuckle, and sucked in a breath that brought with it the tang of marijuana.

Time to take control. He didn't need superpowers to take charge. He was better than them, and they knew it.

"You're one of the Omega gangs, right?"

The men ignored the question and Conroy saw the outline of the baseball cap move again as they muttered among themselves. Conroy puffed his chest out, possibly for his own benefit more than anything. He dropped his voice to a growl that should have been familiar to the two million people living in the city.

"I'm the Cowl, and I need information."

The laughter sprang up again, louder this time. Conroy winced at the sharpness of the sound, the noise of four men high as kites getting a fit of the giggles.

The baseball cap moved forward enough for Conroy to see the man's face. It was thin and spangled with heavy acne.

"Your money," the youth said, eyes narrow. He glanced down at Conroy's shoes. "And duds. You picked the wrong park to jerk off in, my friend."

More laughter, more giggling. The two that hadn't spoken suddenly exchanged words, loudly but too quickly, all street slang and abbreviations that Conroy couldn't follow. The gang members were kids and Conroy was twenty years out of date.

"Smokes and money and make it quick," said the apparent gang leader.

Conroy frowned. "I don't have any cigarettes."

The leader shook his head. "Wallet, my man, wallet. Or we'll fuck you up, and then you'll know who the Cowl is."

The three kids around Conroy exploded with mirth. Conroy knew that he'd made a mistake. There was no way he could convince them who he was – and, perhaps more importantly, it didn't matter anyway. The Cowl, the omega symbol, were an excuse for anarchy. As the city's resident supervillain, he'd given license for the lowlife of San Ventura to think they had some kind of purpose and the freedom to act upon it.

"Too slow, brother Joe. I said give me your motherfucking money and your motherfucking smokes, bitch." Clearly, the concept that not everybody smoked was completely alien to the youths.

A fresh sound, a click and then something soft sliding on something hard. Conroy didn't turn but he knew that one of the kids behind him had pulled a knife of some kind.

"Hey, hey, hey," said one of the group. At once, the other three turned away from Conroy. There, in the yellow spotlight of the playground, was someone else. The black outline was long and flowing –

a woman, long hair and long coat, carrying a bag. She strode towards the group, either not seeing them or determined to make some statement about how the citizens of San Ventura could walk through any damn public place they liked at any damn time of day.

Or, thought Conroy, perhaps she had a death wish.

"Hey, hey, hey," repeated the gang leader. The group of four moved away from Conroy slightly. Conroy relaxed, the tension suddenly evaporating as he realized he was no longer of interest. Money and the possibility of fresh cigarettes was nothing compared to the allure of a woman.

As it was in the beginning, is now, and ever shall be, world without end. Amen.

The group jogged forward to meet the newcomer, who now came to a complete stop. Conroy heard the giggling come again and watched as the four men circled the woman like vultures. He was now forgotten, completely irrelevant.

One of the men reached out and pulled the strap of the woman's bag. She shrieked, and the men giggled. She snapped the bag strap away from the hand easily. They were playing with her. Another orbit and another hand, or the same hand, reached out and pulled at the lapel of her coat.

Conroy blinked. Although it was cooler between the trees he felt the sweat crawl under his hair. He felt the subcutaneous fat over his knuckles roll as he squeezed the rosary beads in his fist.

Contempt of Riches. Love of the Poor.

Conroy walked down the path towards the light.

The street was quiet, and the convenience store was still there with its white lights and red neon sign. Conroy turned, and the playground and basketball court were still there, bathed in the nicotine yellow of the streetlight. The world was dreamlike and Conroy's head was full of cotton wool. Any second he'd wake up, and walk downstairs to the Lair, and look over that night's automated surveillance report on the computer while he sipped freshly brewed coffee.

Any second now. Any second.

It was still hot. Conroy blinked and was surprised to find everything exactly as it was when his eyes opened again. He raised his hand to wipe his face, to get the funk of the night off him, but stopped and changed his mind. He stared for a moment at the blood smeared over his fingers. Confused for a second, he raised the other hand. In the light cast by the convenience store that hand was dipped in scarlet. He moved his fingers and stretched them out, watching the rosary beads shine wetly. The blood went almost to his elbow, and none of it was his.

He felt sick and euphoric and afraid and excited. Then he clutched his stomach, covering his jacket with the blood as a nauseating pulse of adrenaline coursed through his body. His chest felt like it was on fire, his lungs underwater.

What had he done? Oh, what he had done…

He straightened and checked the street. It was deserted, he was alone, and nobody had seen.

He'd saved a life, that's what he'd done. And there was now one less Omega gang in the city. Well… that was… good, right? The woman had run and the kids wouldn't be bothering anyone in the park – or anywhere else – ever again.

But… this wasn't his plan. This wasn't how it was supposed to work. The ends had justified the means but… Jesus, what had he done?

True Wisdom and True Conversion, Piety, Joy of Finding…

Conroy wiped his hands on his jacket as best he could, then slipped it off and dumped it in the gutter. He glanced down at his shirt, keeping his gore-soaked hands far away from it. He felt dizzy and cold and almost staggered but managed to keep himself upright as he realized his mistake.

The sigil. He wasn't wearing the Cowl's suit, but more importantly that meant he wasn't wearing the sigil, the complex array of runes which, when placed over his heart, removed him from God's sight. With the Cowl's suit on he was invisible, free to move and act as he pleased and as he needed. But without it, God could see him.

God could *see* him.

Conroy retched and spat a mouthful of bile onto the street. How could he have been so *stupid*?

That was it. There was nothing else left for him to do.

He needed to talk to someone, one man in particular, and it wasn't far.

It was open, of course. It was open all night, every night, and Conroy wasn't alone. Three people sat at the back, one sat at the front, and there were at least two that he'd seen lying on the pews, asleep. Around the edges of the cathedral lurked a priest, somewhere. Conroy had seen him when he'd come in but the man had vanished with no more than a cursory nod. Maybe he'd recognized Conroy.

Conroy chose a spot three back from the altar, and knelt with his forehead resting on the pew in front. The wood was cold and smooth.

Lead us not into temptation, but deliver us from evil.

"Haven't seen you in a while, Geoffrey."

Conroy opened his eyes but did not move his head. He stared at the dark brown grain of the pew an inch from his eyes. But he did smile, just a little.

"Father Theodore," he said, and he was surprised to find his voice cracking.

A hand on his shoulder. Thick fingers, old but strong. Father Theodore had been a boxer once. One of the best. There was a rumor that'd he even trained some of the superheroes in hand-to-hand combat before turning to God. Conroy knew that rumor to be solid fact.

"Strange time to come to church, my boy."

Conroy lifted himself from the pew and looked at his old friend through wet eyes. Father Theodore was smiling, his thick gray eyebrows pushed halfway up his forehead like the roof of an A-frame house.

The eyebrows stayed there while the smile dropped as Conroy lifted his hand. He kept it low, out of sight of anyone else not sitting in the same pew.

"Oh my Jesus," whispered Conroy, not taking his eyes from Father Theodore's face. "Forgive us our sins. Save us from the fires of hell. Lead all souls to Heaven. Especially those most in need of thy mercy."

Father Theodore looked at the blood-soaked rosary beads, then stood.

"Something tells me you have something to say," he said. He turned, clasped his hands behind his back, and walked toward the confessional that stood to the side of the pew in front of them.

Conroy pocketed the beads, took a deep breath, and followed.

True Wisdom and True Conversion, Piety.

Geoff Conroy breathed the warm air and ran a blood-free hand through his hair. After his confession, Father Theodore had taken

Conroy deep into the workings of the cathedral, through his office and into the private chambers that lay beyond the sight of the general public. Conroy had cleaned himself up, washed his hands and his face, which had been bright red from crying. The priest had taken the rosary and sent Conroy out. He didn't need it anymore – or, at least, not for a while.

Conroy had faced his demons and his sins, and had a new mission.

It was early morning, the sun just kissing the cloudless sky, turning the deep midnight blue overhead to a gentle whitish nearer the horizon. From outside the cathedral, Conroy could see right down the street, one of the main thoroughfares of the city, almost to the famous beaches.

The ground ahead of him was a rainbow display of color, a shimmering, incandescent projection. Conroy watched the multicolored shapes for a moment. He raised his hands in front of him, and turned them over in the colored light, as if he were drying his hands under the fan in a public bathroom.

He smiled and turned. At the opposite end of the street, in a square at the very heart of San Ventura, stood the Citadel of Wonders. It was a giant, triangular crystal shard, magically transparent but multifaceted, clearly an artificial structure but somehow appearing organic, like a natural, perfect slice of quartz. In the bright morning light it acted as a prism, shining the rainbow light across the whole city. And as the sun moved during the day, so the rainbow did as well, spotlighting nearly the entire city as it swept around from dawn to dusk.

Conroy felt his heart race. He had a price to pay, and a duty to perform. His past was catching up with him, but he accepted that. Father Theodore had been right. Penance and sacrifice, but also responsibility and acceptance. God was watching now. God *knew who he was*.

Geoff Conroy, formerly the Cowl, squared his shoulders and walked towards the Seven Wonders.

CHAPTER THIRTY-FIVE

The Lair was dark, the systems on total shutdown. In the dark it was dangerous, with unrailed walkways over abyssal drops. And deep underground, the darkness was absolute.

Tony frowned. He held the white plasma globe as high as he could above his head, not that he could get burnt, but to keep it well away from Jeannie. Even at a distance of several feet, Jeannie's exposed face was red from the heat. But until she could get the Lair systems rebooted, Tony's light was all they had.

They approached the walkway leading to the main control platform, Tony's globe illuminating the dead bank of screens at the opposite side of the cavern. Tony's light didn't penetrate very far into the dark that fell away on either side of the bridge. Something told him it was very, *very* deep.

Jeannie indicated for Tony to head over the bridge, and keeping a safe distance, followed him. Tony found a space on the edge of the platform that allowed Jeannie enough safe room to work, and shuffling his bare feet on the smooth tiled floor, took a good look at the Cowl's abandoned Lair. He didn't speak for quite a time, unwilling to start a conversation he knew would turn into a strung-out exchange, half argument, half prolonged explanation. And besides, Jeannie had brought them here and she needed to get the systems back online. Tony decided that silence was golden.

That worked for a while as Jeannie pulled open panels to check wiring and connections. But as much as Tony tried to keep his mind occupied, scanning the cavernous space with X-ray vision and infrared vision, his mind continually wandered back to the great elephant in the room.

To his surprise, it was Jeannie who spoke first. She must have been thinking thc samc thing.

"Aren't you going to ask about Blackbird? About all this?"

When Tony answered, it was abrupt and came after nearly half a minute's pause.

"Nope."

Jeannie flicked a switch experimentally, and a few blue and red LED pinpricks lit up on the desk. She turned and sat against the edge of the desk, facing Tony.

"This is – was – the Cowl's Lair."

"Yep."

"He's gone, you know. Vanished."

"That a fact?"

"It is," she said, and then paused. "I know where the Lair is and how to get in because I'm Blackbird."

"So I've been told."

"Don't you want to kill me?"

For the first time, Tony stopped looking around the Lair and set his eyes on Jeannie. At this distance, and with the hazy glow of the plasma globe melting the air between them, her expression was hard to read.

He shrugged, juggling the plasma ball and changing the shadows around the Lair. "I don't kill people. I'm a member of the Seven Wonders, remember?"

Tony watched the spittle fly from her mouth as Jeannie laughed, almost hysterically.

"Yeah, and that's going so well, isn't it? I guess police don't count as people now."

Tony frowned. She was right, of course, but the scene back at the apartment was fading from his mind already and even just a few hours later didn't feel real, somehow. Shock, perhaps. Everything felt dreamlike, surreal. He looked at Jeannie and tried to picture her as the infamous Blackbird. She was the right size and shape. And he'd known there was something about her, from when he first met her in the bar. Something which he'd put down to an "X-factor", something indefinable that drew two strangers together on a hot summer night.

No, it hadn't been like that. Tony wouldn't have dreamt of approaching someone like her. *She* had come to *him*. It was so unlikely as to be, well, highly improbable, if not downright impossible.

Tony felt sick. It wasn't about attraction at all. She had chosen him. Then used him, constructing a complex pretense, playing a role with such depth that only a supervillain could.

"That's it, isn't it?" he said at last. "You've been training me all along to be the new Cowl. You picked me from the crowd. A tool to be used. And don't I just feel like one."

The plasma ball in his hand flickered in time with his anger. He felt it grow hotter and was pleased to see Jeannie flinch a little.

She turned back to the control desk and flicked a few more switches. The sound of a generator winding up somewhere behind the rock walls filled the Lair, and soft spotlights came on, strategically illuminating parts of the cavern. Tony flicked the plasma ball up; out of his hands, it sputtered out with a pop a dozen yards above his head. Even the flash as it went out couldn't light the ceiling.

"Very nice," he said. "A secret lair fit for a supervillain." He took a few paces towards the control desk and towards Jeannie.

"Why me?"

Jeannie licked her lips. "It took a while to find the right person. Had to be someone with strong feelings about the Cowl, about the Seven Wonders. Harder than you might think."

"How long did you follow me for?"

"Oh," said Jeannie with a shrug. "A couple of months." She turned and waved at the towering computer screens and panels behind her. "Amazing the kind of search and surveillance you can do on this thing."

"And your boss never knew?"

Jeannie laughed again. "The Cowl is a somewhat self-absorbed individual."

Tony nodded, like an appreciative new employee being given a tour of a particularly fascinating stationery cupboard. Slowly he reached out and wrapped his arms around her waist. Jeannie smiled and returned the gesture, but Tony quickly pulled her against his chest and squeezed too hard to be comfortable.

"So, the thing I'm wondering now..." he said, speaking slowly. Jeannie looked up into his face. He was smiling again, but that in that slightly pissed-off way that people who have just been insulted sometimes do to show they're not backing down. "... is whether we're really in this together, or whether you've been double dipping with the Cowl and I'm just another toy for you two supervillains to play with. Maybe he hasn't vanished. Maybe he's just waiting around the corner, waiting for this diabolical scheme to come to a head."

Jeannie tried to push away, but Tony held his grip for a good few seconds before letting her step back. Time to show her who was in charge of their partnership now.

"The Cowl's gone," said Jeannie. "Trust me, he's not coming back, not for a while anyway."

Tony raised an eyebrow, but said nothing.

"Time for the big reveal then, eh?" Jeannie turned and walked with some purpose back to the computer desk. Her whole posture changed, even her gait. Jeannie had become Blackbird. As much as he hated to admit it, as much as the confusion of the last few hours had clouded his mind, he was impressed. A secret identity was more than just a costume and a funny name. He had to remember that.

At the desk, she stood beside the tall swivel chair and leaned over, typing at a keyboard to bring all seven displays to life, then stood back and gestured at the chair, turning it slightly in invitation. Tony walked over and slumped into it before turning his attention to the bank of active, but blank, monitors.

Jeannie opened a folder of files on the huge main display, then two more folders on two of the smaller secondary panels. The main display showed the CIT directory, the smaller monitors a list of files detailing something called Meta Induction Coupling and Negation. Tony frowned, but Jeannie just waved at the screens.

"Listen to the audios and read *everything*. I'll be back when you're done." She turned on her heel and left the platform via a side bridge, then vanished into the darkness. Tony heard some tapping and a beep as a concealed door opened, and then Tony was alone in the Cowl's Lair.

Jeannie kept walking, away from the cavern, away from Tony, away from the sounds of her parents' screams and the Cowl's taunts that filled the air. She slipped through another door and was finally out of earshot of the horror.

This was not how it was supposed to have played out. Blackbird had started something and Jeannie wasn't sure she could finish it.

Alone in the corridors, Jeannie slid to the floor, and wept.

CHAPTER THIRTY-SIX

An hour later and Tony was still sitting in the swivel chair, stroking his unshaven chin in thought. As Jeannie strode in, soft-soled combat boots silent on the hard polished floor, he flicked the main monitors off and turned the chair to watch her approach. His supersense had picked up her approach – he'd also heard her sobbing in the corridor earlier. He looked her up and down, his expression unchanging.

Black boots over shiny, skintight leather pants topped with a matte-black utility belt. Above this, the leather catsuit continued to the neck, although it was currently unzipped almost to her navel. The suit had other black enameled zips arranged on it, tiny pockets and compartments holding wonderful gadgets and tools. In one hand she held an elaborate mask, a streamlined helmet with a thick, curved triangular beak and large circular goggles. The sides of the mask followed the contour of the beak as it swept backwards and up, giving two wings on either side of the head that were tapered and fluted like feathers carved out of obsidian. In the low light of the Lair, Jeannie's pale skin almost shone behind the open zipper, her short dyed hair glistening blue-black.

Blackbird.

Tony couldn't help but smile at her entrance, and she seemed to relax, and grinned. She threw Tony the item she was holding in her other hand. It was a black fabric half-mask that would cover the face down to the nose, leaving the mouth and chin exposed. Tony held it up, opening the mask with his fingers, and stared at the face of the Cowl.

"You gave me my powers," Tony said, poking his fingers through the eyeholes. "You took the powers from him and gave them to me, with your machine, the Meta Induction thing. He killed your parents." Tony stopped and sighed. "Doesn't explain why you're his sidekick."

Blackbird walked around the chair, making Tony swing around to follow her as she sat on the edge of the computer desk on the opposite side.

"I was his 'sidekick' long before I knew he'd killed my parents. Their death was what drove me to the... well, it was what led me down a dark and dangerous road. I was angry and he made me an offer."

"The master and his apprentice?"

"Not quite," she said. "My parents were involved with top-secret military research at CIT. I'm moderately powered thanks to them. A bit of strength and agility, fractionally above the upper limit of human normal. Not much, but when they died, I felt something else break inside. I had no idea how or why they died, but I felt a rage burning. Hatred of the city and whoever had done it and those goddamn motherfucking superheroes who didn't give a shit. My parents were fucking well working for them, for Christ's sake!"

Blackbird stopped and looked at the floor. Tony kept his gaze on her, waited for the anger to pass, then asked: "So you wanted revenge?"

Blackbird shook her head, nodded, then shrugged. "Yes. No. Maybe. I don't know. But playing by the rules had done nothing for my parents, who gave their lives working to protect the world. Of course back then it wasn't just the Cowl – there were supervillains all over the world, every city had them."

Tony nodded. "And then the superheroes won."

"Then the superheroes won." Jeannie repeated Tony's statement without emotion. "Ain't that a fact. Except not in San Ventura, where the last active superheroes keep the city safe from the last active supervillain. Ever wondered why that is? The Cowl was powerful, sure, but there was only *one* of him and *seven* of them. Not to mention superheroes all over the world, hundreds of them. Their combined might could crack the planet in two."

Tony nodded again. "The Cowl could only exist because they *wanted* him to exist. The Cowl justifies the existence of the Seven Wonders."

"And allows them to maintain their grip on City Hall. And by extension, because the Seven Wonders still exist, so too the global network of superheroes. If the Seven Wonders control San Ventura, then heroes must be in control all over the world."

Tony whistled, but then shook his head, waving at Jeannie and his face clouding in annoyance again. "But you still haven't told me why you're the Cowl's girlfriend when you know he murdered your parents. And what happened to him, anyway? Why did he abandon this place, and where did he go?"

Jeannie sighed and lowered herself to the floor, her tight catsuit stretched even tighter as she dropped into a cross-legged position. She carefully placed her bird mask in her lap.

"I was working on the same project my parents were. MIC-N – Meta Induction Coupling and Negation. It's a machine that removes superpowers. Theories about the MIC-N have been in development for decades, but... let's just say I got a helping hand. The MIC-N is a powerful tool...

"As soon as I found out the Cowl was responsible for the death of my parents, of course I wanted revenge, I wanted personal justice. I'm a supervillain's sidekick, revenge and violence and vengeance are what I'm about. But I discovered the MIC-N has other uses. It can remove superpowers from one person and transfer them to another."

Jeannie fell silent. Tony's expression darkened.

"Wow," he said at last, his voice nothing but the whisper of a disappointed man. "You met me in the bar, got under my skin, and gave me *his* powers. I knew it was too good to be true – I knew *you* were too good to be true." He slapped the computer desk angrily, and spun the chair half-away from Blackbird, covering his face in his hands as he leant on the desk.

"It's not *like* that, Tony." Jeannie could reach his knee from where she sat; he flinched at the touch, turning the chair fractionally away to slip her hand off. "You and me, when we met... that was all real. That was the turning point. You were worried about the city. You hated the Cowl. I could give you his power, enough power to remove him from the city, and even clean the place up, using your powers for good, for doing the jobs that the Seven Wonders never did."

The two sat in silence for a while, the cavern echoing faintly with the sound of a hidden power generator.

After a few minutes Tony moved the chair around slightly, and picked up the Cowl's discarded mask. He held it up, fingers poking through the eye sockets from the inside. Another few minutes passed in silence, then he asked again: "So where is he now?"

Jeannie looked up. She ran her hands over the wings that curved out from the back of her mask. "I honestly don't know. He's completely unpowered now, and the last couple of fights he got into busted him up pretty good – me too. I think he freaked out, ran away. He might be dead, but I doubt it. He's most likely not in the city, anyway. Possibly travelling, trying to get his old friends together to help stage some kind of comeback. But I don't know, I'm theorizing. He's afraid, that's for sure. The removal of his powers had more of a psychological effect than I had predicted."

Tony put the mask down and sat up straighter in the chair. He looked up at the six dark screens, and across the myriad of controls on the computer desk.

"I guess we should finish this then. The Cowl is gone, that just leaves Aurora and the Superfriends."

Blackbird stood and moved towards Tony. She placed her arms around his neck, and this time he didn't shrug her off.

"Whatever you think of me, Tony, I understand. But I thought I was doing the right thing. I fell in love with you. I gave you power - the power to change things, to change the city. The power to change the world. I helped you, trained you. Love me or hate me, I'll understand. But right now you're the most powerful man in San Ventura, and I'm your sidekick. What do you say?"

Tony thought for a moment, then turned to her. He took her chin in his hand, and planted a delicate kiss on her dry lips. They smiled at each other. He glanced down at his tattered pajama bottoms, and held up the Cowl's mask to her.

"The Justiciar needs a new costume."

Jeannie smiled. "The Justiciar also needs to make an entrance, an announcement. He needs to tell the Seven Wonders that there is a new boy in town who's not going to take the same old shit."

Tony straightened, his eyes fixed on the Cowl's mask.

"An... entrance? What did you have in mind?"

Jeannie stood and took the Cowl's mask from Tony's hand.

"Oh, it's just a little idea..."

CHAPTER THIRTY-SEVEN

Sam had only ever been inside the Citadel of Wonders once before, accompanying Captain Gillespie and the mayor on a civic tour last year. She'd found the place showy, fake somehow, but could never quite place a finger on why. Now, following one step ahead of her partner and surrounded by five of the city's superheroes, she saw how the earlier visit had been a charade stage-managed for publicity.

No sooner had they entered the building's magnificent glass lobby, a vast atrium of crystal shards stretching up several stories, sending natural light cascading across the lobby floor in spectacular prismatic patterns, than they turned abruptly through a nondescript side door rather than continue through the grand gateway ahead. Beyond the publically accessible area of the superhero headquarters, the architecture became less decorative but certainly no less impressive. Glass and natural light was replaced by glowing white wall panels and discreet computer displays. Each door they passed was marked with a dense barcode and every corner contained a three-lensed security camera, although Sam wondered if anybody had seen these corridors outside of the Seven Wonders and their immediate associates.

Aurora strode on, forcing Sam and Joe to walk at an uncomfortably fast pace. Sam noticed that Bluebell had the same difficulty, dwarfed at her husband's side and taking small, quick steps to keep level with him. Behind them, the Dragon Star's powerstaff clacked loudly on the floor. The rhythm didn't match their walking pace, and it irritated Sam. She was wound up enough as it was; realizing she was getting unnecessarily tense, she momentarily closed her eyes and took a deep breath.

She walked straight into Aurora's back, the hot surface of his costume causing her to cry out in fright. Joe caught himself just as he was brought up short by Sam, and put a hand on her shoulder. She turned and saw the Dragon Star standing a few paces behind, her hooded and masked face looking at them.

Sam felt the hairs on the back of her neck go up. There was something about the Dragon Star that unsettled her. The superhero wasn't cold, or unfriendly. She was just... blank. Expressionless. Even SMART seemed to have more emotion.

But then not everyone was suited to small talk. Aurora handled all their PR with admirable flair.

Aurora didn't seem to notice that Sam had walked into him. He'd stopped by an elevator. Neither he nor Bluebell, nor any of the others had spoken since they had entered the building. He led them inside the elevator in silence.

The elevator took several seconds to rise, and when the double doors opened Aurora led them directly into a large conference room, a vast, triangular space that, Sam realized, matched the glass pinnacle of the Citadel. Ahead of her, the two great glass walls met, giving a spectacular view across San Ventura. The Citadel of Wonders was the tallest building in the city by at least three or four floors, allowing an almost unimpeded view across the rooftops and out to the coast.

An elliptical conference table in opaque black glass occupied the center of the room. Sam counted twelve chairs around it. As their group walked into the room, she could see that one was already occupied. Such was the splendor of the view – and of the room itself – that Sam had totally failed to see him. The man seated at the head of the table stood and briskly walked around the table to greet the party.

"Aurora, Bluebell." He nodded at the Dragon Star, Linear and Sand Cat, standing at the back of the group, then looked at the two detectives and smiled. "Detectives Millar and Milano, a pleasure to see you again." He extended a hand.

The man was dressed in a black costume, flexible but heavier than the usual spandex and covered in strategic places with sculpted body armor. The exposed fabric visible between the plates had the same metallic, scaly look as the fragment of the Cowl's cloak they'd retrieved from the alleyway. The plates met in the front to create a crucifix-shaped seam, picked out boldly in white across the chest.

The man did not wear a mask. His short brown hair was stylishly coiffed, and his warm smile showed off expensive dental work.

Aurora gestured to the man and turned to the detectives. He didn't say anything and Sam couldn't tell where he was looking, but she was sure his eyes were fixed on hers.

"Detectives," he said. "This is the eighth member of our team, Paragon. Real name..."

Sam stepped forward and took Paragon's outstretched hand. She felt breathless.

"Real name Geoffrey Conroy," she said. "I know."

They shook hands, and Conroy – Paragon – took a small bow.

"Detectives, a pleasure to see you again." He released Sam's hand and shook Joe's. Joe's grin stretched from ear to ear.

"So the Seven Wonders have a secret extra member?" Sam felt breathless at being let in on what appeared to be the city's biggest secret. The city's biggest benefactor and one of the wealthiest men in the world... was a superhero?

Sam's mind raced, and then she saw Aurora's smile twitch, just a little, just enough to indicate that something else was going on. She raised an eyebrow, and found her gaze drawn back to Conroy.

"No, detective. Mr Conroy is a new addition, one who has not been announced publically yet. Formerly, he was known as the Cowl."

Sam stared at Conroy. Conroy smiled. She heard someone else speak, but the world was suddenly packed with cotton wool.

The Cowl. The world's last supervillain. Latest member of the Seven Wonders. One of the country's richest men.

Then her ears cleared, and she felt hot, and she needed to sit down. She turned to Joe. His mouth worked up and down a little before he spoke.

"*Fuck me,*" he said.

CHAPTER THIRTY-EIGHT

The Justiciar and Blackbird flew high over San Ventura, Jeannie clutching to Tony's back as he wheeled in over the harbor, taking in a perfect view of the city as it baked in the summer sun. At this time of day, the Citadel of Wonders was a glowing crystal shard, refracting a rainbow of light across the city. As Tony weaved around the buildings, picking their approach with the mathematical precision of a fighter pilot, they were bathed in a glorious spectrum of color. He heard Jeannie laugh, the beak of her mask brushing the back of his hood, before he called over his shoulder to hang on and put her head down.

Joe saw it first, a small black object flitting across the rooftops. The meeting with the Seven Wonders had been lengthy and exceedingly dull, and it was only his inattention that alerted the others. How could a room full of superheroes not notice a speeding missile heading straight for them? Joe nudged Sam and pointed. A second later she called out to Aurora and the room exploded.

They came in out of the clear blue sky and through the observation deck-cum-conference room of the Citadel in one sudden, subsonic dive. Tony angled his body to protect Jeannie and timed a superpowered punch just as he reached touching distance of the building, shattering the window and filling the conference room with a hailstorm of deadly shards.

Tony came to a standing stop, Blackbird cartwheeling off his back, over his head and onto the conference table, where she quickly struck a fighting pose. They'd caught everyone by surprise, which was the intention, but – unfortunately – nobody seemed to have got hurt. The two detectives from the apartment were there, picking themselves up off the floor at the back of the room, with Bluebell. Aurora and the Dragon Star stood square on either side of the conference table, the leader of the Seven Wonders holding one hand out, projecting a plasma shield protecting one side of the room from the imploding window. Next to him, the Dragon Star had her powerstaff raised, emitting a similar energy shield; where the swirling red of Aurora's field met the translucent purple of the Dragon Star's, the two energies fizzed and popped. At the back of the room SMART began unfolding the arsenal hidden inside its arms and rotated its dome-like head, assessing the threat. Its maker, Hephaestus, stood by the robot's side, brandishing the massive blacksmith's hammer with one hand, and wiping his other on his dirty apron.

Standing before the destroyed plate-glass window, Tony uncurled to his full height, his long scalloped cloak sweeping across his front in the wind blowing in from fifty stories up. The breeze tugged at his hood, giving glimpses of the tight skullcap and half-mask underneath.

"Well now, they say imitation is the sincerest form of flattery." Conroy stepped out from where he had been sheltering behind SMART. As he moved forward, Jeannie dropped her fists and tilted her head in obvious surprise.

Conroy walked as close to the inside of the energy barrier as possible, and reached out a finger to touch it before pulling away and instead clasping his hands behind his back.

"Hello, Blackbird. I assume Cowl the second is something to do with you. Looking good, supervillain, even if I do say so myself." He looked Tony up and down, nodding appreciatively. "Very dramatic. Great design, isn't it?"

Tony hadn't moved; in truth he was beginning to panic. Attacking the Seven Wonders head-on sounded great back in the Lair but was now looking like a fucking stupid idea. Of course, that was why Blackbird had been the sidekick and the Cowl the boss – you could never trust a sidekick to come up with a plan. But there was something in Conroy's words: the hood, mask and swirling cloak... it had a power all of its own. Tony's fear fell away, replaced by confidence. Their entrance had certainly taken the assembled heroes by surprise.

Tony smiled at Conroy and dropped his voice to an imitation of the Cowl's characteristic growl.

"I thought the Seven Wonders had, y'know, seven members. You know this guy, Blackbird?"

She stepped back carefully, retreating along her side of the table top before hopping delicately off the end and moving backwards to stand beside Tony. She nodded, and when she spoke her voice had a low, metallic quality.

"Geoff Conroy, superpowered billionaire playboy, city benefactor, and he who used to be the Cowl." She laughed, the sound filtering through her mask like somebody rubbing bricks together. "Powerless, defenseless, he crawls to the good guys and begs for help. Pathetic."

Truth be told Tony was impressed with her attitude, but then he supposed she'd had years of practice at playing it cool. Even as she stood beside him, she'd struck a pose, legs apart, balled fists held low, head held up, the winged mask elegant and arrogant. She was a pro, no mistake about it.

Tony spoke, and taking a leaf from his partner's book, kept his voice low and even so as not to betray any emotion or surprise he felt at discovering that the Cowl hadn't left the city but had apparently swapped sides as soon as the going had got tough. Estimating the odds, he decided to take down the least-powered heroes first, which meant – apparently – Geoff Conroy, the former Cowl's powers now residing within him. Tony had wanted to rid the city of the Cowl, that was the whole point, but now seeing him switching allegiance to save his own skin, Tony felt even more disgust. Murderer and terrorist to... what? Superhero? Eighth member of the Seven Wonders? What did that say about him, or perhaps more importantly, about the superheroes themselves? Could you change sides so easily? The Cowl was an evil killer, not someone to invite around for afternoon tea.

The Dragon Star twisted her staff into a fighting posture. Tony saw the opportunity, the microscopic breach in the energy shield as the field emitted by her alien device realigned itself. From a standing start he flew forward, several inches from the floor and at near-supersonic speed, punching through the gap in the shield and tackling Conroy, forcing the superteam to separate. Pinning him with one foot, Tony brought the heel of the other down on the floor. The marble split under his boot, then shattered as the structural integrity of the floor failed. Tony leaned down and grabbed Conroy by the shoulders, before accelerating downward in flight, crashing through the floor.

In an instant, Aurora dropped his energy barrier and jumped feet first into the chasm, followed quickly by SMART, blue rocket jets firing from the bottom of its feet to control its descent.

Blackbird stood alone. The remaining superheroes were formidable opponents, although Bluebell seemed to be preoccupied attending to the detectives. Of Linear and Sand Cat, there was no sign; she presumed they had followed the other two, the speedster racing down the stairs and Sand Cat freefalling through the floors in her spirit form. Hephaestus and the Dragon Star stood together, ready for battle. Behind them, the two detectives and Bluebell were talking. Blackbird focused her mask audio on their muffled conversation, but only caught the meaningless end of it before they both darted out of the room, leaving Bluebell to face Blackbird.

Blackbird braced herself. As she tensed, she saw the Dragon Star bringing her powerstaff to bear. She smiled behind her mask.

"Bring it, bitch."

There was a crack and the wind from the broken wall gusted, causing Blackbird to sway on her feet. Then she heard a soft sound behind her, and spun around in surprise.

Linear stood behind her, arms folded, his sleek silver suit gleaming in the sunlight.

"That's no way to talk to a young lady."

Blackbird dropped to a battle stance, but she knew it was pointless. She was a champion fighter, but had only slightly augmented strength and agility. Against Hephaestus, the Dragon Star, Bluebell and Linear, she had no chance. The attack was possibly the biggest fuck-up of her entire supercriminal career.

Then again, if she was going down, she could at least break a few of their bones in the process.

She curled her left hand into a fist, said a quick prayer to the goddess of advanced body armor, and with a feint to the right hooked Linear from the left. The speedster fell for it and was propelled backwards, crashing awkwardly onto the glass-covered floor near the smashed window. Less than a second after her punch landed, Blackbird's mask picked up movement behind her as the Dragon Star shifted her grip on her powerstaff, bringing the weapon to bear as she jogged forward. Blackbird kicked backwards, throwing herself completely off balance but pushing the powerstaff back into the hero's face, to which it connected heavily. She too stumbled backwards, Bluebell stepping forward and around her as the Dragon Star collided with the conference table. The all-American beauty, all blonde hair and blue eyes, had a face as dark as a storm.

"Oh, Blackbird," she said with a smile. "I've been waiting for this for a *long* time."

They fell. As they did, Tony thought back to the bank robbery, to the first time he had met the Cowl in person. So, this was just like old times. He tightened his grip around Conroy's chest, letting just a fraction of superstrength leak out. Even with the too-long cloak flapping around his head, he heard a rib crack and Conroy yelp in pain.

The conference room had been fifty stories up. Tony's intention was to kill Conroy, but he wanted to do it with his own hands. As soon as he had broken through the floor he'd spun onto his back, holding Conroy above him as he pushed himself downwards, flying through floor after floor after floor, rending steel-reinforced concrete like tissue paper. He wanted Conroy dead, but he also wanted to frighten him a little first, terrorize him as he had done to the good people of San Ventura when he had been wearing the hooded mask, the famous cowl that had given him his name and that Tony now wore himself. Tony was pleased with the irony.

Twenty floors and the whole building shook. Positioned above Tony, Conroy had escaped major injury, but the flying debris that swarmed around the pair as they crashed through the building caught his legs and arms. Already his new costume was dirty and beaten. Tony assumed that he was now completely unpowered, which meant no matter how impenetrable the armor was, it wouldn't stop Conroy from hurting.

Twenty-five floors. They weren't alone. Tony was looking directly upwards over Conroy's shoulder. Above, the red glowing form of Aurora, arm outstretched as he flew downwards, his speed flaring his ever-present energy aura into a comet tail. From this distance, Tony could still see the smug smile, the blank white eyes, and the flaming hair pulled into the trail.

Farther up, a flickering, diffuse blue glow that hid whatever it was that made it. But it was growing bigger – Tony assumed it was the Dragon Star, or one of the other energy-based heroes.

Aurora and the blue glow were getting closer. Thirty floors. Tony put the gas on and sped away and downwards, the next floor exploding as he pushed through it. Faster. Forty floors, forty-five floors, then… space.

Tony swore and jerked a look behind him. Had he miscounted? No, it was the atrium, a five-story-high space filled with prismatic light. Which meant the next impact was going to be the big one.

The air around Tony and Conroy flashed red. Tony looked back up, and saw Aurora gathering energy from his comet tail and throwing plasma balls. But not *at* Tony, *behind* him. The plasma took a few seconds to dissipate and with careful timing, Aurora was managing to place them so the expanding globes hit Tony from behind, quite effectively keeping his hostage from harm. For Tony it was only a minor inconvenience, but it stopped him from concentrating. Which, he realized too late, was entirely the point.

Tony was also right about the next impact. This was the atrium floor, street level, the concrete thicker and laid onto a stronger steel framework that provided ground level support. Tony twisted and took the impact with a shoulder instead of his back. The shockwave vibrated through him to Conroy, who cried out in surprise and pain. But Tony didn't let the floor stop him, he powered downwards, rubble exploding out from around him. Two lower levels, much like the ones above, then space again. Tony was in unknown territory now, with no idea how far down the Citadel sublevels went. But he wanted to reach the bottom, and then bring the entire structure down on the Cowl. Flashy, theatrical, unnecessary. The perfect death for the last supervillain on Earth.

The space through which they fell confused Tony, so he turned to the vertical and slowed their descent to get a look. They were in another open chamber, larger than the atrium above but a similar shape. At floor level, the circular walls were lined with large blue server cabinets, LED indicators flickering red and green. From the ceiling hung various arms, chains, harnesses in a dozen different sizes and shapes, clawed arms and mobile platforms. The floor itself was mostly empty space, with only a few wheeled trolleys and cabinets scattered around. It looked like some kind of laboratory or, more accurately, a factory floor.

The workshop was illuminated evenly and brightly by a large circular portal in one wall. At three stories high, it was a brilliant white and yellow swirl of light and heat. The green metal door, three yards thick at least, was ajar. In front of the maelstrom, far too close for any normal person to be able to stand the heat, stood an old-fashioned blacksmith's anvil, and a bath of quenching oil. Tony realized where they were – the workshop of Hephaestus. Everyone in the city had heard of it, although none had seen it. It was too dangerous, nobody except the superheroes – and even then only four out of the seven – could enter the workshop. This was the Nuclear Forge where Hephaestus made superhero weaponry and armor. Where he had designed, shaped and hammered a robotic superhero, SMART, into being.

Tony touched down gently, releasing his bear hug around Conroy but keeping hold of him by one arm. Conroy didn't struggle as he was too busy shielding his face from the furnace. Tony wondered how long it would be before Conroy succumbed to the radiation, and then it occurred to him that he wasn't even sure he was safe himself. This wasn't the best place for a fight. If he brought the Citadel crashing down on top of his enemy, the furnace would go up and take out the entire city. That certainly wasn't the intention.

"Justiciar!"

Tony looked up and then dragged his hostage backwards, towards the Forge. Aurora swept down, hitting the spot where Tony had stood with one knee, cratering the workshop floor. He stood immediately as SMART descended on its blue rocket motors behind him. Tony looked at them both from under his hood, the famous cowl fluttering in the hot wind thundering from the open Forge behind him.

Aurora took a step forward, but seeing Tony retreat an equal distance, stopped and stepped backwards. He held a hand out, but not in anger.

"Tony, we must leave the workshop. The radiation level is too high for normal people. You and Paragon are in great danger if you do not leave now."

Aurora was one of the heroes who *could* enter the workshop. Hell, he could take a walk through the furnace, which would do nothing but recharge his energy aura. SMART was built here; the Forge was its home.

But maybe Aurora was right. Tony felt beads of sweat sliding down his forehead under his mask. He didn't sweat, not anymore, not since he became a superman. Seems he wasn't radiation-proof. Conroy practically hung from his grip, his legs bowed and eyes half-closed. A few more minutes and he'd be unconscious, the radiation poisoning irreversible. Paragon? Now there was a crappy superhero name.

This wasn't the plan. The plan had to be spectacular, historic.

Aurora spoke again, but Tony wasn't listening. He was looking up at the angled ceiling of the workshop, estimating a route. He swung Conroy by the arm, curling him into his chest, and launched himself at a seventy-degree angle. Fist held in front, Tony split the ceiling of the workshop and powered upwards.

Aurora and SMART watched his flight until the rubble from the ceiling stopped falling, but neither launched to follow. A shard of sunlight from the street above stabbed downwards, spotlighting Hephaestus' anvil.

Aurora touched his ear. "Hephaestus, the workshop is breached. Seal the damage to prevent contamination of the city. SMART and I will be in pursuit."

The communication crackled, reception affected by the radiation. Eventually the Greek's deep bass answered in the affirmative.

Aurora aimed for the ceiling breach, and looked over his shoulder at SMART.

"Let's fly."

CHAPTER THIRTY-NINE

Their original plan – such as it was – had been foiled, not by the Seven Wonders, but by his own woolly thinking. *Think*, then act. Have a plan. Consider the possibilities. Do not let emotion rule the mind.

Think.

Conroy had already begun to recover, out here in the open and the fresh air, away from the radioactive glow of the Nuclear Forge. But he didn't struggle as they flew. He was learning; Tony had all the power – *his* powers – and falling from this height would be certain death.

Not that Tony would ever let him go. Oh no. Unable to drop the Citadel of Wonders on him, Tony had settled on something far easier. But in a way, the simplicity of it would send an even stronger message, not just to the Seven Wonders but to the whole city. Execution, in public. In fact, right on the corner of Busiek and Carey – the Moore–Reppion Plaza, the busiest shopping strip in San Ventura, packed on a sunny Saturday in summer.

Tony heard Aurora's call but ignored it, not looking back. To gather his thoughts, Tony had headed east, to the outskirts of San Ventura and had begun an orbit of the city limits. Their destination was only a couple of miles from the superheroic headquarters, but Tony wanted a moment to think and decide and be sure he was right. He paused in the air high out to the west over the coast, then angled down towards the broad pedestrian mall of Lafferty Boulevard and powered forward, carrying his helpless victim with him.

People stopped, and stared, and pointed. Some smiled, enjoying what they thought was a bout of superpowered aerobatics, seeing only a fluttering cloak and lithe, costumed forms, not recognizing the black on black on black of the Cowl from this distance, nor the nondescript black armor and white cross of Paragon, a new hero they'd never even met.

As Tony got closer, some shouted, and some ran as people recognized the costume. San Ventura had a population of nearly two million. All knew what their resident supervillain looked like. Some had seen him in the flesh. A few had felt his power and witnessed his crimes at close range.

Tony smiled, and to ensure maximum attention he dived low over the ground, scattering shoppers and tourists before arcing up into the cloudless sky, catching the top of the curve in a graceful pause, then plunging down again. He hit the ground in a dramatic pose, deliberately so, causing the flashy pavement of the shopping street to crack with a gunshot report. Tony threw Conroy to one side; the former supervillain rolled to a stop and remained still.

Tony had taken too long with the display. Aurora stood on the street, a hundred yards from him, SMART towering behind. They'd been waiting.

The crowd had transformed – half had fled to nearby shops or whisked children away as they raced for parking lots, taxi ranks, anything to get away. The remainder were too foolhardy or too curious – or both – or those unable to distinguish superheroic street theater from real warfare. The crowd naturally moved into a huge circle around the superheroes and supervillain. There was sporadic applause and hoots from the more carefree members of the public.

Aurora and SMART didn't make any attempt to get any closer. Tony suspected they were enjoying the spectacle as well. And then it occurred to him: this is what superheroes do, and *especially* what superheroes in San Ventura do. True, the Seven Wonders hadn't taken down a supervillain since Green Tiger, the last supervillain but one who took a swift one-two from Sand Cat before being thrown out into the bay with a single swipe of the Dragon Star's powerstaff. But they'd done it to ordinary criminals. Powered, superpowered, unpowered. It didn't matter. It was all theater to them. Just like this. This was what they wanted. Tony spit onto the sidewalk and was sure he saw Aurora's permanent smirk twitch just a little higher.

The leader of the superheroes moved his hand to his belt and pressed a button. His voice was loud, just enough for most of the crowd to hear and for the rest to ask friends and strangers what the mighty man had said. Tony was right. Aurora's smirk was now an arrogant, lip-curling smile.

"Seven Wonders, unite!"

With the sound of a low-flying jet, a silver flash streaked just over the heads of the crowd, making a circuit of the shopping plaza before materializing just behind Aurora's shoulder. Linear's silver suit shone in the sun. From out of that sun, the Dragon Star and Bluebell descended together, each with one shapely leg bent upwards in an arrival that was clearly choreographed and much rehearsed.

A murmur rumbled through one side of the crowd, which turned to shouts of surprise as a giant cat made of blue smoke leapt clear over their heads and into the arena, an armored Grecian warrior brandishing a huge hammer skywards riding the creature's back. As soon as the spirit cat touched down, Hephaestus leapt to the ground and Sand Cat spun in mid-air, transforming into her human warrior form.

As the Seven Wonders faced Tony in Moore–Reppion Plaza, Tony's confidence slipped. He wanted to back away… but he remembered Jeannie's defiance in the face of huge odds, and held his stance, fists closed. Shit. This was exactly what they wanted. He'd fallen right into their trap.

"Give it up, Justiciar." Aurora's voice came loud and clear. The assembled spectators hushed into silence, heads turning from superhero to supervillain and back again. "There's seven of us, and one of you, and you can't win. It's time to answer to the city of San Ventura."

Would it matter if he made the first move? Should he wait and see what happened? If they attacked first, would that give him the advantage? Tony wasn't sure. Last time he'd encountered the Seven Wonders he'd fled. Flight had been more important than fight. But now the fight had arrived. He kept quiet, deciding to wait for Aurora's move.

It wasn't Aurora that acted first. Their actions were synchronized, each member of the superteam so in tune with the others that any movement one of them made was matched and complemented by the others.

Linear dissolved into a silver blur as he charged forward, while the Dragon Star ascended vertically and let out a rapid-fire barrage of energy bolts from the glowing end of her powerstaff. Tony dodged these easily, swinging to the left, directly into Linear's path. The speedster collected Tony with a Mach 1 punch to the cheek, sending him flying out of the plaza and through two nearby parked cars and the glass front of a shop. People scattered and screamed, but overall the crowd just buckled before reforming in a slightly larger circle to watch the fight.

Linear stood in the center of the boulevard, the Dragon Star alighting next to him and firing another dozen bolts into the wrecked shop front. Behind them, Aurora, Bluebell and SMART were airborne, hovering ten feet above the paving. After the Dragon Star lowered her staff, the only sound for half a minute was the bleating of car alarms and the chiming tinkle of broken glass falling. Aurora lowered himself to the ground and wound up his aura to a bright crimson glow.

Tony exited the shop at speed, diving head first towards the heroes. Knowing Aurora to be the most difficult opponent, he flicked himself towards Sand Cat, aiming for her head. Sand Cat saw this and transformed with a roar into her animal form, catching Tony in mid-flight. The pair were dragged backwards, wrestling for control. Despite her smoky, translucent appearance, Sand Cat remained a solid object, and grabbing the mane-like hair on the back of her cat form's neck, Tony managed to flip the hero onto her back, and then scooped her up by her two front paws and swung her across the road where she collided with spectators, toppling them like skittles.

Hephaestus yelled and, hammer high, charged at Tony. Tony met the hammer blow with his forearm, but the impact forced him to his knees, where a blast of blue laser from SMART's main gun arm caught him full in the side. Tony staggered sideways, only just blocking Hephaestus' second hammer blow with his other arm. Allowing the Greek's momentum to carry him awkwardly backwards, Tony rolled out and up onto his feet, swinging outward with his left leg as soon as he had purchase. His boot connected with Hephaestus' side, knocking the superhero a dozen yards away. Tony heard SMART adjust its aim, and just as the robot fired a second laser blast Tony shot upwards in flight, leaving the shot to create a smoking hole in the ground where he had been standing.

The air was a dangerous place, being the domain of the strongest of the Seven Wonders. Tony only had time to turn around his axis before blue and red globes of searing energy struck him, spinning him around in the air. Aurora and Bluebell slowly floated towards him, side by side and arms outstretched, Aurora's aura pulsing with each blast and Bluebell's blue and white suit shimmering like water as it channeled her psychic energy into an electrical attack. Tony tumbled in the air but remained aloft, crying out in agony, but he soon realized that the Cowl's suit and cloak did much to mitigate the attack. Summoning his strength, he darted upwards a few yards and with a yell threw white plasma at the husband and wife supercouple. He missed, but Aurora and Bluebell separated and ceased their own attack. On the street below the plasma exploded, throwing several members of the public into the air.

Ah... that was it. Cause havoc, attack the public. Give them reason to hate the Seven Wonders and to fear him, the Justiciar... the new Cowl.

Tony flew down towards the nearest edge of the crowd. Among the screaming and running people he picked an attractive teenage girl, plucking her skyward by the wrist. As she cried out he flew directly upwards.

She was good-looking, and young – maybe seventeen or eighteen, just on the side that any men watching the TV news would not feel too guilty lusting over. Tony allowed himself a smile as he pulled her up alongside him so they were face to face as they sped upwards.

The girl's eyes were wide but she didn't make a sound. Her mouth twitched a little as she looked around and down, seeing the ever-increasing drop between her and the city. Her eyes finally met Tony's, and seeing the black half-mask – the mask made famous by another man – in close up, she drew a breath to scream.

Tony jerked his head forward, catching her with a kiss before she cried out. She struggled a little, but at this height and being held as she was, there was little she could do. Tony finally broke it off, smiling even wider. Then at one hundred feet he dropped her, and *then* she screamed. She'd be fine, as he knew a superhero would catch her, but he'd be feared, and the standing of the Seven Wonders would drop a little as the city saw they couldn't control such an unpredictable foe.

As soon as the girl was clear, the Dragon Star materialized in the sky behind Tony's back. Tony was standing in the air, arms folded, cloak flapping around him, watching his hostage plummet. Immediately, the Dragon Star brought the end of her powerstaff to bear on Tony's back and unleashed a whip crack of energy so fierce it threw her back thirty feet in the air. She recovered, spinning the momentum out and regaining direction, swinging the powerstaff in front of her like a cutlass and sling-shotting a second energy blast. By now Tony was already tumbling towards the ground; the second shot was also on target, throwing him up and away slightly, before he returned to a downwards path, stunned and unable to control his flight. As he turned over in the air, the plaza appeared above his head and he saw his hostage caught not in the air by Aurora or Bluebell, but at ground level by Conroy.

Geoff Conroy the supervillain, the traitor. Geoff Conroy the motherfucking sell-out. The girl seemed to be unconscious and Conroy drew her carefully to the ground as Sand Cat pounded towards him to help. Then Tony's vision went black and red and he carved a trench into the road with his head. When he stopped he lay still, smoke curling from his borrowed costume.

The Dragon Star blinked out of the sky and onto the road as Aurora and Bluebell descended slowly, arms outstretched to cover the prone form of their enemy. Hephaestus and SMART were already at the edge of the trench, poised for a renewed attack, while Linear buzzed around the crowd, helping with the injured. The sound of police and ambulance sirens filled the air.

Tony remained unmoving. Hephaestus looked up at Aurora, who nodded to Bluebell. His wife returned the gesture and delicately hopped into the trench, walking with confidence up to the unconscious supervillain. Satisfied that he was out for the count, she squatted over his chest and placed one hand on his forehead and the other on her own, mirroring the finger position exactly. She closed her eyes, trying to scan his mind, gather data on his strengths, weaknesses and motivation. To assess how deep his level of unconsciousness was and, perhaps most important of all, to discover the source of his powers.

At the edge of the plaza, Conroy and Sand Cat were talking to the now-revived hostage, tearfully reunited with her friends in the crowd. Looking around, Aurora saw a sea of camera phones pointed in every direction – most at him and the churned-up road, ones closer to Conroy and Sand Cat recording their actions. A few people seemed to be smiling, perhaps having recognized the supposedly missing Geoffrey Conroy, delighted in the discovery that he was really a superhero. Leaving his wife to her business, Aurora motioned the Dragon Star and Hephaestus over, indicating the audience. They both nodded and split up, walking to opposite sides of the crowd, beginning the lengthy process of moving people along.

"Aurora." Bluebell's eyes were still closed, but her forehead was creased in confusion. "There's something wrong here. This man... his powers... they're not... they're not, well, real." She shook her head to herself, and screwing her eyes tighter she probed Tony's mind at a deeper level. Aurora joined her in the trench, standing with arms folded and with Tony's hooded head between his booted feet.

"Explain?"

Bluebell shushed him, then her expression changed, almost as though she were surprised. "Oh," she said.

With all his strength, Tony rocketed upwards, catching Bluebell under the jaw with a punch strong enough to melt stone. As she was thrown upwards, he followed a quarter of a second later with a plasma bolt, narrow and focused. Bluebell was flung out of the trench; Aurora staggered backwards and blinked, looking up just in time to see her fly through the upper stories of a nearby office block. The building shook with the impact and most of the floors she hit concertinaed downwards, smashing nearly all of the windows in the whole building. The crowd gasped and pointed; Sand Cat instinctively swirled into her animal form as the Dragon Star flew into the wreckage after Bluebell. Aurora's pause was only momentary, but enough time for Tony to turn just ten feet in the air and slam down on the superhero at twice the speed of sound. The ground exploded as Aurora and Tony disappeared five feet into the road's foundations. For a second the crowd stood silent, then gasped as the road split again in a brilliant red flash as Aurora and Tony rose back into the air, locked together in face-to-face combat. Aurora's fists glowed red as he fed them energy from his aura, and there was a gunshot crack as each blow landed or was blocked by Tony. Tony's strength and speed matched his adversary's, and the pair twisted like cats as they gained height, engaged in an aerial version of a bar-room brawl.

In the square below, the other members of the Seven Wonders were kept equally busy. The Dragon Star had still not returned from the damaged building with Bluebell, and Sand Cat had pounded off to their aid. Conroy and Hephaestus were busy among the crowd, assisting the police and ambulance services that had arrived to deal with the many injured and the few unfortunates who had been killed by Tony's actions. Linear raced among the crowd, collecting the injured and the dead.

SMART stood near the great gouge in the road, optics within its white domed head trained on the fight between Aurora and Tony. The pair had stopped gaining altitude and were now mixing superpowered fists with energy blasts, circling the arena formed by the shopping precinct as they battled.

SMART considered for a moment, calculating probability factors and power requirements. The hypothesis was sound, and the logic of the decision flawless. SMART fired the rockets in its feet and slowly lifted itself into the fray on cushions of blue flame.

If Tony noticed, he didn't pay much attention as the giant white robot hovered nearby, bouncing in the air as the rockets fought to compensate for its immense tonnage and the force of gravity. Unleashing a volley of small, fast, white plasma bolts, Tony yelled in anger and charged towards Aurora. The superhero's aura flickered yellow at the edges and expanded outwards slightly as he swept forward, arms outstretched. Tony took Aurora square in the chest, but the aura flared again and with another dynamite hook, Tony somersaulted backwards. Towards SMART.

SMART rotated twenty-two degrees east, and raised its left arm ninety degrees. The mighty fist at the end of it twisted and retracted into the arm, a spring-like metal coil sliding forward into its place. As

Tony came into range, SMART jetted forward at a slow walking pace, stretching the arm with the coil ahead of it. The coil sparked blue. Tony regained his flight balance and turned upright just as the coil came in contact with his back.

There was a wet sound, an organic *crunch*, and the air around SMART was shot through with blue ozone. Tony stiffened, back arched, and fell silently to the ground twenty feet below. He hit the ground with his neck at an odd angle, and for the second time that day did not move. SMART's feet jets fizzed blue and it sank down to the road. The crowd watching went quiet.

Aurora reached the ground before SMART did, alighting next to Tony's body. His aura faded almost to nothing as he knelt by the body.

"Aurora?" Bluebell called out as she returned to the plaza, carried in an energy bubble projected by the Dragon Star's powerstaff. She was bleeding from a cut above her eye, and held her side awkwardly. Aurora glanced up as they arrived but did not stand.

Linear and Conroy broke off from the crowd and headed to the crater in the road. Something was different this time. Hephaestus' giant robot had descended very slowly and was the last to set down. Conroy squeezed himself into the silent circle. All were looking down at Tony. He tapped Linear's elbow discreetly.

"What's going on? Is the jackass down or what?"

Linear turned to Conroy, his face a smooth silver curve that shone in the sunlight. Paragon could hear the superhero breathing underneath it. Then Linear looked away.

Aurora stood. For the first time, the smile was gone. Even the empty white eyes of the mask seemed now to impart an emotion, the same registered by the slack jaw. Paragon glanced at the circle of heroes. All stared blankly, in shock.

"What? What's going on?"

It was Linear who spoke, his voice weak.

"He's dead. The Justiciar is dead, and we killed him."

CHAPTER FORTY

Sam's stomach flipped as the world pulled itself back together, black and white digital squares coalescing before her eyes until she could see the room she was in. She felt the floor rise up to meet the soles of her feet with a kick, and she bent double at the shock. She felt a hand on her back, and looked up to see Joe standing upright but loosening his tie and breathing deeply.

She knew what the odd sensation was, having been through it once before when the entire SVPD building had been sent to Australia. Teleporting just sucked.

They stood in a glass atrium, a smaller version of the entrance to the Citadel of Wonders in San Ventura. But through the twisted, elegantly fractured crystal shard windows, it wasn't the streets of a busy city on view. Sam stood up and felt immediately dizzy. She could hear Joe's breath catch in his throat as he worked his jaw to say something, but no words came out. He just looked out of the transparent walls of the atrium with wide-eyed surprise.

They were on the moon.

"Shit." Sam was impressed with the view, but her mind had difficulty registering the fact that they'd been transported a quarter of a million miles in a fraction of a second. The last thing she remembered was manning the phones at the SVPD, her and Joe having been sent there by Bluebell not only for their own safety, but to help liaise with the SVPD and prepare the authorities for the potentially city-wide carnage that was likely to ensue as the superheroes fought Tony Prosdocimi, who seemed to have become the new Cowl.

Sam had heard of the Apollo Fortress – everyone had – but she couldn't remember the last time it had been activated. But she guessed that whatever the reasons, they could not be good. Something must have gone wrong, badly.

Sam registered Joe's sharp intake of breath behind her but it wasn't until he tapped her on the shoulder that she could drag herself from the view of the gray plains and craters outside. A maskless Linear shimmered into view, his outline blurry as he vibrated in agitation. He waved a hand in apology and returned to something more solid and less headache-inducing.

"Detectives." He nodded in greeting and adjusted the thick spectacles on his nose. "This way, please." Turning, he led the pair to the main elevator.

The ride was short, nothing like the two-minute journey back in the Citadel of Wonders. The Apollo Fortress was only a few stories high, a truncated version of the Citadel. The remote outpost had been an important surveillance point when the thousands of superheroes of the world were at war with the hundreds of supervillains. In those days, the small lunar base would have been swarming with capes from every country and jurisdiction. Now the base was quiet and still, although immaculate and polished as though it had never really been mothballed at all. The thought that maybe it never had crossed Sam's mind as the elevator swished open, Linear stepping forward and leading them into a conference room.

This room was far less flashy than the Earth equivalent. The low, dark ceiling gave the room an urgency, an importance. Here the windows were flat glass instead of the artistically angled crystal; outside, the moon's horizon loomed uncannily close.

Aurora rose from his position at the head of the table. There were five people seated before him: three of the superteam, Sand Cat, the Dragon Star and now Linear, and...

Sam sucked in a breath. She'd thought, maybe, somehow, it had been a mistake, or a temporary reassignment, or some devilishly complex and cunning plan to get him to reveal his secrets and plans before handing him to the proper authorities for his trial and sentencing. In the confusion of the Justiciar's attack she'd managed to forget, temporarily at least, pushing it out of her mind as she'd dived in to help with the emergency. But surely...

"He's still here?" Sam stared at San Ventura's most eligible bachelor and most wanted criminal. Conroy smiled, his high cheeks squeezing his eyes into tight lines.

"Detectives," he said, but he hardly moved in his chair. It looked like he'd taken quiet a beating.

Joe and Sam looked at each other. Seeing Sam was almost unable to speak, Joe addressed Aurora. "So you're serious about recruiting a murderer and terrorist for your little primary-color glee club?"

Aurora shook his head and indicated for the pair to sit. He remained standing as he addressed them.

"There will be time for explanations later. Detectives, I thank you for coming, although I know you had no choice in the matter. I trust your captain will understand your sudden absence." His smile crept upwards a little. "Or at least he will when I tell him."

Sam closed her eyes, and focused on keeping calm. The Seven Wonders would explain everything. Aurora had said so.

For the meantime, her disgust – and fear – of being in the same room as the Cowl melted into anger and frustration. There was no reason for her and Joe to be here. A secret meeting of the superheroes and her and Joe and an ex-supervillain, sitting at the table like he was an old friend. She and Joe had a job to do, with the destruction at the Moore–Reppion Plaza requiring all members of the SVPD to pitch in. Meanwhile the instigators of – the cause, the goddamned *reason* for – the whole mess zoom off to the *fucking moon* for a meeting, abducting her and her partner by teleport without the consent or knowledge of their captain. Teleport! It was abduction, pure and simple.

But she held her tongue, deciding to bide her time and was glad that Bluebell wasn't in the room. She presumed that the psychic hero would be interrogating Blackbird, no doubt also brought to the moon. But instead, she asked: "What does this have to do with us? We have work to do."

Aurora sat, but he seemed hesitant. Around the table, none of the heroes would meet each other's gaze. Instead they looked variously at the table, at the ceiling, out the window. Everywhere except at Aurora. The only one not distracted appeared to be Conroy. He sat in the middle of the superheroes, hands clasped on the table in front of him. He was waiting for someone to speak, for Aurora to explain the situation, for the other heroes to put their word in. Sam tried not to look at him, but it was impossible, the urge too difficult to resist. Maybe, if she had a chance...

"Where's SMART and Hephaestus? What happened to the Cowl II?" Joe said at last. At his words a ripple of movement shot around the table as the heroes first looked at Joe, then at Aurora.

Aurora's heavy gloves pattered softly on the conference table. He seemed to be staring into the middle distance, but with eyes hidden behind the opaque white windows of his mask it was impossible to tell. That was the point, Sam remembered.

Aurora seemed to sigh, and Sam noticed Conroy settle slightly in his own chair. Still nobody spoke. Joe and Sam exchanged a glance, and then both started a little as Conroy coughed to break the deathly silence and began talking quickly, almost afraid that he would be interrupted before finishing his piece.

"Well now, Bluebell is in the infirmary. She got beat up nicely, but she'll be fine."

Of course, Bluebell didn't need to interrogate Blackbird, if indeed Blackbird was in custody. With Conroy at the table, Bluebell could read the secrets straight from his mind. Blackbird was an accessory – as guilty as Conroy, but useless for information.

Conroy coughed again.

"Hephaestus is busy rebooting his big honking robot downstairs. Seems the Supra-Maximal Attack-Response Titan has a little glitch in his AI that makes him look for... permanent, shall we say... solutions to battles."

Sam cocked her head. "Permanent?" A light eyebrow raised itself at the question. Conroy shuffled a little and coughed again and Aurora took up the explanation.

"SMART killed the Justiciar, aka Tony Prosdocimi, thereby breaking the primary clause of the International Superheroic Justice Pact." He looked at Sam but Sam found herself staring at Conroy again. Under her gaze his internationally famous playboy grin became fixed and cold. Sam felt ill.

Joe leaned back in his tall conference chair. The leather creak that accompanied the movement ricocheted around the quiet room, causing him to wince, then he leaned forward and he folded his arms.

"Well," he said. "That shits that up, doesn't it? The Seven Wonders kill someone and recruit their sworn enemy as a new member of the superteam. You guys need to work on your PR."

Sam pursed her lips, glanced around the downcast heroes. "So the Seven Wonders broke the golden rule, and are hiding on the moon?" She almost laughed at the childishness of it. Aurora had his head inclined, as if he was studying the table, but she could *feel* his eyes watching her. She turned back to Conroy, who looked ridiculous in his black and white costume. It must have been a cast-off from a forgotten superhero, mothballed in the Citadel of Wonders. The Churchwarden, perhaps.

"What's this got to do with us?" Sam waved in Joe's direction before continuing. "And what the hell are you doing here, Mr Conroy? Forgive me, but I'm finding it a little difficult to believe you've renounced your ways and have become the model superhero."

Seated on her left, Linear let out a low whistle and looked away from Sam, who just caught the look on his face before he turned. Awkwardness, embarrassment even. Aurora's gauntlet creaked slightly as he flexed a fist.

Conroy looked at Sam for a moment, then laughed. The humor seemed genuine, and it annoyed Sam. She felt like she'd become the butt of a private joke, but none of the other heroes were laughing. As Conroy's laugh receded, he sighed and the real smile reappeared.

"I've had much to think about recently. I lost my way, but I found an old friend. Friends, actually. Then I had... well, an epiphany. Plain as that. I could talk about the scales falling and seeing the... well, never mind. I came to the Seven Wonders, and they gave me a new name: Paragon. This represents what I've become. You may not believe a man can change, but trust me, he can. If I were not a reformed character, I would hardly be seated at this table."

Sam's world went fuzzy at the edges. The only thing she could remember later was asking someone for a glass of water before she pulled out her gun. Her hand wobbled and her aim was clumsy, but in a red haze she eventually managed to level the weapon across the table at Conroy, who had stopped smiling.

Time slowed. Next to her, Joe leapt from his chair and drew his own weapon through a sea of treacle. Sam watched him lazily out of the corner of her eye then refocused and squinted down the barrel of her gun, which drooped down and to the right, no matter how hard she concentrated on keeping it still. Someone yelled; Sam realized it was her, then she squeezed the trigger. The gun bucked in her hand once, twice, three times. Her scream continued long after she emptied the magazine.

Aurora was standing at the head of the table, one hand outstretched and glowing red. At the opposite end of the table, the Dragon Star also stood, her powerstaff held aloft and pointing not at Sam but at her gun hand.

The air between Sam and Conroy glowed blue and red. Sam could see the neat row of bullets, some heading to the target, some angled badly and heading for the walls or the table. They were caught in two force fields, one from Aurora and one from the Dragon Star. Sam felt faint as she realized what she'd done, then angry that she'd been stopped, then relieved that the rash action – which she would live to regret, she knew that – had been prevented.

She slumped back into her chair. Joe remained standing, gun raised but unfired. Hovering within the force field in front of Conroy, the bullets lost form and began to melt. The Dragon Star snapped her staff back and the blue portion of the field evaporated. Aurora twisted his hand, accelerating the melting process, and when the bullets were floating spheres of silver, he let them drop to the table. They splatted, splashing hot liquid towards Sam and Conroy. She flinched, he didn't. He wasn't smiling.

"There will be no more killing at our hands." Aurora's voice commanded the room, causing everyone to look in his direction. He leaned forward on the table with two balled fists. "Mr Conroy is now a member of the Seven Wonders. He is highly trained, and his skills and experience will be effectively used. He is an exemplar to all the citizens of San Ventura. A *paragon* and–"

"He's a murderer and a terrorist." Sam found her voice and barked the rebuttal angrily at Aurora. "We've spent years trying to bring him down by legal means. And isn't he the whole reason why the Seven Wonders are still active?"

Aurora raised himself from the table and slowly paced behind the seated heroes, his shock of gray hair waving in his crackling aura.

"… *and*," he said, continuing past Sam's interruption, "he will answer for his crimes according to international law. He has offered this condition himself, to turn himself in to the United Nations once his work is done. But for now he will begin repayment to the city of San Ventura by serving us. He came to us for salvation, not just for himself, but for the city itself. He has information to share, and we shall hear it."

Aurora came to a stop behind Sam's chair and she saw Joe shrink back as much as he could as the unhealthy heat radiating from the atomic superhero wafted over them like a desert breeze. Sam looked up at Aurora, shaking slightly, then back to Conroy.

"Why now?"

Conroy held his hands above the table, like he was at a classroom show-and-tell.

"I'm powerless. I've lost it all – in fact, my powers were stripped one by one and given to the now-deceased Justiciar."

"Given?"

Aurora took up the question. "Blackbird is in possession of a device which transfers superpowers. Paragon's account corresponds to the actions of the device."

Conroy laughed. "Quite a little toy she had, and I had no idea." He looked at Aurora. "Was she brought here too?"

Aurora nodded.

Sam leaned forward. "So, epiphany, you say? Don't tell me you mean in the Biblical sense?" She glanced at the peculiar white cross pattern on his chest, like he was some kind of crusader.

"Just so," said Conroy, smiling now. "With no power I am a mortal human like the two million people of the city. I finally saw the world through their eyes. They don't require subjugation, they require *representation*. Everyone in the world does. If I'd turned myself over to you, I'd be rotting in jail or most likely executed. My fate, I think, lies with the United Nations, and the Seven Wonders have promised to hand me over to them when my assistance is no longer required. But at the moment, we face a grave threat, one that I have knowledge of and that I can help with. Without me, San Ventura will fall. Perhaps the whole world will."

Joe remained silent. Sam stared at Conroy, not quite believing what she was hearing. She looked around the table – Sand Cat, the Dragon Star, Linear, Aurora. All were looked at her, nobody saying anything. She turned back to Conroy.

"You murdered my husband, asshole." Her heart thundered in her chest, so hard and so loud she was convinced it could be heard from the Earth.

Linear fiddled with his glasses.

Conroy sat back, a frown crossing his billion-dollar good looks. He flicked a hand through his fringe. "I killed a lot of people, detective. And I shall pay for those crimes when the time is right."

Sam slapped the table hard and launched herself across the black glass surface as far as she could from a seated position. Conroy jerked back and Sam fell back into her chair, Joe's hands on her shoulders as he whispered to her to keep it cool. Sam closed her eyes and breathed deeply.

Aurora tapped his hand on the back of Sam's chair, then quickly strode back around the table to his position at the head, apparently ignorant of her obvious distress.

"Ladies and gentlemen, we face an infinite crisis," he said as he stretched his arms out to rest on the conference table. It was an imposing, powerful piece of body language. Aurora was in charge, and he was talking.

"I apologize to you, detectives, for taking you away from your valuable work protecting the citizens of San Ventura, and I am also sorry, Sam, that you were not prepared to face Paragon. As you know, the Seven Wonders regret the loss of Detective David Millar. He was a fine officer and instrumental in the creation of the SVPD SuperCrime department."

Sam eased herself from Joe's grip and wiped her eyes and nose. She jabbed a finger in Aurora's direction. "You're sorry, Mr Superman? Is that one of your superpowers? You're harboring a criminal, a *murderer.* How does that work, huh? He murdered my husband and took over my life. He's killed hundreds, thousands, reduced parts of the city to ruin, made the whole place almost unlivable with the threat of his superterrorism hanging over everyone." Suddenly Sam found that she was on her feet, but she didn't care. Her hands gesticulated with each point, her voice rising in volume. "And now we find out who the Cowl really is, that he's been under our noses all the time, with the city and the police – with *us* – in his pocket, and you say he's sorry and he won't do it again and that's just OK with you, huh?" She turned to face the imposing, silent leader seated at the far end of the table. "You're supposed to protect us, Aurora. Protect me, Joe, our friends and families. The friends and families of everyone in the city. They used to call San Ventura the 'Shining City'. Look at it now. All thanks to that man."

The heroes remained silent. Sam saw that the Dragon Star and Linear had bowed their heads, clearly hurt by the truth of Sam's outburst. She was sure the superheroes were good people; that was what they were, what they had to be.

But Sand Cat and Aurora did not bow their heads. Sand Cat held her jawline high, ever the proud warrior. Aurora remained still, his face characteristically unreadable. Those two were hardly fucking human anyway.

And Paragon – Geoff Conroy – the Cowl. He sat opposite Sam, regarding her with what really did look like genuine concern. Maybe Bluebell had done a mind trick on him to get him to cooperate. Huh. It was years too late for that.

Aurora sighed. It came as a surprise to everyone. The great and powerful leader showing... emotion?

"You are correct, detective," he said. "That is why I have brought us all to the Sea of Serenity. We have failed the city. We have failed the world. We have failed you, Sam, and you, Joe. We have failed your husband. We have failed your friends and your families. We have squandered our power and influence and grown complacent. It was Paragon that first opened my eyes to the fact – our endless war with the Cowl was a farce, a pointless, futile exercise prolonged by both sides as... as a *game*. And for that I am deeply ashamed."

The superhero stood, and turned his back to the table. Hands clasped behind his cloak, he walked to the vast glass wall and looked out over the inky dark of the moon. Just on the short horizon a diamond of light was growing. Earthrise.

"But today was our ultimate failing, an event which has settled my mind on the course I considered when Paragon first came to us to beg forgiveness. We have broken the one rule that all superheroes must live and die by. We have misused our powers. We have killed another. This is not acceptable, and we regret the loss."

He turned to face the room, looking at Sam and Joe. "That is why you are here, detectives. You represent the finest San Ventura has to offer. We represent the worst. For that reason, once the current crisis is resolved, the Seven Wonders will cease to exist. With the threat of the Cowl eliminated, we have little function, and because of our very nature we pose a danger to the city which we are supposed to protect.

"All law enforcement and security will pass immediately to the San Ventura Police Department. We will transfer all of our records and research to you, detectives. I hope you will act as our go-betweens during the transition period." Aurora sat at the table. Of the heroes, only Linear made a sound, fidgeting with his silver gloves which he had taken off and placed on the table top in front of him.

Joe cleared his throat, and without moving Aurora spoke his name. Joe sat up and adjusted his jacket.

"I hope you don't mind me speaking freely, sir, but hiding on the moon after a single accident doesn't seem to be the best decision. You guys are the best, you're the superheroes, you're an example to the people. Did you see how many people had crowded the plaza to watch your fight? The city is on your side. Surely rather than give up you could just..." Joe struggled to find the right word. "... mend your ways."

"And did you see how many of these good citizens were injured or even killed?" Sand Cat now, her deep, exotic accent a sharp contrast to everyone else. Her eyes flicked towards their leader. "Aurora is right. We cannot continue. There is no need for us anymore."

"Erm, excuse me." Conroy was leaning back in his chair, rocking slightly but hadn't quite got around to putting his feet up on the table. His hand was raised, like a prize pupil trying to get the teacher's attention. "You've got no supervillain to fight, I have to agree there. But you are needed. As the good detective here says, you don't just protect the city, you represent the city. To those who live there and even to those who don't. You are a symbol for the whole country, maybe even the world. The Seven Wonders *are* San Ventura, California."

He paused, waiting for a reaction, but not getting one. Of the people around the table, only Joe and Linear were looking at him. He slapped the table in frustration.

"No offense, detectives, but I don't see the SVPD doing much good against the invasion."

Aurora, Sand Cat and Sam turned to Conroy. The Dragon Star dropped her head, the edge of her wide hood hiding her face.

Linear began buzzing in his chair, a clear sign of agitation and worry.

"Invasion?" he asked, eyes torn between Conroy and his leader. "Nobody said nothing about no invasion."

Sand Cat and Linear exchanged a worried look.

Conroy's smile flickered on and off for a few seconds as he looked at each of the heroes around the table in turn. Emotionless Aurora, proud Sand Cat, unreadable Dragon Star. Only Linear seemed like a natural, regular guy. His silver eyebrows were raised high on his forehead in surprise.

Conroy laughed nervously. "The invasion, yes. The Thuban? The crisis that Aurora just spoke of." He paused, and scanned the room before setting his eyes on Aurora. "You have briefed everyone… haven't you?"

Everyone in the room looked at the leader of the Seven Wonders. To Sam, the whole conversation – no, the whole *day* – had turned into a surreal nightmare. Her head was beginning to ache.

Again, it was Linear who broke the uncomfortable silence.

"No, he hasn't."

Sand Cat thudded the table with a fist. "I am not aware of any 'invasion'." She turned slowly in her chair to face Conroy, eyes dark and brow furrowed.

But now it was Conroy's turn for surprise. "You must know – the Thuban are coming. They've sent an object hidden in the Draconid meteor storm, and once their target is located, they're going to sweep in and pick up the pieces."

Aurora remained silent. Sand Cat turned away from Conroy and toward her leader, but he was still staring at the table, expression frozen.

"This is the first I have heard of this. Why have we not been informed? And why did Paragon not tell us all earlier?"

When Aurora still refused to answer, Conroy laughed in exasperation. "I intercepted Thuban transmissions picked up from your own surveillance satellites. As the Cowl I was in direct contact with the Thuban – I was helping their plans, building a little device for them. Hell, that's why I went after your living vaults, grabbing their secrets. That's why we carried out those raids. But the initial comms were routed through your systems, which I patched into. You *must* know. The communications were two-way. Threat, counter-threat. Someone responded before I did."

Aurora stood quickly, Sand Cat and Linear practically jumping out of their chairs at the same time. The three exchanged glances that, Sam knew, carried a lot of information. You didn't work as a close-knit team of superheroes without knowing what your colleagues were thinking. They didn't need Bluebell for that.

Aurora motioned for the others to sit.

"Like Paragon, I had been intercepting the transmissions as well. But, my friends, I had to be sure. Now with the problem of the Cowl and the Justiciar resolved, it is time to focus on the real threat."

Behind her seat, Sam heard the Dragon Star click her powerstaff against the hard floor. She had remained standing during the meeting, out of her eye line; now, glancing back, she felt that same creepy feeling as she looked at the superhero's expressionless face. The Dragon Star's eyes were downcast, like she was ignoring everyone and everything in the room. Or avoiding eye contact with Aurora. Sam turned back to the table.

Aurora reached down and touched a dull square on the table which Sam hadn't noticed. The panel flicked to a bright red with a beep; looking at the table top, Sam saw that the whole surface was actually covered with touch-sensitive displays. It was an impressive piece of tech.

Aurora spoke into the air as the comm link opened. "SMART, report

ConSat surveillance log and confirm transmission records." The comm beeped off, and Aurora waited for the reply. None came. He pressed the link again.

"SMART, are you back online yet? Report please."

Beep. Silence.

"Hephaestus, what is your status? SMART is offline."

Beep. Silence.

Linear vanished in a silver cloud and reappeared at Aurora's side. He waved a hand over the controls on the table in front of the leader's chair. Several colored panels lit, including a larger rectangular screen that seemed to be an internal security camera. Linear waved his hand, flipping through several views as Aurora watched over his shoulder.

There was a bang, loud enough that Joe and Sam stood and looked instinctively to the door behind them, past the immobile form of the Dragon Star. But the sound had come from Linear's surveillance panel. He and Aurora looked at each other, then Aurora punched another panel on the table.

"Bluebell?"

The link hissed, then her voice came through with a pop, halfway through a sentence.

"... response negative. Aurora?"

"Aurora reading."

"What's going on in the dome? SMART is undertaking unscheduled systems maintenance. I just had the lights go in the infirmary."

"Bluebell, are you still there? Where are SMART and Hephaestus? Have you seen them? They should be in the workshop."

"Goddess protect me."

Aurora and Linear turned at Sand Cat's exclamation. She was standing at the observation window. She looked over her shoulder at the others and pointed to something outside. Aurora and Linear were joined by Joe, Sam and, at a distance, Conroy. Sam edged over to place Joe between her and the ex-supervillain.

On the lunar surface, the perfect, sharp lines of the landscape were marred by a gray and white cloud that hung low on a flat plain, just outside one wall of the Apollo Fortress that curved around and out of sight.

"Dust?" Linear asked. Sand Cat shook her head.

"Look."

The dust was fine and would take hours to settle completely, but had already cleared enough to reveal another shape. Something long, bulky, its pink and brown color contrasting sharply with the monochrome of the lunar surface.

It was a body.

Aurora's aura flared deep red, causing Sam, Joe and Conroy to recoil from the sudden flash of heat.

The comm fizzed again and Bluebell's voice echoed digitally through the room.

"Aurora, it's SMART. I think it's killed Hephaestus."

CHAPTER FORTY-ONE

There was movement outside, near the cloud of dust settling over the body of the dead god. Sam leaned in on the window, its ice-cold surface prickling her fingertips as she touched it.

There, just around the corner of the building, in the bright Earthlight something white flashed.

"There's something out there," she said.

Aurora nodded. Sam found Sand Cat squeezing in beside her for a better view. The warrior's rich, earthy scent filled her nostrils. Outside, another brilliant stab of light reflected off the white object as it moved away from the steely gray of the fortress.

"It's SMART. What's it doing?" Aurora's question was more to himself than the others in the room, but the words reflected what everyone was thinking.

The robot walked toward the body of its creator, paused, and walked back to the airlock which lay just out of sight. As SMART moved out of view, the faint sound of the airlock door being closed and locked echoed, the slight vibration carried not through the airless vacuum outside but through the fabric of the Fortress itself. A moment later and Sam thought she could hear its footfalls echoing through the base, but it might have been her own heartbeat.

Then the group heard the sound of the airlock being opened. Joe glanced at the ceiling.

"What's it doing?" he asked.

Aurora was scanning the view outside. "SMART is still outside."

Linear buzzed around the room, investigating every possible viewing angle offered by the observation windows, before returning to the group. He stopped next to Aurora and looked up at their leader, who stood nearly a full foot taller than he.

"Maybe it's bugged? It killed the Justiciar and now Hephaestus, against all superhero code and international law… maybe it's stuck in some kind of error loop?"

Sand Cat raised an eyebrow. "SMART is a machine intelligence, a digital mind all of its own. It is one of us. If it has broken the laws of Earth, it was its own decision." She didn't take her eyes off the robot as she spoke.

Aurora flicked the comm on his belt. "Bluebell, are you still in the infirmary?"

The comm fizzed with static, making Bluebell's reply difficult to understand. "No, I'm in the lower control room near the workshop. The power went out in the infirmary so I went to check the systems. I just walked in when I saw SMART blow the workshop airlock and throw Hephaestus out."

"Are you able to fight?"

More static. "Yes, I'm fine, really."

"Check on Blackbird and make sure the detention zone is secure. I'm sending Linear to assist you. All superheroes are to work in pairs until we have the situation contained."

Bluebell's voice briefly replied, then clicked out with a pop and another burst of static. A new voice entered the conversation, recognizably male but oddly accented. Synthesized.

"All members of the Seven Wonders will remain where they are until I can attend to them." There was something in SMART's voice that made even Aurora's face tighten. Sam felt Joe's hand on her shoulder, and they exchanged a worried look.

Aurora clicked the comm. "SMART, this is a priority command. Return to the workshop and set power to standby. Initiate systems backup and shutdown. Confirm, please."

The channel was filled with empty static.

"SMART, confirm, please."

The static cleared. "All members of the Seven Wonders located.

Please await assistance," came the robotic voice. The calmness of it was dreamlike.

Linear swore and tore his glasses off. Without them, he looked even older. Sam was fascinated – morbidly, she realized. The price he paid for his accelerated life.

Outside, SMART finally broke its looped routine and thudded back to the airlock, the vibration of its footfalls declining in amplitude as the artificial gravity field of the fortress compensated for its weight. Aurora swung away from the observation windows and returned to his position at the head of the conference table. Without sitting, he swept a hand across the touch panels embedded in the glass surface. An alert sounded and a series of scrolling red characters spun across the table top.

"I've locked the inner airlock door, permanently," Aurora said, tapping the display. "It won't keep it out, but it will slow it down." He flicked on the comm on his belt. "Bluebell, Linear will meet you in the cells. Stay there to ensure the safety of our prisoner. Sand Cat and the Dragon Star will secure the workshop."

Conroy stepped toward Aurora. "Ah, Aurora? You're sending the Dragon Star with Sand Cat? Don't you think, ah, we should keep an eye on... *her*?"

Sam looked at Joe, and together they looked at the Dragon Star. For once, the hero was holding her head high, allowing the deep, wide white hood to fall back slightly. She looked young, just a teenager, half the age of the second youngest person in the room, which Sam realized was probably her. Sam remembered the odd way in which the Dragon Star was detached from the previous conversation, and the look that Aurora had given her. What else did Conroy know about the impending invasion? More to the point, what did the Seven Wonders know but weren't saying?

"The Dragon Star's powerstaff will be needed to contain SMART. She and Sand Cat will secure the workshop." Aurora spun on his heel and looked down at his temporary recruit. "It is you and I who need to talk, Mr Conroy."

Conroy looked around the heroes in the room, then back at Aurora, his eyes squinting with confusion. "Aurora, the Dragon Star–"

he indicated the superhero standing nearby, waving a hand up and down her length like he was a used car salesman "–the entity that animates this body, anyway – *is* Thuban. You guys never got the transmissions, yet I picked up two-way coded messages exchanged between the Seven Wonders' surveillance network and the Thuban themselves. What's going on, Aurora?"

Finally Aurora let his emotion slip. Sam understood totally – the very foundation of the superheroes and their declaration of protection, not just over San Ventura, but over the whole world – had been badly shaken by the death of Tony. Now SMART's malfunction was confirmed, the robot killing its creator and now intent, apparently, on doing the same to everyone else in the Apollo Fortress. And to top it off, the world was being threatened by an alien menace linked somehow to the Dragon Star, which only Conroy knew about, and only because he intercepted secret transmissions coming from within the Seven Wonders themselves.

Only Conroy... and Aurora, Sam realized with a start. Their own leader, keeping secrets.

The superheroes had been shaken to their core, so perhaps it was no wonder Aurora blew his stack. Metaphorically speaking; if it had been literal, chances were this side of the lunar surface would have had a brand-new crater smoking in the Earthlight.

The leader of the Seven Wonders turned on Conroy, his plasma aura flaring bright scarlet fringed with magnesium white. All in the room recoiled from the sudden glare, and Conroy stumbled backward as the edge of the energy field threatened to lick him. Aurora's eyes, those featureless, blank ellipses, flared white with the same limelight intensity. His characteristic enigmatic smile twisted into a snarl.

"Don't presume to instruct me, Cowl!" The volume of his voice was almost as shocking as his flaming appearance. Sam noted how he had slipped and referred to their new recruit by his old supervillain name. Sam had seen many superhero battles – hell, battles between Aurora and the Cowl, the pair now standing just a few feet from her in the same room – but had never seen a superhero lose their cool. And she never wanted to again, glimpsing as she could now a tiny fraction of the power the atomic superhero had at his disposal. The power of the heart of the sun itself.

Aurora took a step towards Conroy, who fumbled behind him with one hand as he hit a conference chair, and tumbled to the floor. The Dragon Star shuffled slightly, and Sam noticed her hand was gripping her inert powerstaff like a vise, stretching the thin white fabric of her elbow-length gloves tightly over the back of her knuckles.

"Sand Cat, with me." Out of her usual silent character, the Dragon Star's assertive instruction seemed to catch even Aurora and the other heroes by surprise. Aurora's blaze faded back to an angry, but more usual, level, while Linear and Sand Cat just stared at her. Her wide hood shifted as she regarded her compatriots. She tapped the end of her powerstaff loudly against the floor and the length of the weapon lit with energy. Sam's nose crinkled as she smelt something hot and electrical and her mouth was filled with the taste of battery acid.

The Dragon Star lifted off the floor and flew across the conference room, disappearing through the main door. Sand Cat leapt into the air, tumbling gymnastically as she did before landing back on the floor as a vast, spectral cat. She galloped out of the room.

Ignoring Conroy, who hadn't moved from the floor, Aurora turned back to his control board.

"Linear?" he asked, without turning.

"On my way," said the older hero, placing his thick-framed glasses carefully in the breast pocket concealed under his sprint suit. He buzzed to the table to collect his gloves and mask, then was gone.

Beside Sam, Joe sighed in relief, perhaps happy at least that the room now had fewer angry superheroes in it. Conroy clattered a chair clumsily as he pulled himself to his feet. Aurora continued to ignore him, his attention instead on the large display in the table surface, which now showed an aerial view of the workshop and airlock bay.

A deep metallic smack resonated through the base. Joe darted to the observation window, then waved for Sam to join him.

As the pair watched, clouds of dust billowed up from the lunar surface in slow motion as the walls of the base shook. Sam walked back to the table and looked down at Aurora's display. On a security feed trained on the workshop inner airlock, the doors started to buckle as SMART attempted to punch its way back into the base. The Dragon Star walked into the view of the camera, and they watched as she angled her powerstaff and threw up a green and blue cone of energy over the door, trying to keep the powerful robot out, while the spirit animal form of Sand Cat paced impatiently back and forth behind her.

Joe looked over his shoulder at Sam, almost to check whether she was still there, and then looked up at Aurora. Aurora's face was less angry now, although his expression was firm. The white eyes of his mask flickered occasionally, almost as if he were blinking.

"We don't want to be in your way," Joe began slowly. He was nervous, and Sam couldn't blame him. She was downright terrified, not just because they seemed to be right in the middle of the disintegration of the Seven Wonders, on the moon, with a homicidal robot trying to kill everyone in the base. She'd seen the rage in Aurora's eyes.

"But," Joe continued, "is there anything we can do?"

Aurora stood from the table, his composure restored in a second. "Indeed there is, detective. *Detectives.*" Aurora stood and joined Joe at the observation windows, motioning for Sam to follow. "We will be able to secure the base, have no fear. But Paragon and I will be needed presently. We are below strength now, and I meant what I said about cooperation. If you would join Bluebell and Linear in the detention zone, I would be much obliged."

Joe nodded. Sam instinctively checked she still had her pistol; her hands met her empty holster, and with a start she remembered it was at the other end of the table, empty of bullets. So, that really had happened after all.

"Happy to help," Joe said with a smile. Sam nodded, still in a daze. Aurora watched the dust clouds outside and flicked his belt comm. "Bluebell? The detectives will be joining you in the detention zone. Release Blackbird, but keep her secure. We may need to move the prisoner quickly."

The comm popped. "Understood."

Aurora swung around to Conroy, aura flashing just slightly. Conroy – as Paragon – did not wear a mask, and his fear was clear to see.

"You and I need to talk, Mr Conroy."

CHAPTER FORTY-TWO

Sam snapped the magazine back into her pistol, and gripped the weapon in both hands with practiced ease as she and Joe rounded another corner inside the moonbase. At least the superteam kept an arsenal of regular ammunition   not that the gun was of any use other than making her feel better. Joe proceeded ahead of her, his own gun at the ready. Sam knew they were over-reacting, knew there was no point in brandishing the weapons, knew that there was nothing to shoot at, and if SMART somehow made it past the heroes in the workshop, bullets wouldn't have any effect anyway.

But the gun made her feel better. It shouldn't have, she knew that. Feeling safe and secure when holding a gun was entirely the wrong path, especially for an officer of the law. But just for now she gave in to her feelings, and let the tension and anger guide her, within limits. Darth Vader would have been proud. That thought made her smile, despite the turmoil of emotions in her mind. Then she remembered what uncontrolled emotion had done earlier in the conference room, and she relaxed her grip on the gun's handle, just a little. She thought of David and what he might have done in her position.

Joe held a hand up, bringing her to a halt. Around the next corner was the main elevator. The lights and life support were on in this section, and the green LEDs of the elevator control panel shone brightly. This part of the base, at least, was unaffected by SMART's shutdown. Sam figured that the robot had more important things to worry about downstairs. And it seemed like it didn't want to freeze or asphyxiate everyone in the base. It wanted to kill with its own hands. Sam thought back to what Sand Cat had said, and wondered if SMART was a machine complex enough to have a truly independent, artificial intelligence. It had been designed and built by someone out of myth, after all.

The air buzzed between her and Joe, and a light gray blur refocused to reveal Linear. He continued to vibrate as he spoke.

"All clear and systems operational. SMART is distracted, I think." Linear laughed. "Seems we're small fry and probably last on its list." He indicated the elevator. "Take it down to four. I'll go back and code the door for you. Laters!" The superhero vanished in a blink, only a buzzing sound and the swinging stairwell access door betraying his trail.

Sam holstered her weapon, but kept it unclipped, just in case. Even with Bluebell in the same room, Blackbird was dangerous. Maybe the gun was not just a psychological comfort after all.

"Me first," she said, striding boldly to the elevator and hitting the panel.

Conroy sat himself in a conference chair. Aurora remained standing, and regarded him with folded arms.

Conroy tapped the table, waiting for Aurora to say something. The hero just stood there. Conroy coughed politely.

"You called me the Cowl."

No reaction.

"Am I still San Ventura's supervillain in your eyes? We had an agreement, didn't we?"

Aurora smiled. Slightly.

"I apologize for the reference. You came to us in surrender, an exemplar of change, a paragon of–"

"Yeah, yeah, I got it." Conroy waved the speech off.

"Those aren't just idle words. Despite our opposition, we have known each other for many years, Mr Conroy. You know as well as I the extent of our agreement with regard to San Ventura. And now Bluebell confirms your allegiance and that your self-sacrifice is just and worthy, at least in your own mind, which is all that matters. You have truly joined the Seven Wonders, for a time. But our situation grows ever more dangerous."

Conroy nodded an acceptance. "So how much do you know about our impending doom?"

"Of the Thuban and their war fleet, only a little. I heard the threats the Dragon Star made to her people, although she thought her secret was secure." Aurora shook his head. "But your own communications with them were concerned more with the retrieval of the power core they are going to hide in the Draconids. Although I expected they would come to collect their fugitive in person, I do not know the extent of their intentions." Aurora paused. "Are we really in so much danger?"

Conroy frowned. "The whole world is. Once I had recovered their power core, I was to use it within a weapon I had built myself, using the plans you had hidden in your vaults. Plans that you don't even remember exist."

Aurora didn't move, but Conroy saw his jaw tighten. Conroy continued.

"You had plans for a weapon, one that could be used against superheroes. It wasn't quite done – didn't have an adequate power source – but before work was completed you ordered the plans and key components to be broken up and hidden. Having such a weapon, even locked inside your Citadel and under the guard of the Seven Wonders themselves, was too great a risk. Too much of a temptation. Even for you."

Conroy sniffed. Aurora turned and gazed out at the lunar surface.

"How did you discover the secret, Mr Conroy?"

"Oh," Conroy said, waving a hand. "That was the easy bit. The Thuban knew about it because the Dragon Star knew about it, and they told me. And the Dragon Star knew because Bluebell's mind tricks don't work on her. So she remembered. Quite an oversight, big guy."

Aurora said nothing.

"But," Conroy said, "we can use this to our advantage. Retrieval of the power core is integral – they're sending it because it can be used against one of their own, the Dragon Star. So I figured we can use their own power against *them*. But only if you're sure you don't want to give her up. The Thuban are very keen to have her back."

"That may be," said Aurora. He sat at the table, and stroked his chin.

"But I want to know why. Threatening the Earth is not the most diplomatic approach."

"Depends what she's been telling them behind your back. She didn't want the Seven Wonders to know about any of this. There must be a reason."

The room shook, and the sound echoed on for too long. Conroy sat bolt upright as Aurora turned back to the table-top display. He passed a gauntlet over the screen, which flickered back on. The workshop was filled with smoke – SMART had rendered the main doors in two, and advanced on the Dragon Star and Sand Cat.

"How long until the Earth crosses the orbit of the Draconids?"

Conroy stood, glancing out of the observation windows, as if he could somehow see the approaching shower. "Less than a day."

Aurora nodded. "Acceptable." He jerked a thumb toward the display, showing the fight in the workshop. "First things first, Mr Conroy. We need to deal with SMART. Ready?"

"Lead the way, Aurora." Conroy clapped his hands, and took a breath. As Aurora strode out of the room, Conroy held back a little, focusing on keeping calm. Powerless, he was about to face a big white robot that wanted to kill everyone, fighting in the tightly controlled and delicately balanced environment of a base on the moon.

This was going to be fun.

CHAPTER FORTY-THREE

Jeannie didn't look happy. She didn't look particularly scared either, but then Sam reminded herself that despite her expression, and despite the shapeless orange prisoner jumpsuit she was wearing, it would probably take more than an insane giant robot smashing its way into the moonbase for her to break a sweat. Instead, she sat in a plain interview room, out of her cell but wrists held by powercuffs, glaring with indignation at Bluebell as the superhero stood over her with hands on hips. Bluebell didn't turn around when Sam and Joe entered. She kept her eyes trained on the prisoner while Linear buzzed around the room in a silver flash.

Jeannie raised an eyebrow when the two detectives walked in. She glanced at Bluebell.

"Police? On the moon? Gimme a break."

Bluebell merely raised an eyebrow to match Jeannie's expression.

Sam looked around the interview room. The walls were alternating white plastic and bare metal panels like the rest of the base, and there was the usual one-way mirror set into the wall, but apart from the slightly odd and clinical aesthetics it could have been any interview room in any police station she'd ever been in. Even with four people in the room, a table and a couple of chairs, it was quite spacious. A classic setup. She wondered when it had last been used… perhaps when the Seven Wonders had taken down the Anti-Man. That, as far as she could remember, was the last superhero battle that had taken place in orbit.

Bluebell saw Sam looking, and tilted her head toward the mirror. Looking at the reflection, Sam saw Bluebell's bruised face, the purple welt a sharp contrast to her otherwise perfect appearance.

"This room has never been used," she explained, having read Sam's thoughts. "By the time the Apollo Fortress was finished, there were no supervillains left."

Sam shook her head and remembered why she didn't like Bluebell. The truth-twisting mind-controlling *bitch*.

Bluebell's reflection smirked, having heard that thought too. Well, good.

"No, there was one supervillain left," Sam hissed. "Not that the Seven Wonders ever gave a shit."

Bluebell ignored the comment. Joe kept quiet, letting Sam vent her frustration.

"What are you going to do with her, anyway?" Sam continued.

Bluebell looked at Jeannie as though she were an art patron regarding an important gallery piece. "Same as any criminal, superpowered or not. She'll stand trial and face justice."

"Won't she join the Seven Wonders? You seem to be making a habit of accepting terrorists and murderers into your ranks."

Bluebell shook her head. "No, Paragon is different. His change is genuine, fundamental, and he has agreed to face justice after he has completed his duties. But there is no remorse or regret in this one."

Jeannie snorted in derision. Linear hazed into being next to her chair and frowned. The room shook as another shockwave rumbled around the moonbase from the battle in the workshop. Linear looked worried, while Bluebell was apparently unmoved, still keeping watchful eye on the prisoner.

"Why is she out of the cell anyway?" Sam asked.

"In case we need to move quickly. The cell release takes a full three minutes to complete."

"And we're safe here?"

"The safest point on the base, certainly. It's also close to the medical zone and the morgue."

Joe blinked. "Morgue?"

Bluebell turned to him, smiling sweetly. "If we have to move, we need to take the evidence with us as well."

"Evidence?" Jeannie squirmed at the table.

"Tony Prosdocimi's body. Exhibit A."

Sam blanched at the thought of wheeling a body bag around the base, then swung her arms to regain balance as the room shook again.

The Dragon Star took a steady step backward every twenty seconds or so. The containment field from her powerstaff only represented about one hundredth of one percent of the alien device's total power output, but operating it at such low levels was difficult. The slightest miscalculation would result in SMART being converted into a slick of molten metal and burning plastic and, most likely, the hull of the moonbase being damaged. It was best, then, to play it slightly under, allowing the robot to fight against the force holding it back until the others arrived.

Sand Cat paced the workshop in her animal form, ready to pounce on SMART if the robot should suddenly breach the Dragon Star's multicolored energy shell. She was a contingency only, while the Dragon Star's field was merely a temporary measure. To safely deactivate SMART without damage, allowing its systems to be restarted and debugged, would require all seven of the Seven Wonders. All six, thought the Dragon Star. Minus Hephaestus, minus SMART, plus Paragon.

Paragon. He knew of the Thuban, he knew of the transmissions. The Dragon Star was also sure Aurora knew of her hijacking of the satellite surveillance systems and the data tapes she had dubbed. But he hadn't said anything, and seemed unwilling to intervene, allowing events to play out while he watched the others deal with it.

But she'd done the right thing. She was no criminal, not by the standards of the Earth, her adopted home. The Seven Wonders and the international alliance of superpowered protectors were sworn to defend life, liberty and the pursuit of happiness. Did such fundamental tenets not apply to her, a citizen of the Earth? Or would her friends turn against her in the relentless pursuit of theoretical justice, no matter how unjust the charges? Would they respect the unjust laws of another sovereign power over the laws of her adopted homeland, a homeland that she had devoted her life to defending?

SMART surged forward a few yards. The Dragon Star refocused on holding the giant robot and flicked her powerstaff a little, allowing an infinitesimally small lick of energy to crack across SMART's armored chest. The robot shook a little and raised its arms up, before shuddering forward another step. They were now halfway across the large workshop space, the destroyed airlock doors behind SMART and the smaller, though equally heavy-duty entrance to the main base behind the Dragon Star.

The doors slid apart from the center, admitting Aurora, followed by Paragon. With each step forward, Aurora's corona grew in intensity, tongues of solar energy pluming outward, arching over his body as he ramped up his own internal magnetic field, channeling the power of the nuclear furnace inside him. Paragon scuttled through the door behind him, keeping as flat against the metal walls of the workshop as possible, face turned away to limit the risk of severe sunburn from being so close to the solar superhero.

"SMART! Stand down and deactivate, pending system check." Aurora's voice boomed in the echo chamber of the workshop. SMART did nothing but gear up a powerful leg to take another step forward into the Dragon Star's shield.

"Confirm!"

SMART took another step.

The Dragon Star and Aurora were the two most powerful of the Seven Wonders, Conroy knew that. But the way they worked together really was breathtaking. Each wielding a different spectrum of energy, the two worked with a synergy that was almost telepathic. Even as Aurora began raising his fists, ready to soften SMART up with low-energy plasma balls, the Dragon Star deftly stepped to one side, yanking the powerstaff up and providing a window in her shield, through which Aurora could direct his fire. Backed into a corner, away from Aurora's radiance, Conroy gasped in appreciation. The initial move took a second, and for the next minute the two superheroes danced around their target, moving the shield and throwing energy at the robot's exposed weak spots. Conroy had no real idea what he was expected to do except stay out of the way.

Eventually, inevitably, one bolt found its mark. One of SMART's legs failed, the machine hitting the workshop floor on one broken knee servo.

That was enough for the heroes. The Dragon Star deactivated her shield, allowing Sand Cat a clear run. The muscular, translucent animal swept into the air with a roar, landing with two heavy front paws on SMART's domed head. Sand Cat's supernatural claws penetrated the covering and tore the dome off, revealing a black, square processing unit, surrounded by wires. SMART's main optics, six rotating red lenses of various sizes, swam on their servos, scanning the attacking enemies. A green laser sight stabbed a target on Sand Cat's muzzle but passed straight through her ghost-like form. Aurora saw his moment and flew in, arm outstretched, and removed the laser and the six optical sensors with a superheated punch. The impact knocked SMART backward, but the robot caught its fall with an arm. Rotating gears switched the damaged knee mechanism for the agile stealth system, and SMART regained proper footing. It swung up both gun arms, the square ends of which flashed blue for an instant as the power coils charged, then kicked back as two violet-blue laser beams caught Sand Cat square. This time at least some of the energy spectrum was absorbed by her form and the hero spun backward through the air, unhurt from the blast but rendered unconscious. By the time she hit the floor she was back in her human form.

Aurora floated himself into the beam, catching one with each hand, waiting for SMART to stop the onslaught before shooting forward with another atomic punch. This one impacted the robot in the center of its curved white chest, but in testament to Hephaestus' mystical blacksmithing, the world's most powerful fists could only cause a shallow dent. But it was enough at least to send SMART sliding backward, sparks cascading from knees and knuckles as it gouged out a path in the workshop floor.

Conroy moved to the stirring form of Sand Cat. The warrior moaned back to consciousness, bright red blood trickling from her nose. She was aware enough of her surroundings to acknowledge Conroy's assistance, but it was pretty clear that she wouldn't be fighting again today.

Aurora lowered himself to just a foot above the floor, the Dragon Star at his side, her powerstaff now pulsing with a radiant intensity, fully charged and ready for a refreshed attack. Aurora held his arm out across her front, however, shaking his head.

"We can't risk it," he said, addressing the Dragon Star but keeping his eyes fixed on the sparking chassis of SMART. "One stray blast and we'll tear out a wall. All of the base control systems are being routed through SMART – we wouldn't be able to contain it in time."

The Dragon Star said nothing, but lowered her staff, just a little. Overhearing, Conroy called out across the workshop.

"If SMART controls the base systems, why hasn't he just shut the life support down and voided the base? It would be an easy way to get rid of us."

There was a pause, a beat of just a second, then the lights went out. Aurora flared his aura and the Dragon Star cracked her staff on the floor, the high metallic ring sounding out across the workshop as a brilliant white glow emitted from the weapon, re-illuminating the room. Aurora took a breath to berate Conroy before the room shook and the sound of rushing water filled the workshop. No, not water. Air. Conroy swore under this breath.

Aurora's comm beeped. He flicked it on. Bluebell.

"Aurora, the power is out up here, and it's getting cold. Are you OK? Has the base been breached?"

"Affirmative, Bluebell." Aurora had to raise his voice against the steadily increasing roar as the base atmosphere began to equalize with the vacuum of the lunar surface. "SMART is still in control of all systems, and has compromised the integrity of the base. We must regroup."

The comm buzzed as SMART again attempted to override the link. Conroy could hear Linear talking in the background, and Bluebell agreeing to something. "We're on our way," came her final communication.

Conroy jumped, and turned. Standing directly behind him was Linear, Sam and Joe, Bluebell, and a powercuffed Blackbird. Sam looked around in bewilderment, her blonde hair still moving in the breeze brought up by Linear's speedy delivery. Conroy slapped the speedster on the shoulder. "Nice trick."

"It's getting cold," said Sam, stating the obvious and absently rubbing at her arms. Conroy glanced around the room. The Dragon Star's light threw odd shadows upward, while Aurora's red swirling aura projected organic, rippling shapes across the walls. He nodded.

"Indeed. We don't have much time."

Aurora and the Dragon Star looked at each other, then he nodded and she turned away. She floated backward, head down and hood completely hiding her features. She raised her powerstaff up over her head, holding it at one end like a gigantic battle-axe, poised over SMART's frame.

Bluebell reached out to her husband, apparently immune to his fiery radiation. "Aurora! We can't risk it. Even the workshop isn't that strong."

Aurora's mouth twisted below his half-mask. SMART had remained motionless, apparently locked into a crouch position, gears sparking as it struggled to regain movement. But even paralyzed, the machine operated all base systems remotely. It was a threat that needed to be eliminated.

Aurora began to speak, but was cut off as a beam of blue light struck his head. He cried out and was floored, dropping vertically. His aura dimmed and cooled to a deep burnt orange.

Linear sped forward, catching his leader before he touched the ground. But Aurora was already regaining his footing, shaking his head to clear it.

"Bluebell, Sand Cat is hurt – see to her. Linear, Dragon Star, it's time to end this. Paragon, maintain vigilance on the prisoner."

Conroy's mouth pursed, half in surprise, half in embarrassment. Blackbird fluttered her eyelids at him and smiled coquettishly, before spitting in his face.

SMART rose, leg gears grinding as they found a happy medium between regular systems and the agility/stealth setting. The robot wavered slightly with each step, but soon compensated for the altered balance. Swinging its guns around to cover the heroes, it opened fire with everything it had.

The Dragon Star's shield stopped the initial blasts, allowing Linear to fly in, spinning a silver blur around the robot as he attacked weak points and attempted to find gaps in the armor plate. Distracted, SMART took several hits from Aurora's plasma blasts before the hero came to touching distance and threw a right, then a left, then a right again.

The first two punches landed with awful metallic clangs, but on the third the robot ceased fire and blocked Aurora's attack with its own armored fist. Aurora's knee came up and connected with the underside of SMART's arm, forcing the robot to release him. Advantage on his side, he lifted up a few feet, then brought his elbows down onto the exposed head unit. SMART shook, but this time a waist servo snapped and it fell sideways. Linear's silver glow changed trajectory, avoiding being crushed by the immense machine and turning his attention to newly exposed weaknesses.

Aurora pummeled SMART's casing again and again, each blow weakening the robot, just a little bit.

"Aurora!" Bluebell called out over the cacophony of sound. When he turned to look at her, she indicated Joe and Sam, who were beginning to suffer in the increasingly rarefied atmosphere.

Conroy wasn't doing much better, but found the strength to be heard. "She's right. We can't last much longer. We have to regain control of the base and turn that damned robot off."

The Dragon Star flipped her shield off for a moment, collapsing the energy shell into a series of powerful blasts that struck SMART, causing the robot to rock but apparently inflicting little damage, then turned the shield back on as another volley of blue laser bolts flew towards her and the civilians.

"Paragon speaks the truth, heroes." The Dragon Star spoke for the first time in the fight. Even Aurora backed away from the robot and came closer to the hero, interested in her appraisal.

"We can only destroy the robot if we use maximum effort, which will breach the workshop," the Dragon Star continued.

"There is another way."

Everyone turned. Blackbird waved her powercuffed arms toward SMART. "If he's linked to the system, the system is linked to him. Five minutes." She waggled her cuffed wrists. "If you want us all to live, of course."

Aurora looked at her, then Conroy, his face lit by another barrage from SMART, held in check by the Dragon Star's shield.

Conroy stepped forward. "She's right. Jeannie's primary expertise is electronics and computer systems." Aurora remained silent. Conroy searched his expressionless face, then sighed in exasperation. "She patched us into your secure satellite system, for goodness' sake! Do it!"

Aurora tilted his head toward the prisoner, then nodded curtly. Bluebell moved to release Blackbird from the powercuffs, tapping out a sequence on its keypad. The cuffs clicked open and Blackbird let them drop to the floor.

"Control room?"

Bluebell nodded. "Hephaestus' lab. This way."

The lab was an annex to the workshop, and was cast in deep shadows. The only light came in from a large reinforced viewing window that looked out into the main workshop. The glass was thick and tinted, but there was enough illumination cast from the Dragon Star's powerstaff in the other room for Blackbird as she tore at a control panel on the wall. Bluebell kept her distance, watching the now-freed prisoner but ready to knock her out with a psychic punch if she tried anything. But soon Blackbird was peering into the wall cavity up to her shoulders, and Bluebell couldn't resist moving in for a closer look.

"What are you going to do? And *how*, exactly, do you know what to do?"

Blackbird's head emerged from the access panel. She reached in deep with both hands and dragged out a thick, weave-bound cable, joined at the middle with a bulky metal screw connector. She began twisting its collar to separate the leads.

"The *what* is to turn your lovely robot off, from here." She gestured to the currently inactive main control deck. "SMART and your whole computer system are not two separate units, a computer operating system and a controller, they're the *same* system. There is no separation." She pulled the lead apart then scanned the array of inputs that studded the next wall panel along. "Which is either a very clever way of designing your entire computer infrastructure, or a very stupid one." She glanced at Bluebell, one eyebrow raised, waiting for a retort, but Bluebell didn't say anything. She clearly wasn't the technical brains behind the operation. "Well, just for today, I'll go for clever.

"The *how* is easy. We've got a complete systems readout of the Citadel of Wonders. Well, *had* a complete systems readout. We needed it to patch into the satellite system, and it was also useful for monitoring every move the Seven Wonders made. The moonbase is a carbon copy. I even know your electrical wiring system like the back of my hand."

Locating the required port, she screwed one end of the cable into the wall. The second lead she left dangling from the opened access panel. Blackbird turned to the main control desk under the observation window. Through the glare, she could just make out the red haze of Aurora as the hero pumped his energy up a notch and took another swing at SMART, which had managed to stand again and had both arms raised as it advanced on its former leader.

"Let's get this party started," said Blackbird, depressing a key combination on the control panel, which bleeped in response, a constellation of LEDs lighting all at once.

This was it. Sam was pretty sure of the fact. The environment was too far gone, quickly heading towards being completely incompatible with life. Her face, arms, chest and thighs burned with heat as, in front of her, Aurora maintained his assault on SMART. The two colossi clashed in hand-to-hand combat, while the small, almost frail form of the Dragon Star flitted around, keeping the room lit and her large elliptical shield up to protect everyone from the seemingly random blue laser of the robot.

But the back of her legs, her shoulders, they were as cold as ice. With the moonbase life support off, it was only the heat of Aurora's battle that kept her, Joe and presumably the Cowl from freezing to death. She presumed that the superheroes were immune to the cold anyway, although it crossed her mind as to how Blackbird was managing to stay alive in the workshop control room. She and Bluebell had vanished into the annex and had been gone for what seemed like hours while the superheroes fought to keep their robot – and former member – in check.

There was a brief blast of siren, the squawk of an emergency PA, and the workshop lights came back on. Immediately the Dragon Star quenched her own light and redirected the energy back into the offensive. Her shield began to pulse as she used the excess power to fire round after round of pink fizzing energy bolts at SMART. Most were absorbed by its miraculous white armor, but it proved to be an admirable distraction. Momentarily confused, assessing the new threat, SMART paused, allowing Aurora in closer for a colossal underarm charge. Aurora and the robot swept backwards, colliding with the rear wall of the workshop. Aurora pressed the machine into the wall, crumpling a large area with a fingernails-on-blackboard screech.

Next to her, Joe let out a sigh. Sam looked over at him, and saw him smiling as he clutched his chest. He was breathing easier, and she realized she was too. The air didn't have the deadly icy quality to it any longer. Blackbird had managed to regain control. Joe winked and gave a thumbs-up.

Aurora floated backwards from his handiwork, with SMART embedded in the workshop wall. While normally this would only be a minor hindrance, the robot did not attempt to extricate itself. The Dragon Star allowed her shield to fall as she approached the robot, and Linear reappeared, a handful of wires and twisted plastic in one hand. He tossed the debris to the floor and peered at SMART. The robot's red optics were dark.

"Was that me?" Linear pulled his mask off and scratched his beard, then kicked the discarded components out of the way with the toe of one boot.

The PA barked, and Bluebell spoke from the annex. "Blackbird's disconnected SMART from the system. We've got control back."

Linear grinned at Aurora. Even from her position near the workshop exit, Sam could see the superhero's face back in the usual smirk. She smiled herself, finding Aurora's clichéd tough-guy expression strangely comforting.

Bluebell and Blackbird emerged from the annex doorway. Sam watched them cross the floor, noting that Blackbird remained uncuffed. Conroy walked over to where Aurora, the Dragon Star and Linear were poking and prodding at the deactivated bulk of SMART.

"Ah, Aurora, we don't have much time here." As he spoke, Conroy glanced at Blackbird, who was watching him with an expression of complete hatred. He cleared his throat and turned back to Aurora.

Aurora stepped back from the robot's carcass. "The Draconid meteors?"

Conroy nodded. "We have to be ready, intercept the package in space before it even reaches the Earth."

"Understood." Aurora waved over at Blackbird, and pointed a heavy gauntlet at SMART's dead optics. "Can you remove SMART's data core and install it in the base computer?"

Blackbird strolled over, somehow maintaining a casual, indifferent air. "Why can't you do it?"

"Hephaestus was our technical expert."

Blackbird's mouth curled up in an unpleasant smile. "You want to mount his core like an external drive?"

"Allowing access to the file directories, yes."

Blackbird squinted, tilting her head as she looked at the black cube of SMART's processor, nestled within the wires and loops of its exposed head mechanism. "Yeah, should be easy. Got a terminal?"

"Main conference room." Aurora turned on his heel, striking out for the workshop door. "The meteor shower approaches, but before we can act we need to get to the bottom of this mystery."

He paused, mid-stride, and turned to slowly walk back towards the Dragon Star. Hands on hips, he towered over her.

"We must know everything, my friend. The fate of the entire world hangs in the balance." He turned to face the room. "Everyone, follow me."

Aurora strode back to the main door. Linear and Bluebell helped a still-groggy Sand Cat up and out, and they were followed by Conroy, Joe and Sam. Blackbird clambered over SMART's collapsed form to reach the head. The Dragon Star stepped backwards, sweeping the powerstaff around to cover Blackbird, still technically their prisoner. Blackbird heard the movement, and looked over her shoulder at the gently pulsing superhero.

"Gimme a break, kid. I've got work to do." She turned back to her job. "So, on the run from the Thuban, eh? Well done on keeping that a secret. I guess Bluebell can't read that dead head of yours, eh? No electrical activity, is there? Brainwaves at zero. Handy. I'll see what I can do with the memory readout from this thing, but I can't promise anything. You'll need to face up to the consequences yourself."

Blackbird jerked SMART's memory cube from the robot's head and turned, but the Dragon Star was gone.

CHAPTER FORTY-FOUR

With Bluebell's help, Blackbird jury-rigged SMART's memory cube into the system controller that formed part of the conference room table within two hours. Aurora's display panel was active; he tapped at it, navigating through system folders and directory displays, waiting for SMART's isolated memory core to become available. Blackbird had been surprised to find the Dragon Star already sitting at the table, at her customary position at the opposite end to Aurora. Already the two heroes had exchanged glances a few times, or was that just her imagination? What was the link between the two? Did it go as far as telepathy? Given their almost symbiotic relationship in battle, it wouldn't have surprised her. Aurora was stoic, emotionless, and the Dragon Star silent, expressionless. Quite the crime-fighting pair.

"Are we ready, Blackbird?"

She looked up at Aurora. The memory cube had been active for a few moments, and she'd let herself drift off into her own thoughts. That kind of carelessness was dangerous, especially with Bluebell at her shoulder.

Blackbird nodded, and Aurora's gloved fingers moved over the touch panels.

"Of course, what readout SMART's systems will provide is merely the missing link," began Aurora. "As part of his agreement with us, Paragon placed all files and data once in the possession of his alter ego known as the Cowl in our hands, and with his direction, retrieval of the power core from the Draconid meteor shower will be a matter of routine." Conroy nodded, almost sagely. Blackbird snorted. The creep.

"What *is* new information is that in addition to the power core, the Thuban have sent a warship to collect their bounty." Aurora sat down, and leaned back, causing his chair to creak loudly. "That bounty, of course, being our guest from the Thuban, the Dragon Star." He gestured towards the opposite end of the table. The Dragon Star was looking downward, and appeared not to notice the entire room was looking at her.

Linear buzzed. "Bounty?" He looked around the room. Nobody was saying anything, or even daring to move. Linear's chair rattled against the floor as his outline faded into a blur then snapped back into sharp focus. He looked around each of the people seated at the table in disbelief. "The Dragon Star is a dedicated protector of the Earth, and a sworn member of the Seven Wonders… right? Are you telling us she's a criminal? Some kind of alien con on the run from her own people?"

Aurora said nothing, but the Dragon Star raised her hood and met her leader's empty, masked eyes. He inclined his head slightly, and she began.

"Linear is correct. I am an escapee of the Thuban. I am a wanted criminal on a hundred worlds and a thousand moons. The bounty on my head exceeds the value of the mineral wealth of your entire solar system. If I am captured, I will be imprisoned until the end of the universe and tortured beyond that time point."

As the Dragon Star spoke, for the first time she appeared to become animated, a real, living person, even though Sam knew the horrific truth about her. The words were stilted, odd coming from this all-American teenager, apparently no older than sixteen, but the voice that spoke them and the alien intelligence behind the young face was ancient beyond all understanding; a bodiless, abstract entity merely re-animating the dead body of a teenage murder victim. Sam knew, unlike most members of the general public, about the Dragon Star. She'd investigated the girl's death: it had been her first assignment when she'd joined SuperCrime, the case that had brought her and David together. Perhaps, she thought, that was yet another reason among many why she didn't like the superheroes in general, the Dragon Star in particular. She shuddered inwardly as more gory details of the case swam into her mind… but then here was the girl, the dead cheerleader, all hope and promise for the future extinguished violently, sitting at a table of superheroes in colored spandex, wielding an awesome alien artifact, and describing an impossible life the girl could never have known. As she listened to the Dragon Star's explanation, Sam didn't know whether to weep or be sick on the floor.

"My crime is a simple one, according to the Thuban. Freedom of thought. The Thuban are a collective, a group intelligence into which each individual is absorbed. While each Thuban retains consciousness, intelligence and awareness, identity is forbidden.

"But this is not a choice we make. For many, assimilation is a living hell, entered into unwillingly. But more than that, as the Thuban hive expands outwards in space from our home, Alpha Draconis, the Dragon Star, so intelligent life and civilizations old and new are absorbed into the collective. The Thuban are consumers, absorbing and destroying all that come near. So I made my decision where billions of my kind would not. I declared an identity and left the collective. I was not stopped, because no one had ever left before. Such an act was beyond all reasoning.

"I could not fight the Thuban on my own, so I fled as the declaration of my outlaw status was pronounced. I flew across the universe, and to the Earth, where freedom and identity are paramount. It is here that I found my home, defending those very principles, with my new friends. The superheroes of the Seven Wonders."

The Dragon Star dropped her head back down and stared at the table top, her hood slipping forward to shadow her face. Sam wasn't sure, but she thought she could see the wet tracks of tears on the dead girl's face.

"Well, they're coming to get you," Conroy said. He slouched in his chair, stroking his chin in thought. "After the initial transmission, I negotiated a bounty and they agreed to send one of their own power cores, providing enough raw energy for me to take you out once I'd built the supergun – Hephaestus' design, I'm guessing, which you've all forgotten even exists."

Conroy paused and allowed himself a chuckle. He glanced at Bluebell and a murmur rippled around the room. Conroy raised an eyebrow and continued.

"Oh, I don't blame you. You got Hephaestus to design a weapon that could be used against other superheroes. That kind of thing is too dangerous to have lying around, even locked in the Citadel of Wonders. So it was never built and all memory of it erased. All you were left with was the knowledge that there was important information entrusted to a series of individuals. What that knowledge was, you'd forgotten."

Linear sighed dramatically and shook his head. The other superheroes remained silent. Conroy turned back to Aurora. "After assembling your weapon with the Thuban power core integrated, I was to hold the Dragon Star's body until they arrived to collect."

Aurora drummed his fingers on the table, then paused, and fixed Conroy with a look.

"But...?"

Conroy smiled again. "*But* is right. As your friend here said, the Thuban expand by absorbing civilizations they come into contact with. The Earth is no different. Sure, they're coming to collect their outlaw, but sure as hell they'll collect the other seven billion people on the planet while they're dropping by."

Conroy pointed at the black memory cube from SMART. "After months of regular communication, Blackbird intercepted the *other* transmissions, the ones routed through your satellite system that you never received. SMART, I presume?"

"Not SMART." The Dragon Star turned her hood to him, and reached into the folds of her cloak. She removed a small plastic disk, two-inches square. The metal spindle embedded in the center glinted as she held it up. "Me. I received the transmissions, but fearing for my freedom I hid this from my friends. I feared they would not understand my position. I am the very thing the Seven Wonders exist to fight, a criminal."

Aurora shook his head. "You underestimate us, Dragon Star. We uphold natural justice, a universal tenet." He raised a gloved hand and gestured at Paragon. "But Paragon is correct – SMART was not a part of our computer system, it *was* the computer system. I'm afraid, Dragon Star, that the messages you received were not only read by me, but were also received by SMART. Here we failed – Hephaestus' skill was too fine. He created an infinitely logical machine intelligence with a mind and will of its own. Seeing a traitor in our midst, it did what it was designed to do – protect the Earth, at any cost. I fear SMART saw first the Justiciar, then ourselves, as the primary threat, one that had to be eliminated in order for the Thuban menace to be neutralized."

The room was silent after that for some time, each person around the table lost in their own thoughts. The Seven Wonders were disintegrating just as the world faced one of its greatest threats.

Joe cleared his throat, and had the attention of the whole room. He nervously adjusted his tie and rubbed the top of his closely shaved head.

"So, what are we waiting for?"

Sam looked at him, shaking her head in confusion. Linear buzzed on his chair. The others sat and stared. After a few more seconds, Joe tapped his fingers on the shiny table top, leaving big smeary fingerprints.

"The Cowl built a weapon specifically designed to take out superheroes. The Thuban have sent the power supply so we know it works against their own kind."

The detective looked around the room, waiting for the penny to drop. Conroy sat back in his chair, a broad smile across his face.

"So goes the theory," he said.

Joe made to move from the table, then sank back into his chair.

"So let's go get the power core and shoot some aliens."

The Apollo Fortress was, quite literally, a smaller version of the Citadel of Wonders. Same layout, same facilities, all just a little *reduced*. Control One, with its conference table and observation windows. A Nuclear Forge, with yard-thick walls half the thickness of the furnace's cover itself. Sleeping quarters that were never occupied. An infirmary.

A morgue.

The room was lit in clinical blue, as if the choice of lighting somehow reinforced the chilled temperature within. Since the Apollo Fortress had been built, the morgue facilities had never been used. And now it was doubling as an evidence locker. Exhibit A lay on the slab, his skin washed a flat white by the blue lighting, a sheer plastic sheet draped over his body from head to toe.

Tony Prosdocimi, electrocuted by SMART. The first deliberate killing of the Seven Wonders in the team's history. His death, the pivot on which the future of the Seven Wonders, of San Ventura, of the world, perhaps, turned.

The morgue was quiet and cold, much like Tony's body. The gentle hum of refrigeration was amplified a little by the general hum of the moonbase's life-support system. While the latter wasn't of much use to Tony, not anymore, someone would have to perform an autopsy at some point, and it was easier to slice into a cadaver that wasn't a flash-frozen slab of meat.

The air moved. A light on a console flashed green as the environmental systems compensated. Balance restored, the morgue lay still.

A rustle of plastic, a tug at the sheet covering Tony's body, a nudge at the table on which he lay, a tap reverberating around the flat, hard walls.

The light flashed green and the air moved again. But this time, balance was not restored. The green light was joined by an orange light: something wrong, something beyond the control of the automated systems. An alert sounded, a faint *ping* echoing in the morgue quietly, almost as if it were impolite to disturb the sleep of the dead. The alarm sounded again, and apparently satisfied that all attempts at gaining the attention of the morgue technicians – who weren't there, who never *had* been there – had been made, fell silent. The orange light remained.

The air moved with more force, like someone rushing around the room, looking for something, in a hurry. The movement rattled the table and swirled the heavy condensed mist on the floor up into the air. The mist spiraled clockwise and anticlockwise as it was drawn through the currents of air, caught in the wake of the hurried actions of... nothing.

The table rattled and there was a tap again, and the air rushed to fill space which had been occupied a second before with a faint pop.

The plastic sheet which had covered the body of Tony Prosdocimi sank several inches, flattening itself against the sucking coldness of the morgue slab. The orange light went out and the green light came on.

The morgue was quiet, the air still, and Tony's body was gone.

CHAPTER FORTY-FIVE

An infinity of light, and infinite color. Tony closed his eyes against the endless void and screamed forever.

When forever came to an end and his scream faded out across the universe, he stopped, and waited, not breathing because he did not breathe anymore, not moving because there was nothing for him to move. His eyes – what he thought, believed were his eyes, what *felt* like his eyes – were screwed tightly shut. All around him, the voices murmured, so many that they were an indefinable rush of white noise. For a hundred thousand million years the voices increased in volume until Tony could take it no longer. He opened his eyes – what he thought, believed were his eyes, what *felt* like his eyes – and looked at the world around him.

There was no form, no shape, just… an awareness of space. Tony knew that he really had no senses, no form or substance that could perceive form or substance. But he retained an awareness of his being, his mind attempting to map his twenty-three years of body memory onto the curve of space-time, the ultimate phantom limb syndrome. Finally, Tony formed himself, his being, his existence, into a single coherent thought.

So, this is what it's like to be dead?

As soon as he thought it, the voices ceased their murmur and began shouting. Infinite sound, a three-dimensional weight, crushing Tony to a singularity. He cried out again, and pushed at the void. His arms stretched out for light years in either direction, sweeping the sound away, pushing the void to the ends of the universe, clearing a space for his own formless, non-existent existence. He closed his eyes.

Good.

The thought was not his. In his mind, his eyes opened, he spun around, searching for the hidden presence. He ran, looking under things, behind things, opening doors, drawing curtains, racing up stairs. He ran across oceans and through cities. He was not alone.

We are the Thuban. You are the Thuban.

Tony stopped, and drew deep, calm, non-existent breaths. He closed his imaginary eyes and opened them again to look out at the void of no particular color that wasn't real. His mind told him that he was swimming upwards, being pulled, drawn by an invisible force to meet his new friends. No, not friends. His new masters.

Life exists in many forms. The man called Tony was but one. But he was nothing, his existence was merely infinity divided by zero. So one phase of existence ends, so the next begins.

Tony understood. Calmer now, he could gather his thoughts. Gather himself. He was dead. He remembered.

remembered the summer sun and the million windows of the city catching it and throwing the rays up to him like spotlights as he flew low over the plaza picking up the girl and dropping her and letting the wind catch his cloak and the cowl and the power shimmering beneath his skin and infusing his mind and he was the most powerful man on the world and it was his for the taking and nobody could stop him and

Tony shook his head, then jerked as the memory of pain exploded brilliantly inside him.

Nobody could stop him, except the Seven Wonders. The Seven Wonders killed him. They broke the rules, and they killed him. He had left the world, that wonderful, shining, sun-soaked world.

The Seven Wonders killed him. The Seven Wonders killed *me*.

Tony wept for eternity, and then when eternity ended the Thuban spoke again.

Do not lament the passing of an age. Our eyes are now turned to the Earth. The Earth will be welcomed to the Thuban. Through you, we will bring them to the Next Age.

Tony spoke. He found it was just the same as speaking when he was alive, except he had no larynx and no voice, and his words made no sound, and there was no air to carry the sound that wasn't there.

"Why have you chosen me?"

The void rippled, and the infinite opaque kaleidoscope shifted. Was this Thuban laughter? The sound of the group consciousness of the gestalt gasping at the stupidity of the question?

We have chosen you because you are our choice. You are powerful, a superman among your kind. You have the ability and the will to see to this new task. That you were sent to us now is fortuitous. Nothing in the universe happens by chance.

Tony felt a flush of pride. He was special, he was powerful. *They* knew it, they said so. This was... justification. An elucidation of truth, and confirmation that he had a purpose and that his actions had a meaning.

Tony smiled to himself with a mouth that was not even yet a thought-form. Not even death could stop him. Here he was, still in existence, freed from the limitations of humanity, in communion with the powers of the universe, chosen by them to be their tool on the Earth. Tony smiled again and his silent laugh echoed without sound down the corridors of space-time.

"What is my task?"

The void rippled again. A thousand million voices whispered into his imaginary ears at once, answering his query.

You must collect our power core, sent to the Earth as part of our earlier, illogical, disagreeable plan. You must return the fugitive to us, as our earlier, illogical, disagreeable agent has failed us. You must destroy the superhumans who protect the world. You will give us your life and that of all your kin. Together you will help the Thuban transcend humanity and join the glory of the light in the Next Age.

"How do I do this? I'm dead. The Seven Wonders killed me."

Your life was merely one state of being. We can fashion another for you. We have already claimed your physical form and we will use this as the template for something new. You shall return to the world with the meteor shower. You will rain down upon the city with a might that no human has yet seen. There are none who will be able to prevent this.

Tony spun on his axis, imagining his arms outstretched as he flew on the wind, exhilarated and bewitched and filled with a joy and happiness that belonged only to the insane. But Tony had read once, in his old life, that if you thought you were mad, you probably weren't. Tony wasn't mad. He never thought he was. He was happy. He was an angel sent from above, a specter of vengeance and justice, a power beyond the pathetic abilities of the Seven Wonders. The Thuban would turn his old body into something new. He would be a god – a living god, the embodiment of light and good and all that is right. Converting humanity to the Thuban was not punishment, it was reward.

And even as he thought it, the Thuban looked into his mind and saw the image there. Crowned and winged, smiling beneficently over the spires of San Ventura with a shadowed face.

As you wish. It is time for you to return to the world and do our work. We are transecting the space between worlds to reach the Earth, but you will be there to prepare for our arrival. Go to your task.

Tony screamed. The mental projection of his old form was suddenly as heavy as a planet, as a solar system, as a galaxy. He flexed his arms to pull against the weight, and found he had arms again. He pushed upwards, finding feet and legs and a torso and launching himself against the void. Then the infinitely open and light space split in front of him and folded in on itself, becoming a tiny, sticky cell filled with darkness. He turned again, punching and kicking at the ever-decreasing sphere which threatened to crush him. The walls of the void closed in and adhered themselves to him, a brilliant plastic envelope of fire and pain. Tony screamed again, but the taut substance would not let him open his mouth.

Eventually he opened his eyes. It was night, and the ground was wet and sharp. He felt outwards with one hand, his new-old body registering the textures and the temperature and the form.

He stood up on the damp grass under the street light, which dimmed the instant he looked at it. Around his feet, the dull dark of the grass took a monochromatic tone as his shadow, thrown from a sun that did not exist in this plane of being, spilled downwards and outwards from him.

Tony smiled, and looking up, regarded the night sky above his head. Already the first few slivers of the oncoming storm of solar flotsam and jetsam were scratching at the Earth's atmosphere, leaving white marks that faded in a second.

Tony took a breath, and found he did not need the oxygen. The night stretched out around him, and soon the grass and the street light and the small block between a football field and a grandstand in which he stood grew to an inky black.

Power. The Thuban had looked into his mind and saw his new self-image, and had crafted the form perfectly. An angel of light and glory, bringing new wonder to the world.

The Living Dark that had once been Tony Prosdocimi lifted from the wet grass and flew into space.

CHAPTER FORTY-SIX

They flew in fast and low, not that up or down had any meaning in the vacuum of space. Above/below them an ocean of rock and dust swept downwards/upwards, its direction shaped by the Earth's magnetosphere as the planet gently tugged what would become the annual Draconid meteor shower into its fateful orbit.

Linear, protected in space by the Slipstream and holding his mask in one hand, pirouetted, and Sam gasped. Enclosed in an almost undetectable energy shield tethered to the Dragon Star's powerstaff, she lay on her back/on her front and absorbed the sights offered to her. Linear came to within touching distance of the detective, winked at her, then curved back above them all before repointing towards the Earth. Behind him was nothing but open space, but without the filtering, obscuring atmosphere of the Earth – and the air pollution of San Ventura – it was a dazzling hemisphere of lights, so bright and dense that they left Sam's vision dotted with purple smears. She blinked, and turned like a swimmer, risking another glance at their destination.

The Earth. It was bright, too bright to look at directly, like looking at the sun on a clear day. If she brought her fingers up to her eyes, the energy envelope around her was thick enough to shade some of the glare, and peeking between her fingers she could, after a moment to let her eyes adjust to the light, just make out North America. There were no clouds over the West Coast at all. It was another beautiful day in California.

She turned over again and watched the mini-fleet of superheroes streaking home. Next to her, sharing the life-support bubble, Detective Joe Milano had his hands behind his head, looking for all the world like he was sunbathing on one of San Ventura's famous beaches. Away to their left, Aurora blazed red, from the waist down a miniature comet, his arms outstretched as he streamlined himself for re-entry. The Dragon Star's cloak billowed and her wide hood rippled in... Sam had no idea what. It was a vacuum, as close to perfect as to make no odds. She supposed the fabric was caught in eddies of invisible energy streaming out from the powerstaff held at the perpendicular in front of her. Two further white tendrils coned out from each end of the device, providing transportation shields and a supportive atmosphere for Bluebell, who was escorting Conroy and Blackbird. Beside them, Sand Cat was in her animal form, the translucent blue shape running, pounding on nothing but space as they headed towards the Earth, leaving a wide blue wake behind her.

Joe shifted onto an elbow and pointed.

"It's starting."

Sam watched as the leading edge of the wide, black silhouette she knew was the meteor cloud began to flare white and transform into the annual fireworks display that was the famous Draconids.

Sam decided that flying through space beat the hell out of the teleport, although the journey would take several minutes rather than be instantaneous. But there was no telling what systems had been affected by SMART's shutdown of the moonbase, and which systems were fully operational after Blackbird had got the power back online. Teleport was too big a risk.

So flying it was. And they were running ahead of the meteor shower. There was time to spare.

The Earth loomed large and Aurora sped off to take point. Linear came in close to the bubble shared by Sam and Joe and reached out his hand to touch the wall near Sam's.

He smiled, then fitted his facemask with one hand.

"Sit back and enjoy the ride!" he said, but separated by a couple of feet of space, Sam couldn't hear a thing.

Houston, we are cleared for re-entry.

CHAPTER FORTY-SEVEN

Gillespie hadn't slept for what felt like forever. In reality it was more like thirty hours. It wasn't like he hadn't done it before; it came with the job as police were fond of saying, and the job was his decision, but it wasn't a *common* occurrence and maybe he wasn't as young as he thought he was. Any job that required continuous overtime or out of work hours just showed, according to this police captain, that they were understaffed. And true enough, the SVPD, like every single police department in the country, probably the world (except maybe North Korea) fought a continuous battle for adequate funding and resources. But really, they got by. They had the Seven Wonders, after all, and the federal government considered the city to be a shining example of the future, of good housekeeping and of the rule of law and justice.

Yup. Uh-huh.

Gillespie considered this as he drank his fourth straight robot coffee. He'd stopped tasting the metallic sharpness of the black liquid that was supposed to be a double espresso after his second, but over the brim of the paper cup he regarded the hopelessly optimistic, Photoshopped image of an antique coffee pot and steaming cups on an elegant tray that adorned the dirty front of the machine with deep suspicion. True enough, the department was a 24/7 operation and while SuperCrime was closed up, the station was full of life downstairs and the canteen ran twenty-four hours. But the chief didn't feel like taking a walk. He wanted to be right there when Detectives Millar and Milano returned.

He'd rehearsed the dressing-down he planned to give them over and over in his head.

Gillespie blinked furiously, realizing that his overtired mind was starting to drift. He slugged back another hot mouthful and began the too-long walk back to his office.

Sam's chair was empty, and on her desk her phone flashed an angry red in the dim light. Joe's phone on the desk next to Sam's remained dark. Gillespie sighed, deciding not to clear another batch of messages. When his detectives had vanished, he'd soon given up trying to reach either of them on their cells, but he'd started answering her phone to see if it was her (although why Sam would call her own desk, he really had no idea). Sick of jotting down illegible messages on Post-it notes, he flicked her line to voicemail.

Of course, Gillespie knew where they were. They'd been kidnapped by the goddamn superheroes. Gone, *zap!*, blinking out of existence just as the smoke was clearing at Moore–Reppion Plaza, leaving their captain and the uniforms to clear the crowds and coordinate paramedics and traffic.

Gillespie shuddered at the memory, then thought he needed to stop drinking the robot coffee and start thinking about going home. He'd been shaken by the events of the last two days, and as he remembered the scene at the plaza he felt his heart begin to pound. It wasn't the superhero/supervillain smackdown, the wrecked buildings, the torn-up road, even the injured – *killed* – bystanders. He'd seen that before, dozens of times. The whole police department had, every staff member from the top down. It was part of living in San Ventura, that wonderful shining jewel of the West Coast.

But it was the way the Seven Wonders had stopped, frozen, when the Cowl – the *new* Cowl – had dropped from the sky and not got up. The way they'd gathered so fast, quickly – too quickly – abandoning people in the crowd who were hurt and who needed help and the beautiful, concerned face of Bluebell to reassure them and the cocky manner of the speedster to cheer them. The way Linear swore and Aurora stood, apart from the rest. Hesitating. The look on Aurora's face. The emotionless, all-powerful leader of the Seven Wonders, defender of San Ventura, icon and idol to millions.

Fear. And perhaps worse than that, *uncertainty*. If Aurora didn't know what to do next, then heaven help us.

Gillespie reached his office just as his own phone rang. He slumped into his chair and picked up the receiver as he swiveled to the dark window behind him. A split-second spit of white crossed the sky. A meteor shower. *The* meteor shower, which meant…

"Gillespie."

"Dispatch, sir. We've got trouble up on Melville Rise. Officers request assistance."

Gillespie sighed, then took a slow breath. It happened every year. A hot summer's night and the annual free lightshow. Mix in teenagers and alcohol and the big, open, wide roads on the hills above the city, and you had a street party turning to riot.

Still, it wasn't like he had anything else to do, other than not going home and waiting for his two detectives to rematerialize and explain what the hell was going on. Gillespie smiled. Yeah, like she'll teleport straight into her office chair and start filing a report. And it wasn't a job for SuperCrime anyway… but he knew by the end of the night damn near the whole police force would be called out to assist.

"Call everyone in. I'll join you myself."

Gillespie dropped the phone back on its cradle, finished his coffee, and headed out.

Less than an hour later, Gillespie ran a finger over the roof of the patrol car. It came back smudged with black: a slippery, moveable residue, something like printer toner. He looked up at the night sky as the meteor shower drew a thousand trails of superhot gases across it. This was a big one, that was for sure. Unusually large, maybe a record breaker. Gillespie wiped his finger on a trouser leg, but the dust from the car was difficult to shift. Looking around the gaggle of cars parked at odd angles nearby, he saw the vaguely translucent sheen adhering to them all. What, was the dust falling from the sky? The incinerated remains of meteor rock? Gillespie shook his head, and frowned. He wasn't entirely sure meteor showers worked like that, but in a town like San Ventura he'd learned to live with the strange and unusual. He half-wondered if the vanished superheroes had anything to do with it, but was distracted from his thoughts as a uniformed officer pushed an only slightly uncooperative young man in a sleeveless basketball shirt against the hood of the car. The officer shouted something in his ear, but Gillespie couldn't pick out her words, not over the sounds of the crowds and the music. He sighed, and hands-in-pockets, turned to view the carnage.

Actually, the uniforms were handling it, and a part of Gillespie felt it was a total waste of his time being there, that inner, automatic part of him that just insisted he did his eight and got out the gate. He sighed again, his breath tasting of stale coffee, and wished he could muster up some enthusiasm. He guessed he was supposed to be setting an example; the vigilant captain out on the scene.

But drunk teenagers weren't exactly what he'd signed up for when he joined the SVPD. The assembled crowd on Melville Rise was bigger than most years, numbers swollen by the notable awesomeness of the meteor display. This high on the hill there were only a few houses: big ones that could barely be seen at the end of long drives and gargantuan football field-sized front lawns. But they were the houses that really counted, at least as far as the residents were concerned. And, it had to be said, once the outer fences were scaled, the wide open ranges of soft, level grass formed the perfect staging areas for alcohol-fuelled punch-ups. Gillespie wondered – not for the first time – whether this was another bad influence of the superheroes, with all the angry, testosterone-fuelled young men of the city being taught that their problems could be solved with a fist-fight, or whether all towns in the US had a problem and he just had a need for San Ventura to feel special. He shook his head. Of course they did. San Ventura was special, but not that special.

A group of six girls sat silently along the curb. Gillespie couldn't tell whether they were trying to stay out of the way, or had been told to stay out of the way, or were just happy to sit and watch their boyfriends push and shove at the gathering police. With only a handful of houses, street lighting was fairly sparsely spaced along the roadway, so most of the light came from the half-dozen police cars and wagons parked in the road and the nearest driveways.

The captain strolled up past the girls, keeping his eyes on their reactions. One noticed him, and nudged her friend, who looked up and did the same to the next girl, a domino effect of glance, nudge and snicker. Gillespie sighed a third time, and decided to take his mind off the night, off the absence of Sam and Joe and the superheroes by lending a hand to the officers managing the increasingly rowdy crowd. He smiled, and adjusted his stab-proof vest.

There was a hot whoosh, like a large firework. Gillespie ducked instinctively, feeling heat crawl up the nape of his neck. His nose filled with a sharp, earthy scent. Fights and fireworks? Like the natural beauty of the meteor shower wasn't enough for these punks.

"Sir!" A short female uniformed officer was running towards him as he turned to meet her. He couldn't quite recognize her face in the half-light, but then there was a second rocket sound and she was lit up for a second by a bright, moving white light, revealing her identity as Catherine March, one of the precinct sergeants.

A third whoosh, accompanied by a bang that sounded very much like a small sonic boom.

"What the fuck was that? Is Linear back?" Gillespie was surprised he'd been startled so much by the flash and bang, but looking up into the sky, he saw the meteor shower intensifying, the shooting stars leaving thicker, brighter trails. The shower was getting *lower*.

A shot of adrenaline punched through Gillespie's chest. That was bad, wasn't it? Since when did meteor showers get so big and scary? Was it going to be dangerous? Another whoosh. This time, followed by a delayed echo, a muted thud that was unmistakable: something had impacted the ground, maybe a few miles away from the hill. There was another thud, another flash of white light. The air felt hot, although whether this was due to the meteor shower, or his increasing anxiety, Gillespie couldn't tell.

Even the kids on the street had paused, their attention wavering from an impending police-monitored punch-up between rival jocks from two local school football teams to the light show above. A few hooted as meteors streaked low and fast, while others stood silent, necks craned upwards. A lot of the police had joined them; Sergeant March quickly reminded them of their duty.

Impact thuds came more frequently now, and were louder. Gillespie gave an order to disperse the crowd from a purely safety point of view, but thirty seconds after he said it, the first meteor hit their immediate vicinity. The sound was shockingly loud as it punctured the roof of the garage of the house nearest. At this, the group jumped in collective fright, a few of the teenagers – male and female alike – shrieking in surprise. And then they started to run.

Gillespie ducked to one side as panicked teenagers began filing between the bottleneck formed by the patrol cars and vans, Sergeant March in the middle trying to organize her troops. More meteor impacts now, hitting the road, the dark, empty grass of the hill above, even a patrol car. Its rear windshield shattered and the whole vehicle bounced on its suspension, throwing the blue and red siren lights over the retreating partygoers.

More blue and red light caught Gillespie in the face, brighter somehow. He raised an arm reflexively to shield his eyes, then realized the light was not coming from the car. Another whoosh, and he looked up.

This shooting star was different. It was smaller and perhaps higher than the most recent low-entry space rocks. But it was a brilliant red. Behind it, a wider cone of bright blue light followed in a similar trajectory. Obscured by the glow of these colored trails, a series of softer, thin lines.

Gillespie swore, as much in relief as anything. He'd seen those colored contrails before. Blue and red and mysterious – the Seven Wonders were involved with the meteor shower somehow, and were heading towards the city at high altitude.

Gillespie shouted at March, and she shouted back, but neither could understand what the other had said. That didn't matter. Gillespie swung into his car, Kojak flickering on top, and flicked on the siren as he forced his slow way through the crowd and down the hill road, back towards the lights of San Ventura.

The Earth spun 25,000 miles below him. The Living Dark that had once been Tony, the Justiciar, locked himself into geosynchronous orbit and kept the city of San Ventura directly beneath him. The Draconid meteor shower from here was an unbelievable spectacle, a chain of brilliant white lights, woven into a rectangular strip, trailing off from the black of space into the Earth's atmosphere, where they flared red and orange and streaked as the rocks were vaporized by re-entry friction.

But the Living Dark did not notice, did not register the splendor of it. Arms outstretched, he tapped into the magnetosphere of the Earth, tweaking the parameters here and there, curling the normally innocuous belt of space rocks down a gravity well he'd placed over Southern California.

The Living Dark smiled. As the moon rose from the Earth's sharp blue horizon, there, at the edge, tiny insignificant points of light skipped the atmosphere under the meteor shower, leaving a bright red and blue trail. The superhero protectors of San Ventura were returning to the Earth.

The Living Dark was pleased. The Thuban would be pleased, and would reward him. He would collect the power core and dispose of the heroes and detain the Thuban fugitive that dared to name herself after her home system.

The Living Dark waited, measuring the trajectory of the Seven Wonders. Then he swept in, down towards the Earth, leaving nothing but a trail of ultimate blackness behind him, through which not even the brightest star could be seen.

CHAPTER FORTY-EIGHT

"Where are we?"

Conroy couldn't see. The constant, strobe-like flash of meteors above them, combined with the orange spurts on the ground as the meteors hit the soft earth, was enough to render him almost completely night-blind. He blinked, trying to keep one arm over his face and his eyes trained on the dark grass at his feet, but it was little use. Oh, what he'd do for image intensifiers, augmented optical processors, a full heads-up display with adaptive AI. Exactly what the inside of Blackbird's mask provided. Hell, what he'd do to get just a fraction of his powers back. Then he might have been of some use. Unlike now, at the mercy of the falling space rock and the red and orange smear across his retinas.

"Somewhere near North Beach." Conroy saw Linear's silver boots vibrate into solidity in his limited, downturned line of sight. As soon as they'd touched down, the speedster had taken off on a reconnaissance trip, probably covering several dozen miles in every direction. He'd been gone two seconds. The mess of lights in the night reflected over Linear's boots, before a red glow pushed the other colors out. Conroy screwed his eyes tight again, angry thoughts crossing his mind as he attempted to will his eyes into the correct adjustment. He opened his eyes and risked looking around.

Aurora stood right in front of him, next to Linear. Behind, Bluebell (blonde hair immaculate), Sand Cat (in her human form), the detectives (blondie with a bad case of bed-hair and the tough guy looking around all serious and nodding like he knew what on Earth to do next) and Jeannie (orange prison jumpsuit almost glowing in the dark) were lit by soft blue light cast from the Dragon Star's powerstaff as she projected a shield over the top of them. Beyond the shield, they seemed to be standing in what could have been a golf course, all softly rolling knolls, dotted with handsome trees here and there. Of course. The hills above the city – right in Conroy's old neighborhood. His mansion, swapped for an isolated private island in the Caribbean with a difficult Qatari sheikh after six weeks of painful negotiation, was a stone's throw away. And below, the Cowl's Lair. He laughed. The relics of a past life.

The hills of North Beach were being struck with considerable frequency by the meteor shower. A continuous rain of particulate stony material – from slick black dust to rocks the size of golf balls – struck the ground, sending up chunks of turf with little orange flashes. The material bounced audibly as it struck the Dragon Star's shield before rolling off and to the ground. It was like being caught in a hailstorm from hell. Conroy muttered a short prayer of thanks.

Sand Cat surveyed the area. "This is not like any meteor shower I have ever experienced."

Aurora nodded at her assessment, looking around himself, as the warrior stepped closer to Conroy. "Is this increased impact density a result of the Thuban power core?"

Conroy blew his cheeks out, then sucked in another lungful of air. It had a sharp, tangy quality from the smoke thrown up by the meteor rocks. "Tell the truth, I really don't know. There was no description of the meteor shower, or whether the power core would have any effect on it." He looked around. They were in a hollow between several natural mounds of the hill. On one side, the yellow glow of the city itself competed with the near-endless shooting stars above, although from where they were standing, San Ventura itself could not be seen. Jeannie turned from the group and walked up the rise for a better look across the harbor.

"This is unnatural." Aurora's expression was characteristically unreadable below the half-mask, his white eyes glowing like low-power flashlights as he looked around. He knelt by the edge of the Dragon Star's shield, and without pause pushed his hand through the energy barrier to pick up a golf ball-sized chunk of meteor that lay smoking in the grass.

Bluebell looked over Aurora's shoulder as he held the rock in both hands. Manipulating it between fingers and thumbs, he gave a twist and split the rock in half. Holding each piece at an angle to catch the light, he looked closely at the shiny, gray interior.

"Iron and nickel," Bluebell said. "Just an ordinary meteorite."

"But not an ordinary meteor shower." Jeannie's voice carried down to the group from her position at the top of the rise. Everyone looked up at her, but she was facing away, towards the city, hands on hips. "You need to come and take a look at this."

The group walked up the rise, the Dragon Star maintaining the protective shield against the hailstorm of rock. Conroy recognized the rise as one of the highest points on the North Beach hills. In front of them, the hilly terrain gradually sloped down to North Beach itself. The harbor lapped at the sand, reflecting the lights of the night in the gentle waves, and curved around and almost out of sight to the right, a mostly undeveloped area of parkland. Immediately across the bay, a mile or two distant, stood downtown San Ventura. At night, the city was spectacular, a dozen impressive skyscrapers lit by their own light and also reflecting the multitude of colors displayed by the glass shard of the Citadel of Wonders, the proud center of the city.

"Holy Mary, Mother of God." Conroy couldn't help himself. Linear opted for something more down-to-earth.

"Shitburger."

The city was lit, in the twinkling white and blue of the skyscrapers… and in the raging orange and yellow of fire. Impossibly high flames licked the bases of the tallest buildings, while the harbor shopping area and pedestrian plazas of the waterfront appeared to be completely consumed, the devastation reflected as an awful mirror image in the harbor waters.

No skyscraper was intact. Mighty constructs of glass and steel, they were no match for the meteor shower. The rock fall on North Beach was a gentle nothing compared with the debris that was hitting the city. Rocks the size of cars and buses roared down from the sky, white-hot and ablaze, tearing through the artificial construct of the city center as they headed to the ground. As the group watched, a rough spherical mass itself the size of a small building struck the side of the Prudential Assurance and Life Building, the second tallest structure in the city after the Citadel. The building went dark as the power cut, only to be lit half a second later by a colossal explosion. The giant meteor, unhindered and moving almost in slow-motion, continued downwards at a forty-five-degree angle, throwing up a second explosion and cloud of deep black and brown debris as it buried itself in the bedrock of the city. Even as the debris cloud from the impact continued to fan outward, the Prudential Building cried out with a metallic ache, buckled on one side, and telescoped downwards. A second explosion and dust cloud added to the first.

There was no let-up in the intensity of the storm. Before the night was out, San Ventura would be destroyed. Conroy looked around the group, awestruck at the terrible sight. All were too shocked to react; Linear and blondie had tears in their eyes.

Aurora flared, causing Conroy to flinch away. His cloak swept out and up, carrying on a blazing red aura. As he raised his arms, he lifted off the grass and hovered maybe a foot.

His eyes flashed white, and his famous sardonic smile twisted into a determined grimace.

"Seven Wonders, unite!"

Heeding their leader's call, the superheroes and their friends lifted into the air and shot across the bay to save their city.

The closer they flew to the city, the more dangerous and difficult it became. Dangerous for the unpowered or almost-powered humans, anyway – for Sam and Joe, and Conroy and Jeannie. Difficult for the superheroes, keeping their four vulnerable charges safe while trying to save the city.

Halfway across the bay, small meteorites sank into the harbor with the velocity of small-caliber bullets. Once again, Sam and Joe shared one support bubble, Conroy and Blackbird another. As they flew over the water Sam watched the other bubble. It was a bad idea, letting the two ex-accomplices stick together. She knew it. They'd reconcile somehow and plot an escape, or a takeover.

Looking up, the Dragon Star's shield was pitted with water-like ripples as it protected her and Joe from certain death.

Two-thirds of the way across the bay, Aurora came to a halt and drifted into a standing position to survey the city ahead. No further rocks of gigantic proportion had fallen, although meteorites as large as refrigerators still cascaded downwards, alight with magnesium brightness.

Linear buzzed next to his leader, shaking his head. "This isn't a meteor shower. Meteors of that size are like nuclear bombs. These, they're more like crashing airplanes. This is an artificial, controlled descent, designed to do what? Cause significant damage, incapacitate the city, keep us busy. Instill fear… but what for?"

Aurora nodded, arms folded. "You are correct. This is not a meteor shower, it is an attack on the city."

Bluebell gasped. "Space terrorism?"

"Perhaps."

"From where? The Thuban?"

Aurora paused, his own aura burning brighter than the light from the flaming city. "According to Paragon, the Thuban power core was to be hidden in the meteor storm. The mass of the meteors would shield any small object from detection as it made landfall. This..." He gestured to the guttering skeleton of San Ventura. "this is not a distraction. The Thuban would not have miscalculated to this extent. This is something else entirely. A third party."

Sand Cat brandished her fists before her, head down in a fighter's stance. "If this is how a new supervillain introduces himself to our city, he has made a mistake."

"Patience, Sand Cat," said Aurora. His voice was quiet as he stared at the hypnotic oranges and yellows of the fire of San Ventura. "We must locate the power core before anyone else. We should assume we have competition."

"Competition?" Bluebell's brow creased in confusion.

"There may be no connection, but somewhere in the city is the Thuban power core. Even if no enemy agent intends to take it, we must not be complacent. It is a device of terrible power. Retrieval must be our top priority, but we must save the city."

There, high above the harbor, Sam's jacket pocket buzzed. It gave her a fright, and it was a few seconds before she realized Joe was pulling at her shoulder. She turned and looked him in the eyes, her own wide in panic. He shook his head and gave a smile.

"Your phone is ringing. You've got it on vibrate."

Sam felt relief drop over her, then a punch of excitement as she read the caller ID.

"Chief!"

The line was terrible. Sam took the phone from her ear and checked the display. Only one bar of signal. Figured. Most of the city masts would either be pulverized metal or out of power.

"Detective Millar. Nice of you to drop by. You can tell me later about where you and your superhero friends flew off to, but right now we need all hands on deck. Where are you?"

Sam hadn't quite heard over the roar of the city and the bad line and her own excitement. She began to speak, so quickly she tripped over her own tongue. She stopped, took a breath, and started again.

"We're here, over the harbor. We were on the moon. Sir, the city's getting a pasting. The heroes are going into the CBD to save as much as possible and protect what's left. Where are you?"

"North Beach. The interstate is out – I had to abandon the car at the bridge. Everyone's leaving the city, heading to the hills. I'm heading back on foot to help coordinate."

Sam turned and glanced up. She saw Blackbird waving from inside her bubble. Their eyes met, and Blackbird shook her head. Sam grimaced, trying to ignore the criminal, but Blackbird called out.

"Go in there and we're toast." She pointed over at the city center. "It's a fucking inferno. And if we don't burn to death, we'll be crushed by a meteor. Let the heroes deal with it."

Sam knew it, fucking knew it. When the going gets tough, the villains turn tail and only think of themselves.

"Sam? You still there? Can you get to me?"

Blackbird wouldn't give up.

"We're no good in there. The city needs these guys." Jeannie pointed at the superheroes floating nearby. They had all turned to face the support bubble, listening to the conversation. Blackbird continued.

"You, me, Geoff, Joe, we can help at the bridge, at North Beach. The meteor shower is focused on the city, not the suburbs. It's just like a hailstorm with a bit of kick out here."

Sam blanched, feeling the color drain from her face as though Blackbird had slapped her. She was right, and that was... confusing.

"Sam." Gillespie's voice came through a wave of static on the phone, still at Sam's ear. "Move it, pronto."

Sam paused. She and Blackbird were locked on each other's eyes for seconds until Blackbird cocked an eyebrow.

Sam brought the phone up to her mouth. "Stay put, I'm on my way. And I'm bringing help."

"An excellent course of action, Blackbird." Aurora was floating right behind Sam, his voice causing her to spin around. "The Dragon Star will accompany you. Her powerstaff will be of use in protecting the innocent," Aurora continued. He then flew up and back towards the other heroes. "Bluebell, Linear, Sand Cat, with me. We will secure the city and locate the power core. Move out."

The superheroes flew towards the city, accelerating so quickly that they drew a vapor trail over the harbor in the hot air. The Dragon Star watched them go, then turned to her wards. She held the powerstaff horizontal, bringing the two support bubbles together until they merged. Sam and Joe found themselves standing next to Conroy and Blackbird.

The Dragon Star looked up to the horizon.

"Let's go."

CHAPTER FORTY-NINE

Abandoned by the superheroes once more, the moonbase was devoid of life, but was not empty.

There had been no time for a full shutdown, including a total security sweep and standardized mothballing and lockdown of systems. They'd left quickly. There would be time for that later, when the crisis was over.

Aurora's chair at the conference table was swiveled at an angle and the panels in front of it were dark. If there had been anyone to stand by the observation windows and look out across the plains of Taurus–Littrow, they'd see the dust had finally settled around the frozen corpse of Hephaestus, which lay undisturbed, abandoned but not forgotten. There would be time for burial and remembrance later.

Contrary to popular urban myth, human bodies don't explode in the vacuum of space. Sure, fluids phase into gas, water puffs to vapor in seconds, but the mechanical strength of human skin is more than enough to keep it all contained. Not that Hephaestus was strictly human. Bare skin tough enough for the god to plunge his arm to the elbow into the Nuclear Furnace would not be affected by the moon's lack of any tangible atmosphere. So his body lay still in the silent gray dirt, the Earthlight reflecting sharply from the mirror polish on his breastplate.

Aurora's control deck flickered, nothing more than a blip of power, like a half-plugged-in television set getting a signal for a second then powering off. As soon as it went off the OLED display embedded in the glass table top glowed blackly in the dark room.

And then another light. And another. Tiny, insignificant, unimportant. The hard drive spin of data retrieval, a standard, ordinary green flicker of network activity.

Snik snik.

Detecting a lack of activity within, the automatic systems of the moonbase went into an efficient power-save mode, gently dimming unused portions of the base and dragging the internal temperature down slightly, every infinitesimal decrease in ambient life support prolonging the lifespan of the solar power arrays by months.

As the air cooled and thinned, sound became indistinct, hard to get a direction on. But the corridors of the base were metallic and hard, and the sound that echoed down them equally harsh.

Snik snik.

The lights on Aurora's display went out. SMART's memory core sat on the table, connector lead still plugged in, the LED on the plug still a strong green.

Snik snik.

Down, levels down, ground level. Compared to the rest of the base, the workshop was hot. It had its own furnace – a smaller, safer version of the great atomic maelstrom back in the Citadel of Wonders – but even though the furnace shield had been undamaged in the superheroic battle with SMART, energy leaked from it, warming the huge space, filled with a chaotic mess of twisted componentry and solid metal debris. SMART's headless body lay where Aurora had put it, fused into the buckled wall of the building with his atomic punch. There was a breach here, a tiny tear from the fight. The atmospheric leak was small but significant; the life support in this section of the base was running a little over norm to compensate.

On an undamaged wall opposite SMART's resting place, a rack of servitor drones hung in various stages of deconstruction. In the building of his super robot, Hephaestus had constructed separate sections and tested each by attaching them in sequence to a basic robotic skeleton. While SMART had been built in the Citadel Forge, the servitors were useful tools and the blacksmith kept a stock in both bases. The ten servitors hung on a rack, a loose and heavy chain drawn across each. They were a mix of mismatched robot parts – a slim mannequin form with oversized prototype gun arm, one with augmented leg pistons, one with a gigantic test claw. Each was different, none were whole.

Snik snik.

One was more complete than the others.

In the annex control room, a panel flashed, ran an automated script, then shut down once the *ping* of command completion sounded to nobody.

Snik snik.

The servitor that was more complete than the others had a whole body, legs and head, and one thin arm. The other arm, from the shoulder to articulated five-digit hand, was a wide, white metal construction, a freshly repaired spare arm from the SMART robot itself. Compared to the rest of the robot the arm was ridiculous and huge, like something out of a badly drawn manga.

Snik snik.

A light sparked in the servitor's optics, and the black fingers of the SMART arm flexed again, *snik snik.*

Lunar dust kicked over the threshold as the door closed. High above, the view from observation windows in the conference room would show more reflections, more moving lights. Everything on the moon that wasn't rock or dust acted like a mirror at noon, lunar time. The thing that moved was mostly dark brown and dark blue, but the wide, lopsided robotic arm was white and dazzling in the vacuum.

The robot's feet crunched forward, making no sound but sending an uneven vibration up and down the frame as the servitor continually tried to rebalance the SMART arm. Gears spun and pistons pulled. More vibration, more unsound.

The lunar dust was disturbed again as Hephaestus' body was dragged by one foot, turned roughly in a semicircle, leaving a scour in the dirt that would remain until the end of the universe.

The black hand on the end of the white arm reached down and took hold of the blacksmith's hammer. The dead hands refused to surrender the weapon, but were no match for the superpowered mechanical systems, and the frozen flesh and bone snapped clean off.

Wielding the hammer with SMART's arm, the servitor limped back to the airlock.

CHAPTER FIFTY

"Captain!"

Gillespie turned, scanning the mass of people weaving through abandoned cars on the packed highway and wishing he had a cigarette.

Everyone was heading away from the city in one great tide. Gillespie couldn't see a single person coming back towards the interstate bridge that connected North Beach to San Ventura proper.

Then he noticed that what he thought was the blue and red flicker of his Kojak was actually a blue glow from over his head. Looking up, he saw the Dragon Star descend, alighting on the only clear surface – the roof of his car. As her feet touched it, a translucent glowing bubble floated down behind her, attached to her powerstaff by a fine tether. Inside, the chief watched his two detectives gingerly find their footing, accompanied by billionaire industrialist Geoffrey Conroy wearing a strange black costume with a white cross on the front, and a woman with short black hair wearing... an orange prison jumpsuit? He recognized her at once, pleased at least that *somebody* had managed to take Doctor Jean Ravenholt into custody.

As soon as the Dragon Star snapped the bubble off, the group dropped another inch onto the roof of the car. Sam slid off the side straight away, then snapped a salute to her captain with a smile.

"That's quite an entrance, detectives," said Gillespie. "I'll take the cost of roof repair out of your next checks." He glanced up at Conroy and Ravenholt, still standing on the roof, and raised an eyebrow.

"Good evening, Mr Conroy." He turned back to Sam. "I'm gonna ask you about them later. First up, we need help."

Sam nodded and quickly surveyed the roadway. Most people were walking towards the suburbs. What space there was on either side of the highway on the narrow isthmus was packed with more people standing and watching the burning city. The area was a popular spot for watching city displays on the Fourth of July or similar occasions for those who weren't committed enough to camp for hours farther up the hills in the prime viewing positions. But this was something else entirely. Everyone looking back towards the city was doing so in complete shock. Well, most people. Some were crying, but some were laughing and pointing too. Assholes.

The meteor shower seemed to be passing. Although the sky was still filled with shooting stars, no further debris was falling on the safe side of the harbor. A few rocks, much smaller than the devastating lumps that had pelted the city earlier, but still large enough to be seen as they streaked downward, fell on the city. Their falls were slow, sickly somehow, almost drifting downwards in a steady tumble. It was surreal and frightening, like CG from a movie. Sam shook her head and turned away. Joe had his arms folded and watched with a grim expression. He nodded back to his captain.

"OK, what do we need to do here?"

Gillespie pointed back down the bridge. "There are police down the opposite end of the bridge. No one is answering their cell, and the radio in my car seems to be out as well. I don't know what's going on in the city, but if we can liaise with the patrol at the end of the bridge, perhaps we can get these people moving farther up into the hills."

Joe nodded, then looked at the one-way push of pedestrians walking between the stationary cars. A lot of vehicles were empty, engines cold, the drivers and passengers having abandoned them on the bridge and roadway to join the exodus on foot.

"Talk about pushing against the tide. Come on."

"Hey!"

Doctor Ravenholt shouted from the top of the car, and jumped off, pointing a finger in Sam's face. "What about us, peaches?"

"I'm hoping she is in custody and you aren't trusting her an inch," said Gillespie, glancing at her orange jumpsuit. He watched as the detectives fumbled for a concise explanation, but he'd already turned around.

"I can vouch for Jeannie," said Conroy. "We're all pitching in tonight."

Gillespie held his hands up. "OK, whatever, time's a-wastin' here. Let's clear this up first, then we can debrief." He began to walk off.

The Dragon Star pushed off into the air. Already the flow of pedestrians had snarled around the vehicle on which she'd landed as people called out to her with outstretched arms, begging or demanding assistance. She flew up just a few yards, but enough so everyone could now see her, from the end of the bridge to the furthest line of people halfway up the North Beach highway. Her powerstaff flashed, calling everyone to attention.

"Enough," she said, the authority in her voice overcoming her physical youth. "We have come to help and we expect full cooperation. You will obey all instructions of the law enforcement authorities." Her voice was loud, *superpowered* loud, and echoed out in the night. Everyone heard, some people cheered and clapped, and the exodus resumed their slow shuffle into the hills, perhaps at a slightly faster pace than before.

The Dragon Star lowered herself, and pointed her staff at the five unpowered humans. Gillespie took a step back and held his hands up.

"I'm needed here. You take the others wherever is best."

The superhero indicated her understanding. "Come," she said, a blue bubble of energy growing from the end of the powerstaff and enveloping Joe, Sam, Conroy and Jeannie. The Dragon Star turned and pulled her charges behind her into the air as she flew to the city side of the bridge.

Gillespie watched them for a moment, then turned back to his other officers. He really wanted a cigarette and, against all odds, he really wanted a robot coffee.

Sam had no clue how long they'd been chaperoning pedestrians and directing traffic, trying to get the bridge clear. She needed to rest – she and Joe both did – as they hadn't really stopped since the battle in

Moore–Reppion Plaza that had killed Tony Prosdocimi, but so long as men, women, children, babies, even cats and dogs needed assistance in reaching the relative safety of the North Beach hills, they'd keep working.

It was only when Joe started talking to her that she realized she wasn't listening. She'd spent the last couple of hours on autopilot, her conscious brain taking a much-needed break.

"I'm sorry, what?"

Joe raised his voice, thinking perhaps she just hadn't heard him above the hum of the crowd.

"I said, it looks like the main fires are under control."

Sam craned her neck over her shoulder at the cityscape behind. Most of the skyscrapers were now dark, not only because the power grid had either been shut down or burnt out, but because the ferocious yellow of the fire had almost vanished completely. Sam half-wondered what Aurora had been able to do, his power being based on channeling nuclear energy from the sun – fire from the stars, quite literally.

"Do you think they found the core yet?"

Sam shook her head, then shrugged, then rubbed her forehead. Now she really was too tired for such advanced thought processes. "I think we would know by now. Any news, Dragon Star?"

The superhero had just arrived from the opposite side of the harbor, where she had ferried a disabled man and his family over the top of the still-thick stream of people. There was little room on the roadway, so she hovered above Sam and Joe, forcing them to crane their necks awkwardly to see her. Sam wished she could lift the whole crowd across, but it was impractical and she knew only a select few – the disabled, infirm and elderly – could get a ride in the Dragon Star's magical bubble.

The Dragon Star stared into the city, then spoke. "I have not heard anything."

Joe nodded. "Well, yeah, we'll find out when they do, I guess. How's the progress on North Beach?"

The Dragon Star rotated on her axis in the air, gently coasting around to face away from them. Sam didn't know how far she could see, or hear, or whatever, but it was a little unnerving. Still, she'd been a tremendous help, moving not only people but cars and even buses.

"The beach and foothills are becoming crowded, but the area is safe. Regular law enforcement and emergency ambulance services will be able to get in soon. There are helicopters there already, both police and rescue. People are traumatized and unprepared for a night in the open, but they still hold hope."

"To be expected," Sam said. "We've been lucky. The city is used to weird happenings. Even on such a grand scale, they've handled it well."

There was a crackle, and right above Sam's head, the Dragon Star's powerstaff kicked in the air. The hero gained height a little, and the staff twitched again. Her cloak billowed in the breeze, lit from underneath by the pulsating light of the device.

Sam could sense something different about her. The superhero may have the body of a teenage cheerleader, but Sam had to remind herself that the alien intelligence animating the body was just that, alien, a fact betrayed by incorrect body language and, well, an inhumanly cold manner. Right now, she was rigid, tense, listening and looking for something. The Dragon Star raised her powerstaff, which buzzed hotly in the air.

"The power core. Come, we are in danger."

Sam looked at Joe, who stared back. She then looked around the immediate area, turning a complete circle. Three patrol cars, a handful of uniforms, some taking a break, the thin trickle of stragglers from the city.

"Where are Conroy and Blackbird?"

Joe's eyes widened as he joined Sam's search, their whiteness contrasting even more against his dark skin in the artificial light cast by the patrol car lights. "Oh shit. Not…?"

Sam met his eye. "The Cowl and fucking Blackbird. God*damn,* I knew it."

Before they could say anything else, the air fuzzed blue and purple, the Dragon Star's bubble surrounding them again and lifting the pair from the ground with a sudden jerk which threw them against the side of the sphere. Sam felt the bubble tingle against the heel of her hand.

"Hey! Where are we going?"

The Dragon Star pointed with her staff. Soon they were flying over the interstate bridge and to the North Beach hills.

"There. The power core is there. But..." She paused, and their flight stalled.

Sam looked up at her. "But what?"

The Dragon Star didn't reply immediately. When she did, Sam could see her mouth was pulled downwards at the edges, the closest that she'd ever seen the alien had got to an emotional expression.

"I cannot contact Aurora or any of the Wonders in the city. Even Bluebell's mind is closed."

Sam took a breath. Joe looked like he was ready to say something but she held a hand up, motioning him to keep quiet while she thought things through.

"First things first," she began slowly. "If the Cowl and Blackbird get the power core, the city really is history. That's number one. Number two, once we get the power core and those two assholes sewn up, then we go into the city and check on the heroes. For the moment we just have to assume they can handle themselves."

Joe's mouth closed, then he nodded. "Agreed."

"I too agree," said the Dragon Star, turning in the air and pulling the detectives behind her.

CHAPTER FIFTY-ONE

"Ah, a home away from home," said Jeannie. "Such sweet memories."

Conroy couldn't resist a laugh, but as he did he tripped and bumped into the corner of the building. Here, on the side facing away from the city and harbor, it was quite dark and he was forced to feel his way forward around the back of his old North Beach mansion.

"We do it your way, this is gonna take all night."

Jeannie strode past him, her bright overalls nothing more than a deep gray shadow. He took a delicate step forward, then tripped again as he started at the sound of breaking glass and splintering wood. He swore, called for Jeannie, then stopped as the outside lights flooded on.

"OK, that works."

He stepped around the corner, grimacing at the smashed French windows of his former mansion. Jeannie stood inside an airy dining area, furniture covered with white sheets.

"So what are we doing here, exactly?"

Conroy clacked his tongue against the roof of his mouth. "Well, seeing as we were in the neighborhood, there was just something I wanted to pick up."

"What about the evacuation of the city?"

Conroy waved a hand. "The heroes have that under control."

"Uh-huh." Jeannie put her hands on her hips. "I thought *you* were a hero now?"

Conroy laughed. "You could say that, yes, but a hero without powers? Useful, but only to a limited degree."

"Still feeling... impotent, eh?" Jeannie snorted.

"Oh, catty. I like that." Conroy hopped down a short flight of three wide stairs that led down into a broad lounge area. A massive copper-faced hearth stood cold against one immaculate white wall. Jeannie went to follow, then paused on the steps. On the floor in one corner was the crumpled cloak The Cowl had dumped millennia ago.

"And what are we looking for?"

"Oh, we're not looking for anything. I've found it." Conroy reached under the artfully angled frontage of the hearth, groping for a secret compartment. He let out a long "Ah-ha!" and withdrew his hand. He turned to Jeannie and held up a thick black cylinder, its surface shiny and glass-like.

"Prison life rotting the brain, eh?" he said with a smile. "We only raided a dozen secret locations and killed even more to build this."

"So that's where you hid it," said Jeannie. She frowned. "I didn't think we'd finished that project?"

Conroy rolled the device over in his hands, running his fingers over every square inch of its smooth surface.

"Oh, we didn't," he said. "There's no way to couple it with the core itself and charge it up, and of course we never got to the gun part. But it'll help locate the core, anyway. The city is a mess, I thought we might need it."

Jeannie reached out a hand, palm up. Conroy hesitated for a second, then handed the slim device over. It was featureless and smooth, with no controls or readout. Jeannie handed it back.

"I prefer my alien artifacts to have buttons. You know how to use it?"

Conroy looked at the cylinder. "You don't need to know how to use it. It'll do all the work."

Right on cue, the device blinked into life. The black metal surface changed hue, becoming a shiny gray like a TV set that's just been turned off in a dark room.

"Drop it!"

The blonde detective stood in the smashed doorway, legs splayed, pistol held firm in a two-handed grip. Behind and to her left, her partner adopted the same position, aiming squarely at Jeannie. The Dragon

Star hovered at the rear, head and shoulders above the two detectives and hefting her powerstaff horizontally over her own head.

Conroy took a step forward. The color of the wand shifted to a lighter shade of gray. "Sam, I..."

"That's Detective Millar, SVPD, Mr Conroy. Another step and I'll put a hole in that fancy suit of yours."

"It's armored, detective."

Sam twitched the gun up a fraction, maintaining her precise stance. "Well I'll just have to aim a little higher, won't I?"

Conroy raised his hands in surrender, making sure the power core detector was as visible as possible.

"Sam, you're making a mistake. I came here to collect this–" he waggled the device in the air "–which I thought would be the easiest way to find the power core."

Sam's expression didn't change. "Yeah, right."

Jeannie threw a sideways glance at her former lover. "Now what?"

"Now what nothing."

"No, like now what, what are we going to do?"

Conroy shrugged. "Like, nothing." He nodded at the Dragon Star. "Will this be useful? Take it."

The Dragon Star floated to the ground, and walked around the two detectives, obscuring their line of fire as her cloak spread out behind her. She walked up to Conroy, close enough that they almost touched. The Dragon Star looked up into his face, her eyes searching his features. Conroy imagined the alien mind inhabiting the body trying to read the expression and judge what the true intentions of this human were. Conroy smiled, and brought the device in front of the hero's face.

The Dragon Star reached up and took it. Conroy let got with no resistance. "I told you. I wouldn't betray the Seven Wonders."

Jeannie hissed. "You sonovabitch. You really have changed, haven't you?"

The Dragon Star took a step back and Conroy used the space to turn to Jeannie. "Damn right, honeybun." He looked at the detectives. "Happy?"

The Dragon Star turned and walked back up the stairs and towards the exit, holding her powerstaff in one hand and the detector in the other. Without stopping, she walked past the detectives and out into the grounds of house.

"Paragon speaks the truth. The power core is near – come."

Joe relaxed and holstered his gun, shaking his head but not arguing. Sam held the gun a moment longer, keeping Conroy in her sights.

"Sam?"

Sam's face was flushed red and her eyes were wet. But she took a breath and lowered her gun. She fixed Conroy with a dark look for a few seconds, then turned and followed the Dragon Star outside.

CHAPTER FIFTY-TWO

Sand Cat opened her eyes, seeing nothing but a rough, monochrome surface. For a moment a memory of the moonbase flashed before her eyes, and she wondered what she was doing lying – impossibly – outside on the desolation of the moon.

Then the fire. She sucked in a breath, the air bringing with it a choking grit. She coughed, her back arching from the uncompromising surface with each spasmodic expulsion of air. The movement was good, clearing her mind. The first thing she saw as she coughed was a hand attached to an arm – the hand was bare, the arm wrapped in a striped blue and white spandex sleeve. The fingers of the hand twitched as the owner groaned, Bluebell's face also pressed in the ground.

Sand Cat coughed again and was soon on her knees. Each spasm of her lungs helped push blood back into her head, clearing synapses and shocking her body back to normal function.

The fire, the city. She focused on the black chipped rock that covered the tarmac on which she had lain, the color far darker, she realized, than the light gray of the moon. Next to her lay Bluebell, unconscious. Next to Bluebell, Aurora and Linear. Neither moved except for slow breaths. Bluebell was the second to stir.

They were in a city square, small and plain and gray, nondescript bench seating surrounding a featureless paved open area. Sandwiched between high-rise office blocks, this secluded spot would be busy on a weekday lunchtime with office workers eating salads and drinking coffee. Around, the buildings were smoking shells, their glass-fronted facades shattered.

It was dark. Sand Cat stopped coughing and blinked, her magical vision gifted by the Goddess enabling her to see in low light. But this was different. It was night but the square, the buildings, were… *veiled,* somehow. It was like looking through a muslin sheet.

Footsteps, behind her. Sand Cat was on her feet, crouching low, spinning around in preparation for a fight. Nothing. The footsteps stopped, then restarted on the opposite side of the square. She turned again, calling out a challenge, curling her fists as she readied herself for a quick transformation into her spirit form in a heartbeat. The footsteps stopped, to be replaced by laughter. It was loud, brackish, the laugh of a drunken oaf at a frat house party. It bounced around the square then sounded immediately in Sand Cat's right ear. She flinched, ready to strike, but was met with a punch just as her head turned. She flew across the square, landing badly against one of the bench seats. She slumped to the ground, cried out and closed her eyes, but immediately started to pick herself up. The fight was on.

The man walked toward her, stepping over the comatose forms of Bluebell and Linear that lay in his path. Sand Cat squinted, trying to focus on him, but there was something odd about his costume. Like an optical illusion, as soon as she could make out a feature, more of the man's shape became indistinct, one part coming into sharp relief only for a different part to dissolve into headache-inducing fuzz. What she could see was simple enough – humanoid, male, a black silhouette, white eyes with black pupils. There were no other features, no depth at all to his shape or form. From her position, as he walked across the square, Sand Cat could only make him out in two dimensions. And then a white-toothed smile split the face, too wide to be human, teeth immaculate but monochromatic, like a child's drawing of teeth in chalk on a blackboard.

The shadow stopped. As he did so, Sand Cat saw the black haze around the square shimmer, ripple almost. Particulate black matter, dust-like but fine and smoky, hung around the figure, increasing in density around his neck and stretching out to envelop the square. A cloak of dust and shadow, of darkness, un-light. Hovering above his head by a good six inches was an indistinct shimmer of spikey shapes; Sand Cat realized with a start it looked like a crown.

The superhero drew herself up, ignoring the white-hot sear of pain that cut across her back after her violent impact with the bench. By the time the fighting began, it would be healed. Her balled fists fizzed with magnetic animal power.

"Who are you?" Sand Cat spat the words through teeth clenched in pain and anger.

The figure's smile broadened, the white shape sickly against the flat blackness of the face. "Oh, Sand Cat, what's the matter? Don't you recognize me? Don't you recognize one of your own?"

Sand Cat's eyes darted to the slumbering forms of Linear and Bluebell, lying on the ground. Bluebell continued to move her limbs in a very slow recovery.

One of our own? Who was he?

"I repeat, who are you?"

The smile shrunk. "I'd say I'm disappointed, but that would be a supervillain cliché." He walked up to Sand Cat, and bent down, bringing the black mask-like face to within an inch of her own. Sand Cat did not shrink back, did not show any sign of weakness, but even so close the man's face was... indistinct, indefinable.

"See," the man said, his voice now a whisper. "You should know me, and know me well. You're responsible for my death. Fortunately, I have new friends who are responsible for my rebirth."

Sand Cat expelled a short breath of surprise.

"The Justiciar?"

The figure smiled, and inclined his head in mock politeness. "Once, yes. Once a man called Tony. But now I bring the Living Dark to the city. I've been sent on a mission, you see, by friends who know what trust and responsibility are."

"Is that so?"

"It is, because–"

The Living Dark dropped from Sand Cat's eye line. She stood, and looked up to see the resurrected form of Tony being carried by the ankle into the sky by Aurora, corona blazing in anger. So close to the unleashed solar energy of the hero, the Living Dark appeared to whither and become thin and stick-like, his cloak of shadow all but vanished. Even with the increasing distance between them, she could see the sharp white outline of the mouth curved into a circle. The Living Dark cried out in pain, a wail so terrible that Sand Cat was forced to cover her ears.

Linear twitched with a shout, dragging himself to his knees and pressing his hands against the sides of his head to block the sound, a movement powered solely by his autonomic nervous system. Sand Cat could see Bluebell's mouth grimace in pain, but she remained unconscious.

Above, Aurora swung the Living Dark up, throwing him like a tennis ball about to be served. The Living Dark's emaciated body twisted like a rag, and Aurora powered a haymaker into the side of his head. There was a bang as his fist crossed the sound barrier and connected with the insubstantial black form, which bent around the impact like rubber before recoiling and flying back to the ground. Aurora wasted no time, powering down directly after the falling creature, catching it with a *one-two-three* just above the ground, pounding the Living Dark into the pavers. Aurora hovered, fists ready, waiting for the next attack.

Sand Cat raced across the square, somersaulting over Linear and transforming into her spectral form to gain speed, then twisting in the air back to human form as she reached Aurora. The two stood, looking at the twisted black figure lying motionless in the cratered ground.

"Something else hidden in the meteor shower? Or was this thing in the city already?" Aurora flexed his gauntlets, reducing his aura a fraction. White flame flickered from behind his mask and through the blank eyes.

Sand Cat shook her head. "It's the Justiciar – Tony Prosdocimi."

Aurora turned to Sand Cat, mouth moving in surprise. Finally he found his voice. "What? How do you know?"

"It – he – told me. Said he had new friends that brought him back to life. The Thuban?"

Gravel crunched behind Sand Cat. Her animal senses had realigned themselves after her period of unconsciousness, and she could smell the electric buzz of Linear as his molecules vibrated to a different rhythm to everyone else.

"One, my head frakkin' hurts like a... a... well, something painful. An elephant with a headache? That would hurt, wouldn't it?"

Aurora raised an eyebrow. Sand Cat stared at the speedster, never sure if the aged one was being serious or not.

"Two," Linear continued, oblivious and rubbing the back of his neck, "where are we and what's going on? OK, that's two and three. End of questions. Answers please, and an aspirin."

Aurora gestured to Sand Cat. "Fill him in." He walked between them and over to his wife, Bluebell, who had begun to stir again.

"I suggest you take a moment to clear your head, speedster." Sand Cat noted the slightly glazed look in Linear's eyes. They'd all been laid out by something – the Living Dark, probably – and would need time to fully awaken. "Do you not remember where we are?"

Linear craned his neck, looking around the square and the ruined and still-smoking buildings. "Oh I remember what we were doing and where we were, all right, I was just wondering where we were *now*."

"I do not understand."

"Well," he continued, still rubbing his neck with one hand while waving at the buildings around them with the other. "This doesn't look much like a real city to me."

Sand Cat snapped her head up, looking around the flat building faces quickly. The black haze was odd, certainly, rippling, causing the view of the buildings to curve out of true.

"You're half-right." Aurora re-joined the pair, supporting a groggy Bluebell on one arm. Bluebell had one hand on her forehead and her eyes were closed, but seeing the concern of her friends, she managed a smile and a nod.

Linear looked at Aurora. "Half-right?"

Aurora waved his hand in the air. There was some kind of smoke, a fine gray mist in the air. "We're in the city, but we're inside some kind of field, or bubble. Something artificial, a construct."

Sand Cat's animal hearing pricked, and she felt a light breeze on the back of her neck, as though someone was standing right behind her. She spun, but there was no one else in the square.

Then the laughter came again. Quiet at first, then building, a chuckle, a polite smirk at an inside joke, then expanding. A laugh, a gale of hilarity, then an insane scream.

The Living Dark rose from the crater where Aurora had put him. He floated in the center of the square, arms outstretched, white smile splitting the black face almost in half. The air swirled thicker now, the dusty shadow coalescing around his neck and spreading outwards once more, forming a cape made of night. The black crown flared over his head.

"Welcome, oh Wonders of the world, to the city of shadow. My city, where I am king. Where I am good and evil, where I am superhero and supervillain."

Linear huffed. "Just another crazy supervillain." He nudged Aurora. "Loop-de-loo and ready for the asylum. Quite like the old days, eh?"

Aurora flared and rose into the air, matching the Living Dark for height. "What do you want?" His voice boomed like an avalanche.

"I want for nothing. And nothing is what I deserve. A world of nothing."

The air darkened further, the black haze becoming black fog. The light from Aurora's rippling corona cut through it, but the edges of the square vanished into ink.

The Living Dark's eyes, the black pupils in the white ovals, darted around, looking at each of the heroes. Still the monster smiled.

"The Dragon Star is not here. No matter."

Quicker than Linear, the Living Dark reached out a pointed claw and grasped Aurora by the neck. Aurora struggled, caught by surprise by the impossibly fast motion. His aura exploded as a yellow and white solar flare, blasting the shadow shape before him. Plasma arced around invisible magnetic fields as Aurora became a tiny sun, striking the Living Dark from all sides and angles. The creature did not appear to notice. With a flick of his arm, the flares flashed out and Aurora flew to the ground.

Bluebell was at his side first, even before Linear managed to turn and reach him. Aurora lay on the ground, in the dark, dark himself. Above his mask, his red and gray hair hung limp, his ever-present halo of fire extinguished. His normally blazing red and yellow costume was dull, the colors still. And his eyes, once glowing white with the power of the core of the sun, were visible behind his mask. Normal, human eyes. Closed.

The Living Dark's laugh echoed around his mist-shrouded domain once more.

CHAPTER FIFTY-THREE

The Dragon Star was high above the hills. Sam got tired of looking up at her. It wasn't like she'd ever go out of sight. The night sky was clear and starry as the Earth passed clear of the Draconid meteors. Against the backdrop of night, the Dragon Star was a blazing beacon, her powerstaff pulsing rhythmically as she hovered, darted, hovered, darted. All the while she stayed on the north side of the harbor, not crossing into the mostly dark city which now sat silently smoking. The superheroes seemed to have done their job, putting out the main fires, but it worried her that the Dragon Star had been unable to reach them.

"Hey, Conroy, Cowl, Paragon, whatever you call yourself."

"Angry eyes, detective, angry eyes."

Sam squinted in annoyance and she huffed, her breath catching in the cool night air as a thin mist.

"Shut up." She waved his comment off. "Don't you have some kind of superhero communicator? Have you tried contacting Aurora and the others?"

Conroy held up his left arm, facing it out towards the detective. He pointed at a flat rectangle of plastic across his wrist. "Yes, I do. Yes, I have. No, they don't respond."

Blackbird coughed.

"What did you say?" asked Sam.

Blackbird looked sideways at Conroy, then back at Sam. "Oh, nothing, officer."

Snik snik.

Sam went to speak, but Conroy held up a hand. The large grounds of the hillside mansion were well lit after Blackbird had found the switch, and quiet. Night insects stirred in the immaculate garden that bordered the wide tennis lawn, but that was all.

Snik snik.

Sam took a few steps towards Blackbird, who stood resolutely with arms folded. "You got something to say, Agent Orange?"

Blackbird screwed her nose up. "Seriously, go fuck yourself."

Sam felt her temper rising, but Joe's call distracted her.

"Seems some meteorites hit your country pad, Mr Conroy." Joe reappeared from the far end of the lawn, out of the shadow cast by a fine, old tree. Sam turned, but couldn't quite see what he was holding.

"Where did you go? What's that?"

The lawn was swept by blue and white light as the Dragon Star returned to the Earth. Her powerstaff was a Christmas tree of flashing colors, and the metallic detector held in her other hand was glowing a light gray. Most surprising to Sam was her face. Beneath the hood, her mask came down and covered her forehead, the area around her eyes, and the top of her cheeks, leaving her nose, mouth and chin exposed. She was smiling, broadly, making the alien superhero look, for the first time, like the dead cheerleader whose body she inhabited. Sam didn't like it.

Conroy folded his arms, and tapped a finger against his lips. "I have a feeling that the detective has just detected what we've been looking for."

Joe's mouth opened. He was holding a multi-faced crystalline rock, the many dull facets making the object roughly spherical. It had a natural, organic, metalloid quality that implied it was just another meteorite, but perhaps one of those rare, special ones that always got their own special case in a science museum. Joe stretched both arms out full, moving the core as far away from his body as he could while still holding it. He whistled, low.

Everyone took a step back as the Dragon Star flew forward. As she got closer, the flat faces of the object changed color, moving to match the reflective gray of the detector.

Snik snik.

Sam glanced around, the sound again at the edge of her hearing. But there was nothing. High on the North Beach hills, the main road and the refugees from the city were half a mile down Conroy's exclusive driveway, their distant chatter a static rush blending with the sound of water in the harbor. But other than that, there was no sound except for the crickets in the grass.

Snik snik.

"Geoff?"

Sam turned at Blackbird's call, and saw she was not the only one casting furtive glances. Conroy nodded.

"You get the feeling we're not alone?"

The Dragon Star reached out towards Joe, who was more than willing to hand the power core over. "How come it landed so far out of the city anyway?"

Conroy turned to scan the edges of his property. "The Thuban were never clear on where it would come down, hence the ability of that little doohickey to detect it like a dowsing rod. I guess they homed in on here as some of our original transmissions were relayed through the satellite dish." He pointed up at the roof of the house, where a perfectly ordinary subscription-television antenna innocently stood. "I guess. I don't know. Dragon Star, ma'am?"

Snik snik.

The Dragon Star touched the power core.

Snik snik.

Blackbird yelled out as Joe was dragged to one side with a shout, his upper arm enclosed almost completely in a black robotic hand. The hand – and the arm to which it was attached – was thin and wiry, but there was enough power in the servitor's basic frame to crack Joe's humerus in two places. He sagged to the ground, the power core slipping to the clipped grass. The servitor flexed its other arm, the wide, white armored limb looking ridiculously large and out of proportion, the large black hand on the end gripping something small and club-like.

The Dragon Star kicked back, feet six inches from the ground but the base of her staff embedding into the dirt, propelling her backwards like a gondola punt.

Sam swore as she saw Joe fall, but Blackbird pulled her back by her shoulders, overbalancing the pair of them. They rolled back onto the grass. Conroy was still on his feet but not far behind.

"What the fuck is that?" Sam asked with surprising calmness.

Conroy frowned, but it was the Dragon Star who answered. "It's a servitor from the workshop of Hephaestus."

"And that," Conroy pointed, "looks like one of SMART's arms."

Snik snik.

"KAPPA-DELTA-ALPHA-ALPHA" The robot's voice was thin and far-away. It repeated the code then uttered a second string. "SIGMA-TAU-OMICRON-OMICRON."

The robot didn't move. It just stood, apparently scanning the group in front of it, twin red optics shining brightly. Between it and the Dragon Star, the power core glowed darkly in the grass.

Joe carefully reached under his jacket with his good arm and gripped his pistol. He didn't draw it, but he was ready. He gasped for breath, fighting the pain, and hissed at Sam. "I thought SMART was destroyed – deactivated?"

Sam nodded. Jeannie cut in. "Destroyed, yes. Deactivated? Doesn't look like it. We left SMART's memory core plugged into the moonbase computer."

Conroy sighed. "And SMART *is* the computer."

"Well," said Joe. "Don't you feel silly."

"Yeah thanks, detective."

The Dragon Star touched down on the grass, bringing the powerstaff around. The power core was only a few feet away, and the robot wasn't moving. She took a small step forward. Nothing. She took another step forward, swinging the crystal-tipped end of her staff to point at SMART 2.0. Nothing. Finally she walked up to the power core and reached down for it.

She never reached it. As the top of her hood obscured her face, the servitor swung the SMART-arm out, raising the hammer of Hephaestus high. Sam and Jeannie saw it, and called out, but it was too late.

There was a slap as the hammer connected with the top of the Dragon Star's head and a flash that left the humans staggering backwards. When the spots had cleared from their vision, the Dragon Star lay on the grass, face down. The robot kept the deadly arm outstretched, but did not move. The exposed servos in its chassis clicked into a new position as it rebalanced the too-heavy arm, *snik snik*. The power core remained untouched.

"ALPHA-OMEGA-MISSION-ONE-SUCCESS."

Joe emptied the magazine into the robot. Unlike the original super robot, the servitor was no more than a skeletal robotic frame, all motive units and mechanisms exposed. But the metal was the same with which the Greek god had built the original SMART. Although Joe's aim was true, his regular firearm was useless. The night was lit with showers of orange sparks as the bullets uselessly hit their target.

As Joe's gun clicked to empty, Sam dropped and moved forward in a soldier's crawl. Within reach of the Dragon Star's feet, Sam grabbed her ankles and pulled. The superhero's body was surprisingly heavy, but moved just a little. The servitor watched her with its twin optics, but made no attempt to intercede. Sam swore as her grip on the smooth spandex-covered calves of the Dragon Star slipped. Blackbird stepped forward, hesitated, and then ran in to help her. She grabbed one leg with one hand, and yanked at Sam's collar with the other. Sam got the message, stood, and together they quickly dragged the Dragon Star back a few yards from the robot, out of the reach of the white arm. Joe reached for a spare magazine, but Sam called him back. He nodded and limped back to join the others, his injured arm held firm across his chest.

Someone had turned the Dragon Star over. Her eyes and mouth were open. The body was dead – it had been for several years, and Sam really had no idea whether the Dragon Star breathed or bled or had any semblance of life when she was up and moving anyway. But now the body seemed empty somehow, just a teenage girl in weird fancy dress. Despite the violent impact of the blacksmith's hammer on the top of her head, there appeared to be no physical injury.

"Where's her staff?"

Sam looked back at the servitor. While they'd been arguing, it had picked up the magical alien artifact and was holding it in the heavy SMART arm.

"Fuck."

The powerstaff had gone dark after the Dragon Star had fallen, but as the robot's thick fingers moved over the shaft, the bright glow from within the weapon relit. The robot flexed the arm, swinging the staff with little effort, and took a step forward. There no longer seemed to be balance issues as power from the staff was transferred into its own systems. It shook slightly, and the red lenses in its head flared brighter.

Jeannie frowned, her hands on her hips. "Now what, superheroes?"

Sam thought. She was unpowered. So was Joe, so was Conroy. Jeannie was a halfling, moderately powered, but only to just beyond regular human performance. Which would mean she'd be fast. Sam glanced down and saw the cylinder portion of the Thuban device was still held in the dead Dragon Star's hand.

"Blackbird," Sam said. "The power core."

"The what now?"

Conroy crawled forward on one knee, reaching over the Dragon Star's inert form to place a hand on Sam's shoulder.

"We can't use the power core. We have no idea what it is capable of. It's dangerous, far too dangerous for any of us to try to use."

Sam turned to him. "The Cowl – *you* – were planning on using it to take out the Seven Wonders, right? All of them. It wasn't just the Dragon Star. The opportunity was too good."

He hesitated. "Well yes, but the Cowl never finished building the power coupling device. The only thing that got done was the detector wand."

"Then what do you suggest? The Thuban sent it for a human to use, so there must be a way." She looked past Conroy at Blackbird. She took a breath to speak, but the Cowl's former sidekick was already shifting into a runner's crouch.

"You guys talk too much. Do or do not, Yoda said." She bent her head down, eyed up SMART, and took off.

And she was fast. Not Linear fast, but she would set a new record in the one hundred meters. Even on the smoothly trimmed grass, she hit a sprinter's pace in seconds, tearing up the turf. It was only a couple of dozen yards to where the power core lay under the swing of SMART's arm. Blackbird turned as she ran, skidding into the soft ground, mud and grass showering the robot. By the time she was level with the power core, she was already turned to run back.

And then she skidded too far, her center of gravity in the wrong place, and she collapsed onto her front, thudding her breastbone onto the power core. She cried out, and scrabbled to get traction. Behind her, SMART's eyes swiveled and fixed on her prostrate form. It raised the powerstaff in a series of jerky movements, the mechanics still adjusting to using the overly long weapon.

"Blackbird!" Conroy called out. Joe swore and ran towards her. Sam's eyes widened in fear as the powerstaff crackled. Blackbird rolled onto her side and fumbled underneath her. She pushed the power core along the grass a little, finding a one-handed grip awkwardly on its wide surface. She shouted something, and tossed the object towards Sam. Joe watched the throw as he ran, then dived for Blackbird's outstretched arm.

Sam caught the power core as the servitor fired the powerstaff at Blackbird. Sam watched as the staff glowed, a liquid ball of white energy coalescing at its tip. It detached itself from the staff with impossible slowness, and crawled through the air towards Blackbird's back, just six feet away.

Sam wondered why it was taking so long to hit her. She stepped forward, finding herself instantly standing in front of the robot. That was strange. Beside her, the glassy blob of plasma was tracking an inch at a time towards its target. Sam reached out gingerly and touched it. It was warm, and slightly tacky. She laughed, and plucked it out of the air. She held it for just a minute, then squeezed her hand. The blob compressed, then popped, miniature drops of the glue-like energy flying into the air.

SMART was still aiming the powerstaff at Blackbird, but wasn't otherwise moving, and a second shot did not appear to be forthcoming. Sam stepped over Blackbird, reached up, and tugged the staff. It wouldn't budge from SMART's grip, so Sam pulled the huge arm off the skeleton and threw it clear.

The servitor was really a fascinating object. Taller than a person, it was little more than a frame of some coppery metal, the bulk of it filled out with pipes, electronics, gears, levers, all manner of moving parts. Sam wasn't really sure what was important or not, so she reached into the open abdomen and smashed it all. The robot still stood, so she snapped the thick framework in several places and pushed the robot backwards. It took forever to hit the grass – Sam walked around it as it toppled through treacle. She gave it a shove a couple of times to hasten the fall, which seemed to accelerate it, just a little.

There was a flash. Sam doubled-over, breathing hard, then looked up. The air she sucked in was cold and hurt her nose. In front of her, she was surprised to see the servitor scattered across the lawn in several smoking piles. The powerstaff lay nearby, remnants of the black robotic claw still attached to it.

"What the fuck have you done?"

Sam turned. Conroy and Blackbird were on their knees, looking at her with wild, shocked looks, eyes and mouth so wide in... fright? Sam smiled, and saw Blackbird raise a hand to her mouth. The hand shook.

Sam laughed, and in a second she found herself standing close – too close – to Conroy and Blackbird. How had she reached them so quickly, in the blink of an eye? The pair jerked backwards in surprise. Sam frowned, and reached out to help them up. Then she saw her arm, and stopped. It was bare, white, *glowing*. She moved it experimentally, and the white glow left a dusty trail in the air. Looking down, she saw her whole body was the same. She was naked – *felt* naked – but the glowing white mist swirled around the appropriate places, wrapping her in light, almost like a... costume?

Sam turned. On the grass, where she had been standing with Conroy and Blackbird and Joe just a few moments ago, lay the power core. It had split along the sharp faces of the polyhedron, six sides cracking open. It lay, spread like a flower, hollow and empty. Sam looked at her hands and arms again. She glowed in the night. The power core had given her its power.

"If that's still Sam Millar in there, you need to control the power!" Conroy was speaking. Sam didn't turn, but listened to his voice as she examined her forearms. She felt light, energetic.

"Because if you can't control it, you'll kill us too!" A pause. "Sam, look!"

Sam turned. Conroy was approaching her on foot, one arm outstretched in a nervous, almost pleading gesture. Blackbird sat on the grass behind him, keeping her distance.

As soon as Conroy saw Sam was paying attention, he pointed with his other hand to his left. Sam looked, seeing only a long gray shape lying in the grass.

Joe.

She was at his side in an instant, but his body flopped unnaturally at her touch. His skin was warmer than the air, but only just. Square in his chest was a circular burn. Sam tore his shirt off, the body arching as her miraculous alien strength wrenched the fabric apart. The burn was deep, a crater of cauterized flesh reaching down into his chest cavity.

"What is this? How did...?"

Conroy approached but kept a fair distance, and even then, kept his legs tense, ready to retreat from the glowing figure that had been Detective Sam Millar.

"It was a blast from the powerstaff. You stepped in the way and deflected it with your hand. Remember? There was an explosion, energy showered the whole place. One hit Joe – he was running to help Blackbird." Conroy looked Sam up and down. "You've absorbed the power core. Blackbird threw it... I didn't see what happened, perhaps nothing happened. One minute she threw it, the next you were dismantling SMART with your bare – glowing – hands."

Sam listened, kneeling by Joe's body. She'd caused his death. She was just trying to stop SMART killing Blackbird. Killing a criminal. Executing a criminal. Joe had died for... Blackbird? It was her fault. She threw the power core because she ran too fast, she slipped, she didn't think. It's all a game to her. To Blackbird.

Sam stood and Conroy darted backward. She bunched her fists by her sides, and they flared with streaky white light. Jeannie saw the look on her face and scrabbled to her feet.

"What?"

Sam took a step forward, the grass beneath her smoking with each footfall. "You. You did this." Her voice echoed, energy crackling like fire underneath each word.

Conroy placed himself between Sam and Blackbird, holding his hands out. At a few yards' distance, Sam's uncontrolled energy burnt the palms of his hands.

"Wait there, superhero. It's nobody's fault. Somehow the power core opened, and you used it to destroy SMART there. That's all according to plan. If it wasn't for you, we'd all be dead, and there'd be nothing to stop that thing going after the Seven Wonders."

Sam stopped. The Seven Wonders. Was she a superhero now? Was she more powerful than Aurora? Where were the Seven Wonders?

Sam lifted one hundred feet into the air on a pillar of white smoky light. She rotated to view the city, still dark without power. There, near the center, near the base of the Citadel of Wonders itself, something darker, not the night or smoke, something artificial, energetic. She listened for a moment, to a thousand conversations on the harbor side as city refugees passed the night watching the dead city, to police radio, fire radio, civil defense. To people trapped in the city, to their rescuers freeing them. To falling masonry and broken glass, to the steel skeletons of the skyscrapers groaning as they cooled in the aftermath of the fire.

She could see the city in her mind, every sound and sight mapped, giving her a complete three-dimensional view of San Ventura from every angle. At the center, there was no light, no sound. Energy bent around the envelope of darkness, an egg-shaped hemisphere.

She listened again, just to be sure. A million million sounds and voices. Not one of them from the Seven Wonders.

Conroy and Blackbird forgotten, Sam flew off to the city to save the superheroes.

CHAPTER FIFTY-FOUR

Conroy watched Sam skyrocket towards the city, a blazing white shooting star that would not have been out of place in the Draconid shower. Jeannie joined him, following his gaze out to the city.

"Well, shit."

Conroy hrmmed. "You're lucky she – *it* – has a short attention span."

"Do you think there's anything left of the detective in there?"

"She's strong. It might be the power doing the thinking now, but she'll learn to control it."

"And if she doesn't?"

He turned to Jeannie, then looked over her shoulder at Joe's body. "You have a point there."

"I have a point there, yes." She walked over the lawn, ignoring Joe and stepping over the Dragon Star's body. The alien's powerstaff flickered, lighting the blades of grass up around it. "At least we have this thing."

"You think you can work it?"

Jeannie sank to her haunches, observing the staff but keeping her hands tucked into her stomach, unwilling to touch it. It was a dark metal, the surface covered with thick seams and hieroglyphs. Here and there the hieroglyphs shone brightly. Others glowed with a dull light. Jeannie and Conroy had both seen the staff in action many times.

"I'm not even sure I want to touch it. Could be dangerous."

Conroy joined her. He gave the staff a nudge with his toe. It rocked on the ground, but there was no change in the pattern of illumination.

He nudged it again, rather pointedly, out of Jeannie's reach. She looked up at him from her crouched position.

"Dangerous, yes." He smiled. "In your hands."

Jeannie stood quickly. "In my hands? Oh come on. I'm still a prisoner? After all this? San Ventura burns to the ground, the Seven Wonders are missing, and what, you want to get me in powercuffs? Just try it, Captain Virtuous."

Conroy held her gaze. In her anger, Jeannie had come to within an inch of his face, and their noses almost touched. Jeannie's breath was hot and fast, Conroy's calm, almost imperceptible.

"When this is all done," he said, "we'll see what we can do. In the meantime, I have need of Blackbird's special skills."

Jeannie raised an eyebrow, then smiled as her former lover used her supervillain name. "You do… or the Cowl does?"

"Like I said, let's see when all this is done. But in the meantime, our problems are more pressing, and I have a better idea."

"That so?"

"That so."

"And it is…?"

Conroy looked at her face, holding the gaze a moment at such close quarters. Then he stepped back, turned around, and walked back to the house. He called over his shoulder for Jeannie to follow.

Inside, Jeannie found him in his den. As with the rest of the house, everything was covered in white sheets, matching the white walls and giving the place a quiet, reserved dignity even though it was mothballed.

Conroy swept the dustcover from the large desk, revealing a stylishly expensive glass and steel table, still covered with papers and paraphernalia. Ignoring the computer, he fiddled with the edge of the table. There was a click, and a section of white wall behind the desk slid open. Inside the dark cavity, two fireman's poles glinted in the dim light thrown from the approaching dawn through the French windows that were ubiquitous to the whole building.

Jeannie leaned over the desk, looking at the poles and then to Conroy. He grinned and gestured to the poles with an expansive sweep. This entrance hadn't been used in years. Jeannie raised an eyebrow but her smile matched his. Conroy placed one hand on the pole closest.

"I know how you gave Tony his power, and I know you two went down into the Lair. But I'm assuming your lab is still operational?"

Jeannie hesitated. Conroy watched her face for a while, then continued after she failed to respond. "The antidote to the power core will be the MIC-N, correct?"

Jeannie nodded, slowly. "Aurora told you, right?"

"He told me a lot. About the MIC-N. About you."

Jeannie looked away, changing the focus of the conversation. "You're right. If we needed to, we could drain Sam's power off."

"And transfer it back to the power core?"

Jeannie shrugged. "Maybe. We won't know until we try it. It should be possible. Do you think we'll need to use it on Sam?"

Conroy nodded. "Yes." He pulled himself onto the pole, clinging to the smooth metal with his arms and legs. "We'll need to," he said, sliding into the darkness below.

In the damp grass, the light of the powerstaff remained strong, but as the rising sun began to compete with the alien light, the staff seemed to dull, the light diminish. The sunrise crept over the crest of the North Beach hills, the first rays striking the staff's shaft, rendering the dense, dark coppery metal from which it was made a flat, almost plastic hue. Lying next to the staff, the morning light reflected brightly from the white sections of the Dragon Star's spandex costume. Even after numerous battles and, ultimately, her death, the costume was as immaculate and colorful as ever.

There was a muffled sound, a slippery rustling, as someone walked across the dew-damp lawn. Feet in black leather shoes carefully stepped over the Dragon Star. They stopped for a moment over the body, then continued their tread.

As dawn broke a hand reached down and picked up the powerstaff. A strong, male hand, the skin as dark as the burnished metal of the staff.

Ripped shirt flapping in the wind, the former SVPD detective, the late Joe Milano, rose into the air and flew towards the darkness at the heart of San Ventura.

CHAPTER FIFTY-FIVE

Bluebell closed her eyes. Hands to her forehead, she desperately reached out to her husband. He was alive, his mind floating on the sea of unconsciousness. Bluebell sighed, unable to communicate with his subconscious mind, but relieved nonetheless. His body lay on the ground, still dark, but breathing. She hoped that his fire would reignite when he came to, but this was the first time he'd been knocked out – the first time he'd ever not been *awake* – so all she could do was hope.

Linear completed another lap of the night bubble perimeter, skidding to a halt next to Bluebell, shaking his head. Sand Cat stood in the center of the square in a fighter's crouch, looking directly up to where the Living Dark hovered, white gash mouth slicing an evil smile into the otherwise featureless face. The creature seemed content to just watch.

Linear knelt over Aurora. Bluebell looked at him, uncertain, delicately touching her husband's face. Aurora moaned, but his eyes remained closed.

"Come on, big guy. We need some firepower here." Linear reached down, brushing Bluebell's hand away, and slapped their leader hard across the face. Aurora's head jerked, but he did not wake. Bluebell yelled, but Linear took hold of Aurora's shoulders and shook them violently.

"Dude, wake up and start kicking ass."

Bluebell finally managed to pull Linear off. The two sat back on their haunches, watching the steady, slow breath of Aurora. Bluebell spoke quietly.

"He's never been unconscious before." She looked at Linear, eyes moistening.

Linear stood and scratched his beard. The Living Dark and Sand Cat seemed to be in some kind of Mexican standoff. He looked around the dark square again.

"Maybe if I can find the frequency at which his night-shield, or whatever it is, vibrates, I can set up a counter-vibration." He took off again, becoming nothing but an indistinct silver flash around the edge of the bubble.

The Living Dark laughed, and began to spin on his axis, watching Linear's trail and eventually matching it for speed, sending out a shockwave which knocked Sand Cat to the ground, Bluebell falling a second later. As Bluebell hit the dirt she saw a flash of blackness connect the Living Dark with the wall of the night bubble. A second flash and Linear somersaulted through the air, colliding with the opposite side of the bubble and bouncing to the ground not far from Aurora. Bluebell leapt to her feet and ran to him. He was awake, conscious, blood streaking his face. He writhed a little, one hand to the back of his head. His glasses were broken.

There was a bestial roar. Bluebell looked behind, over her shoulder, to see Sand Cat in her animal form pogoing upwards, snapping at the Living Dark. His shadow cloak swirled around her as she clawed the air. One paw caught his leg, jerking the black figure downwards, but even as he reached the ground there was another flash of black as the Living Dark's fist connected with Sand Cat's muzzle. Bluebell watched as the insubstantial black fist and forearm traveled all the way through Sand Cat's head in one sweep. The superhero roared and blinked back into her human form. She remained upright for a moment, but then her head slumped and her legs slackened, and she toppled to the ground.

Bluebell stood. That was it. She was the last hero standing. Electrical energy caressed her body as her suit helped channel psychic energy into something more tangible, more *offensive*.

In the past, in the golden age when superheroes from all over the world battled supervillains, there had been bad guys like the Living Dark. Supercharged supervillains like the Black Mass, who drew power from a sentient black hole at the center of the galaxy. Magical anti-heroes like Twenty-Two, immune to all laws of physics. They'd been defeated and imprisoned or banished, when the superheroes had united. The Seven Wonders of San Ventura and the Chicago Nightguard. The Seven Wonders plus the Hyper-Committee plus the Ancient and Artful Legion versus the Sultan of Space. The Seven Wonders and United International taking down Death Route 66. Funny how it always seemed to be one single supervillain, one entity that required a superheroic team-up of ten, twelve, twenty, one hundred superheroes. But that's the way it always was.

Those days were gone. Sure, a lot of the superhero groups were still around, enjoying comfortable celebrity, staying out of the business of the world now that all the supervillains had been defeated. A few were stationed on alert, but only in a very casual, part-time manner. If any trouble flared up, if any supervillain returned, they would just contact the Seven Wonders. The rest were tour guides or charity mascots.

Except the Cowl. Except the Seven Wonders. That was a special case. A game: super cat and mighty mouse. It had gone on too long, too far. And now it had cost the city, and the lives of the people of San Ventura, and had destroyed the Seven Wonders. It had brought the Living Dark down upon them. Bluebell was the last hero standing.

She took a deep breath, and took a step forward, playing it slow to allow her power to build up. The Living Dark stood in the center of the square, watching her approach, the monstrous smile fixed.

Bluebell thought about saying something bold and meaningful, lecturing the creature on its evil ways. Something stirring, something American.

And then she thought about saying something funny, caustic. Make a joke about his face. Crack wise about his mother.

Arcs of electricity crackled over her body.

After five more steps, Bluebell realized she didn't have anything to say. Heroic speeches were for Aurora. Quips about poor performance in the bedroom were Linear's ticket. She didn't have any material to play, and she wasn't in much of a mood to come up with something.

She was the last hero standing.

Instead, as she tensed to charge, arms outstretched ready to unleash a volley of electrical psychic energy, she screamed.

"Get the fuck out of my city, you sonovabitch!"

White lightning, blue at the edges, zigzagged towards the Living Dark. In the split second before the arc of energy connected, Bluebell saw the white smile drop, just a little. Then the world flashed blue and white and blue again, the walls of the night bubble around the square reflecting the bursts of color back like a camera flash.

Bluebell took another step forward, took another deep breath, and whipped her hands forward again. A second blast of energy, more powerful than the first, focused by concentration and training and fuelled by anger and hate. She didn't even see the Living Dark, but she could feel the resistance as the bolts of psychic lightning found their target a second time. Her leg muscles tensed as her upper body absorbed the kickback from the blast.

When the flashing stopped it took Bluebell a moment to be able to see again. The brilliant strobe of her attack had rendered her blind in the darkness, but the building charge in her suit for the third attack threw more than adequate light across the whole square.

The shadows moved, dusty smoke coalescing into a figure, a figure which flexed its arms and rolled its neck like a prize fighter. The eyes opened, white with fixed black pupils, and the figure smiled, a white diagonal streak across the blank face.

Bluebell dropped to her knees, the realization that the supercreature was immune to her powers suddenly draining the fight from her. She felt tired. Parts of her body throbbed in protest, recovering still from her earlier injuries. Her suit channeled her telepathic abilities into pure force, but there were limits, and her attack had nearly drained the battery. She looked around, at Aurora and Linear and Sand Cat, each alive but in varying states of consciousness and injury.

If she'd been in the open, she could have made a call, either by her wrist communicator or by mental projection. She could have called some of her old friends. Captain Captain for sheer muscle power. Or maybe the Absolute. Or better yet, both.

But the wrist comms registered no signal, and her telepathy was unable to penetrate the night-shield thrown up by the Living Dark. He was a formidable foe, and part of Bluebell saluted the fact. The Seven Wonders had come up against the best, the most powerful, and had been overcome. They'd paid the price for their mismanagement of the city. But at least, at the end she'd given it all she had.

The square exploded with light. The light was yellowish, carrying heat, and… promise. It was the light of a dawn, of a new morning. It flooded the square as the curtain of darkness shriveled, evaporating into a slick dust that stuck in Bluebell's hair. Bluebell spun around, towards the source.

Surrounded by the light of mornings, the Living Dark cowered. His mouth-slash became a circle, the white eyes wide and the pupils tiny pinpricks. He held his arms in front of his face, and Bluebell could see how thin and insubstantial they were. It was the same for his whole body. In the light he seemed to dry out, desiccate, trailing the black dust behind him, somehow blown off his body by the falling rays of sun.

Bluebell followed his gaze upwards. She was grateful for the sun – from the moon to the Earth, she'd experienced a night far longer than was natural.

Except this was not the morning sun. The light radiated from a central point – Bluebell could see the spokes angling down through the dusty air. The rays rotated, widening, as the source came closer and closer. It was a figure, flying fast…

A superhero.

Bluebell stared until her vision almost whited out, ignoring the stabbing pain along her optic nerves as the whoever-it-was flew down into the square. Judging distance was hard, and then as Bluebell got to her feet and scrambled backwards suddenly the superhero was there, on top of the Living Dark. The light was bright, like a physical presence, pushing Bluebell to the ground. Beneath the white envelope, she saw the Living Dark shrink to nothing more than a skeleton, a bundle of black sticks quivering in fear. It was screaming, mouth open, but Bluebell couldn't hear above the roaring in her head. The light was too much. She closed her eyes, the insane bright white turning to a maddening bright red. She rolled onto her front, retched, and felt about a thousand years old. A wave of nausea spread up from her stomach. The red of her vision became spangled with white stars.

The last thing she heard as she passed out, the impossible force of light sitting on her back, pushing the consciousness out of her head, was a powerful female voice, swearing, making threats, talking about the city and her parents and *whathaveyoudonetothecityyousonovabitch*?

Bluebell blacked out as the superpowered Detective Sam Millar unleashed her years of fear and anger on Tony Prosdocimi, the Living Dark.

CHAPTER FIFTY-SIX

"Just like old times."

"Huh?"

Jeannie raised her voice. "Just! Like! Old! Times!"

"Oh yeah. F'sure." Conroy gunned the accelerator, twisting the handgrip the full way around and leaning to one side. Jeannie matched his movement, and the motorcycle smoothly skirted another torn-up patch of road.

They were traveling on a superbike, but not one built by the Cowl or augmented by Jeannie. Well, maybe just a little. It wasn't a hog, but it was still huge. Sleek Japanese lines and streamlined shell for aerodynamics. A racing bike, perhaps not strictly street-legal. Just one of billionaire Geoff Conroy's many playthings.

It was the best way into the city – hell, short of flying, it was the *only* way in. The crowd at North Beach parted as the motorcycle roared towards them. The bridge was still packed with cars, most abandoned, doors open, but there was plenty of room. And then in the city itself, the roads were a mess of craters big and small, abandoned cars, destroyed cars and debris fallen from buildings, not to mention some buildings in their entirety, collapsed as the unnatural path of the meteor storm intersected with the city.

Even with the colossal damage to the civic infrastructure of San Ventura, they made superb progress. The bike was fast, punchy, and Conroy was an expert rider. All they had to do was point a route straight to the Citadel of Wonders, which had escaped the meteor strike and was apparently the only thing left with power. In the dark heart of the city, its crystalline walls projected a rainbow of colors across the devastation.

Jeannie held close to Conroy's back, feeling his muscles flex as he controlled the machine, leaning in with him with every agile turn. As she felt his new superhero armor, she realized that while Jeannie and Geoff had often gone riding or driving or flying (conventionally speaking), Blackbird and the Cowl never had. The Cowl liked gadgets but not machines. With his innate superpowers he had no need for cars or bikes. So when Jeannie had shouted that it was just like old times over the howl of the engine, she realized she hadn't been talking about riding hell-for-leather through the city on a supermachine, she meant it was just like old times with him, going on an adventure, a caper, something dangerous. She felt that spark somewhere inside flicker, and her heart race. She breathed in the smell of his hair.

Another sharp turn, and the machine in the bike's tiny cargo box rattled. The power transfer device – the MIC-N – was small and portable, and for that Jeannie thanked her not-insubstantial technical skill. They'd collected it from Tony's apartment, which thankfully had sustained only minor damage in the meteor storm. She only hoped it would work, and that the broken shell of the power core wasn't just a disposable, single-use container. She edged a hand farther around Conroy's chest as the bike bumped over more debris.

Conroy slowed the bike, and Jeannie saw his head angled downwards. She peered over his shoulder, the floodlit square ahead too bright for him to safely steer towards. Not for the first time, Jeannie wished she had her Blackbird mask.

Conroy pulled the bike into the shadow of an alleyway; Jeannie hopped off the rump and hefted the MIC-N from the cargo box.

Conroy squinted at her.

"We good to go?"

Jeannie nodded. With no further debate, Conroy turned and sprinted towards the light, head down, dodging between rubble in his limited field of vision.

The being that had once been Sam Millar stood in the center of the square, holding something in front of her. Around her, splayed like the picked petals of a flower, were Aurora and Sand Cat, Linear and Bluebell. All were face down, although whether they were dead or not, Jeannie couldn't tell. There was no time to check.

She looked at Sam, her eyes popping with pain until they adjusted as best they could to the light. She could just make out a smooth, curved female form. One arm out in front held a thin, scarecrow-like figure by the neck. The figure was thin, almost two-dimensional, its black outline streaming ash in the radiant energy. Jeannie had no idea who it was, or what was going on, or even if their plan was a good idea or even if it would work at all and what were they thinking and what would happen afterwards and wasn't this a new superhero now and…

She jumped as Conroy clapped a hand on her shoulder. Keeping his back to the light, he pulled the shell of the Thuban power core from inside his tunic. He turned to Jeannie and nodded.

Jeannie snapped out of her reverie, and brought the MIC-N to bear on Sam.

Sam turned her head, and looked at Jeannie. Jeannie felt a rush of adrenaline punch through her chest, almost enough to physically knock her over. Sam's expression was beyond anger or rage. It was hate. Superheroes were supposed to be stoic, epitomes of fair justice. Whoever it was in her grip, Sam was killing him or her or it. Surprised at her own moral judgment, Jeannie realized that Sam couldn't be a superhero, wasn't ready for it or capable of handling the power and responsibility. She was operating on instinct. Revenge.

"Fuck this shit." Jeannie flicked the machine on with one hand and dragged the power sliders to full with the other.

Instantly, Sam released her captive. Caught in the light, the figure collapsed downwards, nothing more than a tangled mess of dry rags. Jeannie saw Sam turning her body to face her, raising both arms in front, her once-blonde hair streaming behind in a crown of white flames. Jeannie held her breath, and closed her eyes.

She felt the machine kick, and had a vague feeling of space beneath her. Then her back hit the ground and the back of her head bounced sharply against the surface. Disoriented, the blackness spun behind her closed eyelids like she was drunk. She reached out blindly, realizing that she wasn't holding the machine anymore. Then she gasped as a hand took hers. Its fingers locked around her hand and she was jerked forwards – no, *upwards*, the world spinning back to level. She opened her eyes.

It was Linear, mask missing, broken glasses haphazardly sitting on his face which was cut and covered in soot. Under the dirt and bruises he smiled, the eye behind the one good lens sparkling.

Jeannie looked around in confusion. It was morning, still early, but the square was bathed in the yellow light of dawn under a sky that was filled with smoke rising from the city, but otherwise clear. Linear released her hand and went to re-join the other heroes – Sand Cat, Bluebell, Aurora, all alive and well (and in Aurora's case, blazing) and standing in a tight circle around something folded up in the center of the square.

"Welcome back to the land of the living."

Jeannie turned. Conroy stood, apart from the others, running some kind of scanner over the ground. He flicked it off, flipped it in half like a cell phone, and stowed it in a belt pouch.

"What happened?"

Conroy laughed. "Oh, you were out for a while. The others–" he nodded toward the heroes "–gave up trying to wake you about an hour ago."

Jeannie raised her hands, expecting the MIC-N to materialize in them. She looked around in a slight panic, then exhaled as she saw the gizmo on the ground, stacked safely next to a pile of rubble.

"Did it work?"

Conroy nodded. "It worked."

"The power core?"

"Ask Aurora." Conroy turned and walked towards the others. Jeannie followed.

Aurora watched the pair approach. Jeannie flinched at his heat, at first, then found it strangely reassuring. She pushed her way in next to him. Sand Cat moved and, amazingly, didn't complain.

On the ground, two figures were entwined in fetal positions. One was Sam, arms and legs curled around her naked form like an angelic painting, a look of peaceful contentment on her face. The other... the other was *Tony*. He was alive, breathing. His body – dead body – had been in the chiller on the moon. Now, here he was, in San Ventura, naked but covered in soot. He twitched occasionally, dreaming.

Jeannie stuttered her words. "I... Tony? He's alive? But... I... What happened? Where's the power core?"

Aurora turned to her, eyes afire. She backed away instinctively as he faced her, opening his cloak and stretching out his arms theatrically. She swore, lip curling upward out of instinct, confused at what he was doing, behaving like some kind of superpowered flasher.

"We'll fill you in. But the power core is safe, for the moment."

As Aurora spread his arms, his personal superhero symbol on his chest – a stylized sun, surrounded by a moving, swirling corona, flared into life. Jeannie squinted to shield her eyes, but they could not help but widen in surprise as Aurora's *chest* opened, split apart like a jewelry box. The heat was like a punch in the face, the light as bright as the sun on a summer morning.

There, swimming in yellow energy, the familiar multi-surfaced form of the power core sat, spinning gently, red light radiating from the seams along each facet. The power core was inside Aurora, part of him.

Aurora smiled. Jeannie thought his expression was cruel.

"The danger is not over. The Thuban are still on the way, but we can deal with them. It is time for all the superheroes of the world to join in battle once more."

Jeannie looked around the superteam. Conroy was the only one smiling.

All the superheroes? Jeannie sighed.

"Well," she said. "Hot dog."

CHAPTER FIFTY-SEVEN

Sam awoke on the third day, to noise and light. People talking, feet pounding. Everything echoing down hard corridors, everything lit with controlled, artificial light. She felt fine, and got out of bed with little difficulty, noting the slightly odd pull on her limbs as she walked around the functional but well-appointed quarters. She didn't know quite where she was, or what was going on, or what had happened, but she was of sound body and mind at least. She opened the cupboard next to the bed experimentally. Inside she found her clothes – not the ones she'd been wearing, but a selection of work wear from her own home. She frowned, then shrugged and made her choice, replacing the clinical, hospital-like pajamas with something at least more familiar.

Fragments of memory came back to her as she pulled her boots on. She paused, on the edge of the bed. She remembered light. She remembered the city under attack, not from supervillains or terrorists but from space. She remembered Geoff Conroy's hillside mansion. And then… nothing.

She stood, then realized where she was. The artificial gravity, the conditioned air. She was on the moon again. But unlike the mausoleum it had been on her first visit, this time felt different.

The door slid open and she stepped into the corridor, then shrank back.

The moonbase was full of people.

Dozens strode past in both directions. Some smiled as they passed, others ignored her. A lot were in a generic blue uniform, support staff of some kind. But their lack of color and distinction was more than made up for by the eye-popping variety of the rest.

Red, white and blue. Orange, yellow. Flat colors, glowing colors, colors on fire and leaping from backs, shoulders, heads. Acres of cloth like decorated circus tents sweeping any available airspace between the throng of pedestrians. Skin completely covered, head to toe, or skin almost entirely exposed with only some tiny, daring coverings – on both men and women. Soft, organic, friendly people with smiles and perfect muscled forms. Mystery men and women in hoods and cloaks and shadows. Hard, metallic, robotic forms, shiny and percussive as they marched down the corridors.

Sam took a breath and found she was leaning back against her door, making herself small if not actually shrinking back in… fear? No. Surprise, for sure, but something else.

She smiled, and laughed, and pushed off from the wall, joining the walkers and matching their pace as she strode with confidence toward the conference room.

The moonbase was full of superheroes. They had returned.

The conference room was filled to standing room only, every available space – extending even to the wide observation windows – packed with superheroes. Somehow Jeannie had managed to find herself seated at the conference table, ingratiated into the inner circle of the Seven Wonders. She wasn't quite sure how or why or even quite when the transition had been made, or even how long it would last, but she wasn't complaining. She was still in the fluorescent orange prison jumpsuit, but she was among the least brightly dressed in the room.

All but one chair was occupied. Aurora sat at the head of the table, Bluebell on his left, Sand Cat on his right. Then Linear and Conroy, left and right. Jeannie sat next to her former partner. She wasn't sure whether she'd intended to or not, but they naturally gravitated to the same side of table. Opposite her sat the last member of the core team. Holding the powerstaff in one hand, he was perhaps the most out of place in the room, dressed in a cheap blue suit and white shirt, tie loose at his neck. Jeannie supposed a new costume for the Dragon

Star's new body would come later. She smirked. His former partner was going to get a hell of a shock.

As Jeannie counted the places she realized with a jolt that perhaps this really was it, and they were the new superteam, the new Seven Wonders. Her mind raced. She wasn't sure this was quite what she wanted. Or perhaps she was jumping to conclusions. Then there was the mystery of the empty seat. Jeannie frowned.

The entire room stood silent, waiting. They'd been like that for minutes now. Jeannie was pleased she had a seat. Even the all-powerful supermen and women squeezed into the room shifted slightly on their heels, arms folded, expressions set, waiting, waiting. A room full of good guys, as many of the best of the best that would fit – leaders of other teams, mostly, and a few solo heroes deemed to be most senior. But even Jeannie was sure that at least a few of them were eyeing the others up, flexing biceps, pushing out breasts. A multicolored display of superpowered masculinity and femininity. The most perfect of the human race.

They'd all come. It had taken two days, but all, *all*, had heeded Aurora's call. They came in groups: the Chicago Nightguard, United International, the Army of One, the Coven, the League of All-Stars, the Computer Council, the Manhattan Manhunters, Volcanic, the Pan-African Hero Society, the Devils You Know, the Phenomenals, the Scienceers. The superteams alone counted for more than one hundred heroes. But that was just the start. Over two days, the remaining superheroic population of the Earth had journeyed to the moon – by ship, teleport, magical portal, elemental transduction – mostly alone, some in pairs or small groups, not big enough (or so self-important) to have given themselves a group title, but small teams or collectives, and solo protectors: the H-Man, Pangolin the Protector, Glass Tambourine, Omega-Mur, Hammer and Sickle, Jackdaw, the Infinite Wisdom, Doctor Mandragora, Czar and Tzar and Star, Kalamari Karl, Lightning Dancer, Doctor Chlorophyll, Jack Viking, Monomaniac, the Gin Fairy, the Holy Ghanta, the Bandolier, Vengeance, the Gray Claw, Senny Dreadful, Batmonster, the Nuclear Atom, the Mysterious Flame, Moonstalker, Cataclysm and Inferno, the Skyguard II, Your Imaginary Pal, Dark Storm, the Hate Witch, Psychofire, Rabid, Riot,

Fox and Hound, Hydrolad, Captain Fuji, Captain Cape Town, Captain Australia, Captain… Jeannie lost count, one uniform and one costume blurring into another. Behind Aurora, on the right. Was that Doc Madness, or the King in Yellow? Or Strange Dynamic in a new cape? And farther back, head visible a full two feet above everyone else: Iron Giant, or the Steam King, or Train? Jeannie really didn't know. Some of these heroes were still in the public eye but a lot – most, even – had long since retreated from the world. Over there, standing behind Linear: Colonel Storm and his partner, Spacelord. Jeannie had thought they'd both died years ago, yet here they were, as large as life. Larger, even, in this moonful of superheroes.

The conference room door swished, and people shuffled. From her position at the table, Jeannie could see the crowd parting, letting someone in. Everyone at the table turned to see, except Aurora, who just sat, staring, his powerful arms outstretched on the table before him.

Sam walked in, the superheroes parting on either side like a multicolored sea. Sam stopped at the end of the table, opposite Aurora, by the empty chair. Jeannie wondered what she was waiting for, then almost as one everyone in the room turned to the Dragon Star.

Sam sat gently. Her expression was fluid, betraying a mix of emotions and the turmoil she felt in her mind. Nervousness, confusion, fear, uncertainty.

Hope.

"Joe?"

The Dragon Star flexed the fingers of his right hand, adjusting their grip on the powerstaff. The man met Sam's eyes, but did not nod or shake his head or offer any form of expression. He spoke softly, in Joe's voice, but it wasn't Joe.

"I am sorry for your loss, Detective Millar. I am the Dragon Star."

The day passed, although on the moon it was hard to tell. The nightscape beyond the observation windows didn't change. The superheroes stood as the meeting continued, except for the Seven Wonders, and Sam, and…

No, it wasn't Joe. Sam knew that now. It had taken an hour to fill her in on a day of missing time. The power core, SuperSam, the Living

Dark. How Joe had died trying to help. How the Dragon Star's body – the anonymous cheerleader – had been killed, but how the alien life force within had found a new host. Detective Joe Milano. Now, the superheroes said, Joe could live on, fighting for justice and avenging his death. So the superheroes said. Sam's face was hot and her eyes hurt. The only thing she wanted to do was run back to her quarters and throw up.

But then the Dragon Star in Joe's body had done something that made her want to stay and watch and pay attention. He – it, she? – rolled his shoulders, loosening his neck muscles, as he sat quietly, listening to Aurora's appraisal. It was not an uncommon movement, a typically human fidget. Except the Dragon Star was not human, and in the body of the cheerleader had never so much as twitched all the time Sam had spent with her.

There, again. A shoulder roll, smaller this time. The body language was like a signature. Detective Joe Milano. There was something left, something buried beneath the alien intelligence that had occupied the still-warm body, repaired the plasma wound, and flown it to the moon.

So Sam tried to stop rubbing her eyes, and sat and listened.

She'd never been sure of the hierarchy of command of the Seven Wonders, aside from Aurora being the leader. The other six had always seemed to rotate as deputy as the needs demanded, the expertise of each coming into play when Aurora asked. Right now, Aurora and Conroy were leading the discussion and battle plan.

The news of the San Ventura disaster – Sam was sure a neat-o soundbite title had been devised by the news media already, but she didn't know it, and the superheroes didn't use it – had been followed by all of the superheroes of the Earth, and they all knew that that was not the end of the danger, given Aurora's summons to the Apollo Fortress. The revelation of an alien attack from the Thuban was something of a shock, but these were the best the Earth could provide, and in such numbers, there was an air of confidence in the room. An air that was steadily sapped as Aurora, Linear, Bluebell and Sand Cat gave a detailed analysis of the fight with the Living Dark and the powers granted to him by the Thuban. The atmosphere cooled and quieted as the magnitude of the threat became apparent.

Supercharger clicked his fingers with a spark. He was another speedster, a former classmate of Linear caught in a bizarre repeat of the disastrous college science experiment that had granted superspeed to his friend. Supercharger was faster than Linear, but he couldn't fly. They were the only two superheroes who drew their power from the Slipstream.

"We've been supposing and maybe-ing for hours. Isn't there someone in this moonbase that could just go and suck the data out of Mr Prosdocimi?"

Bluebell shook her head and began to explain that Tony – the Living Dark – watched in his quarters by members of Force 10, had no memory of his resurrection or link to the Thuban, but Supercharger's comment stirred something in the audience. Sam realized that the superheroes were impatient.

"There must be a residual trace," said a tall woman in a striking black and white checked cloak. She wore a simple domino mask and her black hair cascaded to her shoulders through a white tiara. "Something beyond the abilities of Bluebell?"

Ouch. Bluebell's lips pursed. Aurora shifted his white-eyed gaze to the speaker, just slightly. "The prisoner is not dead yet, Veil. While he remains on this side of the void, your powers will not be required."

The Veil said something to the hero next to her, a muscle-bound wrestler in skintight blue costume and red bandana wrapped around his bald head. His folded tree-trunk arms shook as he suppressed a laugh.

"Ladies and gentlemen, we waste time." Lady Liberty. And now everyone shut the hell up.

Lady Liberty didn't need to push her way to the front to address the conference table, the crowd just made room for her. She was only one row back anyway, but Golden God and Killswitch stepped to one side each way, giving plenty of room for her copper-green cloak to open as she raised her right hand into the air, famous torch flaring as all eyes fell on her.

If any superhero team could be considered celebrities among celebrities, it was Lady Liberty and the Presidents of the United States of America. Sam shrank back in her chair a little, feeling hopelessly inadequate to be sitting in such a presence. She heard leather creak and chainmail rattle as all in the room paid her very close attention indeed.

Behind Lady Liberty, Sam could just see her team of android presidents – WashingtonX, Jefferson 2.5, TR (aka Robot Roosevelt), and Absolute Lincoln. She'd seen Lady Liberty in person, just once, when she visited San Ventura and there was a governor's reception. And she'd seen the robot Presidents on TV, but being in the same room as them was – even under such intense circumstances, sitting on the moon amid hundreds of superheroes – quite a thrill. Each of the robots, constructed for ill by Lady Liberty when she was being mind-controlled by prospective alien invaders, was a perfect clone of the original leader, crafted out of an alien metal, and possessing superpowers of varying sorts. Each stood proudly in the correct period dress, their unearthly silver skins with riveted seams where one metal plate bonded to another the only indication they were not human beings.

Aurora stood, and gestured to Lady Liberty with a gloved hand. "Please, Lady Liberty."

Lady Liberty nodded, and stepped forward again. "We need to cast differences aside if we are to fight. We are fighting not just for our own cities and homes. We fight to defend the entire world."

She paused and turned her verdigris features to Aurora. "Before we left Mount Rushmore, we detected the passage of the Thuban at the orbit of Saturn. Mr President?"

It was unclear to which of her team she was referring, but it was Absolute Lincoln that jerked into life, clasping the lapels of his coat. His voice was coated in silver and mercury.

"Madam, thank you. Fellow superheroes and patriots. We are met today on a great battlefield of war, and I know we are all in agreement that it is the responsibility of those such as ourselves, so blessed with special powers, to protect the nations of the world as one. The task is mighty, but we shall prevail."

There was a murmur of agreement among the superheroes. Sam couldn't resist a smirk. Lincoln cleared his throat and continued.

"I propose we defend the Earth on two fronts. Firstly, all those heroes with powers that will allow the operator to function in the vacuum of space will form a perimeter around the Earth, at a latitude and orbit to be decided. Secondly, all those heroes who cannot survive in space, or who do not have superpowers but instead special talents of unpowered nature, will travel in spearheads and enter the Thuban warship itself, once breached by the first group."

Aurora nodded. "An admirable solution, Mr President. I shall lead the defense of the Earth. I propose Paragon leads the assault on the ship."

Another murmur sped around the room. Lady Liberty said nothing, while the Presidents conferred behind her. Finally Kalamari Karl spoke the question all were thinking.

"Who's Paragon?" The king of the fish folded his wide, finned arms, his tentacled mouth twitching in the inky water that filled his translucent, spherical helmet. "Ain't nobody heard of him." His accent was pure Louisiana Creole.

Sam saw Jeannie smile. It was all a joke to that bitch. Conroy coughed politely, and looked toward Aurora. All of the Seven Wonders followed his gaze, and the room drew quiet again.

"Paragon is the newest member of the Seven Wonders. I imagine most of you have recognized him already. May I introduce Mr Geoffrey Conroy, noted industrialist and benefactor of the city of San Ventura. Perhaps better known as the Cowl."

Sam found herself at the infirmary. After the furor in the conference room, when Conroy's former identity had been revealed, Sam managed to excuse herself. The superheroes continued to argue; she could still hear them as she entered the elevator at the end of the corridor. Those not in the conference room milled around the corridors of the place, debating among themselves about the nature of what they might be facing.

Sam was actually surprised to find herself at the infirmary. She just wanted to walk, to give herself time and space to think, but some instinct or curiosity had led her there. Despite being secured for the duration of the emergency, the door opened at her touch.

There were two superheroes in the room – an immense man made out of shiny black stone, known as Monolith, and a small, slightly short but athletic-looking superhero in a red and white head-to-toe costume, the cape of which came to just above his waist. Sam hesitated, recognizing the hero. Lawmaker, an ex-cop from San Francisco sucked into the Earth during the quake of '89, who returned with superstrength, indestructibility, and no sense of humor. Before his happy accident, he'd been reassigned to San Ventura, and to this day stories were told about him, like he somehow belonged to that city rather than his own.

Sam knew his reputation: Lawmaker was uptight and worked strictly by the book. He nodded Sam a greeting, and continued gently punching his fist into the palm of the other hand as he stood guard over the bed. Monolith stood silently on the opposite side. Force 10 must have been on a break, which was a shame, because the decuplets were a cute family and, from what Sam could gather, far more sociable company than the two heroes currently on duty.

Tony Prosdocimi was asleep. The twin prongs of an oxygen hose trailed from his nose, and he was still on a drip. Sam had no memory of what she'd done to him when she'd had powers, but whatever it was, it had been enough to drag his formerly deceased human form back from whatever Thuban nightmare he'd been trapped in.

"Detective Millar?"

Sam didn't turn from the bedside, recognizing the voice but not wanting to look.

Joe.

She heard the powerstaff clack against the floor as he approached. He was too close, and she flinched, then cursed the involuntary movement and turned around, holding her breath. She had to deal with it sooner or later.

Joe looked just like Joe. Same suit, same shirt, still torn, same shoes. Just her old friend and partner from SuperCrime.

But his face was different. The muscles beneath the skin seemed to hang differently on the cheekbones. His mouth was at an expressionless horizontal. Sam released her held breath as she looked into his eyes – far from the glassy, dead look she had expected (the Dragon Star was some kind of parasitic zombie, right?), they glittered with stars, the once-brown iris now a gold-speckled emerald, gently spinning like clouds seen from space. They were deep, and beautiful, and like no human eyes could ever be. She found herself moving closer.

"The Thuban are approaching Earth orbit. Aurora wishes to speak to you."

Sam nodded. She wondered if Joe would get a funeral. She wondered if she would have time to mourn. She wondered if she would be able to, with his body apparently walking around in good health.

She wondered if whatever spark of Joe was left inside would ever come to the surface.

The Dragon Star seemed to hesitate for a second, then he looked down. Another recognizable motion, but this time not one from Joe. The female version of the superhero had had a habit of avoiding eye contact.

"I am sorry for your loss. But the survival of many depended upon my claiming this body. Do not fear. I shall do your friend a great honor."

Sam nodded again. She understood, or perhaps she understood enough to cope with the situation for now, until the emergency was over and the Earth was safe. The Dragon Star was no body snatcher. He/she/it was just trying to help the Earth, his/her/its adopted home.

The Dragon Star said nothing more, but when he raised his head again there was something in his eyes, something that seemed to indicate an understanding had been reached.

The two left the infirmary.

Monolith and Lawmaker watched Sam and the Dragon Star walk away, then Monolith turned back to the bed and resumed his impassive, unmoving position. Lawmaker looked him up and down, pounded his fist into his open palm again, and stood tensely at the bedside, ready for anything, anything at all.

A minute later Tony's breathing hastened, he turned his head, and opened his eyes. The sclera was entirely black, with no iris or pupil discernible.

Tony screamed.

CHAPTER FIFTY-EIGHT

At this distance, the Earth was a hemisphere almost too big to take in, blue and green and white and shining with the blindingly bright light reflected from the sun. Bluebell had forgotten how, well, amazing the view was. Ever since the moonbase had been mothballed the exhilaration of working in space had been pushed to the back of her mind. Now, floating in the infinite ether, it all came flooding back. The first trip to intercept the meteor storm had been too fast, her mind too focused on the task at hand to appreciate the beauty of nature. Now the danger was even more acute, but Bluebell lingered in the calm before the storm, maintaining her position in the assembled force, facing away from deep space to view her home.

Space was not unoccupied between her and the Earth. Although the brightness of the planet obscured most of the superheroes waiting at a lower altitude, some of the more flamboyant could be seen as colored specks remaining perfectly still as the planet rotated under them. A blue star that was Polaar, a mix of red and orange dots flaring in the upper atmosphere as the Merchants of Freedom held a grid formation. Slightly closer, two flickering, interlocking squares of pink energy that were the weapons net stretched out by the members of Shibuya ichimaru-kyū. Just a few of many.

Aurora buzzed in her ear, addressing the entire assemblage. She turned, pushing herself around with her arms like a swimmer even though the motion was largely meaningless, her movement controlled by her psychic power converted to electrical energy. All around her, she saw the rest of the armada clearly against the black of space. Superheroes ranged from just a few yards away to a few miles. A multicolored scatter of figures, forms and dots. The raiding teams stood by on either side of Bluebell, half a dozen magical platforms and life-supporting energy bubbles of various shapes and sizes carrying the heroes incapable of spaceflight.

A historic gathering.

Ahead, at a distance of something like one hundred thousand miles, the moon was a nothing, a void of black that blocked the star field beyond. Aurora was ahead of her; he floated backward and pointed for the benefit of those heroes close enough to follow the direction.

At the moon's empty horizon, a star appeared. At first nothing more than another white dot in space, perhaps another superhero moving into position. Then the edge of the moon flared, like the diamond ring effect during a solar eclipse. The Thuban moved from the far side of the moon into range of the Earth, and of the superhero army.

Bluebell couldn't make out much detail of the Thuban ship – if it could be called that at all. It appeared to be a series of cuboidal sections, moving, undulating like a mass of growing and shrinking bubbles which changed behind the curtain of light to become hundreds of polyhedral angles. It reminded her of the power core, now placed in a stasis field in the Apollo Fortress. But whatever the shape and design was, it was growing large as it approached. Very large. Her comm buzzed again as Aurora called the superhero army to bear. Everyone seemed to speak at once, individual heroes confirming their readiness while superteams called their members in. Bluebell made out just a few in the immediate rush of sound.

"Seven Wonders, unite!"

"Chicago Nightguard, TEN-HUT!"

"Power ready and waiting!"

"Let the Circle of Magi be one!"

"Logarth of the Dereni affirms his readiness."

"United International standing by."

"Lady Liberty and the Presidents standing by."

"Connectormatic standing by."

Bluebell tuned the rest out, focusing instead on building power through her suit. She could see her increasing blue glow reflected against the backs of the nearest heroes, before it was completely overwhelmed by Aurora's corona exploding outward in a red haze. She looked sideways at her husband. He was smiling as he raised a fist toward the enemy. His voice buzzed again as the last of the heroes signaled in.

"Let's tell the Thuban it's rude to visit without calling first."

Aurora yelled and shot forward, and the space around Bluebell exploded with an endless rainbow of silent firepower.

The view from the moonbase was as spectacular as it was terrifying. Sam watched as sheets of color swept between the superhero armada and the gigantic, amorphous glow that was the Thuban. It was impossible to judge any progress. The superheroes kept shooting. The Thuban kept moving.

She wanted to say something, to comment on the battle, but caught her tongue just before the words blurted out. Jeannie was standing next to her in the corridor outside the infirmary, far too close really, but Sam was prepared to suffer the company so long as she could pretend she wasn't there. Fact was, there were only five people on the base now anyway, Monolith and Lawmaker keeping watch over Tony, and her and Jeannie. All of the heroes had gone, Force 10 included, and all of the technical staff supplied by the United Nations Superheroic Council had been evacuated back to the Earth, as if that was somehow safer. The moon might take collateral damage, she supposed. Maybe it did make sense. Maybe she shouldn't be here at all. But she was just a regular person, after all, who...

"We should go to the conference room," Jeannie said, breaking the silence and Sam's train of thought. Sam's brow furrowed in annoyance, and she shook her head slightly like she was brushing off a distracting insect.

"The view is better from here."

Jeannie clicked her tongue in impatience. Sam heard it and shook her head again.

"The view is pretty but you can't see what's happening, *detective.* Up there we can listen to the comms and follow the battle."

Sam jerked her head over her left shoulder, met Jeannie's eye, then walked off. Jeannie had been right, but she'd be damned to admit it.

She came to a halt immediately, her shoes squeaking on the polished floor. Beside her, Jeannie swore.

"Tony!"

He stood in the doorway of the infirmary, wrapped in a blanket. He balanced uncertainly, one arm against the wall to support himself. He smiled weakly at them, risked moving his hand to push the hair from his eyes. He bunched the blanket up at his neck, trailing it like a superhero cape as he stepped forward.

Jeannie rushed to help him. "Should you be up? I..." She didn't finish the sentence. Tony looked into her eyes with his own. The uniform blackness of them was horrifying. Tony saw her expression and smiled.

"Yeah, I need to do something about that. Either somebody's got some magic juju they can wave at me, or I'll need to splash out on those Ray-Bans I've always wanted." He kept smiling until Jeannie's face broke into a matching grin. She hugged him.

Lawmaker and Monolith appeared in the doorway. Lawmaker rolled his fists like a champion boxer ready for the next round.

"Ma'am, keep away from the prisoner. He vanished from the bed and appeared in the doorway here. He must have residual power remaining." He paused, seeing that Tony and Jeannie were locked in an embrace that showed no sign of finishing. "Ah, I'd advise caution, ma'am."

Sam waved the annoying hero away. "Leave it, Lawmaker. Blackbird?"

Jeannie turned her head over Tony's shoulder and nodded at her. Sam in turn nodded to Lawmaker. "That will be all, thanks."

Lawmaker straightened up and walked back towards the door. He didn't look happy and flexed his fingers, clenching and unclenching his fists. "I'll maintain watch in the corridor, ma'am." He paused, as if waiting for someone to tell him to stay instead, but when no such invitation came he turned and jogged down the corridor. The footfalls stopped as he put himself on guard at the far end. Monolith stayed close.

"Allow me to escort you to the conference room," he said, then turned and walked away without waiting for a reply.

• • • •

Jeannie led Tony around the table and pushed him gently into Aurora's chair. She turned it to face the observation windows, and together they watched the fireworks in space for a moment. He exhaled sharply.

"What's going on?"

Sam pointed out the cluster of multicolored dots. "Superheroes." She then pointed at the yellowish glowing oblong that moved incrementally from left to right. "Bad guys."

Tony frowned. Jeannie saw his expression and knelt on the floor next to him. "What's the matter?"

Tony waved his hands at the window. "The superheroes are attacking the Thuban?"

"Yep," said Sam. "Spaceworthy superheroes are defending the Earth and trying to breach the hull of the ship. Once an entry has been made, the terrestrial heroes will join the others aboard and try to take out the crew from the inside."

Even before she had finished, Tony was shaking his head with increasing urgency. With blank black eyes it was difficult to tell where he was focusing, whether it was on Sam, or the window behind her, or just the empty middle distance.

Jeannie looked at Sam, who just shrugged. She shuffled closer to Tony and put her arms around his shoulders. "What's wrong? Is there something the superheroes should know?"

Tony nodded, rubbing his forehead. "It's not a ship, it has no crew. They're all going to die."

"Who? The boarders?"

"No, no, no, no, no." Tony's voice became increasingly fraught, words tripping over themselves as he struggled to speak. "All of them, they're all going to die. It's not a ship, it's part of the Thuban themselves. It can't be stopped. They'll all die and the Earth will be absorbed. It can't be stopped."

They were losing, and Aurora knew it. In fact the superhero armada was bound to fail, Aurora had seen it from the first few minutes, but he hadn't been sure and could never have given up. He was in charge, responsible for the whole assault. There was a lot of data to assimilate from two hundred solo superheroes and superteams, the constant cross-communication, endless chat in two dozen different languages. But he knew it, could feel it when he first sped towards the glowing Thuban form. Something wasn't right.

For a while anyway, the superheroes put up a spectacular display. No, not spectacular. *Textbook.* Perfect formations, perfect maneuvers. A thousand forms of energy, technological, scientific and magical, unleashed the rage of the Earth at the aggressors. Aurora sped straight and true, opening with a sucker punch against the hull powerful enough to crack the continental shield of Australia. He unleashed a second, a third strike, then peeled off as the surface became an inferno. He flew up, then curved away, the Thuban now above his head. He flew and saw the enemy enveloped in a nova of energy. Superhero after superhero raced in after him, unleashing bolt upon bolt of energy while those with more one-to-one abilities closed in to melee the vast structure. Aurora steered between his soldiers, registering Linear streaking past, trailed by Supercharger running on a bridge of light projected by Silver Ghost, floating nearby.

At the edge of the armada the raiding parties waited on their platforms. Aurora smiled, seeing how they itched to join the battle. Several saluted as he passed over the top, and he gestured towards those projecting the support structures – Helix, Lucifer Now, Doctor Mandragora, A Terrible Aspect, the Dragon Star and Mr Baltus Carnay acknowledged his fly-by as they protected their charges, waiting for the moment the Thuban ship was vulnerable enough for them to deliver the attackers.

But as Aurora swept back around and over, his corona dragging a terrible wall of red fire behind him, he realized he'd been right in his first estimation.

Something was wrong.

The superheroes flew with astonishing speed and skill, unloading their payloads against the target, which glowed and fizzed and vanished now and again in flashes of light that seemed to illuminate all of space. But still the object powered on towards the Earth, its shape and form and speed unchanged. And, as Aurora noticed, without returning fire, apparently ignoring the army before it. He paused, hanging in space for just a moment to assess the battlefield. The attack had passed through at least four separate waves, and even now the superheroes had slowed, observing and assessing the results of their effort before plowing onwards with the defense. Aurora's ear crackled with seventy-five heroes asking him the same question all at once.

"I'm not sure," he muttered to himself just before he touched the comm link on his belt. "Press the attack. Bluebell, Dragon Star, let's take a closer look."

Both heroes affirmed the order, and Aurora swept upwards and forwards, the Thuban vessel looming suddenly in his vision. The Dragon Star hitched his support platform to Mr Carnay's beside him, and together with Bluebell joined Aurora.

"Assessment, Dragon Star."

The former detective floated in space in his blue suit, powerstaff raised outwards, bright colors shimmering over its entire length.

"I fear the nature of the Thuban makes them invulnerable to us."

Bluebell swore, uncharacteristically. "Why couldn't you have told us this to start with?"

The Dragon Star shook his head. "I am sorry, I did not know. The Thuban have many forms. When I knew them, conventional technology was used as well as energy forms such as this. The communications I received were transmitted with technology."

"You mean you assumed?" Aurora's question was put plainly, but Bluebell could detect anger underneath it.

"Assumed, no," said the Dragon Star. "The inference was logical. But I have not seen a craft like this before."

The ship seemed to move so slowly through space, but Bluebell knew it was deceptive. The vastness of space and the size of the object offered no point of reference. She noticed the assault lull as the superheroes re-gathered, awaiting further commands.

"Are we safe?"

The Dragon Star nodded. "The warship is pure energy, configured to consume the Earth. That is its sole purpose. We cannot stop it, but it cannot attack us."

There was no sound in space, but Aurora's head exploded with noise. He cried out, clutching the sides of his head. He spun out of control, and saw Bluebell and the Dragon Star likewise writhing in torment before they were all caught in a ray projected from the Thuban, sweeping like a searchlight across the battlefield. The psychic cries of the superheroes pummeled Aurora's mind. Aurora shook his head and focused, realizing that if the psychic trauma of the assembled heroes had managed to penetrate his mind, Bluebell must have been in serious pain. He turned again, and reached out to his wife.

Aurora held Bluebell, and they tumbled through space, free now from the Thuban beam as it passed over them. Bluebell lost consciousness. Aurora gritted his teeth as his sun powers burnt out the alien attack from within him. He realized his eyes were shut. Opening them, he saw nothing but carnage.

Bodies, floating in space. At least half of the superheroes, if not more. Those that had survived the blast, or had been beyond its reach, swooped in, collecting the incapacitated and wounded. As the static in Aurora's comm finally cleared, and the ringing in his ears started to subside, he began to hear the reports. Many, many, many dead. Many not responding. Some checking in injured, some reporting as they flew in to assist. Looking back towards the Earth, Aurora could only count two out of the four support platforms for the raiding parties. Farther below, black shapes drifted down towards the Earth's atmosphere. Aurora searched and saw that Paragon was safe, for now, in the support bubble held by Helix, Sand Cat running in her spirit form beside them. The feeling of relief was mixed with one of guilt as he recounted the names of the heroes who had died in the vacuum of space as their supportive environments collapsed. Just a small handful were saved by the quick action of Helix and Doctor Mandragora, who both shot out capturing energy streams to collect those they could reach.

Bluebell's eyes fluttered open. She was alive, but her fight was over. She needed to be taken back to the moonbase, quickly. Aurora patched in Linear and a second later Bluebell was taken from his arms in a silver flash.

Aurora's comm began filling with static again, and he realized that this was the "ship" charging the weapon again. He made the call. They had no alternative.

"Retreat. All superheroes, retreat. Move behind it, back to the moon."

Responses came, a mix of protest and agreement, but were soon drowned out by the rush of white noise. A point on the glowing, amorphous form of the Thuban warship flashed brighter, and the cone of death swept outwards again. The heroes were ready for it, and as Aurora watched the beam cross the battlefield he saw the remaining heroes fly up or down, out of its path. Numerous bodies were caught in the ray again, thrown twisting and turning through the vacuum. They'd be able to recover most, but some heroes were doomed to a grave in space – perhaps all of them, himself included. The thought caused Aurora's aura to flicker and cool. Hanging in space, the leader of the Seven Wonders faded from a bright red to a dark blue.

The Thuban death ray snapped off, and the ship continued on its inexorable journey to the Earth.

Tony staggered into the armory. The chamber was buried at the center of the moonbase to protect against meteor strike and supervillain attack, but was unlocked. The only people who ever entered the moonbase were superheroes, so there was no need for internal security. If any supervillain could penetrate the heart of the base – and none ever had, and there were no supervillains left, so it was academic anyway – then stealing some small arms and laser blasters wouldn't have done the bad guys any good, not when faced with the solar explosion that was Aurora, or the alien power of the Dragon Star.

Currently, the armory was empty anyway. Tony leaned heavily on Jeannie. The room was a pointed ellipse, like an eye, the curved walls concealing the weapons racks. At the far end, in the opposite point of the ellipse, was a floor-to-ceiling steel column with a square door set at head height. A safe of some kind, designed to hold the most dangerous of weapons. Aurora had been quick to place the supercharged power core in it.

As the trio approached, Jeannie went on about quantum stasis fields and the reversal of entropy, but Sam just tuned her out. She didn't care whether it worked, only if Jeannie could open the safe.

"Are you sure this is a good idea?" Sam asked. When she'd wielded the power – which she had no memory of – she'd killed Joe and the Living Dark. The fact that Tony had somehow survived and even been brought back to life was another issue. The power had been too much for Sam to bear. If she hadn't been stopped by Jeannie's box of tricks she had no idea what she might have done.

Tony was looking at the floor. He seemed to be getting weaker. "There's nothing else for it. The superheroes can't stop the Thuban. The only chance is to use the power core."

"Fine, whatever," said Jeannie. She was impatient, unwilling to make important decisions, and clearly wanting to hand the responsibility to someone else. She looked up at Sam.

"Think you can handle it this time?"

Sam's eyes widened.

"Ah... what?" She looked at Jeannie, then pointed to the still-closed safe. "Last time I played Supercop I killed my partner and whatever the thing was that possessed your boyfriend here."

"You're the only one who has used it. You're our best chance."

Sam folded her arms. She felt defensive and scared. Like Jeannie, she feared the responsibility. Unlike Jeannie, she had some idea of the corrupting power of the alien device. No matter how much she tried to convince herself, she wouldn't be able to handle it. She knew now that a superhero was more than just a fancy costume, a firm bust and being able to shoot whizz-bang laser beams out of your eyes. Being a superhero required a quality within, some indefinable facet of character that she now knew she didn't have. She was a cop, a detective, and a good one at that. She could help San Ventura and work for the citizens in her own way, but that was it. There were too many flaws, too many impulses both buried in her mind and quite openly bubbling on the surface. She was no superhero. She couldn't use the power core. Power corrupts, and absolute power...

"No," she said at last. "It can't be me."

Jeannie looked at Tony. His eyes were closed now, and he crouched on the floor. He was breathing normally, but very slowly.

"It'll have to be me then." Jeannie stood and took a step toward the safe. Sam grabbed her arm.

"Excuse my French, but no *fucking* way." Her face was set, eyes hard. Jeannie met the stare and didn't back away. "You're a criminal and a supervillain. You were the Cowl's sidekick. Hell, you're still technically under arrest."

"Oh, come on, detective." Jeannie shook her head, moving a step closer to Sam. Sam still did not move. "We really don't have time for this bullshit. I don't know if you noticed, but I seem to be on your side."

Sam raised an eyebrow. "For now."

"Yes, for now!" Jeannie said. "And the Earth now has two hundred dead superheroes for new satellites. Until the Thuban eat it for brunch, that is." She pulled her arm out of Sam's grip and gave her a look that suggested she was about ten seconds away from cracking the detective's skull on the wall opposite.

"No," said Sam. "Wait. We'll call a superhero, get one of them to take the core."

"What do you think will happen if Lawmaker got his hands on it? He's fucking nuts. And Monolith? What do you know about him? Anyone else in space is too far away. In fact, for all we know they're all dead out there now and the Earth is getting munched on." Jeannie waved her arm behind her, in a vague approximation of the direction of the planet they orbited.

"We have no option, Blackbird. I know I can't handle it, and you can't be trusted with it."

"Oh, fuck this, detective..."

Tony stood quickly, the gray infirmary blanket dropping off his shoulders. He wobbled a little on his feet, black eyes blinking at the arguing women. Sam and Jeannie stopped and watched him.

"Jeannie's right, there's no time for this. And you're both right, neither of you can be trusted. It must be me."

He pushed past the two women and opened the safe hatch without difficulty, somehow negating the locking mechanism with a residual superpower. The power core sat in a yellow box of light, gently rotating in free space as it was held in stasis. Jeannie and Sam both spoke at once and made a grab for him, but it was too late. His hands were already around the core. The stasis field blinked green twice to indicate deactivation, and the safe went dark.

Tony pulled the object out and clutched it to his chest, arms folded over it and body hunched forward. From behind, Sam and Jeannie could see him backlit in purple. The room filled with a peppery smell, and Sam felt her ears pop. She and Jeannie exchanged a look.

Tony turned around. His featureless black eyes had become deep wells, purple sparkling spirals twisting in each. He smiled as his skin darkened, taking on a shiny, purple hue, and as he pressed the split shell of the core to his chest it dissolved into him, becoming part of his skin. He then flexed his arms in front of him, watching his own transformation.

"Come," he said. Waving a hand, Jeannie and Sam were enveloped in a thin, violet light, and the moonbase armory faded from view.

CHAPTER FIFTY-NINE

Sand Cat paced back and forth, her steps alternating between the soft pad of her animal form and the hard tack of her human boots against the transparent, glassy floor of the platform. Conroy wished she'd stop, but knew that starting an argument now was a bad idea. Instead he stepped closer to the wall of the bubble projected by Helix and watched the ineffectual attack of the superheroes.

Just how powerful were the Thuban? His original calculations when he'd called himself the Cowl were well, well off. If the Thuban were an amorphous, gestalt energy intelligence, how could they be stopped before they got to the Earth? And even if this "warship" was somehow destroyed, would that save the Earth, or just anger the aggressor? The warship was merely one projection of the Thuban. Size, shape, mass, number – these were irrelevant to them. They could send another, and another, and another. And that was if the superheroes managed to defeat this single "ship". Which, from where he stood, on a hard energy platform one hundred thousand miles above the surface of the Earth, surrounded by a life-supporting force field, didn't look likely.

The others sharing his platform had been shaken by the collapse of two other bubbles, but were trying to remain stoic. Only quick flying by Helix had moved them out of the path of the death-ray-thing, followed by a second quick movement that had thrown them all into a tangled heap in one corner as the superhero grabbed a few comrades from their collapsing bubbles and brought them into his own. Terra Nova, Armistice, the Man With The Gun In His Hand, and another that Conroy didn't recognize... Pangolin, perhaps, a small man in an armored tortoise shell and, bizarrely, top hat. Helix had also managed to capture two others, although one (Warhog or War-something) was already dead, and the other, Miss Magic, was injured. Conroy's team was fortunate to have a magical hero, the All-Star, who had used a spell to anesthetize Miss Magic and an incantation to repair the third-degree burns that covered nearly all of her body.

The heroes were lit by a rapid-fire burst of red flashes. Looking up, Conroy could see that Aurora had gathered the remaining heroes behind the Thuban, and they were concentrating their fire on a single spot. If it had any effect, Conroy couldn't see. The Thuban ship still moved, although it hadn't brought the ray to bear to the rear. Perhaps Aurora had found a weakness in its structure. Or perhaps he was just trying to keep the superheroes alive.

"We are impotent against the enemy!" Sand Cat spat, ceasing her constant pacing to address no one in particular, although she was facing Conroy at the time. She waved a hand dismissively at the scene before them. "We can do nothing!"

"Steady, sister," Conroy said. Sand Cat was jumpy in a corner. He knew that from his previous life. It was exactly the kind of thing that had made him laugh when they'd been sworn enemies. Now it was just annoying and impractical. He turned back to watch the other superheroes. "I'm sure Aurora has a plan."

Aurora didn't have a plan.

Moving behind the Thuban seemed to be a safe spot, but the attack was having no effect. They'd seriously underestimated their power, and now the alien force was going to absorb the Earth as punishment for harboring their fugitive, the Dragon Star. This was not what Aurora intended.

He called in another check of the roster. From two hundred superheroes, eighty were alive, sixty-two uninjured and able to fight. Thirty of these were in waiting on the raiding platforms, unable to fight or survive in space unaided. That brought it down to thirty-two. A dozen were assisting the injured, ferrying them back to the moon or to the raiding platforms, and tending their wounds, some of which were terrible. Bluebell was with them, injured herself but able to use her psychic powers as a sort of metaphysical anesthetic for those who needed it.

Eighteen superheroes floated in space behind Aurora and the Thuban. The glowing, blurry mass of the warship itself cruised forward sedately, now no longer concerned with the inconvenient heroes buzzing around it.

"There must be a weak point, a line of fracture," said the Dragon Star. He was at Aurora's shoulder, suit jacket flapping in the solar wind that streamed off Aurora's back.

Aurora focused himself. It was not the Dragon Star's fault. The Thuban were a vast complex, a gestalt beyond human understanding. They were not to know what form their attack on the Earth would take. But right now, the Dragon Star was perhaps their best hope. The powerstaff had been able, at one point, to penetrate the shield that surrounded the warship, and do damage, however minimal. Aurora had read the spectrum reflected off the object's surface with each attack that found the target. Only energy blasts from the powerstaff showed anything different – traces of elements heavier than hydrogen. Material from the surface, sloughed off into space. Just a little.

"Can you breach the object with your staff, Dragon Star?"

There was a pause as the Dragon Star considered. "I do not know. A sustained strike on a single weak point, perhaps. But I fear the process would take too long, and the Thuban would have time to retaliate before the structure of the warship was breached."

"What if... Can the staff be overloaded? If the warship is susceptible to its energy signature, could we fly it in close and detonate it, somehow?"

Another pause. "This is possible. However, I am tied to the staff. I would not be able to reconstitute an existence again."

"You mean you would die?"

"Yes."

"OK..." There was a glint of light at the edge of Aurora's vision. At the same moment, his comm popped and twenty voices spoke all at once. Linear darted into his view, between Aurora and the warship, and pointed back over Aurora's shoulder. Aurora turned.

At the center of the black disk of the moon was a white light. It grew larger very quickly, and in a few seconds it streaked over Aurora's head and towards the enemy. It was a figure, another hero. Not Sam again? Aurora touched the comm link on his belt.

"Aurora to Apollo Fortress, come in please! Do you read me, over?"

The channel was still heavy with static. Aurora blinked the comm on and off a few times to try to improve the signal. Finally, he got a voice through that was clear enough to understand. The voice belonged to Sam. Aurora listened as he watched the burning figure streak towards the warship.

"Aurora! It's Tony."

"It's Tony what? Detective, explain!"

"Tony used the power core. He says it's the only way to stop the Thuban. He said the heroes will all die with the Earth if he didn't stop it himself."

As he watched, the warship was suddenly surrounded by flashes of violet light. The object seemed to slow and turn slightly as the flashes increased in frequency and intensity.

"Aurora!" Another voice now. He heard half of a muffled argument and then Jeannie came on. "He's brought us into space as well. We're almost there."

He turned and saw a purple globe approach, untethered and drifting. Linear nodded and flew towards it, gingerly nudging the surface and pushing it towards Aurora. As soon as it was close enough, the Dragon Star hitched it with a thread of energy from the powerstaff. The globe sparked as the two energies met, then the globe stabilized. Sam and Jeannie stood impatiently inside, sharing a single communicator taken from the moonbase. Jeannie held the MIC-N loosely at her side.

Aurora drew as close to the support bubble as possible, his aura flaring red in anger and licking the smooth purple membrane that separated Sam and Jeannie from cold space. But before he could say anything, Sam grabbed the communicator from Jeannie.

"Aurora, it wasn't us. He grabbed the core and used it on himself."

Jeannie snatched at the comm, but Sam held her grip. Jeannie instead tugged Sam's arm up in front of her face so she could talk. "You can put the angry eyes away, dude. He said it was the only way to stop the... whatever it is. He said you'd all die and the Earth would be eaten. So go stick that in your pipe and smoke it. Look. Seems he was right."

She pointed, and Aurora turned. Around him, the superheroes floated into a tight pack, drawn by the spectacle of the one-man assault on the Thuban. The blackness of space flickered with violet light that made Sam and Jeannie cover their eyes. Even some of the superheroes with regular or unshielded vision were forced to look away, or peer as best they could from behind raised arms.

The Thuban creation was darker now, losing the bright yellow glow to become a dull orange. Surface features and shapes could be seen, the whole structure appearing to be a rotating complex of polyhedrons, similar in design to the power core shell. From this distance, Tony was a brilliant purple streak, spinning around the superstructure, diving in and around, each orbit coinciding with a flash of light.

"Get those who cannot fight back to the moon, now." It was Tony. Linear and Supercharger looked at each other, then at Aurora. All around, the superheroes murmured to each other, then looked at their leader. Tony had patched into the comm link somehow. Everyone had heard him. Then he spoke again.

"The rest will attack the Thuban on my mark. Aurora, gather the force and lead them in when I'm ready. Please confirm."

Aurora flicked his communicator. If this was humanity's last stand, it was best not to delay with argument or discussion. The Thuban were weakening. Tony had been right.

"Confirmed. Awaiting further instruction." He snapped the comm off, but it buzzed with static again almost instantly.

"You sure about this?" Bluebell, aboard one of the raiding platforms. Aurora looked for them and found the yellow domes floating some distance below.

"Affirmative. Helix, Doctor Mandragora, move the platforms back to the moon. Secure the base and await further orders."

Doctor Mandragora's hiss was difficult to discern through the constant static of the comm link, but Aurora recognized the snake-man's tone at least as one of protest. Aurora's corona snapped out angry tendrils of energy that flickered into space. He snapped the comm on quickly again.

"You have injured personnel. Bluebell and Sand Cat will assist in the infirmary. Move!"

Aurora watched as Helix and then, after a pause, Doctor Mandragora flew back towards the moon, pulling the slightly elastic energy tethers of the two support platforms behind them.

"What about us?"

Aurora turned back to Sam and Jeannie. He pointed at the MIC-N hanging from Jeannie's hand. "We need some insurance." He glanced around the superheroes who were staying, keeping in steady three-dimensional formation in space around him. Some were slightly too far off to be identified by sight. He opened the channel on his comm again.

"Are there any magical superheroes present?"

A single voice popped through the interference. "The Malice Dawn reporting, Aurora." Her accent was European. Aurora couldn't resist smiling – the Transylvanian sorceress was another supervillain turned good. He was glad that she was on their side, and also glad that she had survived the Thuban death ray.

"Teleport Paragon into the Dragon Star's support bubble, please."

From somewhere above, he saw a superhero break out of formation and fly towards the departing platforms. The sunrise icon on the front of the Malice Dawn's cloak glowed brightly as she accelerated towards them.

"Those present in each bubble, hold hands, please. Effecting teleport in three, two, one." She raised both arms as her voice increased in volume. *"Shala-tyr karr'kara-cho!"*

Two sequential flashes, so fast as to be almost instantaneous, and Conroy stood between Sam and Jeannie, clasping their hands in his own.

"Impressive," he said. The corner of Aurora's mouth raised in a smirk.

Tony's voice, remarkably clear, cut through the comm link. Aurora noted that the link wasn't even on, Tony was merely channeling his thoughts through it. A surprisingly powerful trick, done so easily.

"You may commence your attack, Aurora. There is no specific target other than the substance of the Thuban itself."

Aurora clicked the comm on. "Confirmed. Superheroes, when you're ready."

Linear and Supercharger buzzed nearby.

"Light 'em up!"

Two dozen shouts followed the superheroes as they charged through space towards the Thuban, Aurora at the head. As soon as he was within range, he focused his magnetic field into a narrow cone in front of him and summoned the full power of the Earth's sun. His aura shook, then exploded outwards in a yellow-red nova of energy, striking the Thuban with such force that the massive warship shifted in space, tilting upwards as it was pushed by the energy cone. The dull glowing orange of the surface darkened until nearly the whole side of the object turned as black as the space behind it, then it shattered like glass, throwing a billion shards in every direction. Aurora pulled his aura back again and projected it as a spherical shield around himself, vaporizing the debris that was blasted towards him. The other superheroes did the same, those capable of producing shields protecting themselves and others, while a few sped onwards, blasting the glassy rubble with lasers and energy bolts.

The success of Aurora's attack was all the others needed. As the battlefield cleared, the carcass of the Thuban ship could be seen as it spun, end over end. Tony appeared from the far side and flew to Aurora. His body was featureless, violet-glowing black, his smile the same empty white gash as when he had been the Thuban's avatar. He gestured towards the falling enemy with an expansive arm, and the superheroes flew in, opening their superpowered arsenal at it.

The warship was rocked by explosions as the surface was bombarded. As the shattered side rolled into view again, the superheroes retargeted, firing deep into the heart of the thing. Finally it sheared in half, and the heroes spun around each section, dividing it further and further. In a final effort, the last remaining large pieces were destroyed, until nothing was left but glass splinters a few inches in length.

Aurora called the superheroes back as the splinters drifted towards the Earth's upper atmosphere, some already beginning to trail red and white as the friction of re-entry atomized them. Below, the West Coast of the United States was again in night. California – and San Ventura – would have a second meteor shower.

CHAPTER SIXTY

There was something about Tony, something wrong. Sam watched him talk to Aurora, unable to hear them as they didn't seem to be using the comm links, and unable to lip read anything useful. Tony kept glancing at them – or at Jeannie, anyway – whenever Aurora spoke, almost as though he wasn't giving the leader of the Seven Wonders his full attention. There was also something about the look, something not quite right. Sam could see it clearly, despite the black and purple of his skin and, like Aurora, the emptiness of his eyes. Tony looked like he was treading water, unconsciously moving his arms and legs in empty space as he kept level with Aurora, who hung in the vacuum without movement.

And then he looked again, and Sam shivered. It was unnerving, inhuman somehow, and it had nothing to do with his bizarre appearance. She nudged Jeannie and whispered, unsure of what Tony would be able to somehow hear.

"Something's not right."

Jeannie joined the conspiratorial tone. "Something's not right in your head, correct."

Sam sighed and nudged her in the ribs again, harder this time. "Can it, will you? When Tony was sent back to the Earth by the Thuban, he wasn't Tony anymore, he was something else."

"What do you mean?"

"Well, when I was... SuperSam, or whatever – that wasn't me either. Neither I nor Tony can remember anything about when we were powered. It was us, our bodies, but our minds were locked somewhere deep inside while the 'power', or whatever it was, took over, feeding only on our basic instincts and behaviors to create... something else."

Jeannie looked at Sam, then at Tony. Tony looked in their direction again, but this time the smile was different. Jeannie flinched. She clearly saw it too this time. Could he hear what they were saying, or read their minds?

"You mean that's...?"

"That's not Tony."

"You are correct." The purple barrier shimmered in front of them. Sam and Jeannie turned around to find the Dragon Star inside the support bubble. He held the powerstaff vertically, the ceiling of the support bubble dimpling inwards to connect with its tip, like a balloon.

Sam automatically took a step backward, but hit the wall of the support bubble. It fizzed noticeably at the contact, and Sam's eyes flicked downwards in apology. Talking to the body of her dead partner was going to take some getting used to.

"So that's *not* Tony?" Jeannie asked. The Dragon Star nodded.

"Tony is somewhere within, but the power core is part of the Thuban, and is alive. That would have been part of the original plan, not only to grant the Cowl enough power to capture me, but to also control him themselves. He would have been nothing more than a puppet."

Conroy laughed. The unexpected reaction caught Sam and Jeannie by surprise, but the Dragon Star seemed to ignore it.

"Something funny, Cowlboy?" Sam's question wiped the amusement from his face.

"Far from it. I'm starting to think I got off lightly when Jeannie here pulled the trigger on that thing." He knocked the side of the MIC-N with the toe of his boot.

"This may be true, Paragon," said the Dragon Star. "But we now face another dilemma."

Jeannie exhaled slowly. "Tony?"

The Dragon Star inclined his head. "The Thuban power that lives on, using Tony, yes."

Sam squinted as a thought dawned on her. "But Tony's still in there, right? You just said so. So all we need to do is use that thing again, drain the power off, and we're safe."

"Could work," said Conroy. He folded his arms and carefully looked over his shoulder. Aurora and Tony were still in conference. They hadn't appeared to have noticed the other discussion going on inside the shield.

Jeannie shook her head. "No. This thing doesn't work like that, remember? It doesn't just drain power off, it *transfers* it. The shell of the power core was absorbed by Tony when he became the man in black there. Where do we put the power if we can drain it off? It can't be one of us, or one of the other superheroes, or we'll just be back to square one."

Sam looked the Dragon Star up and down, trying to ignore the fact that the blank expression on his face was nothing like an expression Joe would – used to – make. The powerstaff pulsed gently.

"The staff? It's the same tech, isn't it? Can it be the receptacle?"

Conroy and Jeannie looked at each other. "Worth a shot?" asked Conroy.

The Dragon Star nodded. "Prepare the machine."

The conversation had grown cold, and Aurora was growing wary. After Tony had described his method of attack, the topic had now moved to the superheroes – Tony asked not just about the Seven Wonders, but about all of the groups and individuals who had joined the attack. Aurora had humored him politely for a while, but Tony's questions pressed on. The superhero armada had begun to move back to the moon, after a few had broken off to return to the Earth to mop up any shards of the Thuban that might have survived re-entry, and to liaise with the authorities to assure them that the threat was over.

But now Aurora had had enough. Tony's conversation had the relentless, repetitive nature of a child. He held up a hand and after a few moments, Tony stopped talking. He looked at Aurora, his gash-like mouth turning into a child's drawing of a petulant frown.

"Tony, we should return to the moon. We have much to discuss with the others."

Tony was looking at the Earth, watching a handful of heroes spin through the atmosphere.

"Yes, much to discuss."

Aurora nodded, waited for a moment, then flew upwards, relative to Tony, and curved over the purple bubble holding Sam, Jeannie and Paragon. He saw the Dragon Star, and gestured to him as he passed over. The Dragon Star seemed to see, but made no movement.

A hundred yards later, Aurora stopped. He was outstretched, pointing towards the moon with one fist, looking up as he flew towards his destination. Except he wasn't moving, although his flaming trail streamed out behind him as though he were still in flight.

"Did I say you could go, Nikolai?"

Aurora didn't speak, couldn't speak. His head was fixed, looking towards the moon, as Tony glided serenely beside him until his eyes were the same level as the frozen, horizontal superhero.

"You see, Nikolai, now that I removed the Thuban for you, it seems I'm owed something. What, I hear you ask? Oh, *lots* of things. There's Bluebell of course. As chairman of the Seven Wonders, I need a consort. And Bluebell – Alexandra – is such a rare beauty."

Aurora's aura swelled, just a little. Enough for Tony to see.

"Ah, no no no. I don't think so." He flicked a hand, and Aurora went dark, superpowers extinguished. His eyes became visible under the mask, wide and bloodshot, as Aurora began to asphyxiate and freeze. Tony laughed and flexed his wrist again. Aurora's body shone with solar energy again.

"And then there's the Earth. You owe me that. I mean, I wanted it before, I could have had it before. Then you killed me." He floated closer, maintaining eye line with Aurora but pressing in so close their noses almost touched. Tony's voice was reduced to a whisper. "You killed me. Remember? And superheroes never kill. And you know what that makes you? A supervillain. The Seven Wonders are no more superheroes than the Dark League or the Steel Council. Perhaps you killed them too. Where did all the supervillains go, Nikolai? Nobody ever saw them again after they were sent to one of the UN superprisons."

Tony stopped, and floated back a little. "You may speak."

Aurora said nothing, but his mouth moved, muscles now freed from Tony's control.

Tony was impatient. "Well?"

"Now!"

Tony had ignored the humans in the support bubble. They were of no consequence, and if the Dragon Star had dared take any action, he would have shut the bubble off in an instant before throwing the Dragon Star into the sun, leaving the three humans to die in the awful hostility of space. Tony had ignored them at his peril.

A beam, undulating and twisted, projected itself through the support bubble and played across Tony. At first he did nothing but smile, dazzled just momentarily by the brightness of the light. Then the beam, plain white, began to tint, turning first a light purple then increasing in intensity to an electric, shining violet.

Tony twisted, realizing what was happening, but it was too late. The alien energy of the Thuban was drawn off, drained away. He tried to fly up, out of the beam, but like Aurora, he was unable to move. His mouth opened in a scream, but without the power to break into the comm link channel, nobody could hear.

After a few seconds, his black skin began to flake off like ash. Underneath, his pale, human flesh appeared in patches, exposed to the vacuum. Tony writhed as the Thuban power was drained and his human form was exposed to space.

Freed from Tony's grip as his power faded, Aurora dropped away, avoiding the beam projected by the transfer machine held by Jeannie inside the bubble. He could see the Dragon Star holding his power-staff to the machine's output, enabling the power to flow into it. The entire surface of the weapon was a moving rainbow of color. At the back of the bubble, Paragon and Sam crouched, arms over their heads.

Aurora could feel the detritus fizzing in his aura. Turning, he saw Tony was almost completely free of the covering. As the last of the material was shed into space, the beam snapped off. Aurora sped forward, tapping Tony with enough force on the head to render him unconscious, then scooped him up. He made a tight turn to fly back toward the bubble, but in the blink of an eye found himself in the moonbase infirmary.

Someone touched his shoulder. He turned to find it was the Dragon

Star. On the infirmary floor, Sam and Paragon slowly unfurled themselves. With a crash, Jeannie dropped the MIC-N and collapsed.

"The threat is eliminated," said the Dragon Star. His powerstaff glowed white, infused with the energy from the race that had created it. Linear buzzed and lifted Tony from Aurora's arms, and in a second had him connected to the monitoring equipment. Monolith and Lawmaker, ever vigilant, resumed their guard as Bluebell turned her attention immediately to the medical readouts.

Aurora looked around, just in time to see the Dragon Star walk from the room. He glanced at Sam and Jeannie, who stood. Sam blew out her cheeks.

"I thought the teleport was busted?"

Aurora licked his lips. "I think it still is," he said, then followed in the Dragon Star's footsteps.

CHAPTER SIXTY-ONE

Three days later and the conference room was full again, but this time with a new mix of heroes. Sam hardly knew any of them by name, but scanned faces and costumes in morbid fascination, seeing who had made it, and who hadn't. Of the eighty who had survived the Thuban attack, three more had died on the moon. Most of the injured were now up and mobile at least, and a mix of science and magic was being employed in the infirmary to heal the remaining few who were in critical condition.

Sam had slept most of the three days. She realized she'd never really recovered from absorbing the power core back in San Ventura. Like an unprepared runner attempting a marathon, she felt drained, lethargic, and she suspected she would for some time.

She sat at the table in the conference room, again unsure of her right to be seated among the Seven Wonders when so many powerful, important, and famous heroes stood around her. Immediately opposite, standing behind Linear's chair, was Lady Liberty and her robot Presidents. They'd made it at least. Beside Absolute Lincoln, Sam recognized X-Realm and Might, four others she knew by sight but not by name, as well as Lawmaker and Monolith. Pangolin too. She was glad about that – the diminutive hero was most definitely B-list or lower, and she doubted he'd ever faced such a challenge before. The little man saw her looking and nodded a greeting, his snouted face beaming in delight.

Then again, none of them had. Never before had so many fallen in a single day.

She gave up her game of spot-the-hero after that. It wasn't important.

All chairs at the table were occupied – Sam, Jeannie and Conroy as the "humans" on one side, Sand Cat, Bluebell, Linear on the other as the "superheroes", Aurora at the head as usual. Sam felt uncomfortable at being included at the table, and tried to ignore the fact that she had to sit next to Jeannie. The former Blackbird appeared to have taken to wearing her orange prisoner jumpsuit like a costume itself. It had been three days, and Sam realized that she'd even changed into a fresh one.

Sam looked around the table and squirmed in her chair. She felt like Aurora's blank eyes were constantly watching her, and she was very aware of the Dragon Star standing behind her chair. She could hear his powerstaff humming in her left ear.

"Detective?"

Sam blinked. The whole room was looking at her, silently. After a moment, Linear waggled his eyebrows discreetly and made a small motion with his hand, encouraging her to respond. She rubbed her forehead, looked around the room, then met Aurora's look.

"I'm sorry, what did you say?"

It was clear that she had been miles away, but Aurora let it pass and repeated his question without pause.

"Do you accept our invitation to join the Seven Wonders?"

Sam felt her chest tighten as her lungs refused to exhale. A second later she forced the air out herself. It came out quickly, and ended with a small laugh.

"But I'm not a superhero."

Aurora smiled. "Superheroes are not defined merely by special powers or abilities. Character counts, perhaps above all else, as well as dedication to a cause. You have demonstrated both. The first task for the Seven Wonders is to help rebuild San Ventura, and for the superhero community at large it is to re-join the world we have all neglected for too long. The Seven Wonders have a vacancy, and we need someone to both liaise with the city authorities, and to provide law enforcement and detective skills to our team. These qualities we need if we are to fight crime once more."

Sam coughed, very aware of the masked eyes on her, and the ever-present hum of the powerstaff just beyond the edge of her vision.

"I thought the Seven Wonders were seven heroes, until the Cowl killed David, my husband. You did nothing to stop him and your inaction brought destruction to our homes." She paused, and looked at Jeannie and Conroy sitting next to her. "Destruction directed by these two. I cannot believe you would welcome such people to the team."

Linear buzzed. Aurora and Bluebell exchanged a look.

"You are correct, detective. The Seven Wonders will remain as five to honor the memory of our fallen friend Hephaestus, and his remarkable robot, SMART. Now that the Earth is safe, Paragon will honor his agreement and go to the United Nations voluntarily, where he will stand trial. Blackbird also."

Jeannie snorted but kept her eyes on the table.

Sam turned in her seat and looked up at the Dragon Star. The face of Joe Milano looked down at her, the eyes an infinite starscape. It still felt like a dream.

"What about the Dragon Star?"

The superhero shook his head, and for the first time since taking his new body, smiled. Sam's heart raced – the smile was instantly recognizable, a signature expression. Joe was in there, somewhere, he had to be.

"My new powers are not needed on the Earth. With the superheroes returning to the world, the Earth has more than enough protection. I have been given a gift, a new chance and new powers. I am not the only member of my race to crave identity and freedom. I shall return home to fight for them. It is the power of the Thuban themselves that enables this, thanks to the machine of Paragon and Blackbird. I feel… I think Joe approves."

The Dragon Star smiled again, and later Sam would swear he winked at her.

"Your first task, I should add," said Aurora, "will be escorting Mr Conroy to The Hague as his arresting officer."

Sam looked at Aurora, then around the table. Sand Cat and Bluebell were smiling; even Conroy was, apparently content with his fate. Jeannie's lip was curled in disgust.

Linear buzzed impatiently, then mouthed something which Sam took to be "just say yes, dammit!"

"What about Tony?"

Bluebell answered.

"He is not fit to stand trial, yet, but will be held at the UN as well. We will prepare a holding cell for him."

Sam considered. Slowly, a smile spread across her face.

"Yes, I will."

The room broke into applause, and Sam laughed. Her, a regular detective from San Ventura, just trying to keep her city safe and to bring the Cowl to justice. Now she was a superhero, and would be able to serve the city like never before, having a direct hand in the rebuilding. San Ventura would, once again, be known as the Shining City.

Detective Sam Millar, superhero? No way. No *freakin'* way. Captain Gillespie was going to spit.

CHAPTER SIXTY-TWO

The cell was a spacious cuboid, one hundred feet in length, half that again in width, and with a ten-foot stud height, laid out as a stylish studio apartment, complete with study, den, bedroom, bathroom. The ultimate bachelor pad – simple, basic even, but not entirely uncomfortable. Most of it was glass, transparent or frosted. Privacy was not high on the list of required features. The box was suspended in space, without any physical contact with the concrete walls that surrounded it, offering a complete three-hundred-and-sixty-degree view of ninety-nine percent of the interior, from any position on the gantry that ringed the equator of the chamber in which the cell floated. The remaining one percent of the cell was opaque to the visual spectrum only – and the selected superheroes that formed part of the guard rotation did not see in the visual spectrum.

Tony was aware of this as he showered. He'd grown used to it over the past six months. As he was left alone, mostly, the lack of privacy ceased to become an issue. He was comfortable, he didn't care.

The superheroes had grown bored of him too. For the first few weeks of his captivity, Bluebell had tried to read his mind, Linear had tried to strike up friendly conversation, and that lame-ass detective (Sam the superhero? Puh-lease!) had just come and stood on the gantry and stared.

Then one day Bluebell didn't show. Tony hadn't seen her since. Sam was the only constant. She came every day and sat and stared, teleported from the US to Europe in the blink of an eye. Tony had no idea what she was doing. Perhaps the Seven Wonders were giving her training in Jedi mind tricks or some bullshit. Whatever. He ignored her. That was easy. She'd always been a wallflower.

Except Sam hadn't turned up today. Tony registered her absence early, and found himself pacing the cell all morning. He didn't care, tried not to care, didn't want to care, but her absence made him anxious. His routine was spoilt. He wanted to sit and read and ignore her. If she wasn't there, he couldn't. It bugged him. Eventually he stopped pacing and stood by the wall of the cell, looking out at the gantry.

Tony tried to remember what San Ventura had looked like before the meteors came. He frowned. He couldn't remember anything. San Ventura had been totaled, that he did know. He probably wouldn't recognize the place now, rebuilt with the help of the superheroes of the world. Not that he'd ever be in a position to visit the outside world again.

There was a bang, far away. It was hardly a sound at all, more a subtle thud against his eardrums from somewhere way beyond the security area. It was only because the cell, and the surrounding security zone, were so completely silent that he registered it at all. His superheroic guard was also absent.

There it was again. Louder this time. Judging direction was meaningless, but perhaps it had come from the other side of the door. Or perhaps the door was thinner than the walls and acted as a natural soundboard. Who knew?

The door to the gantry opened. Someone ran in, and the door stayed open behind them. Black-skinned, lithe, athletic, female. Not black-skinned, someone wearing a skintight black suit. A costume. The weird head bobbed as she got closer, until Tony recognized the angled triangular front of the mask and the twin curved surfaces that swept back and up past the back of the head. Tony's flat, empty black eyes blinked and he smiled for the first time in half a year.

"Stand back, pretty boy," said Blackbird. She fished something out of her belt, some small, silver rectangle. A red LED flickered madly on its front edge as her thumb caressed the upper surface. The light switched to a steady bright blue, and the transparent cell door swung open and down, forming a twenty-foot drawbridge connecting the box to the gantry.

Blackbird pocketed the device, stood for a moment, then cocked her head. Her mask exaggerated the movement, making it look like the inquisitive stare of a magpie.

"You coming or what?"

There were two more thuds from beyond the main door. Blackbird half-turned, her right hand slipping down her thigh to slide an impressively large gun from a holster. That was new.

"Tony, hurry the fuck up. I'm rescuing you, like, now. Come on, dammit."

Tony smiled again and stepped onto the bridge.

ABOUT THE AUTHOR

Adam Christopher was born in Auckland, New Zealand, and grew up watching Pertwee-era *Doctor Who* and listening to The Beatles, which isn't a bad start for a child of the Eighties. In 2006, Adam moved to the sunny North West of England, where he now lives in domestic bliss with his wife and cat in a house next to a canal, although he has yet to take up any fishing-related activities.

When not writing Adam can be found drinking tea and obsessing over DC Comics, Stephen King, and The Cure. He is also a strong advocate for social media, especially Twitter, which he spends far too much time on avoiding work.

adamchristopher.co.uk
twitter.com/ghostfinder

ACKNOWLEDGMENTS

This book is the result of years of reading and enjoying and loving comics. I'm something of a latecomer to the medium, having waited until the ripe old age of about 23 to pick up my first issue of *2000AD*. I was hooked from page one, and after a while decided to give Marvel and DC Comics a go. It was then that I made a somewhat surprising discovery: I love superheroes. Discovering superhero comics was like *coming home*. Maybe it's the heroics. Maybe it's the ideals. Maybe it's the spandex and silly names. But superheroes changed my life, and all for the better. So I owe a huge debt to the legion of creators, writers, artists and editors going right back to the late 1930s. It would be foolish to try and name them all (I don't have that much room here!), but if it weren't for the greats of the Golden and Silver Ages of the American comic book, *Seven Wonders* wouldn't exist. My thanks then to Otto Binder, Steve Ditko, Bill Finger, Gardner Fox, Carmine Infantino, Bob Kane, Gill Kane, Jack Kirby, Stan Lee, Jerry Robinson, John Romita Sr, Julius Schwartz, Jerry Siegel, Joe Shuster, Curt Swan, and of course Major Malcolm Wheeler-Nicholson, as well as a thousand others who over the span of the 20th century created a body of work truly mythological in scale.

Their work is continued, of course, by the modern greats. Once again they are too numerous to mention, but my special thanks to Kurt Busiek, whose epic *Astro City* remains a fundamental to my love of superhero comics. And thanks also Ed Brubaker, Darwyn Cooke, Geoff Johns, Paul Levitz, Grant Morrison, Greg Rucka and Gail Simone.

And if we're talking about inspiration, long before I started reading comics, the spark of *Seven Wonders* was lit many, *many* years ago by one of my favourite bands, Pixies. Interested readers may want to check out their 1988 album *Surfer Rosa,* in particular, track nine: "Tony's Theme". If *Seven Wonders* ever needs a song to play out over the end credits, that's the one.

My thanks to my dynamic duo of beta-readers, Kate Sherrod and Taylor B Wright, and to my international league of super-friends who I can rely on for support, encouragement, and the occasional saving of the Earth from diabolical masterminds: Lizzie Barrett, Lauren Beukes, Joelle Charbonneau, Paul Cornell, Kim Curran, Dale Halvorsen, Nick Harkaway, Tom Hunter, Laura Lam, Mur Lafferty, Matthew McBride, Lou Morgan, Tom Pollock, Adrian Tchiakovsky, Chuck Wendig and Jen Williams. Special thanks also to Mark "The Cowl" Nelson, Emma Vieceli, and the superhero known only as Your Imaginary Pal over at the Comic Book Resources forum.

Thanks as always to the Angry Robots themselves, Marc Gascoigne and Lee Harris and the rest, and to the remarkable Will Staehle. I'm a lucky boy, and I sure know it. And thanks to Stacia Decker, my exceptionally kick-ass agent, for being exceptionally kick-ass.

Finally, to Sandra, my wife, who puts up with late nights and lost weekends and still continues to provide all the love, encouragement and support her writer husband needs. *That* is what I call superheroic. I love you.

DELETED SCENES

#1: TONY AND THE ATM

Author's note: Some parts of Seven Wonders *were written as a series of vignettes, as I wanted to explore all the different things Tony might do as his superpowers developed. This deleted scene originally took place after the police raid on Tony and Jeannie's apartment and the pair flee. It was supposed to be the first time Tony killed anyone, fuelling his journey to the dark side. However, after shuffling the book's timeline a little, it made more sense for Tony to take the police out in the apartment, so this sequence became superfluous. The* Smallville *reference is a nod to the second episode of season three,* Phoenix, *in which Clark smashes ATMs to steal thousands of dollars while under the influence of red kryptonite.*

Tony eyed the machine with vague uncertainty. Being in a less-travelled back street behind the Moore-Reppion shopping plaza, the ATM was an older model, scuffed but functional, a half-hearted attempt at graffiti scrawled across the sliding panel that hid the keypad. Tony hadn't seen a machine this old for a long time. He looked around, but at four in the morning there was nobody around except Jeannie.

Jeannie took a couple of steps backwards, unconsciously checking around her like Tony did, just in case. She rolled her hands together, motioning towards the cash machine.

"Go on!"

Tony frowned. "I don't know about this."

"Tony," Jeannie hissed. Tony didn't find her quite so attractive when she was like this. "We need cash. You think being a superhero comes cheap?"

"Um..." Tony turned to stare at the machine. She was right. His job was history. So was the apartment. They needed fundage, but... *stealing*? Didn't that kinda go against the whole superhero thing?

"Old machines like this don't hold much cash," said Jeannie. "The bank'll just write it off."

Tony shuffled. Jeannie sighed.

"And when you're a member of the Seven Wonders and money is no object, you can make it up with a charitable donation, okay?"

Tony nodded, trying to convince himself. She was right, right? A little cash would go a long way. The ends justified the means, right? If he could clean the city up and remove the Cowl, nobody would begrudge him a few readies.

He glanced at Jeannie. "Like in *Smallville*?"

"*Just* like in *Smallville*."

Tony balled his right hand into a fist. Still uncertain, he raised it to his face and inspected his knuckles. He ran the fingers of his other hand over bones, almost testing them to make sure they were as solid as he remembered. Actually, they were nothing like he remembered. They looked the same and felt the same but he knew that somehow, miraculously, they were as hard as diamond. Even the skin, warm, pale, stretched over the knuckles on a bed of subcutaneous fat – even that soft, pliable surface was completely impenetrable. Tony frowned again, then took a step back himself.

"Stand back."

"Standing."

Tony aimed for the center of the machine, throwing his fist forward with as much force as he could muster. He had no idea of the internal schematics of an ATM, but assumed that the money would be inside some kind of safe. He half-remembered stories of crooks ripping machines out of bank walls with tow trucks, then spending a month trying to cut the intact machine open with blowtorches in an abandoned farmhouse somewhere in the country. ATMs were tough to crack. On the face of it they were easy targets, so they had to be.

Tony's train of thought was only broken when he realized he'd punched through the machine's front as far as his elbow. The tiny green computer monitor (hell, this really was an *old* machine) popped with a sharp bang and a flash, and somewhere inside the severed electronics sparked, lighting Tony and Jeannie up briefly with flickering blue light. Tony swore and looked around, but they were still alone in the street. He extricated his arm from the hole and tried to decide what to do next. Jeannie peered into the machine's dark innards.

"Cash?"

"Not sure…" Tony reached in again. "Can't feel anything."

Jeannie tapped her foot. "Pull it out. Let's get a better look."

Tony reached into the hole with both hands and tugged. Part of the plastic façade of the machine flew off. He tried again and gripped something more substantial, and lifted. The heavy frame of the machine squealed in protest as the ATM was pulled from the wall, shattering the brick on either side. Tony dropped the machine onto its back on the pavement and leaned over it. He pushed at the sides of the hole he'd made in its front, splitting the workings of the machine like papier-mâché. A black metal box lay at the center, with a variety of slots and metal attachments surrounding it.

"Bingo," said Jeannie. Tony saw her grin caught by the dim streetlights. He couldn't stop himself from smiling either. How much money did an ATM hold? If this machine was a less-used one, and one of a virtually antique design, did that mean it was full, or did they only load it with enough cash to meet demand?

Tony realized it didn't matter. Cracking the machine had been easy. Too easy. And the city was full of them. They were going to go home with pockets of cash after just a couple of hours work. Wherever home was now of course. Jeannie seemed to know where she was going, at least.

Tony allowed himself a smile. It would be okay, once he'd saved the city. Cash would rain down on his head.

"Open it, come on!"

Tony felt around the edges of the black container and, not entirely sure what he should do, pulled a few wires and a couple of support brackets out to separate the safe from the machine itself. It slid without much difficulty from the heart of the ATM, but when he set it down on the pavement the thud was audible – the thing was heavy, and he hadn't even noticed.

He turned it over and found the door at the back. That looked like the easiest option, but when he yanked the handle but the heavy steel snapped in his hand. He swore, and resorted to something more primitive, punching the door until it caved enough to give him an edge to get his fingertips on. Then he pulled, bending the door around its locking mechanism which rattled but remained otherwise intact. Eventually, he managed to pull enough of the inch-thick metal down to see the stacked cartridges inside.

The cash.

He tore a little more of the door open and reached through the gap until he could get a grip on one of the cartridges. He yanked, and the thin metal box shot out of the safe, Tony tumbling onto his back. The cartridge hit him in the face, and he swore again; blinking in surprise, he looked at the box sitting in his lap. He smiled, and ripped the thin lid off.

Cash. Twenties, stacked high. He laughed and fingered a wedge of bills, leaving dark indelible marks.

"What the fuck?"

Jeannie moved closer to get a better look.

"Shit!"

"What?"

Jeannie looked down her own front. She was splattered with thick blue ink. The ink covered the interior of the safe. Tony's front was almost entirely covered, and it was splashed up on his face. His hands were completely blue, leaving stains on the ATM cartridge and the bills inside.

"What the fuck is this… is this ink?" He wiped his hands on his shirt, but it made no difference, only spreading the security dye further. Jeannie saw the pavement shine in the streetlight. The pavers around the crushed ATM were slick with it.

"Some kind of security thing, marks the bills," she said. "Fuck, I didn't think."

Tony laughed, but it had a nasty, ragged edge. "You didn't think?

Well, great. Now what?"

"Any bills clean?"

Tony dropped to his knees and flipped the cartridge upside down. Green paper spilled out, those that were not already smeared in the ink landing in the spreading ooze on the ground.

"Not anymore."

Jeannie stood and looked around. The street was empty, but… was that a car coming? Tony saw her eyes widen in panic; following her gaze, he saw something flashing on the lip of the bank's overhanging frontage. A square alarm box, blue light rendered grey in the yellow streetlight. Flashing, silently.

"Gotta go, lover boy." She grabbed Tony's shirt at the shoulder, a half-hearted attempt to pull him up that was symbolic rather than practical. He got to his feet, slid a little in the pool of thick ink, then righted himself. He held his hands out in front of them like they were injured or contaminated. He looked at the wrecked money machine and the half empty cartridge. There were a few twenty dollar bills stuck to his jeans.

"What about all this?"

"Gotta leave it. No one will touch the bills now. Even if we can clean it off that shit will glow under UV or something, marking it as stolen."

"Well, fuck-a-doodle-doo."

The pair turned, ignoring the wreckage left behind – the rectangular hole in the bank wall much larger than the square machine itself, which lay on the ground, split and bent like an old trash can – and ran for somewhere, anywhere, that was off the main road.

Too late. The car Jeannie had heard earlier pulled up at the corner ahead of them. A police cruiser. Tony saw it first and swore, too loudly, and pulled Jeannie into the shadows of a narrow alley at the side of the bank.

Also too late. Two officers leapt from the car, torches on and handguns held at the ready. The officers approached at a run, then slowed as the searched for the felons, torchlight playing over the dark alley between buildings. One spotlight fell on the wall of bank, and the officer holding the torch let out a low whistle.

Tony made a break for it, mistimed. The second policeman shouted, the first spun the flashlight towards the alley, both trained their weapons on the retreating forms of Jeannie and Tony. Tony almost tripped as he shot towards a street across from the alley, slowing their escape. Jeannie didn't wait for him.

The first cop was now radioing in for help. While he waited for dispatch to squawk through on the radio clipped to his shoulder, he nodded to his partner, who immediately took off in pursuit.

Reaching the other street, Tony saw Jeannie had finally paused to let him catch up. As he approached, he stopped, confused. He wasn't quite sure this was the right direction. Covered in security ink, he and Jeannie would leave an obvious trail for anyone to follow. Clothes, shoes, everything would need to be ditched. If they could get to the park, maybe the worst of the ink would come off in the fountain, at least enough that they could be confident they wouldn't track it all through the city.

"Freeze! Get on the ground! On the ground! Now!"

Jeannie turned first. Tony turned and stumbled as he was dazzled by the flashlight shining into his face. The policeman repeated his order. Tony could just see the man behind the light, legs braced in a shooting stance, flashlight held expertly along the barrel of his gun.

Tony began to raise his arms, but the look from Jeannie gave him cause to stop, just halfway. He glanced down and saw she her arms were still firmly by her sides, fists clenched.

"What?"

The corner of Jeannie's mouth crawled up into an unpleasant smile. "What are you doing?"

"I'm doing what the nice policeman wants."

The nice policeman took a step further. The flashlight flicked between Jeannie and Tony's faces. He shouted something else, but neither Jeannie or Tony were listening.

"He's just a cop, Tony. You're bulletproof." Jeannie's curled lip made Tony feel uncomfortable. This night wasn't going how he imagined it. Nor was this the most prodigious start to a career fighting crime.

"So," Jeannie continued, "what are you doing?"

Tony thought of his future career again. So, this was a mistake, but he could fix it. He could get them out of this and they could start again. He was strong, bulletproof, a goddamn superhero. What was one cop against him? One policeman with a gun, against a superman?

Tony lowered his arms and smiled. Well, there was no harm in having fun, right? He flicked Jeannie's hair around her forehead, leaving light blue marks from the ink on his fingers. He smiled, and she laughed, and he launched himself at the officer.

The policeman was just quick enough to see the initial movement, and fired his weapon. By the time the bullet had reached the end of the gun's barrel, Tony's had cupped the muzzle with his palm. The barrel flash lit his hand, and the strong stench of black powder filled the air, far stronger than was usual after a gunshot. The policeman had already squeezed the trigger a second time. The second bullet collided with the first in Tony's hand, splitting the gun's barrel and backfiring the shot into chamber. The gun kicked as the mechanism jammed and the hot combustion gas tore the weapon apart at the seams. The cop screamed in pain as half his hand was blown off, his cry vanishing in a wet choke as Tony reached through the man's chest with his other hand, tearing a hole clean through the torso. The cop looked down in disbelief, an action movie cliché, then his head didn't rise. Tony slid his arm back, almost shaking the cop off.

Shit.

He hadn't meant to do that. He heard Jeannie's boots pounding the pavement as she ran towards him, then felt her hands on his back as she came to stop and looked down at the corpse. The policeman's radio popped a few times as his partner tried to make contact.

"Nice."

"What?" Tony tore his eyes from the body and looked at Jeannie. She was smiling. "Nice? I just killed a guy. Killed a policeman. Holy fucking shit Jeannie, we're in it."

Jeannie punched his shoulder. The gesture was almost playful and Tony felt the world go fuzzy at the edges. What the hell had this night turned into?

"It's nice work, is what it is," said Jeannie. "Congratulations, you're a supervillain."

Running in the distance, more cars. More police. Tony bounced on his heels, eager to run but unsure if that was the right thing to do. He was a cop killer. A *cop killer*. He was *in* it.

But… what could they do? He was strong, invulnerable, fast. A superhero.

No. Not a super*hero*. Jeannie had said it. A super*villain*. Something stirred in Tony's chest. Maybe it was the adrenaline, maybe it was the shock, the realization that he had gone too far and that there was no going back.

Tony shook his head and found himself smiling.

A super*villain*?

Well…

If he was going to clean up the city, working within the rules, within the law, was a hindrance. You couldn't get anything done, always had to be careful, had to operate within the insect-like boundaries of normal people so nobody got hurt. It was a waste of time. He had power, potential, ability, but couldn't use it.

Unless… unless he actually got to work, turned the city around. Turned the city around to his way. That would solve the problem, wouldn't it? No more corruption, no more superhero games. The city would be his. Jeannie was right. It was the best way.

Tony wobbled on his feet and he rubbed blue stain over his forehead.

And what was a supervillain anyway, except a superhero who actually got stuff done?

He smiled, picked Jeannie up in his arms, and together they flew up, out of the range of the police and out of sight of the city. He wasn't worried about the ink, or the dead cop, or the Seven Wonders.

The city didn't have a new superhero. It had a new supervillain.

#2: THE START OF SOMETHING BEAUTIFUL

Author's note: This scene is a flashback that was originally placed as the book's epilogue, but it was just a little confusing to jump back so far in time, having just seen Blackbird rescue Tony from the superprison. But it does give a little hint about how deep the Seven Wonders were in it – was Aurora planning to use the MIC-N on the Cowl, or did he have a more sinister purpose? And what hand did he have in the secret origin of Blackbird, anyway? Perhaps we will never know!

The laboratory was ship-shape and Bristol fashion. So said Frank Cane anyway. The aged scientist had been imported from Britain especially for the occasion. Jeannie had only been there a week, but she bet the lab hadn't looked this tidy since it had first opened. On that occasion they'd had the mayor and some charitable big wig, Geoffrey Conroy, cutting the ribbon. Jeannie had seen the photos. She suspected that Frank Cane had been shipped in for that too. He was at that rarefied level of academia where he didn't actually do any work, he just toured universities and institutes the world over to frown over expensive equipment and drink brandy with deans. Not to mention put his name as the first author on scientific papers, even though Jeannie was sure he had no idea who she was or that she was the one not only doing all of the work but writing up the results for publication.

But so it goes. That was how academia, how science worked. She accepted that. It was the price she paid, and at least she knew that one day that would be her. By the time she reached Frank's age, she hoped to be driving a solid gold car, thanks to the proceeds of electronics patents. And this baby was the biggie, the one that the whole event had been organised for. The shindig would eclipse the lab opening too. Aurora's Light was here with a posse from the Seven Wonders.

Jeannie straightened her lab coat and adjusted her glasses, instantly feeling like a heel. For the occasion she'd even tamed her short black hair from its usual vertical position to something resembling a fringe and parting. She'd even gone so far as to swap the gemmed stud in her nose to a subtle pewter button.

Aurora and the Seven Wonders was big news. Even back home in Albuquerque she knew who they were. While the rest of the superheroes of the world had either retired (White Nancy), vanished (the aptly named Secret Sin), or gone into the cosmetics business (hello, Doctor Litewave), the Seven Wonders still held San Ventura, protecting it from the Cowl. Everyone in the country knew that, and not a week went by without a news report about the latest diabolical scheme foiled by the all-powerful Aurora and his team. Of course, if he really was all-powered and the Seven Wonders really were the world's last-standing super-team, then surely the Cowl would have been disposed of long ago, like every other supervillain in the world.

She pushed the doubts to the back of her mind and sucked her teeth as a distraction. She was nervous. Aurora was a celebrity, his wife and co-leader Bluebell a famous beauty. Not only that, they were here to talk to her about the big project. Okay, Frank Cane would do the talking (and take the credit), but it was all down to her. That's what she'd been hired for after finishing her post-doc at the University of New Mexico and...

Someone nudged her in the ribs on the left, and someone said something on her right. She half-turned to ask the speaker to repeat, but Frank Cane was too busy shaking Aurora's hand to answer. Making her way down the row of scientists and officials next to her husband was Bluebell.

Aurora. Tall, broad, handsome even though only the lower half of his face was visible, but the jaw was chiselled and the mouth was set into an expression that at first looked like a smile, but it was slight and raised at one end more than the other. A smirk, but not an impolite one. It was confident, bold. *Superheroic.*

And then he was past her, and she realised she'd shaken his hand and said something nice and friendly and hadn't even registered. Her hand was grasped by Bluebell's. Jeannie smiled and said hello, but there was something behind Bluebell's perfect smile she didn't like. Maybe it was just Bluebell herself, perfect in every way and from every angle, her short blonde hair expertly coiffured and tousled just like she did with her own when she wasn't trying to look more like a scientist and less like, well, a vaguely cool person. Jeannie's smile tightened and she felt even more stupid.

No, there was something else. Bluebell was looking into her eyes but it felt like she was looking past them somehow. The moment passed, Bluebell smiled, and moved on.

It was later. The drinks were out. The only time you can ever drink actually inside a laboratory is when there is a party, or an opening, or royalty comes to say hello. This occasion definitely fell into the latter category.

Frank Cane held court as Jeannie chatted to a lab tech, joking about the definition of interstitial time. Out of the corner of her eye, she watched Aurora and Bluebell. They stuck together throughout, Aurora doing all the talking and Bluebell laughing at the appropriate points. But there is was again, that look, that intense... look, that wasn't a stare and it wasn't rude, but there was something else. When Bluebell met her eye with a smile the back of Jeannie's scalp would itch.

Jeannie watched as Bluebell took Aurora aside by the elbow and whispered something over this shoulder. He nodded, and for the first time they split up. Bluebell returned to Dr Cane, and placing a friendly hand on his shoulder, asked him something about his home town back in England. She'd done her research.

"Dr Jean Ravenholt." Aurora held his champagne in one hand, and had the other extended. Jeannie shook it, remembering this time. His gloved hand was hot and the champagne in his other hand appeared to be steaming slightly.

"Mr... Aurora's Light, it's a real honor to meet you."

Aurora laughed like a Hollywood film star of the 1940s. His eyes flashed white and his flame-hair swirled. "Just Aurora is fine." He took a sip of his drink. "I understand you developed the theory of the black light converter back at Albuquerque."

Ah. Forbidden territory. It was true, she had, but Cane took the credit. Even though he lived in an entirely different hemisphere, he was the spokesperson for the lab. Jeannie had to tread carefully.

"Hmm," said Aurora, half into his glass. "Don't worry about Dr Cane. Bluebell has his full attention. I just need to know that the black light converter theory is actually yours, not his."

Jeannie's eyes flickered to Dr Cane. He and Bluebell were laughing together like old friends. Aurora smiled.

"She can have quite a way with people."

"I'm sure."

"Like you wouldn't believe."

Jeannie took a gulp from her own drink, slightly too large than intended. The champagne was too dry.

"The converter is built on my design, yes. The whole thing is, truth be told."

"Ah." Aurora smiled, wider this time. His teeth we perfect. "How have the tests been so far?"

Jeannie relaxed. Aurora the superman was trusting her to a conversation she shouldn't really be having. Fuck it, go for broke.

"Well, actually," she said. "Energy transfer and absorption has been eighty per cent, which is beyond our initial hypothesis and more than enough to depower a hero." She paused, aware again of who she was talking to. "Of course, in theory only. We have only tested it on controlled power outputs."

Aurora nodded. "Of course, of course. Would you be interested to know that with just a few adjustments you can actually transition the energy source from one type to another, transferring the electron balance across space and time to another target?"

Jeannie stopped with a mouthful of champagne. She swallowed only when the fizzing on her tongue became too sharp. "Are you sure about that?" She raised an eyebrow.

Aurora raised his glass. "Quite sure, yes. I will transmit the schematics to you in the morning."

"Ah. You will? Okay… what for, exactly?"

"You've made an admirable start here, Dr Ravenholt. But we need the device a little off-spec, shall we say."

"You need?"

Aurora smiled. The warmth had gone. "Who do you think is funding this project? Funded your post-doc? Arranged the opening in San

Ventura?" He gestured to Frank Cane with his now empty champagne flute. "Found you a suitably senile and absent boss?"

Jeannie gulped. Despite the radiant heat from Aurora, she felt cold in her chest. Her eyes flicked the Bluebell. The beautiful superheroine was looking at her again, the smile as perfect and charming and fake and dead as Aurora's.

"What do you want?"

Aurora sighed. "Dr Ravenholt, I want a weapon that will let me steal the superpowers of other heroes and transfer them to me. And I'd like your help with that."

He clinked his empty glass against Jeannie's half-full one, that hung at a limp angle from her hand.

"Here's to the start of something beautiful."

MEET *CHESNEY ARNSTRUTHER*... A VERY ***DIFFERENT***
KIND OF SUPERHERO!

ANGRY
ROBOT